MILLEN COUNTY STANDOFF

MILLEN COUNTY STANDOFF

A Novel

Bill Spevacek

iUniverse, Inc.
New York Lincoln Shanghai

Millen County Standoff

iUniverse books may be ordered through booksellers or by contacting:

iUniverse
2021 Pine Lake Road, Suite 100
Lincoln, NE 68512
www.iuniverse.com
1-800-Authors (1-800-288-4677)

Because of the dynamic nature of the Internet, any Web addresses or links contained in this book may have changed since publication and may no longer be valid.

This is a work of fiction. All of the characters, names, incidents, organizations, and dialogue in this novel are either the products of the author's imagination or are used fictitiously.

ISBN: 978-0-595-46785-3 (pbk)
ISBN: 978-0-595-91077-9 (ebk)

Printed in the United States of America

CHAPTER 1

Tad Coburg sat on a rock. His feet dangled over the clear waters of Midewiwin Creek. Twenty or thirty thousand years of swirling at that bend in the river, high water and low had carved a hollow in the limestone, creating a perpetual eddy in perpetual shade. It was a spot where trout could hang out without fighting the current, a fish cafeteria where bugs and larvae drift past to be eaten or ignored. Morsels surviving that eddy were recaptured by Midewiwin's flow to tantalize trout and smallmouth bass in other eddies downstream, or bullheads, chubs, and redhorse in the slower sections of the river. Or to escape Wisconsin altogether and feed the bass, pike, catfish, and carp of the Mississippi River, thirty meandering miles to the west.

This particular swirl in the Midewiwin, Tad recalled from his childhood, would be home for at least one hefty trout in any given year. He had never landed more than ten or twelve inches of brook trout there, nor did he know anyone who had. Still, the myth of the husky, resident trout was enough to draw him back to the fishing hole after a thirty-year absence.

Midewiwin Creek at that point was too wide to jump but too narrow, shallow, and overgrown with bank-side brush and trees to permit navigation. It flowed through a deep, wooded ravine, and was fed from springs in other ravines in the driftless area of southwestern Wisconsin. The creek at that point was reasonably clean, although you wouldn't want to drink it, given the deer, raccoons, coyotes, and smaller beasts that used it for drinking, standing, moving their bowels, and dying in.

For the last 10,000 years, glaciers had avoided that part of North America, leaving steep hillsides with sandstone and limestone caves and outcroppings.

Ridge tops and flood plains were covered with rich, brown loam for alfalfa, corn, soybeans, and grazing.

The rock Tad sat on that June Saturday afternoon was strangely comfortable, with two bun-shaped indentations, formed, according to legend, by the buttocks of 500 generations of Woodland Indians and their ancestors, sitting on that exact rock in the hope of luring the fabled trout that resided below.

Tad was among a handful of people who knew about the fishing hole. In the ten years since his father had stopped grazing cattle there, wild blackberries, gooseberries, burdocks, thistles, and other varieties of nature's barbed wire had joined fallen limbs and tired old trees that had leaned over and died, to form a nearly impenetrable defense of the spot. All but the most intrepid hunters who wandered into the area in the fall conceded that stretch of Midewiwin Creek to deer, not worth the wear and tear on their blaze orange gear.

A pruning shears, sturdy boots, jeans and long sleeves were needed to get through the tangled briars and down the rocky hillside to find that spot on the creek bank. A hat and lots of Deep Woods Off kept mosquitoes, ticks, and deer flies away.

Today, Tad's spinning rod and reel were on the bank beside him. Nylon line and unbaited hook were not in the water, the tackle box was unopened, the fabled lunker in Midewiwin Creek was safe.

Today, the steep walls of the ravine, with hickory, black cherry, and century-old oak trees filtering sunlight like church windows, formed his personal cathedral—St. Thaddeus' Basilica of Red Oak, Wisconsin. It was a place for solitude, contemplation, prayer, a place to sort out the bewildering temporal and religious forces working against him.

Today, eight months after he returned to Wisconsin, a stranger in his own county, two zealous and well organized groups of otherwise ordinary people were plotting to destroy him. One in the name of the Constitution of the United States of America, the other in the name of Almighty God.

Last fall, in the middle of an October Saturday afternoon, Father Tad Coburg had been seated no more or less comfortably with fellow priests at a café terrace on Piazza Navona in Rome, sipping Valpolicella, discussing Edward Schillebeeckx and Rosemary Radford Reuther, Islamic fundamentalism and the 9/11 attacks in the United States a month before, along with Vatican politics and standard college faculty gossip. Surreptitiously, through dark glasses in the Roman tradition, they surveyed the passing dark-haired, finely sculpted Italian women and shapely, sunburned tourists. Fishing without a line in the water, you might say.

Tad was one of the world's leading scholars on a subject professed several times a day for two millennia by billions of people, ninety-nine percent of them with only the faintest understanding or interest in the subject of Tad's insights. He was officially on the faculty of The North American College in Rome, but studied and taught around the globe, wherever religious thought leaders had an interest in the Christian doctrine of the Holy Trinity. He was also the Vatican's resident expert on the subject, and was called on occasion by the Curia for clarification of some point—not often, as the Trinity has little to do with the way people behave and is rarely challenged by infidels or heretics in the late twentieth and early twenty-first centuries.

A messenger pulled his bicycle up to the sidewalk café and inquired at four tables patronized by priests before he was directed to the table where Tad sat with three friends. "*Padre Coburg?*"

"*Pronto,*" Tad replied.

"*Messagio.*" The messenger gave him a letter-sized envelope.

"*Grazie,*" Tad said, reaching into his pocket and handing the messenger a few liras.

He almost put the letter in his pocket for later reading. Then he read the return address: the Dean of the Faculty of Theology at North American College, Tad's boss in Italy.

The envelope contained a faxed note, brief and stunning. It was from Bishop Robert Ardito of the Madison, Wisconsin, diocese. Tad was a priest of that diocese, on loan to North American College and teaching among the Jesuits at Gregorian University there. "Tad," the note read, "I'm sorry to be the one to have to tell you, but we received word an hour ago that your father is near death. I know your mother needs you. Please leave for home at once, and take as much time as you need to help your family through this difficult time. You, your father and the rest of your family are in my prayers. Bob Ardito."

Tad had known that his father was ill, in a nursing home for the past six months from the complications of a stroke that had left him partially paralyzed and unable to speak. He had planned to visit him in July, but had postponed, instead substituting on a panel discussion at an interfaith conference in Geneva. He had prayed that God not let his father suffer further. Apparently, those prayers had produced results.

"Leave for home at once" was not as easy as it sounded. He had to arrange for someone to cover for the classes he taught. A younger colleague, from Limerick, Ireland, was sympathetic, understanding, and willing. There were plane reservations to be made, Rome to Madison and back. Change currencies. Pack.

The quickest way home left him with some sixteen hours—ten in the air, two changing planes at London's Heathrow Airport, two more changing planes at Chicago's O'Hare Field and two more driving from Madison to his parents' home in the hills of southwestern Wisconsin. Sixteen hours to sort through the first eighteen years of his life, the kind of reflection that comes with the impending death of a parent. Memories were distorted by time, some pleasant, some not, a few that he, like anyone else, wished he could edit or delete.

Life on a dairy farm is not for the lazy or weak. Dairy cows are among the most demanding and least forgiving slave masters anywhere. Work twelve or fourteen hours a day, seven days a week, never take a vacation, sweat the balance of checkbook and milk check month after month, year after year, and all of life becomes one, exhausting, tedious, frustrating effort to make a living. Throw in a capricious God who sometimes grants prayers to make it start or stop raining, sometimes doesn't, and it explains why Henry and Ruth Coburg attended Mass on Sunday (just in case), but had little use for religion beyond that.

It's why Tad's father had both hips replaced before he was sixty, why he had to give up farming when he was sixty-two. And maybe why he had a debilitating stroke at the age of seventy-one.

It's why Tad Coburg decided early in life that he would be something other than a farmer. To devote his life to God through the priesthood was quite another matter, as much in love with Miriam Baumer as he was when he and beautiful Miriam graduated, valedictorian and salutatorian respectively, from Red Oak High School. Miriam, however, took love out of the equation with her blunt announcement, three weeks after graduation, that she would enter the convent.

The likelihood of getting killed in the service of his country as a draftee in the Vietnam War didn't appeal to Tad. A safer, albeit longer, alternative was a tour of duty in the Navy. He enlisted for four years. That turned out to be no better than the infantry. He spent almost twenty months on Navy river patrol boats getting shot at from both banks. The carnage of that senseless war was a major factor in Tad's life decision, especially with Miriam Baumer out of the picture.

The sun was low in the west when he guided the rented Ford Taurus along Norse Road toward the Coburg family farm. Despite the fact that he had nothing but catnaps on the plane over the past twenty-four hours, he was alert enough to appreciate and marvel at the beauty of a Wisconsin autumn. A soft breeze from the southwest pushed the temperature into the low seventies. Maples, black cherry, hickory, a half dozen varieties of oak, as well as sumac and untold numbers of shrubs and weeds were at their color peak. All shades of the spectrum, from yellows through reds to browns through the purples of late blooming wildflowers, were punctuated by green pine, spruce, juniper, and cedar. Farmers with their combines were in the contoured fields harvesting corn.

The drive from Madison was slowed by Tad's hesitancy to greet his mother. Most mothers would be oh-so proud of their son, the priest. Not Ruth. His announcement thirty years ago that he was off to the seminary had been met with indifference and some hostility. Neither Henry nor Ruth favored the idea, and the years only hardened their attitude.

Tad as a priest meant the end of that branch of the Coburg family name. It also meant no Coburg to inherit the farm that had been in the family for over a hundred years, through the Depression and all manner of peril from nature and the commodities markets. And perhaps no son to watch over their inevitable years of infirmity between the time they could no longer farm and the time the Lord would free them from the bondage of their rheumatic bodies.

By choosing the priesthood over a good, traditional occupation like farming, or masonry or welding or auto repair, or even going to college and studying agribusiness, in his parents' eyes Tad had chosen the softest and least productive of the options Red Oak offered in the nineteen-seventies.

The Coburg farm was a half mile off Norse Road. Tad stopped at the mailbox and found it full. A quick pass through the stack of mail revealed a handful of what appeared to be get well cards addressed to his father, and a dozen or more offers of Visa and MasterCards from financial institutions that obviously had no idea of the Coburgs' meager demand for earthly possessions and complete inability to repay.

The gravel road to the farm was rutted and pot-holed. He noted that fields along the right, downhill side of the road, rented out most likely, had been planted in corn, not yet harvested. The fields along the uphill side had not been tilled in years; brambles, burdocks, and huge patches of Canada thistles had claimed the land for the devil.

He rounded the last corner and saw the farm, his home, now almost entirely in shadow from wooded hills to the west. The buildings were decrepit, and the shadows didn't help. The cow barn tilted dangerously to the east. Once bright red with white trim, it was now mostly gray. The milk house, formerly white, was bare, weathered wood, and was surrounded by thistles and nettles. Tad had expected some stage of disrepair, given his father's ailing hips and his stroke. But not that bad. The Roman Coliseum was in better shape.

Nor did he expect the appearance of the house where he grew up. The covered porch across the front and east side of the house was once a great place for playing with toy cars and tractors, or reading, or for the family sitting around after a big meal. Today it leaned precariously in two directions and looked unsafe for even a cat to tread on. The lawn had not been cut all summer. Shades were drawn on all the windows upstairs.

No one came out to greet him. He got out of the car, and surveyed the ailing porch. He took a chance and stepped gingerly on the steps. They held. The doorbell didn't work, but the front door was unlocked.

"Mom?" No reply. No sounds.

"Mom?" Still no sound, but he detected the smell of cooking. Onion and something else. He headed for the kitchen.

"What are you doing here?" His mother was seated at the kitchen table, empty coffee mug and an open Bible in front of her. She apparently was not thrilled to see him.

"I came because of Dad."

"He's dead."

Tad's turn for long silence. "When?"

"This morning."

"I'm so sorry. That why I ... I thought I could do something, help out, say Mass."

"Would've done him more good if you'd been here when he was alive. What's a Mass going to do for him now?"

"How do you feel, Mom?"

"Lousy."

"Had anything to eat tonight?"

"Stew's cooking. But not enough for both of us."

Tad walked to her and stood behind her, hands on her shoulders. He kissed her cheek. He wondered,k *Where are the neighbors, the ladies of the parish? Why aren't a half dozen of them here with the new widow, bringing casseroles and pies and cakes?* Silence, an immense wall between them, was his to breach.

"Why don't you put the stew in the fridge and let's go out for dinner tonight?"

She didn't answer for so long that Tad speculated about hearing loss or Alzheimer's.

Finally, she pushed her chair back, leaned on the table, scuffed her feet into position and pushed herself up from the table. "Okay," she said, and began a slow and obviously painful journey to the bathroom.

Tad couldn't remember a bathroom on first floor. "That bathroom new?"

"Your dad had it installed when he had hip surgery."

The fact that Tad hadn't known about such a basic modification to the house to accommodate his ailing father, or had simply forgotten it, added another layer to what was threatening to develop into a hefty load of guilt. It was true that his visits home had been seldom and short, the most recent being three years ago. But he was busy in Rome. And in Paris and London and Geneva and Toronto and New York. Doing the Lord's work. Shaping the theological underpinnings that were supposed to lead multitudes of souls to eternal salvation. Vacations visiting China, the British Isles, and the ruins of lost civilizations were always more tempting than four weeks of helping his father bale hay. He hadn't been home to share and lighten his parents' burden of aging in a world of ones and zeros, a world that celebrated youth and seemed to be redesigning itself exclusively for the young.

All traces of daylight were gone when Tad drove into a brightly lit, nearly full gravel parking lot at the Sandstone Steak House, located at the intersection of County Highways X and Z, halfway between Red Oak and Bremerton. "They seem to be doing a good business. A lot of restaurants aren't even open on Mondays," he said.

"Farmers get just as hungry on Monday as any other day," his mother said.

Despite the cars in the parking lot, the Sandstone had empty tables, and a hostess escorted them to a table next to a window. The window provided only reflections, although Tad guessed the daytime view would be a spectacular panorama of the surrounding ridges and valleys.

"Some farmers must be making money these days," he said. "They seem to be eating and drinking well, having a good time."

"Fact is, it ain't farming money keeping this place going. If you farm a couple thousand acres and milk 500 cows, you come here to eat," his mother said.

"You mean all these customers are big time farmers?"

"No. I mean these customers make more money working in town than they do on the farm."

Tad realized he was really out of touch with his home state. "What kind of businesses do they work at?"

"Not businesses. Business. Distribute Dot Com. Best thing that's happened to these counties since Franklin Delano Roosevelt. Practically every farm family has at least one person, usually the wife, working at Distribute Dot Com. She can make as much money in three days as most dairy herds produce in a week."

He saw the picture. Internet shopping was sweeping the world. But in every transaction someone or something, somewhere, has to pluck an electronically ordered product off a warehouse shelf, put it into a box and ship it.

"The company likes to hire farmers," she continued. "They're honest, work hard, show up every day, don't mind working nights and weekends. They're independent, don't care much for unions. And they're happy with what they get. Company treats them well. Hospital insurance, baby sitting, employee discounts, you name it."

"What kinds of stuff do they handle?"

"Toys. Sports stuff like baseball gloves, fishing tackle. Jewelry. Lamps and shades. Bunch of other things. They've got more acres of warehouse than your father and I have farm."

"That must be a real boon to the economy around here."

"It's kept a lot of people alive."

A young, blonde waitress appeared at the table, pad and pencil in hand. "Hi, my name is Cheryl and I'll be your server tonight. Can I get you guys something to drink?" Another small jolt of culture shock. Tad was accustomed to the swarthy, condescending waiters of Rome.

"Mom, what'll it be?"

"I'll just have water."

Tad wondered what kind of wine cellar the Sandstone might be boasting these days, guessing it would be pretty spare. He was tempted to inquire about a bottle of Brunello di Montalcino, but realized it could sound pretentious, and that would not sit well with his mother. "Could I have a glass of Merlot?"

"Water for everyone and Merlot for you, sir."

They studied the menus. "What looks good to you tonight, Mom?"

"It's all so expensive. Guess I'll just have the fried chicken special."

"Hey, dinner's on me. Pretend you won the lottery. What would you order then?"

"I'm tempted by 'Maine lobster, market price.' But I've never eaten lobster." She decided on prime rib.

"Then prime rib it will be. That sounds good to me too."

A young, skinny boy filled their glasses with water and ice. The waitress brought Tad his wine, took their orders—Tad requesting medium-well, his mother medium-rare—and invited them to partake of the salad bar. Tad felt a toast was in order, but couldn't figure what to toast. "To your health" was obviously many months too late. "To dad" didn't seem right either. He lifted his glass and settled for "cheers."

"Are Janie and Rose coming back for the funeral?" he asked.

"I doubt it. Your Aunt Margaret called them about Henry's death. They told her they didn't think they would be able to come, but they would send flowers. Just what I need."

He realized the estrangement between his sisters and their parents was as wide as his own. Janie lived in Atlanta, sole support of three rebellious teenagers. Ten years ago her husband had made his choice between family and liquor. Rose lived in Phoenix and was currently between husbands. The father of her two adolescent daughters had been killed in an automobile accident eight years before, with no life insurance. Two subsequent marriages had done nothing to improve her lot in life.

The visit to the salad bar demonstrated to Tad that his mother, whatever other physical ailments were slowing her down, had nothing wrong with her digestive tract. She ladled thousand island, ranch, and blue cheese dressing on a mountain of lettuce and adorned it with shredded cheddar, onions, cherry tomatoes, croutons, and red and green peppers. The plate could hold no more.

Ruth Coburg bowed her head before delving into the salad. Tad bowed his and quietly prayed, thanking God for the good food, and the fine harvest, and that was about all he could think of to be thankful for in his mother's presence. He waved a tiny sign of the cross over the table. She didn't notice. Her head was still bowed, eyes shut. Finally she finished, picked up her fork and attacked the salad. She ate it all.

While she was focused on her giant salad, Tad had a chance to focus on his mother. She had once been a beautiful woman, tall and lithe, with rich, black hair, a fair, Celtic complexion that never darkened from the exposure to the sunlight that farm wives endured, and pale blue eyes with a natural twinkle that had always suggested she took nothing too seriously. For the first twenty years of his life, aunts and other Red Oak area farm wives claimed Tad was the spitting image of his mother.

He hoped that was not the case now. Her eyes had lost their twinkle. Ultra-violet rays had won the battle of the skin, leaving it wrinkled and mottled. Her hair was gray and thin, having been treated with nothing more than soap, comb, and scissors for many years. There was no trace of femininity about her thin, C-shaped body.

The prime rib came, servings identical despite their stated preferences for medium-well and medium-rare—brown around the edges, blood red in the middle. Tad wondered how his stomach would handle the rare beef. For twenty years his system had served him well on a diet of pasta, seafood, veal, poultry, crisp vegetables, bland cheese, fresh bread, olive oil, and the right wines. It probably won't know what to do with meat that seemed almost able to walk away from the table. He approached the beef in spiral fashion, starting with the outer, well-cooked layers, saving the rarest for last if, as seemed unlikely, he was still hungry then. None of that bothered his mother. She ate her prime rib as it came off the knife—red, pink, brown, didn't matter. She finished it all, as well as the baked potato with sour cream and two rye dinner rolls with butter.

The waitress reappeared and asked if she should put Tad's uneaten portion of meat in a box to take home. "Yes," his mother said, as he shook his head.

They declined dessert. Tad was calculating the tip on his Visa card bill when a tall man with a massive belly, two or three chins, and hands the size of catcher's mitts walked up to their table. "Sister Ruth," the big man said, "how wonderful to see you."

She stood quickly and they hugged. Finally, she said "Doctor Don, I want you to meet my son, Tad. He's a college professor."

"Wonderful," he said, squeezing and pumping Tad's hand as if it were a hammer handle. "I'm pleased to meet you. So sorry about your father, but I'm sure he's with the Lord at this very moment."

"Yes, thank you. I'm glad to meet you too." The huge man excused himself, caught up with the seating hostess and followed her to a table. He was dining alone.

A roaring case of jet lag and paucity of sleep over the past forty-eight hours were catching up with him, and he was looking forward to a restful night. But Tad was jarred by a grenade his mother nonchalantly tossed his way on the drive back from the restaurant. He had inquired about funeral arrangements, assuming a visitation at the Gregory Funeral Home, followed by a Mass the following morning in St. Brendan's Catholic Church, at which he would preside, probably along with Father Schmidt, the pastor.

"No," she told him. "Doctor Don will handle it."

"I'm not sure I understand."

"Doctor Don will handle the funeral service."

"You mean that, that large gentleman we met at the restaurant."

"He's pastor of the Holy Scripture Universal Church of the Lord in West Charleton. He'll conduct the service."

"Is that what Dad wanted?"

"Yes it is."

"How do you know? He couldn't speak for the last six months."

"But we could communicate. Doctor Don and I had many conversations with him. He could blink his eyes. He could squeeze my hand—just a little, but there's no question that he understood."

"You, are you a member of the Holy Scripture Universal, whatever it is?"

"May seventh."

"What's that?"

"The day I was reborn. The day I found Jesus."

Tad tried not to drive off the road or otherwise reveal his shock. He was speechless, as his mind worked over the latest and most explosive surprise of his homecoming. Finally he asked, "Was dad a member of that church too?"

"Yes. Doctor Don and I asked him directly: Did he embrace Jesus? By the squeeze of his hand and the tears in his eyes, he told us. Yes, yes, yes.I'm sure that if he could have spoken he would have told us he was as joyful as I was when I found Jesus. God wants both of us."

"I won't argue with that. But couldn't I concelebrate with Doctor Don? I mean, I am a priest and the son of the deceased."

"Tad, I know you want to do that, but this will be a Christian service. You haven't found Jesus yet. Doctor Don and I and the rest of our fellowship are praying that you will. And Janie and Rose and their kids too. Until you do, I'm sorry. You can attend, but you can't participate."

Tad lay wide awake in his old room on second floor of the family farmhouse. The room had been used only on his rare returns to the farm—over the past ten years, maybe a total of thirty nights. Door and window hadn't been opened in three years, and the room had the musty smell of an antique shop or haunted attic. The rumble in his gut as the digestive system worked on the strange, red meat was another part of the problem.

The stale bedroom air began to mix with crisp, autumn, country air from the open window, but nothing was clearing up in Tad's mind. *Twenty years a Catholic priest and not a Christian? I've been preoccupied with the big picture and haven't done much for the man and woman who brought me into the world. The least I could do is give Dad a good, Catholic sendoff. But I'm not allowed to because I'm not a Christian.*

The sergeant was exhausted. He showered the dark camo paint from his face, arms and hands and inspected the scrapes and scratches accumulated in his six-hour, cross country walk, stumble and crawl, along with the nicks and dings that had not yet healed from the week before. He and his squad had hauled and stashed in the hillside cave more than a half ton of canned food and bottled water, five semi-automatic rifles, three nine-millimeter semiautomatic pistols, eight cases of ammunition and a box of hand grenades. The nocturnal logistics hikes had stopped being fun weeks ago.

He pulled back the sheet and slipped into bed for three hours of sleep, what was left of the night. Darlene stirred, but didn't wake up.

CHAPTER 2

In less than four days, Tad Coburg had traveled a quarter of the way around the world. He had made the transition from noisy, smoggy, crowded Rome to quiet, pastoral and loosely inhabited rural Wisconsin. He had gone from the companionship and intellectual stimulation of faculty and students at one of the world's premier theological universities to the near impossibility of simple conversation with a woman with whom he had little in common, except genes and his childhood. It was as if a tornado had spun him thirty years back in time and into a land of strange but vaguely familiar people and customs. Most gut-wrenching of all was his role as spectator at his father's funeral.

As a priest and theologian teaching in Rome, Father Tad Coburg was acquainted with the premier thinkers of many of earth's major religions and Christian denominations. Over the years he had discussed, prayed, argued, studied, chatted, dined, joked, and sometimes drank with religious leaders of all stripes—Jewish, Muslim, Hindu, Buddhist and Protestant. He had attended their religious services and they his. He knew the points of doctrinal agreement among them, as well as the points of difference. And he respected those differences. In short, Father Coburg was as ecumenical as you'll find.

Nevertheless, his father's funeral service was a theological and psychological kick in the groin.

The Holy Scripture Universal Church of the Lord was housed in a former Studebaker dealer's garage in West Charleton, fifteen miles from Red Oak and twenty miles from the Henry and Ruth Coburg farm. A local implement seller had stored used farm machinery in it from the demise of the Studebaker until Doctor Don and his followers bought it and fixed it up five years ago. The church members had scrubbed the concrete floor with barrels of strong solvents to remove the grease and automotive odor. Then they had covered it with a clear epoxy. They furred out, insulated, and covered the walls with birch veneer paneling, and installed a dropped ceiling with acoustical tile and recessed fluorescent lighting. Curtains blotted out the industrial-type windows high on the walls. *All in all,* Tad thought, *a nice try. But the Romans, with a couple thousand years of practice, were much more skilled at restoring and maintaining old architecture.*

At the business end of the garage/church was a raised platform, covered by a commercial grade gray carpet, with a backdrop of purple drapery. In the center, three steps higher than the stage, was a pulpit, made of wood several grades up in quality from the building's veneer interior walls. That was where Doctor Don, clad in a gleaming white robe that seemed big enough to cover a volleyball court, held forth in the funeral service of Henry Coburg, former Catholic, and in the deceased's own mind, Tad was certain, Catholic all the way to the end. Doctor Don's job on that day was to dispatch Henry, whether Henry wanted it or not, to a part of heaven reserved for the preacher's followers and out of bounds for those they considered infidels, such as Catholics.

"Brothers and sisters," he began, "Today is the most important day in the life of our deceased brother, Henry Coburg. For the last six months of his time on earth, the Lord withheld from Henry the power to speak to us. Only through his eyes and a slight squeeze of his hand could Henry communicate. Only he and Almighty God knew what was in his heart. But, praise the Lord, God spoke to me and to Henry's beloved wife of over fifty years, our sister in this fellowship, Ruth." He paused dramatically, his gaze swept across the 100 or so in the congregation. "The Father," he said in a near whisper, "through Henry's eyes and the gentle pressure of his once powerful grip, the Father has revealed to me and to Ruth that Henry Coburg had indeed, in his final days, discovered Jesus."

The congregation erupted with joy. "Hallelujah," "Praise God," "Thank you Father," "Jesus, Jesus, Jesus," "Oh beloved Father, we thank thee," "Amen, Father, amen." "Descend on your people, Lord," "Bless your holy name, Lord." A hundred voices in individual expressions of heavenly joy and gratitude, some shouted, some murmured, a cacophony of praise and thanksgiving, accompanied by bodily expressions of the same fervor. Some with arms raised and shouting toward the acoustical ceiling, some bowing with faces almost on the epoxy floor, many swaying as if controlled by erratic breezes. The shouts and body movements of gratitude went on and on. Ruth Coburg was as into the moment as the other followers of Doctor Don.

Tad wondered when, and even if, it would end. He stood self-consciously, aware that he was the only person present who was not in a near trance thanking God for Henry Coburg's supposed conversion.

A song broke out, two or three men on the far left side singing at first, soon joined by others, until the whole congregation was singing in remarkable harmony for an unschooled crowd, and clapping their hands together on the downbeat. "For the Lord our God the Almighty reigns, Hallelujah, For the Lord our God the Almighty reigns, Let us rejoice and be glad, Hallelujah, for the Lord our God the Almighty reigns."

Finally, Doctor Don raised his hands and the crowd became still. "My brothers and sisters," he said, "when God spoke to our sister Ruth, he commanded her to ask the blessing and assistance of this fellowship in bringing Henry across the threshold into the eternal kingdom."

"Amen," "Praise Jesus," "Hallelujah," rejoined the congregation. Ruth right along with them.

Doctor Don continued. "We know that Henry Coburg was a good man. He worked hard on his farm. He was a good husband and father, honest in all his dealings with the people who bought the fruits of his toil and sold him what he needed for his farm and family." Ruth Coburg was nodding her head enthusiastically. Tad wondered when the family history had been revised.

"Henry Coburg's one, nearly fatal failing was his seventy-one years of living without the presence of Christ in his soul."

Tad couldn't miss the preacher's implication, especially since he pronounced that judgment staring straight at Henry's son. If you are not a member of the Holy Scripture church, you are not a Christian, simple as that, was Doctor Don's message to the pagan, the Catholic priest.

"We thank thee, Jesus, for sending the spirit and delivering Henry Coburg to the Father in the nick of time. My brothers and sisters, without your prayers, Henry Coburg would be suffering the untold tortures of hell at this very moment. Let us rejoice, for our brother is now basking in the Father's eternal glory."

"Amen," "Hallelujah," "Praise the Lord," "Thank you Jesus, oh thank you," went the congregation.

"I'm sure I speak for our sister, Ruth, in expressing the deepest gratitude for your prayers that saved her husband."

"Hallelujah," "Amen." "Praise the Lord" and "Jesus, Jesus, Jesus" broke out all over again. Ruth turned to the crowd, smiling and nodding her head enthusiastically to thank them for their devout efforts.

Doctor Don again raised his arms and eyes to heaven, and the crowd became silent. He stood in the pulpit for a full minute to draw their total attention. With a wireless microphone in his hand, only an inch from his mouth, he began softly, "My beloved brothers and sisters." The sermon that followed didn't mention the passing of Henry Coburg. It had no specific theme that Tad could follow, except that Doctor Don was opposed to evil. Four times in the course of the forty-five-minute oration, Doctor Don stressed that it was incumbent on all Christians to turn back the forces of Satan. His ideas and calls to action were flung at the congregation as seemingly random thoughts, but supported liberally with quotations from the Bible.

Doctor Don's final proof in his case against evil and the necessity of confronting it came from the Book of Isaiah: "And I will punish the world for their evil, and the wicked for their iniquity; and I will cause the arrogancy of the proud to cease, and will lay low the haughtiness of the terrible."

The last was delivered in a crescendo that became a roar, sending a chill through the members of the congregation and frightening the ghost of every Studebaker that ever had its spark plugs changed in what became the Holy Scripture Universal Church of the Lord. Doctor Don let the words from Isaiah reverberate and settle into the crania of his followers.

Then his tone became a confidential whisper to every individual present. "Brothers and sisters, who will be the Father's instrument to punish the world for their evil, the wicked for their iniquity? Who will do the Lord's work, causing the arrogance of the proud to cease?" He looked into the pupils of everyone in the room. "Who will lay low the haughtiness of the terrible?" He paused again to let that question settle in. "Brothers and sisters," he concluded, "are we prepared to answer God's call as spoken to us through the Book of Isaiah?" The last words were delivered directly at Tad, who wasn't sure whether he represented enemy, prey or project in the formidable-looking preacher's eyes, but was chilled by the implications in any case.

Tad stood at graveside with his mother, shivering in a blue blazer, shirt and tie, and khaki chino slacks, the only dressy, civilian clothing he had brought with him from Rome. He had started the day in a Roman collar, but quickly changed when his mother threatened to disinherit him if he went to the funeral services dressed as a priest. The thought of losing his share of the run-down farm, which would probably be worth nothing after providing for his mother's final years, didn't bother him. But if it was that important to Ruth, then civvies it would be.

For her part, his mother had spruced up considerably from when he had reentered her life two days before. She owned some basic cosmetics and remembered how to use them. She wore a navy blue, tailored suit that looked fine from six feet and beyond. Her brown, cloth coat was attractive and appropriate for the temperature. In her black, low heel shoes and dark hose, she bore passing resemblance to the Ruth Coburg that Tad remembered from his childhood.

The weather had turned cloudy, late-October-normal for Wisconsin, approximating the depth of winter in Rome. Tad wished for a coat, while the other mourners seemed quite comfortable standing on the damp, still-green grass and listening to Doctor Don transfer custody of the soul of Henry Coburg from himself to Almighty God.

Tad scanned the grieving friends and relatives of his late father standing around the rectangular hole that would soon swallow the low-priced casket and its contents. Faces were only slightly familiar. Thirty years will do that. He sensed they were eyeing him the same way. If forced to put names to faces, Tad would do well to identify three out of the whole bunch.

It was no easier an hour later at the potluck luncheon back at the Holy Scripture church in the former garage. This time, however, his mother took charge and introduced him around. "My son, Tad. He's a college professor."

"Nice to see you again, Tad. I remember when you were this high. Ruthie, you must be proud of him. Such a handsome man, and a college professor!"

Ruth adroitly steered him toward another pocket of people before the questions arose as to his marital status and the field of his professorship. Obviously, to many in this crowd having a son who is a priest was worse than having a son who is homicidal, terrorist, drug addict, or performs abortions. Tad suspected that in a close-knit, small town community such as this, everyone knew the truth about his profession, but out of politeness pretended otherwise.

Tad stood trying to eat gooey tuna casserole off a thin paper plate with a plastic fork, while carrying on an innocuous conversation with an elderly, retired farmer, friend of the family for fifty years. He decided the casserole was not worth the potential embarrassment of spilling half of it on the floor, and settled for black decaf coffee in a Styrofoam cup.

An hour later, the mourners had left, Ruth had hugged Doctor Don and thanked him for his strength and compassion, Tad had mumbled something about Doctor Don's stirring sermon and prayer and had his arm pumped like a hammer again, and the two returned to the Coburg farmhouse.

An envelope, tucked into the screen door, was addressed to him. It bore the address of the chancery office of the Catholic diocese of Madison. The short message asked him to contact Father Frank Donovan by phone.

Tad used his MCI calling card to save his mother the expense of a long distance call, and called Father Donovan. It turned out that he was secretary to Bishop Robert Ardito. "Oh yes, Tad," said Father Donovan. "Thanks for getting back to me so soon. The bishop would like to speak with you. I'll put you right through."

"Hey, Tad. Welcome back to the USA." Bishop Ardito's voice had the slight bit of hoarseness and rough eastern city edge that Tad remembered.

"Bob Ardito. Bishop Ardito," Tad said. "Boy, it's good to hear your voice again."

"Yeah. I'm trying to remember the last time I saw you. I think it was a pub in Georgetown. Can't recall the name of it. We were having a big argument and I don't even know the subject."

"It was 'The Pig's Ear' and we were arguing the relative merits of Big Ten and East Coast teams on the gridiron and the basketball floor. High stakes theology."

"That was it," the bishop said. Turning serious, "Tad, I'm so sorry about the death of your father. I never knew my own dad, but I can imagine how difficult it must be for a priest at his father's funeral."

"More difficult than you can imagine."

"How long before you head back to Italy?"

"I'd planned to stay just a few days. But I think my mom needs some looking after, so I'll probably be here a week or so."

"Can you get over to Madison and see me?"

"I'd love to."

"Tomorrow? For lunch?"

"Well, sure. I suppose."

"Good. We'll have lunch brought in, and we'll eat right here in my office."

Tad hung up wondering whether it would be strictly a social lunch, or if his classmate and racquetball rival at Catholic University a quarter century earlier had something else on his mind. He couldn't imagine the bishop so desperate to talk about the Trinity to insist on lunch the next day. And Tad knew little about intercollegiate athletics anymore.

Their careers as priests had diverged since those fun days at Catholic U., where they had both been outstanding doctoral students. Tad had become the intellectual, a leading academician on the arcane doctrine of the Trinity. Bob had excelled at canon law, church administration and preaching to Catholics of all backgrounds, status, and intensities of faith. His success in turning failing parishes, first small then larger and larger, into healthy, financially sound congregations had caught the attention of the hierarchy. His outspoken and sometimes nonconformist views on certain church matters had also attracted attention. He was viewed in some ways as a cannon loose on the deck of the Catholic Church in the U.S., itself a bit too feisty and independent to suit some Vatican tastes. Nevertheless, Bishop Ardito was widely recognized as good at what a bishop is supposed to do, as measured in census figures, balance sheets, and wealthy donors.

After the depressing events of the past several days and the trauma of Doctor Don's funeral service for his father, Tad was energized by the prospect of seeing his old college friend the next day. He was intrigued by the reason for the summons.

After another plate of warmed-over tuna casserole, Tad kissed his mother and went to bed. It was seven o'clock Central Daylight Time, and who knew what time on his circadian clock. He slept for twelve hours.

Tad turned off High Point Road on Madison's far west side and into the nearly empty parking lot of the O'Connor Center. The center was built in the nineteen-fifties as a seminary, but enrollment had dwindled and it was closed. Current uses ranged from the diocesan chancery offices to summer training for the University of Wisconsin football team.

Bishop Ardito looked like anyone but a bishop when he greeted Tad in his office. He was flushed, perspiring and wearing jeans and a Philadelphia Eagles sweat shirt. "Just got out of the shower," he explained. "I try to get in a workout before lunch. No reason why a bishop can't be as healthy as the next man."

"You look great."

"I'd like to return the compliment, but frankly, Tad, you could lose some weight. Do you get any exercise?"

"I used to run three or four times a week. The last few years, though ..."

"As your bishop, I'm ordering you to start running again and lose twenty pounds."

Tad had looked forward to more than stimulating conversation at his meal with the bishop. He assumed that with his experience and resources the bishop had developed some sense for fine food and would demonstrate it to his pal from Rome, who had grown accustomed to excellent cuisine.

"I sent out for subs," Bishop Ardito said.

The two priests settled into a comfortable corner arrangement of sofa, chair and coffee table, upon which lay two bags of food from Cousins Subs, a tray of cold Pepsi cans and glasses with ice. "I don't think I've had a sub in years," Tad said.

"You haven't gone vegetarian, have you? Or on one of those crazy fad diets?"

"Wisconsin farm boy in Italy? You kidding?" Tad bit into the end of his sandwich and came up with mostly bread. A half inch of lettuce, tomato, pepperoni, onions, peppers, provolone, and vinegar-and-oil dressing shot out the other end. "I forgot. There's a trick to eating these things."

"Right," the bishop said. "Like eating spaghetti. You must be expert by now."

"As a matter of fact, I'm considered quite good at eating pasta. We'll have a contest sometime. Your Italian heritage versus my firsthand experience in Italy."

The talk through lunch was mainly about old classmates, remembering friends and where they are now. Tad had studied for the priesthood at St. John's University in Minnesota. Bishop Ardito had grown up and studied in Pennsylvania. He was up to date with most of their graduate school colleagues. A surprising number were married and had left the priesthood. One had stepped off the deep end and was wanted by the law in connection with a bombing at an abortion clinic. A couple more had met early death by automobile and cancer.

Tad wondered when the talk would turn to business. "Well, Your Excellency," he said, "I have a hunch you'd like to get into weightier subjects than nostalgia."

"First of all, I don't know how they're talking around the Vatican these days, but in my diocese 'Excellency' is banned—symbol of obsequiousness."

"How about 'Most Reverend?'"

"I'd rather you wouldn't."

Tad could see why Bishop Ardito was considered a maverick by many in the church's top echelons, and why he has been so popular—and effective—in the parishes and now the diocese he has served.

"Anyway, I didn't invite you for reminiscing or a cheap meal. I need you. Badly."

"Say that again?"

"I need you back here as a parish priest."

Tad was lucky he didn't have a mouthful of food. He would have either choked or spewed it over the remains of the submarine lunch on the coffee table.

"I'm desperate for priests. They're retiring, dying or getting married at the rate of six or eight a year. We've ordained a grand total of three in the past three years. If every one of our current seminarians goes all the way to ordination—defying the odds, by the way—we'll still fall behind by four or five priests every year. It doesn't take Einstein to figure out that can't continue forever."

"But I'm in the middle of some very important research and writing ..."

"What's more important? A deeper understanding of the Trinity by a handful of university-level priests or the souls of a couple thousand men and women—farmers, farm wives, factory workers, hardware store owners, their children? You get the picture?"

"I understand your problem, Bob, but—"

"Don't get me wrong. What you are doing is important. The church needs intellectuals such as yourself to shed new light on our faith, the big picture. But right now we need workers—foot soldiers."

Tad was silent for minutes. The distance between Rome and the Diocese of Madison was measured in more ways than miles. Finally, "There must be some solution. God wouldn't allow the church to go without leaders."

"There is a solution. And a good one."

"Married priests?"

"Of course. And women priests. they'd both do a better job than many of us old bachelors. Some day, Vatican II will regain its momentum and some pope will realize there isn't a single valid reason why they shouldn't be ordained. Right now the papacy is standing on the shore of tradition, watching millions of Catholics drown or be rescued by main line Protestants or Bible thumpers or New Agers or witches or Druids. Or, most often, good Catholics simply drift away with total indifference to religion of any kind."

"But tradition—"

"Nuts to tradition. Druids have great traditions, older than most of ours. New Agers are coming up with new traditions every day. Traditions are great sometimes, like Christmas. But much of the time they're more problem than solution."

"Don't surveys show more Americans believe in God today than years ago?"

"All the more reason we should have the personnel to serve those people."

Again, Tad fell silent in thought.

"You don't have to give up your academic life entirely. With the Internet, you can work at home a couple hours a day, maybe more. You might even be more effective by computer than in person. Distance learning. Reach more people around the world."

"But ..."

"But your first responsibility would be to your parishes."

"Parishes plural?"

Bishop Ardito went to his desk and brought back a map of Wisconsin. He folded it to display the southern half. "Your home base will be familiar to you. St. Brendan's in Red Oak. You were baptized and confirmed there and went off to the seminary with the blessings of Father Nicholas Schmidt, the pastor."

"Isn't Father Schmidt still there," Tad asked.

"Sort of. But he shouldn't be. Alzheimer's. Should have been in a nursing home six months ago."

"Parishes?"

The bishop pointed to tiny spots on the map. "You will also have responsibility for St. Jude's in Bremerton and St. Joan of Arc in West Charleton."

Tad studied the map. He knew the area. "Can't be done. There's 200 miles of driving involved every weekend."

"A hundred fifty," the bishop said. "Anyway, Father Schmidt's done it for six years. Except today he's liable to forget one or two of them, and parishioners have to go looking for him."

Still more long thought. "I'm sorry, bishop, I just can't do it."

Bishop Ardito's eyes gripped Tad's. "Tad, you can either volunteer to help me out here for a few years. Or I can just say the word and you'll do it anyway. Those are the rules, as you ought to know."

"By the way," the bishop said, "I've talked with the head of your department at North American. He understands my desperation and will do all he can to make this Internet research and teaching work. He needs you too. You'll have two weeks off from parish work every year to attend important conferences, in addition to four weeks vacation."

Tad was out of arguments. He stood slowly to leave. "Wait," the bishop said. "I need to fill you in on some, let's say, special circumstances that exist in that part of the state."

"Don't forget, I grew up in that part of the state. I know every crossroad and hill in those counties."

"But do you know the people?"

"Most of my classmates have left. Their parents are dead or in Florida or in nursing homes."

"If I remember correctly, you served in Vietnam."

"Navy. Two combat tours."

"And won some medals?"

"Bronze Star and Purple Heart."

"I did one tour in Nam. Marine Corps. Infantry. No medals. From my recollection of some of those late night pub discussions in Washington, you came out of Vietnam with the many of the same scars I did."

Tad remembered those talks. Man's cruelty to man, as witnessed by the two veterans, was the jumping off point for some heavy talk about human nature, the relative gravity of sins of malice compared with sins of the crotch, and whether it is even possible to change human nature for the better on any significant scale.

"The war we were in," the bishop said, "was rooted in economics—'I want something you have.' Agree?"

"Yeah."

"But didn't we agree that throughout history, religion—'mine is the only true religion therefore I hate you'—was behind more wars and killing than the rest of the causes combined?"

"I've spent the last twenty years in Italy. Less than 500 miles from Bosnia, Kosovo, Serbia, Croatia, Macedonia, Albania …"

"Which were basically religious wars."

"Sure."

Bishop Ardito recalled, "We concluded more than one of those late night debates declaring that organized religion has produced more hatred than love over the centuries—killed more people than it saved. Was that the beer talking, or did we really believe it?"

"No, it wasn't the beer. We really believed it."

"And didn't we conclude that if we could change that equation, a little more love in the world, a little less hatred, we could consider our lives as priests successful?"

"Yeah."

"Do you still believe it?"

"Yes, I guess so."

"Okay. That's what I want you to do. Less hate, more love in southwestern Wisconsin."

"I would never have imagined hatred as a problem in southwestern Wisconsin. I mean, there's no racial minorities or anything."

"People can always find some reason to hate. Hate is easy. Love's hard work."

"Any suggestions on how or where to start?"

"Too many Catholics are just going through the motions. So do something different. Change the paradigm. Shake things up. Step on some toes. Use your imagination."

"If it's so simple, why hasn't somebody done it?"

"Nobody has the guts. That's why I need you, specifically, not just some warm male body who can drive 150 miles and say six Masses every weekend."

"I still think you have the wrong guy. I'm a professor. I teach at the college and post-college level. I do research. I publish papers. I'm in touch with some of the leading theological scholars in the world."

"Tad, you have three main jobs. First, I want to put an end to religious intolerance. And I want it to begin in southwestern Wisconsin, with you leading the way."

"And?"

"Second, bring back those Catholics that have drifted off. Third, light a fire under those already attending Mass regularly. Build some enthusiasm. Spark some passion."

"That's all?"

"Go back to Rome for a few weeks to pack and wrap things up. Let's plan on this starting December first."

The lieutenant opened and closed the chamber of the Ruger Mini-14, pointed it at an imaginary target over the heads of three fresh, eager recruits and cranked off a half dozen imaginary rounds. "Gentlemen, this is the ideal rifle for our type of action. It uses the .223 caliber cartridge, which packs a high muzzle velocity of over 3,000 feet per second and is capable of penetrating most Kevlar body armor. It's the same ammunition used in M-16s employed by many military forces around the world. Its civilian version is the AR-15, used by police in dozens of countries.

"Soldiers, in my opinion and the opinion of many other experts, the Mini-14 is one of the most dependable firearms in use today. It's rare that a part will fail or break. Jamming is infrequent, and it's one of the easiest rifles to clear when it does jam." He paused. "For a standard, effective, dependable and versatile combat rifle, one that will return our great nation to the people, you can't do better than the Ruger Mini-14."

After a dozen questions, the lieutenant dismissed the recruits, who left singly and melted into the late October darkness.

CHAPTER 3

Packing for the move from Rome to Red Oak wasn't complex or difficult. Most of his clothing went into boxes for shipment and would probably not be opened until late spring, when the Upper Midwest climate began to match Rome's of midwinter. Tad knew one of his first stops in Wisconsin would be a shopping mall for a complete, new seasonal wardrobe, with emphasis on covering as much skin as possible with as many layers as possible.

Goodbyes were hard. In twenty years, he had made many friends at Lateran, Gregorian and Angelicum Universities, in the Vatican and in Rome's secular universities. They all wanted to treat him to a meal, wine, espresso or all three. The body could hold only so much, but Tad did what he could to satisfy their genuine expressions of fondness and best wishes for his future.

Explaining that future was the most difficult. They were all curious about his astonishing decision to forsake teaching theology, where he had carved a worldwide reputation, for that of a simple country priest. And in Wisconsin! None of his friends had ever been there, but they knew it to be cold beyond belief and have a cheese factory on every corner. Some had heard about the University of Wisconsin-Madison and its reputation for biological research, which, of course, had nothing to do with the Holy Trinity.

Tad tried to explain his departure in terms of a desperate shortage of priests, that the United States was becoming a net importer of priests and that he was being imported. That argument, too, clashed with his friends' preconceptions, accustomed as they were to a Roman collar on every third male in that portion of Rome where they hung out.

"Besides," they argued, "how can the United States, the richest nation on earth, not afford to educate all the priests they need and then some?"

Tad suggested the lure of all that wealth might be a part of the problem, although well behind celibacy as a deterrent to religious vocations.

"Ah, well," they would say, shrugging their shoulders. "We wish you success and happiness in your new life, Tad. Please don't forget us, and return to Rome often to visit your old friends."

Bishop Ardito had made arrangements to smooth Tad's reentry into the Midwest and his inauguration into the life of a parish priest. It was Thursday night when his plane landed at Madison's Dane County Regional Airport, a short twenty-five-minute flight from Chicago, fifty minutes if you include taxiing at O'Hare. Tad knew it was cold when he saw from his plane window the ground crew bundled up, looking more like seal-hunting Inuits than cogs in the intricate, high tech transportation system of the early twenty-first century. The walk through the unheated jetway to the terminal almost congealed his thin, Mediterraneanized blood. Waiting to greet him was Father Donovan from the chancery, wearing a heavy blue parka with another, red one under his arm.

"Hey, welcome home, Tad. How was the trip."

"Long."

"You don't look at all prepared to face what we have outside. Too cold for this time of year. Bishop Bob wants me to give you this as a welcoming present. Keep you warm."

Tad tried on the red, hooded parka with the large white "W" and a pugnacious-looking badger on the back and "University of Wisconsin" where a breast pocket would be. It felt much lighter than it looked, but enveloped him and reached halfway down his thighs. "Wear this coat anywhere in Wisconsin you'll be comfortable and fit right in with the natives."

"I am a native," Tad reminded him.

"All the better. Let's go pick up your bags."

Although it was near midnight, Bishop Ardito was waiting for Tad and ready with a selection of cookies and a pot of mulled wine. "Sleep in tomorrow," he said. "Reset your body clock somewhere near central time. I had a couple of volunteers go to Red Oak and pick up Father Schmidt's car and bring it to Madison. It isn't much of a car and you'll probably want to look for something better." Tad thanked him.

"I kept my day pretty clear tomorrow," the bishop said, "so we'll have time to concelebrate a Mass and chat some more. You can leave about mid-afternoon. The parish housekeeper will have dinner hot and ready when you get there."

"Thanks, Bob. Will Father Schmidt be there?"

"Unfortunately, no. Father Schmidt is in a nursing home in West Charleton. He won't be much help. Only things he remembers are his childhood. Sad to see an intelligent and holy man go out this way."

Ruth Coburg had a visitor for supper Friday. She was cooking a three-pound chuck roast, mashed potatoes and gravy, peas and carrots, a tossed salad, Parker House rolls and butter, angel's food cake and coffee. It was the largest meal she had cooked since Henry had his stroke seven months earlier.

Before returning to Rome to pack his possessions and wind down his work there, Tad had explained to his mother that he would be coming back in a few weeks to take over St. Brendan's parish. The facts that Father Schmidt was old and feeble, and that St. Brendan's included two other southwestern Wisconsin parishes, were common knowledge in the community. Likewise, Tad Coburg's vocation as a Catholic priest was known by about everyone, despite his mother pretending he was a plain old college professor. So when word got out that Tad was coming home to take over for Father Schmidt it met with no surprise. Many in the three communities were pleased with the bishop's choice. Many more didn't care one way or the other. Some were troubled.

One of that latter group was Ruth Coburg's supper guest—guest in the sense that she was cooking and he was eating at her house. Not a guest in the sense of having been invited. He invited himself, and he brought the groceries.

After an elaborate blessing of the food, Doctor Don loaded his plate and dug in. Ruth took a smaller portion than she would have liked, not sure there would be enough for the preacher's second and third helpings. There was, but nothing was left to warm over the next day.

Doctor Don pushed his chair back while Ruth cleared the plates, cut large slices of cake and poured coffee. "Now, Sister Ruth, tell me about your son. What kind of man is he?"

For the next three hours Father Tad Coburg was the subject of conversation, Doctor Don asking questions, Ruth Coburg answering directly, frankly and eagerly. Was he an obedient boy? Usually. Was he good in school? Very good. Was he good in athletics? Oh my yes, all sports. Was there ever any indication that he might, well, let's say favor boys over girls? He had a girlfriend all through high school, but I can't remember her name and don't know whatever became of her.

Ruth's answers were not the answers of a proud mother. Rather, she felt herself playing an important, perhaps pivotal role in the eventual rebirth of her son as a Christian, a discoverer of Jesus Christ. She answered because Doctor Don emphasized repeatedly how important it was, how proud she would be when he lowers her son into the north fork of the Midewiwin to wash away all his iniquities and cleanse his soul for the Lord, while the rest of the congregation of the Holy Scripture Universal Church of the Lord sang and shouted "Hallelujah" and "Amen, brothers and sisters, Amen."

The subject of that discussion had arrived at St. Brendan's parish rectory about five that afternoon and had been met at the door by the housekeeper and cook, Mrs. Emma Koch, pronounced Cook. Tad calculated that she must be almost the same age as Father Schmidt, an octogenarian with room to spare. It was quickly clear that she was the one accustomed to giving orders in the affairs of that household.

"Your room is the second one on the left upstairs. Father Schmidt has the first one, and when he gets back from the nursing home he'll expect everything just as he left it. We eat at six o'clock." She turned and disappeared into darkness, presumably to the kitchen. Tad was left at the front door in his red UW parka and holding the two suitcases he brought from Rome. He found the dimly lit staircase and started up, a step at a time, as if expecting an elegantly dressed Transylvanian to appear with designs on his carotid arteries.

He knew from the first breath inside the house that an immediate priority would be a thorough airing of the entire building. Father Schmidt had smoked cigars in the house for more than thirty years. The air in Rome, at its smoggiest, was pristine compared with the stale cigar stench in the St. Brendan's rectory.

He found his room and was mildly pleased that the door had been closed for ten or twenty years, keeping much of the cigar smoke out of the room. The smell inside it was no worse than the stuffiness of his room in the Coburg farmhouse. He opened a window and unpacked.

At one minute to six, he appeared in the dining room, just as Mrs. Koch was carrying a hot dish from the kitchen. "Ah, Mrs. Koch, what are we dining on this evening?"

"It's Friday."

"Yes. What are we having for dinner?"

"Tuna casserole, of course."

A disturbing thought occurred to Tad. "Do we have tuna casserole every Friday night?"

"Of course."

"How about Saturday night?"

"Meat loaf."

"Every Saturday?"

"Of course."

"Sunday?"

"Chicken."

Tad didn't want to hear any more. "Please sit down, Mrs. Koch. I assume you are joining me for dinner."

"Of course."

For the next forth-five minutes, Tad tried to make conversation, without success. Mrs. Koch apparently had few complete sentences in her repertoire. He tried to learn more about Red Oak and how it had changed in the thirty years he had been gone. "Same as ever."

He asked about her family. "Husband dead, son running the farm, other son's a mechanic in town. No grandkids."

"That was delicious casserole, Mrs. Koch. And I loved the lemon pie."

"Came from the IGA."

That was enough conversation for Tad. He left the dinner table, filled with tuna casserole and lemon pie. And ready to choke Bishop Ardito.

The bishop, excellent administrator that he was, had further smoothed the transition by arranging for retired priests to handle services at the two outlying parishes for two more weeks. That left Tad about twelve hours, from seven-thirty in the morning, to prepare for his debut as a small town parish priest at St. Brendan's 7:30 PM Saturday Mass.

The ritual itself, no problem. Same the world over. Finding the vestments and necessary accouterments wasn't difficult, once he found the keys to the church. Familiarizing himself with the day's scriptural readings, easy but necessary.

Preparing a homily was something else. Preaching or teaching before large audiences came easy to Father Tad. But his audiences for the last twenty years had been seminarians, doctoral candidates and Ph.D.s, not farmers, farm wives and shopkeepers. He was tempted briefly when, searching Father Schmidt's first floor office for the church keys, he came across a folder of printed sermons from All-Occasion Homilies, Inc., of New York. Apparently, St. Brendan's parishioners were accustomed to canned sermons. Tad found one roughly suited to the scriptural readings of the first Sunday in Advent, but he tossed the file into the waste basket as unfair to the congregation, who could read the inoffensive and unchallenging platitudes as well as he could.

While Father Tad's inaugural service at St. Brendan's was concluding with a weak and hurried rendition of "Holy God We Praise Thy Name," a seminar on the general subject of loving or not loving thy neighbor was taking place about fifteen miles away.

The venue was Tubby's Tap, which was located in Williamsport, an unincorporated burg where County Highways A and R crossed, many miles from any water in which a decent-sized boat could even float, not to mention tie up. Tubby's was one of two taverns in Williamsport, the other being Bernie & Rosie's. The two remaining corners were occupied by a long-shuttered service station and the stone foundation of what was once a general store. Four ordinary pickup trucks and a jacked up Silverado with oversized tires were parked on the gravel outside Tubby's.

"They're buyin' them places with our tax money, you know," one of the discussion group participants asserted.

"How they do that?"

"Simple. They go to the bank, get a loan and the government pays the interest. All's they pay is the principal, and if they miss a payment or two, so what. Government don't care. 'Pay when you can.'"

"Fuckin' A."

"How'd you know that?"

"My cousin's brother-in-law's girlfriend works at a bank up in La Crosse. My cousin told me. I ain't shittin' you."

The discussion group of five was crowded four in the booth in the corner of Tubby's, the fifth straddling a chair backed up to the end of the booth. Bud Light was the beverage of choice, and fifteen empties stood on the table with five nearly fresh ones. The subject for discussion was the many Amish and Mennonite families from Pennsylvania and Ohio that were purchasing farms in western and central Wisconsin.

"Can't blame the bastards. If the government would pay my interest, I'd let 'em."

"Yeah, but the government don't, and the government ain't about to pay no interest for you and me. All we do is pay taxes and don't get nothing in return."

"Fuckin' A."

"Gets worse every year."

"You wonder whose side's the government on."

"Ain't ours, for damn sure."

"Fuckin' A."

"Know something else. Fuckin' government's buying their seed for them too."

"No shit?"

"You don't see no Pioneer or DeKalb signs on their corn fields do you?"

"Now's you mention it, guess you don't. How does that show the government's paying for their seed."

"Stands to reason. Government can't endorse one kind of seed or another."

"Fuckin' A."

"Them weirdoes is taking over with the help of the United States government and we're the victims. We can't do a goddamn thing about it."

"Boy, you got that right!"

Long swigs on the beers.

"I gotta go. Shoulda started milking an hour ago."

"Me too."

"Old lady'll kill me if I ain't home by eight. She's gotta go to work."

"Hey, Tubby, how much we owe you?"

The discussion adjourned. Participants headed to their vehicles carrying half-empty cans of Bud Light for the ride home, their heads filled with fresh insight, with time to reflect on it and to dream of ways to apply it in the name of justice, as they defined it.

CHAPTER 4

Father Tad Coburg was on the job less than a week, and already he knew more than Bishop Ardito about one task in a bishop's job description. That is, when not to assign a priest to a new parish. The wrong time is the weeks preceding Christmas. It would be a busy time for a veteran with one parish to worry about. For a rookie with three parishes, it was a hellish experience, if that term can be applied to preparation for such a holy season.

To start with, he didn't know a soul in position of leadership in any of the three parishes. That meant going through Father Schmidt's unkempt files, looking for the president of the parish council or some lay person who might know what's going on. In each case, the person listed was not the current president. One parish had not had a council for at least five years. Apparently, Father Schmidt's dementia had been coming on for some time. *Poor old guy,* Tad thought, *he should have been encouraged to retire fifteen years ago, so he could relax and fish or golf for a few years before his mind left him.*

After dozens of phone calls, he hooked up with the people who could get things done. Meetings with parish councils, choir directors, people in charge of Christmas decorations, religious education leaders and the guys who plow snow out of the parking lots—meetings all scheduled at the others' convenience—put a lot of miles on the aging Lumina and a lot of minutes on his cell phone.

But Christmas came together, as it always does, and any lapses in preparations went unnoticed. Tad was as awed and inspired by the Christmas liturgies as all who attended, young and old alike. He had hoped the Christmas season would lure his mother back to the Catholic Church. It didn't. She continued to worship at the pulpit of Doctor Don and his Holy Scripture church.

Nevertheless, it was a successful Christmas, from the religious standpoint. From the human standpoint in his three parishes, Tad wasn't so sure. He knew there must be hungry families and children without a visit from Santa, but he hadn't heard of any efforts to aid those folks, and he hadn't had time to look into it. Next year, he vowed, if I'm not already back in Rome by Christmas.

Tad made a determined effort to get to know his parishioners, at least by their last names. In each parish, he found fully a third grouped under a half dozen surnames, making the job a good bit easier. He stood outside the church door shivering after every Mass, shaking as many hands as possible. Also aiding the memory process were the parishioners' church-going habits. Same people at the same Masses, week after week.

One face, however, intrigued him. The fact that it was vaguely familiar wasn't surprising. Many families in the three parishes were descended from a single boatload of German immigrants who arrived from Bavaria to clear and farm the government-deeded land 140 years ago. There was a bit of sameness to the faces of his parishioners that would have been recognized on the streets of Manhattan. This particular woman attended the 7:30 PM Saturday Mass in Red Oak one week, the 5:30 PM Saturday Mass at St. Jude's in Bremerton another week. Still another week she was seen at the 5 PM Sunday Mass at St. Joan of Arc in West Charleton. Some weeks, not at all. She always arrived late, sat near the back, left early and didn't receive Communion. Middle-aged. Blond or graying hair, Tad couldn't tell from the distance. He wasn't able to shove from his mind her handsome face, weighed down at the mouth and eyes by sadness, fatigue or fear.

Mrs. Koch, the cook, mercifully spared Tad the Hobson's choice of firing her or starving from total aversion to her seven dishes. She quit. Or rather retired. As a retirement celebration, he took her to dinner at the Sandstone Steak House. She ordered the chicken pot pie. He decided that for the time being he would make his own meals and tend to his own laundry, rather than risk hiring another Mrs. Koch.

For the first couple weeks in January, he sequestered himself in the rectory, trying to make some sense of the membership and financial records of the three parishes. Up until about eighteen months ago, they were in reasonably good shape.

From records well before then, however, Tad had the sense that something not quite right was happening to the Catholic Church in rural southwestern

Wisconsin. Contributions had begun tailing off four years ago. Oddly, donations per family increased slightly, as might be expected during a healthy economy. But the number of families giving dropped, and giving reflected attendance. That seemed to buck national data, which showed membership in the Roman Catholic Church in America at least holding its own.

In earlier times, missing Mass on Sunday condemned the soul to an eternity of flames and anguish. Today, no big deal. Despite removal of the threat of eternal perdition, there had to be a reason for the falling attendance. Father Tad and Bishop Ardito suspected it was apathy, competition or both.

Competition is supposed to be the great American way. Brings out the best in competitors. Makes winners out of the lean and mean. Gives us the lowest prices and the best products. But does competition necessarily show us the surest route to happiness? Put two ideologies in the ring, face to face, will the best ideology win? Will truth be determined? Will it be recognized and followed?

Tad had a pretty good idea where the competition was coming from. He had met it at the Sandstone Steak House his first night back from Rome. But he needed a better picture of the religious landscape in that corner of the state.

He started with lunch with Pastor Richard Jensen of Our Redeemer Lutheran Church in Red Oak. Given Red Oak's limited dining choices, Pastor Jensen recommended the Shell Truck Stop just west of town for their meeting.

He turned out to be an affable fellow, small, frail. Father of five, grandfather of eight, planning to retire in two years. They went through the buffet line, muttering about their inability to eat that much, but filling their plates with hearty mounds of truckers' fare just the same.

"Call me Rich," the Lutheran insisted. "A misnomer, if there ever was one."

"Fine, I'm Tad."

"How is Father Schmidt?"

"Comfortable, I guess," Tad said. "He doesn't recognize me. Sad. The man had a profound influence on my life. And all I can do for him in his old age is offer a few prayers. Not that he needs them."

"I agree. When I came to Red Oak, twenty-two years ago, ecumenism was still on shaky ground. Nick Schmidt stopped over the first day we were in town to invite me and my wife for dinner that night. It was a Friday, if my memory serves me."

"Tuna casserole."

"I believe it was."

"Do you suppose too much tuna casserole causes Alzheimer's?"

"Huh?"

"Just a thought."

"From that day on, we were friends first and competitors second. I love the man, even though we have some theological differences."

"As long as you brought up the subject of competition, I'd like to pursue that a bit. How is your membership holding up?"

"It's drooping. Seems I lose a couple families a year. But mainstream Protestantism isn't going anywhere these days. Membership in the Lutheran church has dropped almost fifteen percent in the last thirty years. My numbers are no worse than the Presbyterians or Methodists."

"Are you satisfied with that?" Tad asked.

"No, but frankly, Tad, I'm running out of gas. I'm hoping my replacement, the man or woman who gets the call to Red Oak when I retire, will be young and vigorous. Our Redeemer needs a shot of adrenaline. I don't have any to give them."

Tad buttered his roll and used it to soak up some beef gravy. "We're having the same problem. All three parishes I'm responsible for, as a matter of fact. We've been losing two or three families a year. That's a lot of Catholics going somewhere other than our church on weekends. Apparently they're not turning Lutheran."

"I think we both know where at least some of them are going."

"Doctor Don's Universal, etc., etc.?"

"Yup."

"Why, Rich? What's he got that we don't? Same God, as far as I know."

"Check on the lives of some families that aren't showing up in your churches these days. I believe the pattern will be obvious. They have problems. Doctor Don has answers. Simple answers to complex questions. Some people need that. They're not mentally constituted to handle shades of grey. What won't be obvious is what to do about it. I'm not sure anyone, Catholic or Protestant, has figured out that strategy yet."

"You mean Doctor Don, is out-preaching, out-evangelizing you and me and the rest of traditional Christianity in this part of the state?"

"That's part of it," Pastor Jensen said.

"There's more?"

"I think so."

"Care to tell me about it?"

The Lutheran minister took a long, thoughtful sip of coffee. "No."

Tad mulled that over for a couple long sips of his own. "If I can come up with a credible strategy for doing Doctor Don one better and returning lost sheep to our flocks, will you be part of that campaign?"

Pastor Jensen was becoming uncomfortable. "Look," he said, "I agree on the need. But I'm two years from retirement. I've saved enough to retire, but without a lot of travel and frills. My wife's health is rather fragile. I have too much at stake. And the odds of winning anything in whatever campaign you develop are, let's say, stacked heavily against you. I pray for strength, but God doesn't give it to me. The answer is no. But I wish you well."

The mystery of the lady in the back of the church cleared up suddenly in the meat department of the IGA in Red Oak. He and she reached simultaneously for the same package of chicken breasts. Their hands and arms touched lightly and briefly, but enough to startle him, as if the chilled chicken parts had squawked. "Oh, pardon me," Tad stammered.

For the first time in thirty-four years, they had a chance to look at each other closely. "Miriam?"

"I didn't think you'd recognize me."

"Not across twenty mostly empty pews. But under the bright lights in the IGA, how could I not recognize you?"

"I've watched you."

"I know. Why?"

"I don't know."

He looked into her eyes. They confirmed the sadness he had detected in church, sadness accompanied by a heavy dose of fear and decades of sleep deprivation. "Last I knew, you were in the convent."

"I was. But not permanently."

"There's probably an interesting story there."

"You might find it interesting. I don't."

"What are you doing now?" he asked.

"Existing."

"That's it?"

"That's it."

"Where do you exist?"

"Out north of Bremerton."

"Can we get together sometime for a cup of coffee?"

Miriam looked furtively at the shoppers around her. She shook her head. "Gotta go. I know these people." With that, she abandoned her shopping cart and bolted for the door.

"Wait!" She didn't. He looked into the cart. It was empty. The reunion was as abrupt as the goodbye. The mysterious lady in church had been identified. Except for her last name, her phone number and where she lives.

And why she was so frightened.

Tad had studied fundamentalism in courses on the psychology of religion. He knew, for example, that there are about as many shades of Christian fundamentalism as there are buildings where they worship. No matter where you are in the United States, you can probably tune in to a fundamentalist radio station, and fundamentalist television networks span the country. Most are probably offering a valuable religious outlet to people who might not otherwise concern themselves with God and religion. Some are scams. Catholics have their own brands of fundamentalism, as do Muslims and Jews. Fundamentalist groups range from merely devout to zealous, to weird, to downright dangerous. Most, but not all, are sincere.

Since returning to Wisconsin on what he told himself was a "long-term, temporary basis," Tad made it a point to have dinner with his mother at least once a week, more often twice. Sometimes he brought groceries, always including more than they would consume at dinner that night, leaving the rest for his mother, who had always relished and thrived on leftovers. Sometimes they went out to eat. Tad had an opportunity to sample the roast beef sandwiches at the bowling alley in Red Oak. They were surprisingly good, but he realized no restaurant in this rural area could get by serving anything but quality Angus beef. Occasionally they visited the Sandstone Steak House, where he had become acquainted with the bartender, who was also the owner and a parishioner. Tad had talked him into stocking a couple good varieties of Chianti and a few other wines not normally found in rural Midwest steak houses.

When Tad would arrive at his mother's, either with sacks of groceries or to pick her up to go out, Ruth was always prepared with a few verses from the Bible.

"'And Job answered and said: No doubt but ye are the people, and wisdom shall die with you. But I have understanding as well as you: yea, who knoweth not such things as these?' Job, chapter twelve, verses one to three."

Or, "'And when the Philistines heard that David was anointed king over all Israel, all the Philistines went up to seek David. And David heard of it, and went out against them. And the Philistines came and spread themselves in the valley of Rephaim. And David inquired of God, saying Shall I go up against the Philistines? and wilt thou deliver them into mine hand? And the Lord said unto him Go up; for I will deliver them into thine hand. So they came up to Baal-perazim; and David smote them there. Then David said, God hath broken in upon mine enemies by mine hand like the breaking forth of waters: therefore they called the name of that place Baal-perazim. And when they had left their gods there, David gave a commandment, and they were burned with fire.' Chronicles, chapter fourteen, verses eight to twelve." She didn't know she had mangled badly the pronunciations of almost all the proper nouns.

When she finished such a reading, she would close the book and look at him as mother to son, as teacher to pupil, as if to say, "see, that proves it."

Tad would resist the urge to chuckle, or to shrug and say "So?" Instead he'd deflect what would be meaningless argument by declaring "amen, and let's put on the feed bag." That would be the end of the scripture for the evening. If his mother was looking for a theological debate, she wasn't going to get it from him.

That she was trying to convert him to the Holy Scripture Universal Church of the Lord was as obvious as the eighteen inches of snow that lay on Wisconsin in that mid-January. While it was not his primary motive, learning from his mother as much as he could about Doctor Don was a priority and, Tad hoped, so subtle as to be undetectable.

"Doctor Don is a very impressive man," he said.

"He is the most wonderful man I have ever met. Uh, besides your father, of course."

"And me?"

"You're my son. I'm talking about men that I've met in my lifetime."

"I see. How long has he been in these parts?"

"Doctor Don came to Millen County five years ago last June."

"Where did he come from?"

"Out east."

"Anywhere in particular out east?"

"I think it was Pennsylvania. Or maybe New York. Maybe it was Ohio. Doesn't matter."

"I guess not. Do you know if he went to any theological school or seminary? He seems to have a good command of the Bible."

"He's self-taught. I shouldn't say that. He didn't have to go to a school taught by man. He learned religion directly from the Lord."

"Did he tell you that?"

"Of course. We all were chosen by Jesus Himself. Jesus just had a lot more conversation with Doctor Don than he has chosen to spend with the rest of us. That's why we're so lucky and blessed to have Doctor Don as our spiritual leader."

"Did Doctor Don tell you that?"

"Sure. How could anyone doubt him?"

And so the conversations went between Ruth Coburg, born-again Christian, and her son, the Catholic priest.

One night at the bowling alley in Red Oak, Tad pushed away the remains of his burger and fries—a few fries that he couldn't finish and a slice of dill pickle that was a little too sour—and leaned back in the booth. "Mom, what was life on the farm like the last few years that you and dad farmed it?"

"Awful."

"Drought? Too much rain? What?"

"Too much of everything. Sometimes too much rain or not enough rain. But it seems worst when there's too much good weather."

"I don't get it."

"The better the crop, the more milk you produce because you've got plenty of feed. More milk means lower prices. When crops aren't good, feed is scarce, so you buy it. You get a better price for the milk, but it costs you more to produce it. Either that or sell some cows to save money, and then you produce less milk. Try to figure all that out. Drives you nuts."

"Catch twenty-two."

"Huh?"

"Farmers have been dealing with that for years. What was different the last few years? Why couldn't you get the house painted? The porch fixed?"

"Or the roof fixed," Ruth added. "Leaks like a sieve."

"Right."

"Too much money."

"You're going to have to explain that."

"It's common knowledge. Banks can't get rid of their money fast enough. 'Here, borrow some more. Need a new tractor? Here's the money. New milking parlor? No problem.' Until it comes time to pay it back. We got over our heads in debt, just like a lot of farmers around here."

"You and dad always seemed so smart, so frugal. Couldn't you see that coming? You knew the bank would want its money back eventually."

"Sure. But think of all those starving people in Ethiopia and Africa and India and all over the world. 'What a market,' your dad used to say. Only problem was, they were hungry, we had food, but they didn't have any money to buy it, so we didn't have any money to pay the bank."

"Seems obvious now, but probably wasn't then," Tad said.

"Hard work don't always pay off. That was a bitter lesson for the tough old German. I'm convinced it's what killed him. Almost killed me too. God sent Doctor Don just in time, or I'd be lying in a box alongside Henry six feet under right now."

"Want more coffee?" the waitress asked.

"Decaf," said Ruth.

"Me too."

Ruth opened a couple packages of artificial sweetener and stirred them in. Tad drank his black, but blew on the steaming coffee.

"Mom, is that what happened to the rest of Doctor Don's congregation? Done in by the economics of farming?"

"Not necessarily. Some of them are still farming and making money at it. Some never farmed at all. But they all had problems, just like everybody does. They were lucky. Doctor Don brought them God's message, they found Jesus, and suddenly their problems don't seem so big any more."

"That sounds simple enough."

"Well, it's not. God has to call you. And you have to answer. Just like I'm praying you and your sisters will some day."

While Tad was driving his mother back to her farm from the bowling alley in Red Oak, a motorist, twenty miles to the southeast, was placing a 911 call on his cell phone.

"There's a barn on fire. Better get the fire department out here right away."

"What's your location, sir?"

"I'm on Highway A, about eight or ten miles west of West Charleton."

"Can you pinpoint it any better than that?"

"There's a side road up ahead. Just a second, I think I see a road sign ... yeah, its Section Line Road. The fire is just down the road from the intersection."

"Is anyone injured?"

"I haven't any idea. Better send an ambulance anyway. I can see some people trying to get cows out of the barn. They're having a hard time."

"Thank you sir, for reporting this. We'll get right to it."

Twenty-five minutes later the siren and phone pagers of the West Charleton volunteer fire department and paramedic team were activated. The man who placed the cell phone call had stopped at the scene to help. He was soon joined by a dozen men arriving in horse-pulled buggies. The bearded men were dressed alike in black suits and black, wide-brimmed hats. Their bucket brigade was a valiant but futile effort. The barn and other outbuildings, the cattle herd and several horses were quickly destroyed. The plain white, wood frame house was upwind of the fire and was spared. The owner, dressed like the men who came to help, hugged his wife and children, thanking the Lord there was no loss of human life and no one was seriously injured.

Fifty-five minutes after the motorist placed his call, a single fire engine arrived from West Charleton to sprinkle water on the smoldering embers.

CHAPTER 5

Folklore in the Upper Midwest has it that when the temperature dips into single digits or below it's too cold to snow. People who live through many winters there know that is nonsense. It can snow when it's well below zero. Add a twenty-mile-per hour wind and it's downright nasty.

Father Tad stood bravely in those conditions outside the front door of St. Joan of Arc Catholic Church in West Charleton, shaking hands and chatting with hardy parishioners who had bundled up and attended the 7:30 AM Mass the first Sunday in February. It was two below zero, wind chill factor down around thirty or forty below. The snow that swirled around the church door, huge flakes, consisted of only trace amounts of moisture. It looked scary, but would pose no problems for seasoned Wisconsin drivers.

But, my God, it was cold! Tad had a heavy wool sweater underneath his Mass vestments, but couldn't control the shivering. Most parishioners nodded "Morning, Father" and hustled to their cars. One man, early thirties, sent his wife and two children to the parking lot with the car keys, and stayed to talk with his pastor.

"We haven't met, Father, I'm Bruce Bestman. You'll meet my family under warmer conditions."

"I'm happy to meet you, Bruce. A bit of a nip in the air, wouldn't you say?"

"They're talking about twenty-five below tonight, and maybe colder tomorrow. I think the weather will be my lead story this week."

"Oh, you're Bruce Bestman."

"Right, editor of the *Millen County Reporter*."

"I'm happy to report that I read your paper every week."

"Good. That makes four so far. Father, are you a football fan?"

"I've been out of the country for twenty years, so I'm still catching up on American culture."

"Today's Super Bowl Sunday. Could you come to our house? We're having some friends in to eat, drink and watch the game."

"Sounds great. Time?"

"Four o'clock or around that. We'll catch some of the media hype. Game starts at five. We'll be grazing on chip-and-dip, drinking wine and beer and eating chili until the game's over or we get tired of it, whichever comes first."

"Great," Tad said. "I'll be there."

His parishioners were a hospitable bunch, and he had dined at the homes of a number of them in the two months he'd been their pastor. Good people, good food, but mostly people of his parents' generation and always quite proper. This was the first invitation that sounded like real fun.

Tad had found a well-stocked wine and liquor store in Madison, and he was able to contribute a couple bottles of Brunello to the party. He added his red UW parka to the heap of coats on the Bestmans' bed and was quickly in the mix of partying football fans, friends of Bruce and Ann Bestman. It was apparent the main purpose of the party was the party, not the football game, which, since it didn't include the Green Bay Packers, Chicago Bears or Minnesota Vikings, was of peripheral interest to all but a handful of football aficionados, hunkered down in front of the TV set in the family room.

Recollections from his childhood in Millen County and from visits with his elderly parishioners had given Tad the impression that the area was populated by good, solid rural folks with decidedly provincial views of the world. The Super Bowl party introduced him to an entirely different element. Younger, better educated and in tune with contemporary culture, not necessarily native to the area, some Catholic, many not. All, except for one mixed pair and an openly gay couple, were married. Judging from the conversation, they seemed devoted to their families and up to the minute on politics, world events, the economy, investments, travel and the latest movies. Most appeared to be in their thirties and early forties, although Tad spotted two couples of his own early fifties vintage.

Tad wasn't in clerical uniform. Red shirt, white sweater and gray, wool slacks, from among the closet full of winter apparel he had purchased over the Internet from Lands' End, blended him among the jabbering, laughing guests crowded into the Bestmans' modest, 1960s tri-level home. Nonetheless, it took one introduction by the host to one couple, and quickly all knew he was the new pastor of St. Brendan's, St. Jude's and St. Joan of Arc. That turned out to be a good conversation starter, but religion was not a subject he or the other guests cared to discuss in any depth on Super Bowl Sunday.

"Father Coburg, I'm Jeff Gates and this is my wife Marilyn." Jeff managed to hold an open beer bottle and a plate of finger food in his left hand to shake with his right.

"I'm happy to meet you," Tad said. "This afternoon I'm just plain Tad."

"You in the pool?"

"Ah, I don't think so."

"The Super Bowl pool. The Rams are six point favorites. Cost you five bucks to get in."

"Sure, how …"

"Hey, Gordie. Got another one for the pool. You met Tad Coburg yet? He's a bachelor and lives alone."

"He's not allowed in the pool. He's already luckier than any guy ought to be." Gordie took Tad's five dollars and recorded his prediction of St. Louis by seven. Jeff, Marilyn and Gordie then identified themselves as employees of Distribute Dot Com, the men in information systems and Marilyn assistant vice president in human resources. Tad had a hard time following the shop talk, but was quickly distracted by another outstretched right hand introducing its owner as manager of the local Wal-Mart. Then others belonging to a man and wife who operated a Century 21 real estate franchise. The hosts' son and daughter, ages about ten and twelve, earnestly wound their way among the guests with trays of crackers, cheese and sausages, chips and guacamole dip.

Tad was invited to check out the chili offerings on a counter in the kitchen. One crock pot was labeled "Wuss Chili," another "Challenging Chili" and a third "Sphincter Searing Chili." He wasn't sure what "wuss" was, but was pretty sure he didn't want to be associated with it. Likewise the "Sphincter Searing." He filled a bowl with the "Challenging Chili, topped it with a slice of cheddar," and found it to be spicy and tasty.

By halftime, Tad had met more than a dozen couples and knew right away that he liked them all. He knew from the conversations that he would have to subscribe to *Business Week* and watch more of Jim Lehrer and Lou Dobbs, just to stay in the conversation with this worldly and upwardly mobile crowd. These people could be important to him in his efforts to turn around the situation Bishop Ardito had described and Pastor Jensen had been so reluctant to address.

By the end of the football game, Tad had met the other six or eight couples, had received four invitations to dinner and three more without specified dates. He intended to accept all of them, for reasons having little to do with eating his own cooking. He accepted an invitation to dinner with the gay couple, guessing that some necks would pop out of joint around the community. He was determined to stake out the ecumenical, all-inclusive position. It was part of the vague strategy he and the bishop had developed in that first meeting in late October and in weekly phone conversations since Tad settled into St. Brendan's rectory.

"Sorry you didn't win the pool, father," his host said, handing him his red parka as the party was breaking up. "Your team got nipped by a field goal."

"I had a wonderful time, Bruce, and I appreciate the chance to meet a lot of great people. Would you and Ann and your lovely children be my guests for dinner some night?"

"Sounds good," Bruce said. "But first I'd like to spend some time with you in my capacity as newspaper editor. Could we have lunch Friday?"

"I'd love that. I'll stop by your office about noon. You pick the spot."

The face of Miriam Whatever-her-name-is-now haunted him. Once it was pretty, the prettiest on earth in his biased judgment. For thirty-four years it had never dipped much below the conscious level. What you know you can't have becomes more attractive, more mysterious, even over that length of time. With nothing else to go on, his memory of that face had not changed. Until that sudden and unsettling revelation in the meat department of the IGA in Red Oak.

Now he had two reasons to track down his former best friend. To renew that friendship, which could only be platonic. And to learn why those eyes, which once sparkled like a blue lake in a light breeze, were now encircled with the darkness of many sleepless nights. Tad knew faces aged at different rates, and a long time had passed since he'd last seen Miriam's. But hers was not a product of age. It was a face of immense unhappiness.

His years in academia had honed his research skills. If the information he needed was in a library somewhere, or somewhere on the World Wide Web, he could have it, if not in minutes then certainly in a few hours. But without Miriam's last name, he was stuck. A pass through the thin phone book that included all of Millen County and most of the surrounding counties disclosed no Miriam Baumer, nor any variation of that name. He thought of calling the only Baumer left in the book, one Adolph Baumer, but he knew the man wasn't her father or brother, and something told him that, whatever was troubling her, might be made worse by indiscreet inquiries on his part. The phone book listed many couples by both first names: Thomas & Bertha Fitzpatrick, Ronald & Rita Schoemer. But no Somebody & Miriam Something.

Tad spent a couple hours on Tuesday driving the county and town roads around Bremerton. Nothing on mailboxes or dairy company yard signs yielded a Miriam. He drove past the old Baumer farm, homesteaded by a Baumer ancestor in 1859. The Foremost Farms Co-op sign in front of the house reported that the place was now occupied by Ralph and Patricia Stone, their children Jeremy, Christine and Todd and their registered Holsteins. Tad wanted to stop and revive some of the memories of that house and the family that lived there while he was growing up fifteen miles away. But to stop along a county road for any reason other than to read a map or, in summer, judge the quality of their hybrid corn, was to invite questions for which he had no plausible answers.

He shopped the IGA more often than necessary for his one-person pantry. No Miriam in the meat department or anywhere else in that little supermarket, not while he was there.

As his Friday lunch date approached, he thought of the *Millen County Reporter* archives. It might take days of looking through musty newspapers or clippings for the story reporting the wedding of Miriam Baumer. But it might be the only way.

Bruce Bestman selected the Crazy Quilt Café on Millen Avenue, the main street in downtown West Charleton, for their Friday lunch. Before they reached an empty booth near the back of the restaurant, Bruce had waved at, shaken the hand of or stopped to talk with more than half of the patrons. Tad recognized a few from the previous Sunday's party, and he did his own bit of table-hopping.

The menu boasted of the best hot beef sandwiches and best home-baked pies east of the Mississippi River. Tad couldn't figure how the Crazy Quilt and the bowling alley could both have the best hot beef sandwiches, so he decided to make his own judgment. Bruce ordered a double bacon cheeseburger, fries and Diet Pepsi, acknowledging the caloric paradox before Tad could needle him about it.

"You from Millen County?" Tad asked.

"Almost. I'm from a little town you never heard of in Minnesota, almost straddling the Iowa state line. So I might as well be from here. Same crops. Same people."

"Bruce, maybe you can answer a question that's bugged me since I in was in high school. How did this town get its odd name?"

"What happened to the 's' in West Charleton? It's the most asked question at the Chamber of Commerce. Seems one of the early settlers was from Charleston, South Carolina. He put up a grain elevator, and decided this little crossroads would be the west branch of his old hometown. He hired a sign painter to put the name on the grain elevator. Paid him in advance. But the sign painter forgot the 's' and skipped town. By the time the town found another sign painter and came up with the money to repaint the elevator, everyone knew it as West Charleton, and that was that."

"You'd think a town of 6,000 people, the county seat, would want to have its name spelled right."

They ate and they talked about inconsequential matters until well into what truly was the best blackberry pie east of the big river.

Tad's question sounded nonchalant. "Where are the *Millen County Reporter* archives? In your office?"

"No. Eight or ten years ago, someone much wiser than I realized what a fire trap the old newspaper building is. Had the complete collection of old newspapers, going back to 1892, moved to the Millen County Library. Then the granddaughter of one of the old settlers gave a few thousand dollars to have them microfiched and properly stored. If you want to see them, just ask the librarian. She'll set you up."

"I might do that. Help me get better acquainted with the community. I've been gone for over thirty years."

Tad then guided the conversation in the direction of Bruce's capacity as newspaper editor. A couple of questions established that Bruce loved to write, had an inquiring mind, went to journalism school at Iowa State and aspired, someday, to own a chain of weeklies, small dailies and local radio stations.

"That's a pretty ambitious agenda," Tad said.

"I have no doubt that it'll happen. I've already gotten the *Reporter* almost turned around for the owners. We'll be profitable by the second half of this year."

"You should have bought the paper earlier, while it was losing money. The price has probably gone up already."

"I have to establish a track record before any bank will back me."

"How are you doing that?"

"By giving readers what they want. Today they're not interested in the pap that filled up weeklies years ago. They want local news and they want to be entertained. I'm giving them local news, good writing and a tiny bit of supermarket tabloidism. Stepping on a few toes around town in the process, but that livens things up."

Tad said "You told me you wanted to talk to me in your capacity as a newspaper editor. I take it has nothing to do with your soul, your marriage or your aging parents?"

"You're right. Tad, have you noticed this town is sick? That Red Oak, that the whole county is sick?"

"If you're asking if I'm hearing anything in the confessional ..."

"Oh no. I have my own code about sources of certain information. I'm telling you a lot of folks around here are scared. And I don't know why. You start reaching into certain areas and they clam up or change the subject."

"What areas?"

"Your business, for one. Religion."

Tad was silent while the waitress refilled his coffee cup. It was apparent Bruce had noticed what had come to the attention of Bishop Ardito. The reason why the bishop had pulled him from his life's work in Rome. It was also apparent that Bruce didn't yet know any more than the bishop or Tad did.

"Yes," Tad said. "There is something strange, but I haven't had time to really check it out. All I have is a hunch."

"I wonder if your hunch is the same as mine."

"Which is?"

"Doctor Don and his brain-washed followers," Bruce said.

"How can a group so outside the mainstream and in such small numbers cause the kind of tension in the community that we've both noticed?"

"He's a strong man. One withering look from him can make your knees shake. He's a spellbinder. You can't argue with him, because he throws scripture at you faster than you can duck and dodge it. You walk away like you've been hit by Mike Tyson. His followers love it. They need it. They absolutely idolize him."

"Where'd he come from?" Tad asked.

"He played football, some small college out east. I doubt he ever graduated. Tried out with a couple of pro teams, but never made it. Started his religious career with the Fellowship of Christian Athletes. Innocently enough. Then he got into some kind of doctrinal dispute. Broke away from that group and started his own. Then part of that split away. His religion kept getting stranger and stranger. One day he showed up in Red Oak handing out flyers and inviting people to a prayer meeting at the Orpheum Theater. It just grew from there."

"Can't people see that he's a snake oil peddler?"

"You'd think so," Bruce said. "But his people don't. I'll even give him the benefit of the doubt and say he's probably sincere. Odd maybe, but I think he believes everything he tells his people. His control over them is absolute. If he told them they all had to wipe their butts with their left hands, he'd find something in the Bible to prove it. And they'd do what he said."

"Does anybody ever quit?"

"Some may want to. But they know if they leave that church their family and the rest of the group will never speak to them again. Never. He has them convinced that if they leave the Holy Scripture etcetera church, or even talk to someone who has, it's the same as making a pact with Satan. It's the gravest of sins and they'll instantaneously go straight to hell when they die."

"What are you going to do about Doctor Don?" Tad asked.

"I just report the news. I don't do anything about anything. Question is, what are you going to do about him? He's your competition."

"I don't know. I need information. Background. I need to know who I can talk to and who I can't. Will you help?"

"I'll feed you what information I can on one condition. That is, the story's mine when something happens, and I have a strong feeling something huge will happen."

"Small town weekly scoops CNN, CBS, ABC, NBC, NPR and all the dailies," Tad said.

"Exactly."

Tad and the young, ambitious editor reached across the table and shook hands. "Deal."

The next morning, Rick's Automotive AAA Emergency Service in West Charleton received a curious call from the editor of the newspaper. All four tires of his Chevy Blazer were flat. Over in Red Oak, Tom's 24 Hour Service got a call from the Catholic priest reporting the same problem with his Lumina. Both vehicles had been in locked garages overnight.

It took two hours of squinting at the microfiche reader in the Millen County Library. But Tad found what he was looking for: Dett. The 1974 wedding took place at the United Methodist Church in Bremerton. Miriam Baumer and Myron Dett. There was a comprehensive report on the bride's and bridesmaids' dresses, the color of the flowers, names of the wedding party, and the fact that the young couple would honeymoon in the Twin Cities. But no mention of the occupation of either bride or groom, nor was there an indication of where they intended to live. Tad made a copy of the story.

Snow was falling when he drove to the *Reporter* office. He stomped the slush off his feet on the floor mat inside the door and shook the snow from his parka. Bruce was absorbed in his computer. "Do you know these folks?" he asked the editor. Bruce looked briefly at the copy.

"She's a nurse in the emergency room at Tri-County Memorial Hospital. They have a bunch of kids, and every one of them is screwed up. Him you don't want to mess with. Myron Dett is one of the world's real bad asses. Big guy. Mean son of a bitch. You won't find anyone in southwestern Wisconsin who will say a good word about him."

"What does he do for a living?"

"He farmed at one point. Bought a place outside Bremerton. Went broke doing that. Bought a semi rig when the trucking industry was deregulated. The bank eventually took that away from him too. He worked for a long time at the lumber yard in Bremerton. Outside work. They wouldn't let him near the cash register."

"What's he doing now?" Tad asked.

"They say the sheriff got tired of arresting him for busting up bars and beating up his wife and kids. Wanted him around where he could keep an eye on him."

"How does the sheriff do that?"

"Made him a deputy sheriff."

CHAPTER 6

✿

Society's understanding of human reactions to tragedy and grief is improving, at least at the scientific level. Primitive peoples, who probably knew more tragedy firsthand than we do today, developed rituals and customs that apparently got them through trying times. Since before the rise of civilization, since the Cro-Magnon era and probably earlier, humans have increasingly placed themselves in the hands of specialists—shamans, medicine men, witch doctors, priests, ministers, rabbis—people they believe have insights into what happens after death, to guide them and offer comfort through those times.

Recent decades have seen the growth of secular experts on the subject of dealing with misfortunes ranging from losing a job or lover or championship to the sudden, tragic death of someone very close. Specialties have developed within the fields of psychology, sociology, nursing and education to help people handle those overwhelming moments in life. An elementary or high school student is shot, or killed in a car crash, and counselors are at the school within hours to help classmates understand, as best they can, and work through the trauma. Hospitals and hospices have grief advisors on staff and offer their services as part of the medical care package.

News media recognize that human response to disaster can be as dramatic as the disaster itself, and nearly every evening America is witness to victims of crime, fire, weather or other catastrophe tearfully displaying their grief for the world to share.

Psychology and religions (many of them) have found common ground in assisting individuals and families to confront life's unfair episodes. Most clergy realize that processes go on inside the human brain that are apparently distinct from whatever supernatural processes are at work in those situations. At the same time, a growing number of psychologists and physicians acknowledge mental and physical healing powers in their patients' spirituality.

In short, a whole industry has grown up to help people through the really tough moments in life, to help them make sound decisions at times when the mind is sorely tried and apt to mask self-defeating decisions as fitting and proper for the circumstances.

Such was not the situation in Red Oak thirty-four years earlier. Psychological counseling as a business or as a service of the school district hadn't yet reached that community to any meaningful extent.

Thus, when Miriam Baumer was struck suddenly by the devastating news that her father had perished beneath his overturned pickup truck, only a couple miles from home, she turned to her church for guidance. As expected, Father Nicholas Schmidt explained to her that no one knows what's on God's mind when he permits such inequities. Her pastor prescribed the only medicine he knew—heavy doses of prayer.

Miriam took the explanation to heart and went with prayer in a big way. Within weeks of her father's burial, she made the decision to devote her life to the Catholic Church and to helping others. For Miriam, at the time, it was the only solution that made sense.

Father Schmidt provided brochures from several orders of nuns. Miriam chose a St. Louis order that specialized in care of the sick, owning and operating a chain of hospitals up and down the Mississippi to carry out that mission.

Her good-by to Tad Coburg was brief, direct and, she realized much later, melodramatic and cruel—unintentionally, but selfishly and thoughtlessly cruel.

Their relationship went back to around sixth grade at St. Brendan's school, when they discovered some sort of eleven-year-old chemistry between them. It grew as slowly and naturally as they did. When time came for pairing off in early high school, they were a twosome. In every sense except the physical, by senior year they knew as much about each other as couples married for years. In the physical sense, they fought and won (or lost, depending on point of view) the battle against nature, preserving their chastity for their inevitable wedding night.

That night never came. "Darling Tad," she said, leaning away from him as he sought to embrace her and kiss on the Baumer front porch following a movie and Cokes. "Darling, I have something important to tell you. I have made a decision. On Monday I am leaving for St. Louis, Missouri. I am going to enter the convent. These past horrible weeks after the accident have made me examine my life as I have never before. I've decided to devote my life to Christ and my fellow man as a nun."

Stunned, Tad could manage only parts of words: "Wha? Whe? Wha'bout? Why'n'cha?"

"I'm sorry, my darling, it's what I have to do." In the light of the Baumer front porch, they looked long and deeply into each other's eyes—Miriam's resolute and pleading for understanding, Tad's disbelieving and pleading for a change of heart. The Coburg-Baumer relationship, perhaps as close to true love as any two young, unmarried humans could manage, ended with Miriam's abrupt announcement, corny as an old movie or bad romance novel. But final just the same. They parted with a handshake.

Miriam hurried off to the convent leaving Tad to make some meaning out of a life without her, a loss as sudden, brutal and senseless as her loss of a parent. Except under no manipulation of logic could it be blamed on loose gravel, avoiding an animal or even over-familiarity and lack of respect for a particular curve in the road. Whether Miriam knew what it would do to Tad, she did it anyway.

For twenty ugly, sweaty, terrifying, bloody months behind a fifty caliber machine gun, on the Mekong Delta and jungle rivers of Vietnam, Tad kept her picture in his helmet. Eventually, the high school yearbook photo crumbled from humidity and mold. But it served the purpose of keeping him focused on the future, murky as it was, even though her decision made no more sense than the war itself.

Not long after Miriam boarded the bus for the convent in St. Louis, her three older brothers, never too crazy about agriculture, talked their mother into selling the farm, then bugged out for higher education and careers in Chicago, New York and Denver. Miriam's mother took the proceeds from the farm and moved to Dubuque to live with her unmarried sister. Except for cousin Adolph, his wife and son Adolph, the Baumer name was gone from Millen and surrounding counties.

Miriam was well constituted for nursing. She had paid attention in high school biology, chemistry and physics classes, and easily learned the scientific portion of the profession. She was compassionate and cheerful with her patients. That part of her decision was well matched to her talents and interests. In another, later, more enlightened era, she would probably have sailed through medical school on scholarships and set up practice in Millen County, with the income and prestige that went with the title "doctor."

In retrospect, Miriam acknowledged that she had overdosed on Father Schmidt's medicine. She could not reconcile her zeal for prayer with prayer's apparent futility in helping the objects of her prayers. As hard as she prayed, patients died anyway—mothers with young children, fathers with families to support, bright and promising high school students, children with never a chance to experience life. The God she prayed to, the Virgin Mary and the legions of saints—none seemed to listen.

Two months before the fifth anniversary of her father's death, Sister Miriam Baumer was just plain Miriam Baumer and was employed in the emergency department of Tri-County Memorial Hospital in West Charleton.

The Millen County she returned to was not the county she had left. The most important person in her life at one time, Tad Coburg, was himself studying to be a priest, after healing his left shoulder, messed up by a Vietcong machine gun. Her friends from high school had drifted out of the area for want of opportunities, or had married and were living on farms, up to their hips in children.

Adrift in her home community, Miriam was at the point of sending for newspapers and searching classified ads for nursing jobs in the Twin Cities, Chicago and Milwaukee. One summer Saturday night, around 2 AM, a tall, muscular, handsome man entered her life. Or rather, was wheeled unconscious into her life by the Millen County rescue squad. Fractures to his upper and lower left leg, left arm broken in three places, concussion, an ugly gash from his temple to just below the jaw, and numerous other cuts and bruises had left him in serious condition, an awful mess.

The sheriff's deputy, who followed the ambulance from the accident scene on the west edge of West Charleton, wanted a sample of the patient's blood. Can't be done without the victim's consent, the physician on call told the deputy what he already knew.

"That's okay. There's enough witnesses in enough bars around the county tonight to testify that Mister Dett was so drunk he could hardly walk, let alone drive. The bastard's damn lucky to be alive. Drove his pickup right through a stop sign, never slowed down. Clobbered by an eighteen-wheeler must've been doing forty-five miles an hour."

Miriam, the ER physician and an anesthetist called in to keep the patient at the proper level of unconsciousness, factoring in his high blood alcohol level, worked for three hours to patch Myron Dett up. The broken leg was immobilized to await the orthopedic surgeon's ministrations later on that Sunday morning.

Miriam didn't return to her small apartment after her shift ended at 7 AM Instead, she stayed around to see the crash victim through his arm and leg surgery and his hours in the recovery room. She had never experienced a hangover. But she had heard enough about them to guess that awakening from the night's drinking, along with the other insults to his body and the chemicals used to alleviate them, would leave him in intensely sorry shape. She knew he would require more attention than the floor nurses and aides would be have the time or inclination to provide.

What followed was classic drama; make that hackneyed drama. Innocent, lonely young woman with a passion for helping the sick, the poor, the downtrodden, finds handsome, troubled but misunderstood man who needs only her love and tender care to return to health and to right his listing life.

One version of that drama would lead to a gentle, loving relationship that only got better as children came, the farm prospered and the couple assumed responsibilities in their community and their church.

The other version is the one that actually happened. It followed another shopworn script, the one with rapidly disappearing gentleness and love and the transcendence of alcohol and violence. Hardship did not make Myron Dett a stronger man morally. But it made him stronger in all the ways a sociologist or drama writer would imagine for a character that grew up in a completely out-of-control family.

"C'mon cows, goddamn your black and white asses. Don'tcha even know where to shit? Jesus Christ, dumbest fuckin' animals on the face of the earth." Myron Dett's thirty Holsteins were in their stanchions with full udders. It was six in the morning of what would be a gray, bone-chilling December day, pitch dark outside, milking parlor dimly lit by dusty, fly-specked fluorescent lights, half the tubes burned out. Myron picked himself up from the gutter behind the cows, just as one cow lifted her tail to piss on his face. He had landed in the manure-filled gutter because that cow had moved her bowels more vigorously than the barn designers intended, overshot the gutter and set a slick trap for the dairyman. Manure from heels to the back of his neck and down both arms all the way to the tips of his fingers, that was one consequence of the tumble. Another was further aggravation of the constant aches from the mended breaks in his left arm and leg. Only cold, dismal economic reasons restrained him from kicking the offending cow in the udder; he couldn't afford a case of mastitis. Thirty cows aren't enough to pay for groceries and keep the bank content. Twenty-nine would be worse.

"God, what did you step in?" Miriam was accustomed to the redolence of the barnyard, having lived with it all her life, save the five years in the convent. But it was overpowering, when, following two hours of milking, Myron removed the stinky coveralls, coat, hat and gloves and hung them on the back porch. "If you think I'm going to wash those things in my washing machine you're crazy."

"Then I'm crazy, because that's exactly what you're going to do if you know what's good for you."

Miriam knew what was good for her. Avoiding the kick in the hind end that might otherwise have gone to the offending Holstein was definitely good for her. Most of the dung would have to be hosed off the clothing before she would bring them into the house. That meant hauling the garden hose from the basement, hooking it to an outside faucet, hosing the filthy, smelly garments and returning the hose to the basement before the water in it froze. She'd been through that routine before. A rotten job made worse by near-zero weather.

He sat in his underwear at the kitchen table as she placed in front of him a mound of pancakes and a dozen pork sausages, plus a pot of black coffee. The oldest daughter had been picked from the front of the house by the school bus a half hour earlier. The other two daughters were too young for school and were wrapped in a blanket in front of the television set. Their son was still in the future. Miriam didn't like the idea of their father having breakfast in his underwear when the girls were around. But he'd been known to walk around the house, in full view of all three of them, clad in less than that.

"The bank's going to call this morning," she said.

"Tell them I'm out in the barn."

"That won't satisfy them."

"Then tell them for another twenty grand I can upgrade to Grade A and get a better price for my milk and make the fucking bankers rich."

"They already are. They'll want to know what you did with the last twenty thousand they loaned you," Miriam said, her voice rising. "They've stopped asking about mortgage payments. Now they're counting the days until they own our house, our barns, our land, our machinery and our own sorry asses, and our children as well," Miriam shouted.

The argument ended as many of the now almost daily arguments in the Dett household ended—with the back of his right hand across her face. Such events, often witnessed by some or all their daughters, drew blood or inflicted enough pain to end the discussion.

Inevitably, interest payments and the most essential groceries exceeded the family's income from farm products and Miriam's 11 PM to 7 AM, forty-hour-week nursing wages. Banks, even those as friendly and understanding as they advertise, eventually lose patience with interest piling up and no evidence of principal payments ever materializing. And so it was that, two days before St. Patrick's Day, the bank sold the farm, implements and animals at auction. Myron and Miriam Dett and their three daughters vacated the farm and moved, with a borrowed truck, their few shabby furnishings into a rented mobile home in a park on the edge of Bremerton.

Whatever character flaws Myron Dett exhibited—he showed flashes of most of them—sloth was not on the list. He had worked hard to make the farm viable. Up early, work as long as there was work to be done. But those villains easy credit, leverage, unrealistic optimism, macho pride, and stubbornness, all conspired to nudge him over the financial edge and force him into new lines of work.

First it was unloading and loading lumber and other building products at the Grace Lumber Company in Bremerton, outside, heavy work, and he thrived on it. The job's major drawback was the minimum wage, which the lumber company treated as the maximum wage.

Logic would suggest that when a couple has sufficient income to pay the rent, even for a cramped mobile home, money to feed five people a nutritious diet and pig out occasionally at McDonald's, money to dress like everybody else, money to rent videos and do most things ordinary Americans do, then the family should be reasonably content, at least from a material standpoint.

One thing wrong with that logic, which economic theorists would never understand, was the fact that the wife was bringing home twice the bacon that the husband was. In the macho world of Myron Dett, that was unacceptable. Whether his co-workers at the lumber yard or his after-work friends at Tubby's were aware of the situation, or even cared, didn't matter. Myron knew, and Myron seethed.

So when the opportunity came to invest in a semi-tractor-trailer rig, he grabbed it. The deal was, Teddy Barker would put up the money for the down payment, Myron would drive it for half what a driver would normally get, the other half being his down payment—sweat equity. That would make Teddy and Myron equal partners in the contract hauling business, to split the profits.

For Miriam, the arrangement had at least one good side and one bad side. The good was his long days, even weeks, away from home, time for bruises and abrasions to heal and for Miriam to show her children some of the love that was trapped inside by her husband's violent and unpredictable behavior.

The bad side was once again economic. Owning and operating a semi-trailer rig could, in reasonably good times, provide a decent living. But split the profits with a silent partner and the take-home pay remained substantially below that of an emergency room nurse working nights at the local hospital.

It didn't bother Miriam, who looked upon all family income as going into one pot to pay for rent, groceries, an aging and rusting Buick Roadmaster, and a few of the small town amenities. But it ate at her husband's fragile sense of manliness and self-esteem. And the amenities portion of the family budget contained nothing for future college tuition, down payment on a house or rainy days.

Nor did it allow for drunk and disorderly fines, which began to show up with increasing regularity. One such violation occurred behind the wheel of the semi, and Myron quickly lost his commercial driver's license. Back to the lumber yard.

Two or three times during their eight years on the farm, sheriff's investigators paid visits to Myron Dett concerning allegations of physical assaults on his wife. The calls had been made anonymously by Miriam's co-workers at the hospital, who couldn't help noticing her inability to stand up straight because of abdominal pain that had nothing to do with pregnancy, menstrual cycle, or flu. On other occasions, Miriam only fanned their curiosity by trying to conceal ugly purple-green-yellow bruises with sweaters and makeup. Her friends' insistence on x-rays during quiet periods in the emergency department led to Miriam's acknowledgment of her husband's violent temper and, ultimately, to those friends' calls to law enforcement authorities.

When reports of violence against the Dett children started to come in from teachers at Bremerton grade school, the sheriff's department brought reinforcements from the school district and the county's health and social services agency. Their investigation turned up bruised children, but apparently reasonable explanations for the bruises. It also found three girls who would not look any of the authorities in the eyes, nor would they answer direct questions with direct answers.

When the fourth child arrived, it was a boy. Miriam hoped that a boy would bring out some better instincts in his father. But she was a long way from convinced.

"You have every right to throw the bastard out. File for divorce. Get a restraining order. Keep him away from your battered body. You owe it to your kids, not just yourself. Want them to grow up like him?"

Wanda was dispensing her eminently practical advice over vending machine sandwiches and coffee, lunch in the hospital cafeteria at three in the morning. Wanda had been night supervisor of nursing at Tri-County Memorial Hospital for ten years, and ER nurse for many years of nights before that. Because the ugly side of human nature seems to manifest itself more at night, and often leads to hospital treatment of somebody, Wanda spoke from experience. "He's never gonna get any better. They never do. Never."

Miriam was on the verge, but not quite ready to concede the "never" part. "He has his good points," she said.

"So did Charles Manson and Adolph Hitler."

"He's not that bad."

"To you, he is," Wanda said. "And to your kids, probably worse."

Miriam and Wanda lit cigarettes, violations of otherwise strict hospital policy, but an unpublicized perk of the night shift. Miriam inhaled a lungful of smoke and let it escape slowly through her nose. "I can't fail again," she said, almost in a whisper.

"You been married before? You never told me."

"Not married. I was a nun."

"Oh, I knew that. Six or seven years. Then you resigned. That's not what I call a failure."

"Five years. And yes, I failed. My motive for entering the convent was religious. Big time religious. Mass and rosary every day. I was on first-name basis with the Lord, the Virgin Mary, my patron saint and guardian angel and all the rest. I didn't have a tooth filled without offering it up for the souls in purgatory. It's what kept me going after my father died. Then I lost it."

"It was your crutch."

"I guess so."

"Then along came Myron Dett. He became your crutch."

"Maybe."

"How long have you two been married? Twenty years?"

"Fifteen."

"With four kids under the age of twelve."

"Fourteen."

"You must have been doing something with him under those covers for fifteen years. Being raped once or twice a week?"

"Not exactly."

Wanda pushed her chair back from the cafeteria table. "Honey, you must know by now he's not much of a crutch. Matter of fact, it's the other way around. You're holding him up. Anyway, you're both going to have to learn to walk without a crutch. Or you'll collapse in a heap, him on top, and he'll smother you. Guaranteed."

Lunch break over, Miriam and her boss wandered back to their respective stations. A quiet night in ER, Miriam had all her puttering done, supplies replenished, instruments in their proper places. Plenty of time to think.

Months ago she had reached the conclusion that Wanda had urged on her in the cafeteria. Myron was unsalvageable. She had to stop propping him up. For her own sake and for her children. She had to jettison her husband, gather the children and strike out on her own. Life without Myron was the only life possible. She'd do it. Soon.

But before that oft-postponed breakup, the Holy Scripture Universal Church of the Lord knocked on the door of her trailer. Bernice, a high school classmate, now fifty pounds heavier, married and still living in Red Oak, stood with an invitation. They hadn't spoken in decades, but as they chatted on the trailer's weathered wooden steps, Miriam had a glimmer of those happy school days, the friends and proms and band and cheerleading and homecomings, sock hops and laughter and Pepsi. It was a time of unquestioning faith, enforced innocence and moral certainty that vanished in the last decades of the twentietycentury. Miriam surprised herself by agreeing to attend Sunday services as Bernice's guest and hear the "fabulous" Doctor Don.

CHAPTER 7

✿

"Ye, Gods. That's cold!"

That's what Miriam would have shouted if her head was not under water. Even in July, the North Fork of the Midewiwin ran about sixty-five degrees Fahrenheit, fed by natural springs seeping from the surrounding hills. The dunking lasted only seconds, but enough for a few years of her life to pass before her eyes.

The prospect—Miriam viewed it more as a threat—of the baptismal rite was almost enough for her to call off the whole process of rebirth. To start with, she had an almost pathological fear of water, any amount of water that wetted her face without first passing through a shower head or wash cloth. She had no idea where the fear originated. Nothing in her childhood memories suggested such a problem. Add to fear of drowning a metabolism that left her cold when everyone else was comfortable and comfortable when everyone else was complaining about the heat, and her formal entrance into the Holy Scripture Universal Church of the Lord was less than a totally joyful experience. Her new friends, the church congregation and especially her godparents (fifteen years younger), had assured her that God would protect her from her fears, and that His love would warm her. Besides, they said, it was necessary to suffer for one's past sins to enter the glory of God's love. It sounded logical, but it hadn't made the ordeal any easier.

She stood shivering in the narrow, white canvas tent erected on the creek's bank for the modesty of the baptized members, toweling herself off and telling herself that's that. Born again once is enough. Hell could be only slightly worse than drowning in ice water. She could hear Doctor Don in the creek performing the rite on Darlene, at fifteen the oldest of the four Dett children. "'Jesus replied: I solemnly assure you, no one can enter into God's kingdom without being begotten of water and Spirit.' John, chapter three, verse five.'" Whatever misgivings Miriam had about the baptismal rite itself, she was reassured by the words of John. She had seen them in black and white and they were unequivocal. Doctor Don had assured her that her own rebirth covered her three younger children as well, at least until they reached their fifteenth birthday, that God would not condemn to eternal flames a child too young to embrace knowingly Jesus as his or her Savior. Miriam knew Darlene would enjoy the dunking. Her daughter could spend twelve hours a day in the Bremerton municipal pool if she had the chance.

"I baptize thee in the name of Jesus Christ, our Savior and Lord."

Splash, muttering, spitting, giggling.

"Welcome, my children, into the Holy Scripture Universal Church of the Lord."

Miriam was the last of seven white-robed adults—four women, three men—to undergo baptism that day. Darlene was the first and youngest of three adolescents scheduled.

Myron, that was another story. Her husband's conversion, if it were to happen, would take a great deal more prayer and persuasion. The devil wouldn't surrender that grand trophy without a battle. Miriam and the thirty other members of the congregation were prepared to supply the prayers. Doctor Don would have to provide the persuasion.

The celebratory picnic following her baptism blew away any doubts that lingered about her decision to embrace Doctor Don's new and growing church. Miriam was hugged more times by more people than she had been, cumulatively, since she was a small child.

Miriam brought potato salad, which she had always believed—no one had ever told her—to be among the best in Millen County. Today, nineteen people raved to her about it.

Three families brought fried chicken, different recipes. Miriam was sure all three were better than any she had ever tasted, and were so far superior to what the jolly man in the white beard sold through the drive-in window on the edge of town, that comparison was a waste of time. She told the beaming chicken-fryers so.

She had similar compliments for the makers of the cole slaw—both the creamy and vinegar varieties. And the rolls, white and rye. The lemon bars, brownies and the huge white sheet cake, decorated with green fields, blue stream and huge yellow cross, all rated five-star embraces from Miriam and the other picnickers.

The lemonade was made from real lemons and real sugar. The iced tea from real tea leaves boiled and strained. Missing were beer, wine and caffeinated soft drinks.

The meal began and ended with an extended blessing from Doctor Don, the congregation holding hands, bowing their heads and humming a hymn that Miriam found familiar but couldn't place.

By 4 PM, appetites and most of the food were gone. The women cleaned up, putting leftovers into picnic coolers in time to preserve them for lunch the next day. They talked among themselves about when to expect sweet corn and ripe tomatoes and where to find gooseberries and wild blackberries. Men sipped decaf coffee and talked about gardening and home maintenance. The younger children used the swings and moved trucks and tractors around in an immense sand pile. Four sub-teenage kids were engaged in a self-devised game involving a soccer ball. Three teenagers, including Darlene, were seated apart at a picnic table talking about whatever born-again teenagers talk about when they are by themselves.

This, Miriam told herself, made her descent into the Midewiwin's maelstrom worthwhile. This is what she imagined Christianity was supposed to be. This is what she expected, but didn't get, from her brief stay in the convent in St. Louis. Or from her marriage to the handsome, broken man she met in the emergency room and helped put back together.

The party broke up in time for the two dairy farming families to get home for evening milking.

The Myron and Miriam Dett family sat around the dinner table in the family kitchen. It was Thursday, less than two weeks after the immersion of Miriam and Darlene into the river and into the Holy Scripture Universal Church of the Lord. No one was eating. No one was talking. All were absorbing the impact and sorting through the ramifications, from their individual perspectives, of Myron's latest explosion.

Myron's reaction? Who knows? Probably feeling quite righteous and wondering if another swat across his wife's mouth would be necessary in this particular skirmish.

Darlene: Fifteen years old, no doubt wondering where God was at this moment of extreme need, and counting the days until she can flee this dysfunctional family, never to be heard from again.

Betsy and Maria, ages eight and ten respectively: in tears, but remaining at the table under standing instructions from their father, and probably wondering why their friends' families don't seem to go through similar, periodic, gut-wrenching experiences.

Tony, age five, looking from one parent to the other, developing notions about the respective roles of male and female in a marriage. Preparing, psychologists tell us, for the day when he will carry the banner of cruelty and violence into still another generation.

Miriam sat silent, head bowed, staring at her half-finished supper. But this time she was not cowering. She was accepting her punishment, as Myron probably surmised. But she was also weighing the merits of the plan that she and three of her new-found sisters in Doctor Don's church had concocted. She was not entirely sure whether it would work, but guessed that the only risk was a puffed upper lip to go with her rapidly swelling lower.

Myron had as much power in the back of his hand, left or right, as most men have in a roundhouse right. But a backhand across the face isn't terribly effective in an ordinary barroom brawl. So he didn't use it often. Only at home.

The occasion was her mentioning his modification of his pickup truck by having Rick's Automotive install high struts and oversized tires, setting the truck a good twelve inches higher than its manufacturer intended, for no more practical purpose than impressing his drunken buddies. All at a cost of three thousand dollars the Dett family did not have.

Miriam could taste the blood on her lip and feel the lip growing. Without looking, she sensed tears in the eyes of their two youngest daughters. Darlene's eyes were shut tightly, head bowed, hands folded in her lap. Myron's eyes were aimed at Miriam's right ear, as though it were the next target. She mentally rehearsed her lines.

This time, no tearful flight from the dinner table, dinner unfinished. No futile attempt at response, physical or verbal. If there had been some way to turn her other cheek without tipping over her chair, that's what Miriam would have done. Instead, still looking at her plate, she slowly recited:

"Blessed are the merciful: for they shall obtain mercy."

"What?" If Myron had heard that line before, he couldn't have told you where or what it meant.

"Blessed are the peacemakers; for they shall be called the children of God."

"What in hell are you babbling about?"

"Blessed are they which are persecuted for righteousness' sake; for theirs is the kingdom of heaven," Miriam recited from Matthew.

"Broad, I think you're gone completely crazy."

Miriam braced for another backhand. It didn't come. "Blessed are ye when men shall revile you and persecute you, and shall say all manner of evil against you falsely for my sake."

"God damn. You *are* nuts!"

"Rejoice and be exceedingly glad: for great is your reward in heaven; for so persecuted they the prophets which were before you." It had taken her hours to memorize the passage.

"Holy shit. I gotta get out of here before I catch what you got." Myron shoved his chair back so violently it tipped on the floor. But no more backhand, forehand or even a curse. He stormed out of the kitchen, half a pork chop and a mound of mashed potatoes and gravy left on his plate. He slammed the door, and moments later the over-sized tires of his jacked-up, black Chevy Silverado kicked up a cloud of gravel and dust on its way to Tubby's.

The two younger girls didn't see much difference between that explosion and the scores of blowups that preceded it. Parents arguing about something kids didn't understand. Voices rising. Dad hurting Mom in some way, whether it was a swat with the back of his hand, a twist of her arm or yanking her head back by her hair and simply shouting in her face. The only difference this time was Dad running out. Most times Mom would run crying to her room, not to be seen again before they went to bed.

A new factor had entered young Tony's attempt to solve that increasingly complex equation of life: It looked like Dad didn't win this one. First time ever.

Darlene caught the significance of the moment. Doctor Don had preached the Beatitudes just four days earlier. But after fifteen rough years, she was a hard sell. In her world, it already seemed impossible for the sorrowing to be consoled, for the hungry and thirsty to have their fill, for the lowly to inherit the land. In the Dett family, lowliness was only getting lowlier. But, thanks to Doctor Don and the gospel of Matthew, her mother, while not inheriting the land, at least owned a complete plate of pork chop and mashed potatoes. The poor in spirit had won that round!

Miriam told herself she shouldn't be surprised to be sitting there with her children and her pork chop, and nothing more to show for her moment of independence than a throbbing lip. The topic that precipitated her husband's rage—the extravagance of making a monster truck out of an ordinary, practical pickup—would be there again. She'll have to bring it up next time he complains about the grocery bill. But now she had a new weapon.

❧   ❧   ❧

Miriam was thankful that her job was in the emergency department at Tri-County Memorial Hospital, not on a medical or surgical floor. Her patients were usually in no condition to spot the black, blue, green and swollen portions that showed outside her blue nurse's uniform. Family and friends who brought the patients to the hospital were too wrapped up in the emergency to pay any attention to the condition of the attending nurse. Emergency medical technicians who transported patients to the hospital knew Miriam well and knew well the circumstances that produced her frequent painful but not disabling injuries. But they knew their intercession would be futile. The hospital's ER physicians were either so inured to sprains and bruises, or so wrapped up in their own status that they rarely commented on Miriam's wounds. When they did, she muttered an explanation about playing children's sports and walked away, satisfying any solicitude that might be budding in the docs.

Ice had reduced the swelling of her lower lip to the point where it no longer affected her speech, and cosmetics had camouflaged the discoloration. But none of that fooled Wanda. Three AM, and, as usual, they were the only two in the hospital cafeteria.

"I thought we agreed you were going to throw the bastard out."

"Can't do it, Wanda."

"You want me to come and help you pack his bags? Two of us could have them in boxes and in the back of his truck in about ten minutes. That's only four of his legendary snores."

"Can't."

"You're afraid of what he'll do when he wakes up. Well, the two of us standing together will be more than he or any other man can handle. He'll take one look at these tough old broads and know we mean it. He'll walk out to his truck with his tail between his legs and drive off without a whimper. Forever. Guaranteed. Let's do it. Tomorrow night. What say?"

"Nope." Miriam was resolute.

"Afraid he'll come back? Meaner than ever? I'll take care of that too. I got a brother-in-law's a lawyer in La Crosse. He'll get a restraining order so airtight Saddam Hussein couldn't get around it."

"I appreciate that, Wanda. But I can't do it."

Wanda lit a cigarette and found an empty soda can for the ashes. "Want one?" Miriam shook her head. "You have some explaining to do," Wanda said.

Miriam bowed her head. As if her coffee cup contained the words, she recited what Doctor Don had counseled her: "Wives, submit yourselves unto your husbands, as unto the Lord. For the husband is the head of the wife, even as Christ is head of the church: and he is the savior of the body. Therefore, as the church is subject unto Christ, so let the wives be to their husbands in every thing."

Wanda stared.

"Ephesians, chapter five, verses twenty-two to twenty-four," Miriam added, by way of documentation.

Wanda's cigarette burned to the filter without another puff. She got up, extinguished the butt under a faucet in the sink, dropped it into the soda can and deposited the can in the recycle bin. "Miriam, honey, you're into something I don't understand. Never could. I hope you're right. But I have a feeling some day you're going to be wheeled into your own emergency room right here in this hospital if you keep that up."

"If it's God's will."

"I can't imagine God wants to see your face messed up and your bones broken by that barbarian husband of yours."

"I'm a sinner, Wanda."

"So am I, but I'd rather be a sinner all in one piece."

"I'll pray for you."

"That's fine. But in the meantime, if you want to talk, you just let me know. I'm not interested in your sins, but I am interested in your health and happiness. Call me anytime." She walked out of the cafeteria and returned to her floor.

Miriam sat thinking and praying. A little more thinking than praying. Her lip still hurt.

By Sunday the pain had subsided, the swelling gone down, and Miriam was able to smile, sing and be happy. She was back among her new-found friends. The first real friends she had since high school. The handful of aspiring nuns of her class in the convent might have qualified as friends, if they all weren't as unhappy as she was. But instead of bonding in their misery, like Marines in boot camp or young campers spending a week in the rain, griping about everything while building memories and friendships, they maintained the illusion of piety until the day they packed their few belongings and were out of there. Life with Myron and four kids left no time or energy for openness to those few

Millen County women who would have anything to do with the sad lady in the trailer park.

The members of the Holy Scripture Universal Church of the Lord were at the midway point of the two-hour worship service, the point where the congregation of forty broke into groups of three, four or six and were fervently discussing selected Bible passages and their application to their individual lives. All were sitting on folding chairs, in circles across the ancient garage, voices in check to avoid distracting other knots of Bible students.

Most new members of Doctor Don's church were couples. Discussion leaders were veterans of at least several months in the congregation. Miriam's leaders—mentors would better describe them—were two women half her age. Gloria Stark was from Lubbock, Texas; tall and on the thin side, dark brown hair drawn back severely and tied with a yellow ribbon. Judith Flint was from Jonesboro, Arkansas, short and on the stout side, with unruly ash blond hair that she had to push out of her eyes every ten or fifteen seconds. Both had graduated from an obscure, non-denominational Bible college in Arkansas, had joined Doctor Don's flock soon after arriving in Millen County, and were teaching in Lincoln Elementary School in West Charleton: Gloria second grade, Judith third.

Miriam couldn't figure out what role their husbands, Adam Stark and Joshua Flint, played in the operation of the church. Tall, lean, muscular, crew cut—red hair and black, respectively—late twenties like their wives, they were always present but rarely spoke. They roamed from discussion group to discussion group, listening but never contributing. They sang with the rest, but without the fervor. Once during a hymn, Miriam sneaked a peek at Adam Stark and found him looking at her.

Her mentors were elated at the outcome of Miriam's encounter with her husband over the matter of the jacked up truck. The fat lip couldn't be considered an outcome, since it preceded the implementation of their planned strategy, and was, indeed, a necessary causative factor for the strategy to be put into effect. The outcome was no more violence that evening; in fact, no more violence between Thursday night and Sunday morning.

"What'd he say the next morning?" Gloria asked.

"Nothing. I came home from work about seven-thirty. Darlene had gotten the younger kids up, fed, dressed and out in time for the bus to day camp. I went to bed and pretended to be asleep. He got up about eight-thirty. Smelled like a beer hall, but he made it to work at the lumber yard by nine. Two hours late, but they're used to that there."

"Praise the Lord," said Gloria.

"God is working in the Dett family. Hallelujah," said Judith.

"We'll see," said Miriam. "It's going to take a lot more than one incident and one excerpt from the Bible to reverse the damage to Myron's psyche that's festered over the years."

"Satan had a lot of time to mold your husband in his image."

"Myron is a sick man. He really needs psychiatric care, a lot of it," Miriam said.

"Nonsense," Gloria and Judith almost shouted, almost in unison.

"Psychiatry is the devil's tool," said Gloria.

Miriam was surprised. She wanted to agree with her mentors in everything, but couldn't quite make the connection between psychiatry and Lucifer. "I don't know. I've been around hospitals and the health care business for over twenty years, and I've seen psychiatry do a lot of good for a lot of people."

"Don't you see? Satan would like nothing better than to have a psychiatrist meddling with Myron's soul."

Judith busied herself in her Bible, flipping pages rapidly and expertly. It didn't take her long to find what she needed. "Here it is. Leviticus, chapter nineteen, verse thirty-one: 'Do not go to mediums, or consult fortune-tellers, for you will be defiled by them.'"

"But," Miriam interjected, "psychiatrists aren't mediums or fortune-tellers. They can't tell you what's going to happen. They're mainly interested in what happened in the past."

"Leviticus, chapter twenty, verse six: 'Should anyone turn to mediums and fortune-tellers and follow their wanton ways, I will turn against such a one and cut him off from his people.'"

"I don't really see the connection," Miriam said.

"Here, let me explain," Gloria said, turning to Deuteronomy. "'Let there not be found among you anyone who immolates his son or daughter in the fire, nor a fortune-teller, soothsayer, charmer, diviner, or caster of spells, nor one who consults ghosts and spirits or seeks oracles from the dead. Anyone who does such things is an abomination to the Lord.'"

"We're not talking about burning kids or consulting ghosts," Miriam protested.

"The Bible is for all times. We don't immolate our children today. Granted. But there are diviners and casters of spells today. They are the psychiatrists and psychologists and the others who manipulate minds for the devil."

"But I still don't make the connection. I agree with you on soothsayers, whatever that is, and caster of spells. And I'd add channelers and crystal gazers and that other New Age nonsense. But psychiatrists are medical people. They're scientists."

"Miriam, my dear," Gloria said, "you are still a child in God's eyes. You must learn to trust the eternal wisdom of His word in the Bible. When you have studied it for years, as some of us have, the meaning of these words will become clear to you, as it has for us. Trust us."

Miriam wasn't convinced. But she suspected that maybe the two women had a point. They'd been studying the Bible for many more years than she had. And they seemed so certain. Oh, to be that sure about anything.

"My brothers and sisters," Doctor Don intoned from the two-foot-high plywood platform built over the remains of the hydraulic car jack at one end of the garage, "let us stack our chairs and gather for some final meditations on the Word of Almighty God and sing of joy and celebration."

Darlene, who had been studying with a young adult couple and three teenagers, joined her mother, and together they clasped hands with the rest of the congregation—Gloria on Darlene's left, Judith on Miriam's right—to hear Doctor Don's final thoughts.

"Psalm sixty-two tells us: 'Only in God is my soul at rest; from him comes my salvation. He only is my rock and my salvation, my stronghold, I shall not be disturbed at all.'"

From there the corpulent pastor spoke of rocks and strongholds, using a variety of metaphors from life on farms and in villages of southwestern Wisconsin to buttress the psalm's message of salvation. To Miriam it made all the sense in the world. A good home has a rock foundation, Doctor Don observed; Miriam noted the Dett mobile home stood on rather flimsy concrete blocks. The preacher pointed out that for millennia man had found warmth, comfort and safety in caves hewn by God's hand in rock the Creator had put there for the safety of His children. Miriam reflected that their home was rarely warm enough in winter, and as for the safety of trailers, watch TV after a tornado hits a town. She had no trouble recognizing the contrast between the unsettled life she'd been living and the security promised in Psalm sixty-two.

Doctor Don's voice rose as he neared the climax of that Sunday's worship, taking more from Psalm sixty-two:

"'With God is my safety and my glory, he is the rock of my strength; my refuge is in God.'"

The preacher was thundering now, eyes reaching into the heavens through the garage's ceiling: "Trust in him at all times, O my people! Pour out your hearts before him; God … is … our … refuge!"

From the back a male voice began to hum. Then two male voices. Then more. Soon all forty men, women and children were humming the same melody. The first male voice sang, "God is our refuge." Then the second: "God is our refuge." Then all were singing, Miriam and Darlene as enthusiastically as the other thirty-eight. Words and melody stayed the same, only volume and intensity changed, growing until the rafters seemed to shake. Nothing like this in her five years in the convent had ever reached so deeply into Miriam Dett.

She was flushed, perspiring, more optimistic than she had been in twenty years. She was braced and prepared for whatever surprises Myron Dett might offer, when she and Darlene got into their rusty Honda for the short ride home.

CHAPTER 8

✿

Myron's surprise was that he had no surprises. No vicious outbursts. Not even rumbling or tremors that might warn of impending danger. On the other hand, no signs of affection, either for his wife or for his children. Myron entered a period of remarkable dormancy.

Like Vesuvius or St. Helens, however, the question was always "when," not "if" he would blow his top and unleash his fury. Like inhabitants of the lower slopes of those potentially violent mountains, Miriam chose to remain fully exposed and vulnerable, despite periodic advice from Wanda and still vivid memories of that powerful backhand. Why people consciously ignore such obvious peril is a mystery to folks viewing it from the security of their own worlds. It may be ties to home, no matter how humble or precarious. Or reluctance to change from what you know, bad as it is, to what you don't know, which might be worse. The belief that maybe this time it will be better. It won't happen again. Not in my lifetime.

One more, overriding motive kept Miriam in the mobile home with Myron Dett: the words of St. Paul to the Ephesians about wives being submissive to their husbands, the words she quoted to Wanda on the night of her husband's most recent eruption. She believed them then, with some reservations. As time went by and a form of tranquility prevailed in the Dett household, she cautiously shed those reservations, helped along by substantial dollops of study elsewhere in the good book.

She spent hours in the Book of Proverbs alone, finding comfort in chapter thirty-one, "Who can find a virtuous woman, for her price is far above rubies. The heart of her husband doth safely trust in her, so that he shall have no need of spoil." She quoted that to Myron one evening while he watched TV wrestling, and got a totally blank look, which she took as holding promise. Many of the biblical attributes of an ideal wife, she knew, were meant for another age—obtaining wool and flax and making cloth with skillful hands, planting a vineyard, making garments and selling them. But Miriam figured she qualified on some other of Proverbs' criteria—rising while it is still night and distributing meat to her household, fearing not the snow for her household, for all her household are clothed with scarlet. She understood that in the twenty-first century, she couldn't expect that her children arise up and call her blessed, or her husband to praiseth her. Nor could she expect Myron to extol her. She couldn't picture him saying, "Many daughters have done virtuously, but thou excellest them all." Not Myron.

Nor did she think Myron was prepared properly to carry out the injunction of Proverbs four-one: "Hear, ye children, the instruction of a father, and attend to know understanding. For I give you good doctrine, forsake ye not my law."

Nevertheless, Miriam found fresh guidance among the "He who's" and poetry of Proverbs. She was convinced it could provide a path for her husband, if only she could figure how to nudge him to the starting line. In the meantime, savor the lull in his violent moods and wait for the revelation that Doctor Don promised would bring Myron to his spiritual senses.

Her discussions with her mentors, Gloria and Judith, now moved to the Tuesday and Thursday evening prayer meetings because of expanding Sunday morning services, required some rethinking.

"Scriptures are perfectly clear on raising children," Gloria said. "'He that spareth his rod hateth his son, but he that loveth him chastiseth him betimes.' Proverbs thirteen, verse twenty-four." They had been discussing a discipline problem Miriam had with young Tony.

She had seen plenty of examples of not sparing the rod, in her own home and in the hospital emergency room. In quiet hours at the hospital she read magazine articles about parenting. She mentioned to her young, childless advisors that she had seen nothing to suggest anything but adverse effects from applying the rod.

Judith didn't have to open her Bible for her response: "'Chasten thy son while there is hope, but not to cause him to die.' Proverbs again, nineteen verse eighteen."

Miriam suggested that perhaps it was a matter of degree, something between chastising gently with a wooden spoon on the behind and mayhem that might bring about a death.

Gloria, also from memory: "'Foolishness is bound to the heart of a child, but the rod of correction will drive it far from him.' Proverbs twenty-two, fifteen."

Judith, Bible closed on her lap: "'Withhold not correction from a child: for if thou beatest him with the rod, he shall not die. Thou shalt beat him with the rod, and shalt deliver his soul from hell.' Proverbs once more, twenty-three, verses thirteen and fourteen."

Miriam said, "Somehow, that seems awfully harsh. Proverbs is such a beautiful and reassuring book."

"It's all there. Black and white. The inspired word of Almighty God," Judith said.

Miriam couldn't argue. She didn't know of a countervailing passage in the Old or New Testament. She vowed to herself to look for one. Her instinct told her emphatically that her son Tony had already had all of Myron's generous use of the rod that any boy should bear in a lifetime, that any more rod would make another Myron out of their son for certain, that Tony's greatest needs were plain old love and attention. Miriam shivered at the thought of her son entering second grade in a couple years, with the doctrinaire Gloria Stark in front of the class.

Life post-Beatitudes could not be described as entirely peaceful on the Myron front. Physical force against his wife ceased—or was suspended, Miriam wasn't sure. No more backhands. No more fat lips.

Instead, Myron's overdeveloped assertiveness manifested itself in vivid denunciations of something Miriam or the children did or did not do.

Meals, for example. Miriam's food preparation had never been an issue. Growing up in a farm family and training as a nurse virtually assured that the food would be tasty, plentiful and full of all the essential protein, vitamins, minerals, fiber and everything else it took for lumberyard workers to make it from seven-thirty to four and for children to grow and stay awake in school. Now, however, cuisine in the Dett household was consistently just a little off—too salty or not salty enough, too fat or not fat enough, too hot or cold, overdone or underdone, too heavy on the vegetables and light on the meat and potatoes, or vice versa. Critiques were delivered, not with the grace and sophistication of a restaurant critic, and certainly not in the spirit of constructive criticism. Rather they carried sarcasm and invective to new and sharper peaks:

"This slop tastes like pig puke."

"Where'd you get these potatoes? Dip them out of the septic tank?"

"We got two by sixes at the lumberyard better'n this meat. Need a goddam saw to cut it."

On matters of health, Myron plainly preferred folk remedies to modern science:

"What's the matter with that kid, snotty nose all the time?"

Miriam tried to explain. "She's got allergies. Every spring it's tree pollen. In summer it's grass and ragweed. Fall it's goldenrod. Winter it's mold and dust."

"More of the Baumer bad genes."

"It could be heredity. It could be from living in a musty old trailer."

"Shit," Myron said. "Teach her to hawk it up and spit it out. That's all she needs."

Their respective wages and disposition thereof was the most contentious of Miriam's and Myron's almost universal differences. Here again, Myron could be conclusive, even while illogical.

Miriam began the conversation with a question. "Would you mind telling me what was wrong with your old hub caps?"

"I got a raise. I told you."

"Fifty cents an hour. Minus taxes and social security."

"Fuckin' government."

"Do you know how many hours you'll have to work with that raise to pay for the hubcaps?"

"Mag wheels."

"Look," Miriam said, "between monthly payments, outrageous insurance rates because of your lousy driving record, and horrible gas mileage, that truck just about eats up your whole paycheck."

"But not all."

"No. The rest goes to Tubby."

"Bullshit."

"Bullshit nothing." Miriam wondered on more than one occasion what the nuns would think of their erstwhile Sister Miriam's language these days. The influence of Doctor Don and the two young church mentors notwithstanding, she found it difficult at home to remain entirely above her husband's coarse vernacular, the first and only language he ever learned.

"Truck pays for itself."

"What?"

"You deaf? That truck is a good investment. How else am I supposed to get back and forth to work?"

"You spend almost everything you earn just getting back and forth to work. That's absurd."

"What am I supposed to do, walk?"

"It's only six blocks, for goodness sakes."

"Guy's gotta have wheels."

"Then get yourself a rusty Honda like mine. It gets me to work and that's ten miles."

"You don't understand a goddam thing."

"What's to understand? I pay the rent. I pay the groceries. I pay for clothes, electricity, cable, doctor bills and half your bar bill. You pay for your truck. Period."

"Dumb shit broad," said Myron, closing the conversation with a click to ESPN2, leaving Miriam to shower and prepare for another night in the emergency room of Tri-County Memorial Hospital—to provide for all the Dett family essentials and a significant portion of Tubby's business income.

A nadir in Miriam's born-again life came one evening in early fall when Myron learned about St. Paul's letter to the Ephesians. The issue of the moment was Myron's unilateral decision to purchase a new Weatherby Accu-mark .300 Mag. deer rifle. She didn't begrudge him the time he spent hunting. He was a skilled hunter. Over the eleven-day deer season in November, he could be counted on to bring home a buck and, depending on regulations in effect in a particular year, one or two does. Venison for the Detts for much of the winter. A few ducks and a pheasant or two in October and maybe a wild turkey in the spring were tasty additions to the household menu. Miriam realized that bringing home game provided him a substantial infusion of self esteem, a sparse commodity in his psychological structure. She made it a point to marvel at the majesty of a buck's rack, the beauty of a turkey's tail feathers and the tastiness of all that wild meat. But a new deer rifle when he was already able to kill all the deer the law allows with his old one? Come on.

"Don't forget, woman," said Myron grinning the grin of a man about to play the ultimate trump card. "A wife," he paused dramatically, "should submit to her husband."

"Where did you hear that?"

"Submit to her husband. In everything. All the time."

"Don't tell me you've been reading St. Paul."

"We're not talking St. Paul. What they do in Minnesota is their business. We're talking Bremerton, Wisconsin, where a good and proper wife shall submit to her husband. Period."

"This isn't what St. Paul had in mind."

"Who the hell is St. Paul?"

"Myron …" She stood, expecting a gesture to illustrate his definition of "submit," such as twisting her ear or yanking her hair. She tried to recall The Beatitudes, but got "persecuted" and "peacemakers" mixed up with "sons of God" and "reign of God" and which belonged to which.

"Submit, submit, submit," Myron repeated dramatically. He even tried setting the theme to music, a rudimentary mixture of country, rock and what might pass for Gregorian chant, with air guitar accompaniment. "The woman will submit to her husband, all the ti-ime. Submitting, submitting, submitting. All the ti-i-i-ime." His elaborate bow to accept the applause of a fanciful audience wasn't bad, considering it was likely his first such bow, ever.

Myron was positively gleeful, singing and dancing out the door to his truck for the jaunt to Tubby's and perhaps further scriptural enlightenment. She had never seen him this playful. "Sub-mit-ting, sub-mit-ting," he launched into an off-key rendition of *Jingle Bells*, "Submitting all the way. Oh what fun it is to be a husband …"

The Sermon on the Mount had met St. Paul's letter to the Ephesians. At best, a standoff.

The account in the *Millen County Reporter* was unclear as to who started it. Tubby's had closed at 2 AM. Five or six of its regular patrons had gathered in the parking lot outside with a case of Bud Light. They were continuing an evening of discussion that included farm prices, the Minnesota Vikings, women with big tits, bass fishing on the Mississippi, government interference in individuals' freedom, Ford vs. Chevy trucks, Amish, A-rabs and maybe other topics. Which one actually provoked the melee, nobody could say for certain.

But when Tubby, who was locking up after washing down and restocking the bar, put in the call to 911, quite a bit of blood was already on the gravel parking lot. The two squads from the Millen County sheriff's department were soon joined by EMTs and their ambulance. Only one of the combatants required a trip to the hospital, that to repair a broken right hand and sew up numerous cuts, which could only have been inflicted with something exceptionally sharp—knife or broken bottle, deputies weren't yet sure.

Myron was not that individual. Instead he was treated at the scene by the EMTs for a pretty messed up face and was transported in handcuffs to the jail in West Charleton, along with three other individuals in approximately the same condition.

Miriam and the physician on duty in the emergency room had finished repairs to the broken hand and the various cuts and bruises, when she was called to the phone. Myron. He needed $500 to post bond so he could come home and recover from his injuries, which would include sleeping off a substantial drunk.

Miriam had been through this before, more than once rushing to the sheriff's office in West Charleton with her checkbook, after one of Myron's brawls.

"I'm sorry, Myron. This time I can't. I have two more hours on duty here. Then I have to get home because tomorrow's Saturday and Darlene has Bible class and the kids will be home all day."

"Aw, Mir, honey, you can't leave yer loving hubsand, bubsand, humseth. You can't leave me here t'rot in prism, prisn fr th'resta mlife. Have some pithy on a guy'sa slaven lummeryard all week." The appeal was familiar. In that state, jail was best for him and for the mental health of their children and herself.

"No, Myron."

"Please, Mir?"

"No."

Hiccup. Long pause. Hiccup. "Wife, su'mit. As your husman I'm ordering you to su'mit." The trump card again.

"As your wife, I'm telling you that even if I wanted to submit to you in your awful state, we simply don't have $500. If I write a check for $500, it will bounce and we'll both be in the pokey."

"I'll sell m'deer rifle."

"That's not a bad idea, but nobody's going to buy it at five in the morning."

"Please, honey? I hate jails. I jus' wanna be home in my own bed."

"Myron. No. You are there for the weekend. I'll call the lumber yard Monday and tell them you're sick. Then we'll figure out what to do with you. A couple days in jail will do you good."

✽   ✽   ✽

It wasn't a couple of days. On Sunday afternoon, Myron roared trium-phantly into the mobile home park in his Silverado, skidding a quarter circle on the gravel and kicking up a small cloud of dust to dramatize his arrival and early release from jail. Miriam and the children had returned from Sunday worship services and potluck luncheon at the Holy Scripture Universal Church of the Lord. Darlene was baby-sitting elsewhere in the park. Miriam was help-ing the girls with their homework, devoting seventy-five percent of her ener-gies to trying to hold their attention on a sunny, mild October weekend, and the rest on the lesson itself. Tony was flipping dispiritedly through the chan-nels.

Myron burst into the trailer. He was wearing new jeans and a khaki, but-toned-down broadcloth shirt with sleeves rolled halfway up his hairy, muscu-lar arms. The pony tail was gone, hair two inches long and slicked back in a stylish mousse, beard trimmed, wounds noticeable but starting to heal. He was a man resembling the handsome Myron Dett she had married, but a much dif-ferent Myron than the one who had sauntered off to Tubby's the Friday before. His wife and children gaped. "You were right," he said. "A weekend away, off by myself, was just what this old boy needed."

Myron gave his wife a gentle squeeze on the shoulder, tousled the girls' hair and plopped on the sofa next to his son. "Hey, champ, whatcha watching?" Myron had undergone a sea change. Just as obviously, the news behind his metamorphosis was straining to get out.

He turned from the TV. "Ladies and gentleman," he began. "I wish Darlene was home to hear the news first. And the big news is that starting tomorrow, I will no longer be Myron Dett, lumberyard doofus. Starting tomorrow, I, Myron Dett, your husband and father, will be Myron Dett, deputy sheriff, Millen County, Wisconsin."

If he had said "Myron Dett, multi-millionaire," Miriam would have assumed he had beat the eighty-million to one odds and won the Powerball lottery jackpot. She would have been astonished. But "Myron Dett, deputy sheriff" defied much longer odds.

"Did I hear you say 'deputy sheriff'?"

"Yes, ma'am. That's exactly what I said."

"Starting tomorrow?"

"Yup. Monday."

"The new jeans? The clean shirt, the haircut?"

"An advance against my first week's pay. My uniforms, my deputy sheriff uniforms, will be ready Wednesday."

"What, ah, will be your duties?" asked the still thunderstruck Miriam.

"Jailer and dispatcher. Three to eleven shift. Technically, assistant jailer and dispatcher until the first of November when Taylor Boyd is promoted to patrol officer. Harvey Foster took a job as chief of police in Renfro, over near Green Bay. Shows you what hard work and dedication to duty can do for you."

Finally, Miriam was able to react. "Myron, that's wonderful news. I'm so happy for you."

"That's not the best part. Fifty percent increase in pay. I get six fifty at the lumberyard. Seven bucks as deputy sheriff."

Miriam didn't feel like a lesson in math just then. "That's great, Myron. How did this all come about? I mean, last time we talked you were ..."

"I was a weekend guest of Sheriff Moses."

"That's right."

"Sheriff Moses and I had some long conversations. Must have talked for eight hours. Seems him and me have a lot in common. We agree on a lot of things."

Miriam couldn't imagine what.

"For instance, the importance of law and order. Without law and order, things in this county would keep getting worse and worse."

"Mmm. Yes, I suppose."

"Another thing. Law and order don't just happen. It takes dedicated people. People who don't care how hard it is, or how long they work—I get time and a half for overtime, by the way. Law enforcement is the only thing standing between peace and complete anarchy in Millen County."

"Sheriff Moses told you that?" asked Miriam, knowing a word like "anarchy" would not have been in her husband's vocabulary before then. Nor would such reverence for law and order be in his heart.

"Of course. And he ought to know. He's spent his life in law enforcement. Military police in Vietnam. He was in Border Patrol for a while. Deputy sheriff out west before he got to Wisconsin. Worked his way up in the Millen County department."

"Well, Myron, we're proud of you. I'm sure you will be a very good jailer."

"Deputy sheriff."

"Yes. You'll be an excellent deputy sheriff."

Thus was Myron Dett born again. Not as a believer and follower of Doctor Don. But in his own way, devoted to a cause and no less zealous. Miriam was pleased. For herself, for her children and for Myron. She was not entirely sure the citizens of Millen County should be so pleased with Myron's transformation.

CHAPTER 9

For thirty years, Father Tad Coburg's life had been a thorough immersion in religion. Teaching, studying, writing, meeting with noted thinkers of all faiths, little on the world scene passing without at least a brief examination of its theological implications. Such absorption is found in many pursuits. University scientists are wrapped up in their physics or molecules or fossils from waking until sleeping and in their dreams as well. Show business people think that's all there is in life and everyone in the world shares their passion for the stage and screen. Same with sports nuts, entrepreneurs, political junkies, policy wonks, investors and computer geeks.

So when Tad was whisked reluctantly from life in Rome at the center of his self-contained world to the life of parish priest in rural Wisconsin, the indifference of his flock to what so consumed him was jarring and disturbing.

He could handle the weekend travel among the three towns. He rather enjoyed it, in fact, even on slick roads that he hadn't faced since high school. Financially, the parishes were okay. No debt. Enough from weekend collections to cover maintenance, the pastor's scant budget and various diocesan and Vatican assessments.

But the phlegmatic approach of his Catholic parishioners to their faith, the apathy identified by Bishop Ardito, frustrated him. His oratory from the pulpit seldom brought more than vacant stares from the pews. Handshakes on the church steps were always congenial and pleasantries were always polite and almost invariably dealt with the weather. But never, "You hit the nail on the head that time, Father." Or "I got a question" about this or that, or even "You are full of prunes on that point." Catholicism was a one-hour-per-week pursuit in southwestern Wisconsin.

"You're a scholar. Did you ever think of trying a little market research? Find out what people are really interested in?" Bishop Ardito had a knack for asking the question that makes a person smack his own forehead. The two were meeting for their monthly luncheon, this time at the Brewery Creek Pub in Mineral Point, between Madison and Red Oak. Good beer, and fulfilling the bishop's admonition to get away from the daily grind on occasion.

"Market research," Tad said. "Never thought of that. I suppose if I mail a questionnaire to, let's say, every fifth name on our membership rolls, that would be about 500 families, we get maybe, what, twenty percent reply, which would be a hundred completed questionnaires. Would that be a representative sample?"

"Forget questionnaires and representative samples for now. Even if you got a hundred percent response, it still wouldn't tell you what you need to know."

"Which is?" Tad said.

"Which is what your parishioners are passionate about. What would excite them about their religion."

"My guess is nothing."

"Doctor Don can do it."

"I'm not Doctor Don. He's an actor. I'm a teacher."

"If it was simply acting, he'd get nowhere. People flock to him because he gives them answers. The literal word of the Bible. Overly simplistic, in my opinion, but what the people want to hear."

"So are you saying ..."

"No. If your people want that type of religion, let them go chasing after Doctor Don. Wish them well and tell them you'll meet them in heaven. Your people need two things: First, explain their faith. Second, help them use their minds to apply the teachings of the gospels to the questions and issues of today's bewildering world. A lot of priests, including myself, do a mediocre job at that."

"Where does the market research come in?" Tad asked.

"Who do you know that knows the community? Knows the people. How they think. What they feel. Someone with a good ear and a heavy load of common sense. That's all the market research you'll need for now."

"Father Tad, I pronounce that the best fettuccine between Madison and the Mississippi River."

"It may be the only fettuccine in these parts."

"Almost. Some of the better restaurants—Timbers in Platteville, Silent Woman in Fennimore—may have a pasta dish or two on the menu to satisfy the health crowd. But nothing like the salmon fettuccine you've put together."

"Thanks," Tad said. "Do you think I could serve this to some of our older parish members. I've been free-loading off them for three months and I'd like to return their hospitality."

"Those people know meat, and if it isn't good beef, or high quality pork, they think there's something wrong with the chef. Chicken or turkey, okay. But save the pasta for someone who'll appreciate it."

Editor Bruce Bestman of the *Millen County Reporter* and his wife, Ann, were his guests as Tad reciprocated for the Super Bowl party. They were the first stage of the market research prescribed by Bishop Ardito.

"Now you can earn your dinner," Tad said. "I need your advice. I'd like to light some fires in the three parishes. Rev people up. Get them thinking about their religion for more than just an hour on the weekend."

"What do you have in mind?"

"Small discussion groups. Get people together, six or eight at a time, evenings, here in the rectory or somebody's home. Talk about their Catholic faith. What it means to their everyday lives."

"You mean like the Holy Trinity?"

"Well, sure."

"With all due respect, Father Tad, forget it. God hasn't created desserts tasty enough to draw four American Catholic lay people to a discussion of the Holy Trinity."

"Okay. Give me a few subjects they are interested in."

"Parenting. How to raise your kids as good, Christian, law-abiding citizens in a drug-crazy, sex-crazy, terrifying, materialistic world."

"A media-dominated world," Tad added.

"Right," Bruce said. "And you're talking to the next Rupert Murdoch."

"Give me some more topics."

"How about the extent to which God acts in our lives," Ann said. "Does he answer our prayers? Sometimes? All the time? Never? Does he deliberately throw hurdles in our way just to see us jump, or toss us a bone to chew on once in a while? If so, why?"

Bruce's turn: "How about the legitimacy of other religions? I heard Rome put out a document saying the Catholic faith is the only true faith, everybody else is wrong and it's our duty to convert them."

"Well, Cardinal Ratzinger's Congregation for the Doctrine of the Faith has published a document called *Dominus Jesus* and that's basically what it says."

"Sounds a lot like Doctor Don," Ann said.

"Some say Cardinal Ratzinger represents the fundamentalist fringe of the Roman Catholic Church. He comes down pretty hard on religious pluralism."

"Do you believe it, Tad?"

"Of course not."

"Do you know Cardinal Ratzinger?"

"Well, as a matter of fact, I do, he and I ..."

"Well enough to invite him over here to discuss his ideas with the Catholics of southwestern Wisconsin?"

"Well, ah, kind of expensive, plane fare and all ..."

"We'll sell tickets."

"Well, I don't know if he, that is, he's pretty busy."

"We could arrange an ecumenical meeting with Doctor Don and some of the Protestant ministers."

"Well, I doubt if ..."

"If he can't make it, would you be interested in a debate with Doctor Don?"

"Well, that's an interesting question. I'll have to think about it."

"The point is," Ann said, "Unless you make discussion subjects a better draw than '60 Minutes' or 'West Wing,' don't bother. I mean, like, forget the Trinity. Forget Christ dying for our sins. All well and good, but total yawners. Forget abortion—people are for it or against it and nobody's going to change their mind. Forget contraception; Rome's lost that battle and they ought to get used to it."

It was market research, but the results weren't what Tad had expected to hear. The Holy Trinity, the central focus of his life for the past twenty years, the essence of the Catholic faith—a "total yawner." No wonder the glassy eyes staring back at the pulpit.

"Will you two serve as chairs for the first discussion group to get things started?"

"No," Bruce said quickly. "We report news, not make news."

"Okay, who?"

Tad had swallowed hard, but agreed to the Bestmans' recommendation for co-chairs. Charles and Frederick, the gay couple he'd met at the Super Bowl party, ran a software firm dealing with the bovine genome, working from their

Frank Lloyd Wright-style home in the hills east of West Charleton. Extremely bright, mid-twenties and already, Bruce told him, multi-millionaires.

The first discussion session exceeded Tad's hopes. The co-chairs did a masterful job of setting and following ground rules, including the one that there would be no attempt at conclusion or consensus, the idea being only to get the participants thinking. And did it ever. Charles and Frederick kept the discussion hopping, on subject, letting everyone have a chance to pitch in, quelling arguments just in time, suggesting new avenues to explore when one seemed exhausted.

All three parishes were represented, five couples. The topic was prayer, with Frederick's distinctly updated title: "Does God Micromanage?" The group quickly disposed of the notion that God helps free throws go into the basket and baseballs hit the sweet spot of the bat. Talk ranged from personal anecdotes about God answering intense prayer and restoring the health of a loved one, to real doubts whether God pays any attention at all. Someone suggested that maybe God was simply Mr. Big Bang, who then sat back to watch, once all that matter and energy was set in motion. That led to talk about the nature of God in the context of possible life outside our solar system, then on to new astrophysical concepts such as multiple universes, anti-matter and dark energy and their implications for our understanding of the nature of God and mankind. Frederick eased it back closer to the stated subject of prayer by suggesting that prayer might be one talking intensely to oneself, and that sanguine consequences of prayer were psychosomatic. Or the results of prayer were simply greater insight and understanding of the problem at hand.

"Can a person believe that and still be a Catholic?"

"Why not?"

"Then you're not believing in God."

"Maybe God is inside me, rather than sitting on a cloud out there somewhere."

"Doesn't it say Jesus came down from heaven?"

"Somewhere."

"Apostles Creed," interjected Father Tad, his first contribution since introducing the co-chairs forty-five minutes earlier.

"Gang, we're drifting. The subject is prayer. Remember?" That was Charles.

"I still think God listens. Even doctors are admitting that prayer helps the healing process."

"But other people get well without prayers, and doctors can't explain why."

"But people have been praying in one form or another for thousands of years."

"Billions of people can't be all wrong."

"Anybody here still say the rosary?"

"I do," said Tina of Century 21, the only affirmative response.

"Why?"

"I suppose because I always have."

"When you're praying the rosary, are you thinking about the Joyful, Sorrowful and Glorious mysteries?"

"Sometimes."

"For how long?"

"Maybe a minute or two."

"Is that praying?"

"They say it is."

"How about you, Bert?" Frederick asked the other half of the real estate team.

"Afraid not. Tina keeps asking me, but I can always find something else that needs to be done."

So the discussion went, never ranging too far from orthodoxy, but well outside that normally heard in many Roman Catholic churches.

Tad was struck by the similarities and the differences between the evening's discussion and discussions thirty-plus years before: same topics, same probing and unanswerable questions; the setting and participants couldn't have been much more dissimilar. Tonight's was conducted in the cozy living room of St. Brendan's rectory, insulated from the icy February wind streaming across Wisconsin from Canada's northwestern provinces. Healthy, secure and mostly contented Americans speaking mainly in the abstract, death and judgment being out there somewhere in their distant futures. Thirty years ago the participants were tired, scared sailors, talking in whispers at night on PBR decks on blackened rivers. They talked of a subject they could be facing in the next hour, day or week—what was on the other side when that Vietcong bullet tore life from their fragile bodies.

Tad was impressed with the eclectic interests of the group and the scope of their knowledge of matters outside the tasks of making a living and rearing children. In so many ways, they were better educated and prepared for the complexity of the twenty-first century than the theology students he dealt with at North American College and other seminaries of other faiths. He thought, *Say what you want about the shallowness of television and bullet-point journal-*

ism, these people know more about more subjects than sages, pundits and certainly the Curia give them credit for. And they ask questions folks in Rome can't answer, except in textbook terms—inadequate in most cases.

As the agreed-upon hour and fifteen minutes wound down, Tad had to ask the question that had been building in him for a half hour: "I've heard here tonight a lot of, let's say, independent thinking concerning your Catholic religion. Fair conclusion?"

Nods all the way around.

"To what extent does that reflect all Catholics today—at least the members of St. Brendan's, Joan of Arc and St. Jude's?"

"Most."

"Some."

"A few."

"Good question," said Jeff Gates. "I'd say anyone under forty, make that fifty, tends to think and ask questions about their religion. Anyone over that is pretty locked into what they were taught, whether they actually believe it or not."

"I don't agree," his wife Marilyn said. "I think most people have real questions. They just don't ask them."

"A lot of people, young and old, go to church just in case the priest is right. Hedging their bets." More nods around the room.

This, too, wasn't what Tad had hoped to hear, but he decided he wasn't surprised. Should have known. Yawns, blank stares, all that feedback from his congregations screamed doubt and apathy. His work was cut out for him.

Bishop Ardito couldn't wait. He expected a call at 10 PM, and it was closer to 11 before the last of the discussion participants left. Bruce and Ann Bestman helped put the cake plates, coffee cups and silver into the dishwasher and tidy up the rectory living room.

"Sorry I couldn't get back to you sooner, Bob. Nobody wanted to go home. Couldn't stop talking."

"About religion, I hope."

"Of course about religion."

"Could you answer their questions?"

"Not a one."

"Good," the bishop said.

"Say what?"

"I'd say your first small group discussion session was a total success."

"They asked a ton of questions. I couldn't answer them. Thirty years of seminary education, theological research and teaching and I couldn't answer the questions of ordinary, small-town American Catholics. About prayer, for crying out loud. That's success?"

"It doesn't mean you failed. It only means they are asking the right questions. For centuries the laity have been asking the clergy what religion is all about. The answer has always been a dodge. What we were taught in the seminary or what we think piety and tradition teach us. The answer to the tough question was always 'It's a divine mystery' or 'God is infinite.' In other words, 'Shut up, it's none of your business.'"

"But," Tad said, "some questions don't have answers."

"Jesus made his teaching vivid and understandable. No reason we can't too. Didn't I tell you that your third big challenge is getting people fired up and living the gospel?"

"Uh huh."

"You do that and the unanswerable questions will take care of themselves."

Between the over-stimulation of the evening's spirited discussions, three cups of regular coffee that he knew better than to drink, and the bishop's late night challenge, 1 AM and 2 AM came and went without a suggestion of sleep.

Sleeplessness was not an unusual condition for Tad. The hours of darkness are often the worst part of the day for men and women who have survived many nights of terror in combat.

Add to that the intellectual stimulation of his profession, which often carried well past time to turn off the lights. He frequently would turn the lights back on and return to the computer for an e-mail to a colleague, or revision of a chapter in the textbook or treatise he was working on at that time. Or, depending on the time zones involved, a phone call or two on matters of professional interest, or just a chat with a scholar or friend he hadn't seen in a while.

All too often, those hours of darkness were spent with an ache for a part of life that ended abruptly on the front porch of the Baumer home thirty-four years before. It was a life of shared experiences, thoughts, dreams, fears, hopes, disappointments, sorrows, everything that's better with someone than alone. Until that encounter at the poultry display in the IGA, he had considered that phase of life forever locked behind convent doors.

All that was going on inside the middle-aged priest when the phone chirped beside his bed. It was 2:05 AM Could he come to Tri-County Memorial Hospital immediately? He was needed. Not an unusual phone call for a man of the cloth to receive. Not an unusual time to receive it. The tone of the caller, this time, was different. Not reverent. Not polite. Not apologetic for the hour or the inconvenience. Imperative.

CHAPTER 10

※

At the emergency room door Tad met a thoroughly in charge, thoroughly angry head nurse, Wanda. She led the way.

"No human being should have to go through what this poor woman just went through."

In twenty months in Vietnam, Tad had seen a lifetime of horror, all before he was old enough to drink legally. He knew that Wanda, roughly his own age, had witnessed much of what God can visit on his people in her thirty-some years of hospital nursing. He steeled himself for what she considered the worst yet.

"Brought him in just after one. Ten-year-old boy. Must have fifteen broken ribs. Maybe fractured skull. Bruises everywhere." Wanda was puffing, Tad almost running to keep up with her dash from the emergency room to the elevator. She jabbed the button for the third floor. "Vital signs almost gone when he got here. Doc on call did all he could. Kid didn't have a chance. Doc called me. Boy died with her head on his little chest." A sudden, immense sob competed for what breath was left after their sprint through the hospital halls. "It was her son. She's been calling for you."

The elevator door opened and they hurried to a patient room at the end of the hall. Two athletic-looking men stood blocking the door. "Sorry, no visitors," one said.

"Outta my way," Wanda commanded.

"Sorry, no visitors."

"I'm the goddamn head nurse here and I run this goddamn hospital at night and I'll either throw you out of the way or have you arrested. Now move." Wanda was larger than average, but her presence was bigger yet. They moved.

Tad wasn't ready for what he saw inside. In the bed, IV dripping something into her arm, was the gaunt woman at the back of the church, the frightened woman in the IGA: Miriam Dett. If she had looked tired and scared under the fluorescent lights a month before, she looked just steps from the grave in the dim light of the hospital room. Her eyes were closed.

A man in police uniform sat in a straight-backed chair alongside the bed. He rose and stepped between the patient and her visitors. "Sit down, Bozo." The officer obviously didn't want to reckon with whatever Wanda had in mind. He sat.

Wanda's command presence melted at bedside. She sobbed. "Her own son. Wheeled in on a gurney. Nurses supposed to save lives. Couldn't do a damn thing. Poor dear Miriam. Tried to tell her." Tad put his hand on Wanda's arm. He wondered, whatever the police officer's role in this matter is, he doesn't seem to know how to do it. Tad was no more certain about his own role. Priest? Counselor? Old friend? High school sweetheart?

Wanda blew her nose. "I gotta get back to work. There's a pretty sick woman on two. Don't leave before checking with me, father. I think she's Catholic. If this turkey or the two outside give you any grief, you call me, okay?" She left, and Tad heard her outlining those rules to the two men outside the door in the low but unmistakable murmur of an experienced head nurse.

Tad stood alongside the bed. Miriam slept. He pulled the other straight-backed chair and sat. He looked at the deputy, who was glancing everywhere to avoid the patient's face and Tad's eyes. Tad extended his hand. "Hi, I'm Father Tad Coburg from over in Red Oak."

The deputy's handshake was weak. "I'm Myron Dett, deputy sheriff."

"The patient's husband?"

"Right."

"The boy's father?"

"Uh, huh."

"Please accept my deepest sympathy."

"Thanks."

Tad blessed Miriam with the sign of the cross and prayed silently for her. He could guess what she went through that evening and the horror she would face when the sedative no longer kept it away. He asked God to give her strength, a glimmer of understanding of why these things happen, although he couldn't figure that out in Vietnam and he couldn't in Wisconsin.

"What was the boy's name?" he asked the deputy, the husband.

"Tony."

Long silence. Tad studied Myron, not difficult to do with Myron working so hard at avoiding his eyes. But he detected no sadness, no remorse, nothing on that face. *Not surprising, given the newspaper editor's description of him as a mean bastard. Maybe for such a person this studied nonchalance was as close as he could come to expressing grief. Still, it was his wife in the hospital bed and his son on the way to the funeral home at that moment.*

"How did it happen?"

"Fell down the stairs," Myron said.

Tad thought of the youngster tumbling down a long flight of stairs. But the picture was interrupted when he recalled that the Dett family resided in a trailer on the edge of Bremerton. Something told him not to ask for details.

"Do you have other children?"

"Three daughters. One of them's married."

"Do they know about the accident yet?"

"No."

"Who's going to tell them?"

Shrug.

"Would you like me to go with you when you tell them?"

"No."

They sat in silence. Occasionally Tad detected the door silently open a crack, one of the two men outside peer in, then close again.

"Who are those guys?"

Myron shrugged again, leaving Tad to conjecture. They looked for all the world like detectives. Given what he knew about Myron's treatment of his family, the only scenario that made any sense was Myron in a rage inflicting life-ending wounds to the boy with his hands or a blunt instrument, the detectives there to be sure he didn't take it out on his wife or flee the state.

Tad and Myron continued their silent vigil. The floor nurse, a young man in blue, came in and checked the IV solution and Miriam's pulse and blood pressure. Satisfied, he left. Tad glanced at his watch: 4:50 AM He knew what he saw in Myron's face. He'd seen it in Vietnam. In everybody's face there, but mostly in youngsters just off planes from the states, seeing their first combat. And in the faces of salty veterans, days from rotation back home, afraid the last shot fired at them will be the one that gets them. Myron's face had that kind of fear.

At 6:30 AM, Wanda reappeared. "That lady in 215 seems to be a little better, Father. Maybe you ought to go see her. Now's a good time. She's awake. Be back up here at seven-thirty. Miriam will be coming out of her sedative about then, and the doctor thinks it would be good if you are here at that time. As for you, turkey," she told Myron, "you and your two spooks go sit in the waiting room at the end of the hall. The doctor will decide what to do with you."

Mrs. Schmieden was a member of St. Joan of Arc parish in Bremerton. He recognized her as a regular in the third pew on the right side of the church. The many floral bouquets and stack of cards alongside her bed bore testimony to a lifetime of love and respect in the community. A woman, herself well into retirement age, rose from a bedside chair and introduced herself as Mrs. Schmieden's daughter, her only living relative.

The patient was old and frail, but the bit of animation in her eyes showed she was immensely relieved to see him. The myriad tubes into and out of her tiny body, suggested that she would not leave the hospital alive. It probably would be impossible for her to die without last rites from her pastor; death just would not happen. She would live until he got there, if it took three months.

"Hello, Mrs. Schmieden, are they treating you well?" Whether she heard or understood, it didn't matter. His presence, his blessing and familiar prayers were all that that were important to her. Tad promised to return the next day, but guessed the next time he would see Mrs. Schmieden would be at her wake.

Wanda intercepted him on his way back to Miriam's room. "Coffee, father?"

"Definitely. I'm starting to droop."

Seated at a small table in the cheery cafeteria that served both employees and hospital visitors, Wanda began to answer the questions Tad didn't have to ask. "The two guys outside the room, they're members of the Universal Holy Scripture church, whatever it is, the way-out, Bible-thumping church that seems to be cutting a wider and wider swath through Millen County."

"Those guys are members of Doctor Don's church?" They didn't fit the picture Tad had of someone—his mother, for example—who would flock to an orator like Doctor Don.

"They are. Far as I know, they've been members since they came to town a couple years ago."

"What are they doing outside Miriam Dett's room?"

"Protecting one of their flock."

"Miriam, Mrs. Dett, is a member of that church?"

"Surprised hell out of me, too. I can't tell you why she's a member. And I can't tell you how committed she is. But she's a card-carrying follower of Doctor Don."

It took Tad the rest of his coffee and part of a refill to digest that piece of information. The two men outside her room were obviously there to protect Miriam from him, or anyone else trying to tamper with her soul.

"Does her husband belong?"

"Don't know. He's a jerk."

"So I'm told."

"What I don't understand," Wanda said, "is why Miriam had me call you last night. Why not Doctor Don? Or one of her church friends."

"Miriam and I go back a long way. Friends in high school. Our paths split. She went into the convent. I went into the priesthood. Looks like our paths have re-converged."

"Don't let them diverge again. You may be all that's between her and the loony bin or an early grave."

Over the years, Tad had wondered what a reunion with the only love of his life might be like. The many variations of that picture always involved two healthy, perpetually youthful individuals sharing the intellectual and spiritual passion of their chosen, celibate vocations. Never did the thought of becoming responsible for her mental or physical survival enter that picture. Less than twelve hours before, he had been immersed in the most stimulating discussion since he left Rome, and already anticipating more. Now he is shouldering responsibility for what is left of the woman who might have been his wife, but for a few miles-per-hour too much on a county road many years before.

"I won't abandon her."

"A lot of things about that little boy's death don't add up," Wanda said.

"You mean, like how can a youngster die from injuries falling down steps in a trailer?"

"That part of the story is okay. EMTs brought him to the hospital. They said it wasn't the Dett home. The boy was staying with his teacher that night. Her name is Stark. I don't know any more than that."

"I assume there'll be an autopsy."

"Sure. It's by law. But I'll bet you half I own that the cause of death was multiple contusions, probably a skull fracture, maybe punctured lung, any or all of those."

"Little kids' bones are pretty supple," Tad said. "It's hard to believe just falling down a flight of stairs could cause all that damage."

"For a priest, you sound like a detective."

"Does the sheriff's department have good investigators?"

"You met them last night."

❦   ❦   ❦

Tad had expected the doctor wanted him to be present when Miriam emerged from the sedative. He imagined the picture she would see, with her long-lost boyfriend and her loathsome husband side-by-side, perhaps framed by her doctor and her boss. Instead, Doctor Rashood stuck his head out of her room at 7:35 AM and told the gathered crowd to wait at the end of the hall until he called them. Tad, Wanda, Myron and the two detective/elders trudged to the tiny visitor's lounge. Tad found a spare chair in a nearby patient room, so there was a place for each of them. They sat.

Wanda's glare quickly withered Myron, and his discomfort was worse than in the early morning hours in Miriam's room. Her glare shifted to the detectives. They returned it, kilowatt for kilowatt. Clearly, she was not impressed with their stature in county government or their church. And just as clearly, they did not enjoy being ordered around by the head nurse. Since he was obviously allied with Wanda in the current matter, Tad guessed they included him in their hostility. For almost an hour, nobody spoke.

Doctor Rashood interrupted their silence. He pulled another chair from the nearby room and sat. "I know you are all very concerned about the condition of Miriam Dett. I want to reassure you that her vital signs are all quite positive. When you consider all she's been through in the last twelve hours ... well, she's a very strong woman. Having said that, I must tell you she is a long way from out of the woods. Therefore, I have issued instructions that she is to receive no visitors, with a couple of exceptions, which I shall get to in a moment."

Tad caught a couple of quick glances, between the detectives and between the detectives and Myron. The doctor continued. "I am having Miriam transferred to three south, which as you probably know is the section of the hospital reserved for people facing emotional difficulties of one sort or another."

Translate, the psychiatric department. Tad was sure the doctor's euphemism was not lost on the others.

"I'm asking Doctor Olivia Munoz to consult with me on Miriam's situation. Doctor Munoz is a psychiatrist with outstanding credentials. She's from La Crosse and spends two days a week here at Tri-County Memorial and has a private practice in West Charleton. I don't believe Miriam would be in better hands if she went to Mayo's in Rochester."

By this time Tad was intrigued with the tension rising in the detectives. Both were leaning forward in their chairs, nearly to the point of falling out. One gripped its arm so hard his knuckles were white; the other tapped a rapid rhythm with his right foot. When the term "psychiatric" was mentioned, Tad sensed their stress near the blowing point. But it held.

Doctor Rashood continued. "Our primary concern in this is, of course, the health of Miriam. But her children and their well-being must also be factored in."

"You don't have to worry about that, doctor," one of the detectives said. "Miriam's brothers and sisters in the Holy Scripture Universal Church of the Lord will see to it that the girls are taken care of," wearing his other hat for the moment.

"That's very kind of you," Dr. Rashood said, "and I'm sure Miriam appreciates the gesture. However, she was quite explicit that she would like the two daughters who are not married to stay with her friend, Wanda Goodfeller here. Would that be all right with you, Wanda?"

Caught a bit off guard, Wanda hesitated but agreed. "Well, sure, doctor. We have the room. My mom lives with us, but we've got a big house—"

"No." The detectives were caught way off guard.

"There's a problem with that?" Doctor Rashood asked.

"Well, you see, the members of our church, well, we take care of each other and we can handle this."

"I'm sorry, but we must honor the wishes of Mrs. Dett in this matter. She is quite capable of making such a decision, and under the circumstances I believe it's the correct thing to do at the present time."

"But you haven't even asked the kids' father. Myron, you can take care of them. Tell them. You can handle it."

Myron appeared close to falling apart altogether. "Well, I mean, whatever Miriam wants, I mean, she knows, well, she's …"

"Then it's agreed," Doctor Rashood said. "The girls will stay with the Goodfellers for the time being. When Miriam has recovered sufficiently from her trauma, then we can revisit this. Okay?" Obviously, it was not okay with the detectives, but they were out of arguments. They could only fume and prepare for the next skirmish, certain to be more contentious than this was. Myron became a non-factor. "Now then, as to visitors. I am limiting Miriam's visitors to her daughters, to Mrs. Goodfeller and to Father Coburg. I know that seems somewhat out of the ordinary, but I believe circumstances require it. Are there any questions?"

The obvious question went unasked: Why is the husband not included among the privileged visitors?

"Before you leave, Father Coburg, I wonder if I might have a word with you and Mrs. Goodfeller privately."

"Certainly," Tad said. He was relieved that the Dett daughters would be in far better hands than those of Doctor Don or Myron Dett. But he sensed large battles ahead, and felt Doctor Rashood's request to meet privately was a significant tactical mistake.

Doctor Rashood steered the priest and the head nurse into an empty patient room on the same floor. He told the floor nurse that they were not to be disturbed. Nevertheless, he stopped periodically to check the door to be certain he was not overheard. He began by explaining that he had specific approval from the patient to discuss their conversation with Father Tad and Wanda Goodfeller. But no one else. Wanda and Tad were to respect the doctor-patient confidentiality. When he concluded his description of his hour-long meeting with Miriam, Tad recognized the wisdom of those precautions.

The first concern was the two younger Dett daughters. According to their mother's request, they were to move in with Wanda Goodfeller, Wanda's retired husband, Ralph, and her mother, Isabella Worth. The Goodfellers resided in a large, white frame house, circa 1910, in West Charleton, a half hour's drive from Bremerton. One potentially significant logistical problem turned out to be no problem at all. Ralph would drive the girls back and forth to school.

By the time Tad and Wanda arrived at the Dett trailer, it was well past 10 AM, and, as they expected, nobody was at home. Myron should have been. The girls should not. Accustomed to fending for themselves at ages eleven and thirteen, they would probably be in school by then, so Tad and Wanda surmised. Next stop was Bremerton middle school. The Dett sisters weren't there either. There had been no call to the principal's office explaining their absence that day.

Tad and Wanda got back into Tad's car and considered their next steps. Seeing the heavy-handed attempt of the two detective/church enforcers to keep non-believers away from Miriam, it seemed likely they would apply the same protection to Miriam's daughters. This time, however, Wanda didn't have the authority of her hospital position to bowl or bluff the detectives aside. Tad's position could only harden the walls around the daughters. They felt in over their heads. Time for another "who-do-you-know" call to the newspaper editor.

The lawyer that Bruce recommended had offices in West Charleton and in Platteville. They chose the more discreet location, Platteville. The lawyer wasn't available until four that afternoon, which was just fine with both of them, being in desperate need of sleep, a bit too old for all-nighters. Tad arranged to pick up Wanda at three. He made a couple of calls postponing his Friday appointments, then crawled into bed for a few hours.

Jacob Nicholas listened and took notes on a yellow legal pad in the fashion of pre-laptop lawyers. It didn't take Tad and Wanda long to tell him the story, because there wasn't much to the story yet. The attorney asked many questions, but in most cases got only shrugs.

"We have two immediate legal tasks," he said. "First, keep Myron Dett away from his daughters. There is every reason to suspect him of being an accessory in the death of his son, assuming a coroner's inquest establishes that the boy's wounds caused his death and the wounds could not conceivably have come from an accidental tumble down a single flight of stairs. That, plus Dett's long history of violence, I don't believe a restraining order will be difficult to obtain."

"And the second task," Tad prompted.

"The second will be considerably more complicated. For one thing, since we don't know where the daughters are, we can't very well place them in the Goodfeller household. When we find them, then we try persuasion. You don't seem to think the members of the Holy Scripture etcetera church will voluntarily permit that to happen. Assuming the church members are sheltering the girls, I tend to agree with you. That leaves us to seek legal recourse. A sworn statement from Mrs. Dett as to her wishes in this matter would be looked upon quite favorably by the judge. However, Mrs. Dett is a patient in the psychiatric unit of Tri-County Hospital, and the opposition can be expected to attack her ability to make such a decision on those grounds. That could get very sticky."

Tad glanced at his watch. "It's four-forty on Friday afternoon. Is there still time before the weekend to get a restraining order and keep Myron Dett away from his children?"

"Restraining orders seldom seem to be needed at convenient times. Judges are accustomed to working fast on them when they have to. I'll have our West

Charleton office call Judge Valders and tell him the application's coming. We should have it to him and signed by six. I'll let you know of any complications."

Tad gave him his rectory and cell phone numbers, and stopped to work out billing details (send him the bills) with Attorney Nicholas' secretary. He drove Wanda home and suggested she and her husband and mother meet him in Platteville for dinner. The Timbers has a good Friday fish fry, he said.

Ralph Goodfeller and Isabella Worth turned out to be aptly named. Wanda's husband had nominally retired at age sixty five years before, following a career that read like the Sunday classifieds. He had served in the Army, driven truck, worked in a factory, tended bar, sold farm machinery, helped his brother on the farm on numerous occasions, and, most recently, had been a rural mail carrier. He kept busy in retirement helping the Red Cross blood drive, subbing as school bus driver, helping several elderly neighbors with lawn care and snow removal and driving the van for a local retirement home. He was also able to fix darn near anything, and folks kept him busier than he cared to be doing that. He didn't have enough time for the fishing he had planned when he retired.

Wanda volunteered that she had no intention of retiring. "Couldn't stand to be around these old farts all day."

Mrs. Worth had moved in with her daughter and son-in-law when her second hip replacement started to wear out. The trio got along fine, and she kept occupied quilting and watching television, although there was more of the latter these days, as her fingers began to go the way of her hips.

The Goodfellers were wildly proud of their two children and three grandchildren. "First Goodfellers in history to graduate from the university. Wanda here thought our daughter should go to Southwest Wisconsin Tech and be a nurse like her, and young Tom should be a doctor. But guess what, they both got hooked on computers and are making more money in a month than I ever made in a year."

Ralph, Wanda and Isabella would get away on occasion to do some gambling in Dubuque: "Put your gambling money in your right pocket, your winnings in the left. When the right one's empty, go home. Don't touch the money in the left." Once a year husband and wife got in the car and headed south to visit retired friends in Arkansas and the Florida Panhandle. "I'm scheduled for two weeks of vacation in March, but if the Dett girls are living with us then, we can always postpone it. Anyway, I think our friends might be getting tired of us mooching off them every year when winter drags on up here."

That introduced the obvious topic. Tad, Wanda and Isabella were finishing their wine—Chianti, Merlot and zinfandel respectively—and Ralph his Coors, when the beer-battered cod, fries and cole slaw arrived. "Any idea where the girls are?" Tad asked.

"I'll know by tomorrow night," Ralph declared.

"Not much happens in Millen County that Ralph doesn't know about," Wanda said, saving Tad the trouble of asking. "He's lived here all his life, except when he was in the Army. He'll have the answer after coffee tomorrow morning, guaranteed."

Ralph tried to look nonchalant, but Tad detected a bit of swagger as he pushed his DeKalb seed corn cap back on his bald, freckled head and impaled five french fries on his fork. Being in the know was as important among the retired of southwestern Wisconsin as it was in the top echelons of big corporations and inside the walls of the Vatican.

Wanda's call came as predicted—next morning, well before noon, within an hour after Ralph's daily cup of coffee with the guys in the back booth of the Crazy Quilt Café. The girls were staying with teacher Gloria Stark, the same Gloria Stark down whose stairs their brother Tony had fallen to his death. Supposedly. The more Tad thought about it, the phonier the accidental fall story became. Removing the girls from the Stark house became more than a mere matter of carrying out their mother's wishes.

CHAPTER 11

❀

Tad hoped his persuasive powers would be more effective with a local lawyer at his side. He stood with attorney Nicholas' West Charleton partner, Ellen Killian, and Wanda in two inches of wet snow on the front steps of the Stark home. That was as far as they got.

They were speaking with Adam Stark. His hostility had gone up a few notches since Friday morning. He did not acknowledge that the girls were in the house, nor did he deny it. He simply was not going to cooperate in anybody's attempt to place the girls in the Goodfeller home. "Peah-iod." Stark was from Texas.

"As you are aware," Tad said, "Mrs. Dett's attending physician, Doctor Rashood, has spoken at length with her, and she has conveyed her wishes, rather strongly I understand, that her two younger daughters live temporarily with the Goodfellers as a matter of their own safety."

"Rashood's a Hindu. They don't believe in medicine."

"I understand that Doctor Rashood is from Pakistan originally, although he's a United States citizen now. And I believe he's Muslim. Obviously, he's a believer in medicine and I understand he's quite good at it."

"Rashood's a liar."

"Doctor Rashood would have no reason to lie in this matter. If you would be more comfortable about it, I can arrange for you to meet with him again and—"

"That won't be necessary. Between us and their father, we can take care of the girls just fine."

"Perhaps you haven't heard. Myron Dett is under a restraining order from Judge Valders that he is not to see his two younger daughters."

"Perhaps you haven't heard. Myron Dett and I tore that restraining order up and flushed it down the toilet."

"Ah, do I take it then that the girls' father does not intend to honor the restraining order?"

"You have to ask him."

"Well, do I take it that you are not going to permit the girls to come with us to the Goodfeller home, in defiance of the wishes of their mother?"

"Their mother is a tool of Satan. We will not permit Christian children to be manipulated by the devil. Peah-iod."

Tad, Wanda and the lawyer drove back to West Charleton with the heater on high, hoping to dry their wet feet and revive their soggy spirits. They agreed that the conversation had gone approximately as each had privately expected. Attorney Killian had confirmed the flimsy legal grounds that Attorney Nicholas had outlined the day before.

"What's the next step? Get the sheriff to enforce the restraining order?"

"We could. But first we have to show that Dett is seeing the children. We don't have any proof of that."

"Suppose we park a car out in front of Stark's house and watch for him."

"We don't know for sure they're there. And if we park in front, he goes in the back door. Or waits 'til we get tired of watching. And it helps to remember that Dett works for Sheriff Moses."

"I'll ask my husband," Wanda said. "He knows people in the neighborhood who can keep an eye on the Stark house."

"That's probably the best idea," the attorney said. "Meantime, we wait for the results of the medical examiner's autopsy of young Tony Dett. Our bet is there's enough questions that the district attorney will order an inquest."

Tad asked, "When does all this get underway?"

"Early next week."

"Early next week" turned out to be very early next week. Sunday morning Tad was preparing for 7:30 AM Mass at St. Brendan's in Red Oak when Bruce Bestman walked into the sacristy. "Hi, Father. Special Sunday edition of the *Millen County Reporter*, press run one copy. Just for you."

"Morning, Bruce. I'm honored. What's up?"

"Paper doesn't come out until Thursday, but I'll give you an advance," he said. "Tony Dett case: no autopsy, no inquest. Stick him in the ground, no questions asked. Cover-up of the first magnitude."

"What?"

"That's it. The district attorney told me himself."

"But a kid that age couldn't possibly die falling down stairs."

"That's what the ER doctor said. That's what the EMTs that picked him up said. That's not what the coroner or DA said."

"What's their story?" Tad asked.

"The coroner told me Sheriff Moses investigated himself. Said he interviewed the Stark lady and her husband. They claimed they were in the first floor living room watching TV when bumpty-bump down the steps comes little Tony Dett. He'd been sleeping in the spare bedroom upstairs. 'Must have been sleep walking,' they said."

"I can't believe that."

"There were two more witnesses, said the same thing."

"Who are they?"

"Another school teacher, Judith Flint, and her husband Joshua. They were visiting the Starks that night. Watching TV with them."

Tad shook his head. "Four people with the same story. Two of them school teachers."

"And two of them sheriff's detectives."

"All four are members of the Holy Scripture church, Doctor Don's church?"

"Right again. Four witnesses: Two teachers, two law enforcement officers, all of them righteous, church-going citizens. Coroner and district attorney say that's good enough for them. No autopsy. No inquest."

"That's impossible."

"All perfectly legal. Unless someone can convince a judge otherwise."

"Someone, you mean, like me?"

"You or Wanda Goodfeller."

Two altar boys entered the sacristy, busy with getting water and wine ready for Mass and lighting the altar candles.

"I got to get to work, Bruce. Thanks. If you hear any more news, I'd appreciate getting it first."

"And if *you* have any news, remember who the real journalists are around here."

"You and Annie."

Tad had time before Mass for one quick cell phone call. That was to Attorney Ellen Killian in West Charleton.

So far Tad had not been much help to the ailing Miriam Dett. He had failed in his attempt to remove her two daughters to the safe-keeping of the Goodfeller household. And if there was any justice to be meted out in connection with the death of her son, somebody, such as Tad, would have to initiate it. Driving to the 10:30 AM Mass in West Charleton, he was looking forward to his meeting with Ellen Killian. She and her husband were regulars. They would meet in her office after Mass. In their brief phone conversation earlier, she assured him that all was not lost. Justice would prevail.

"I talked with Doctor Rashood just after you called," she said. "He assured me Mrs. Dett is in complete command of her faculties and perfectly capable of making her own decisions. By the way, he suggested you stop in and visit her as soon as you have the time."

"I'll drop in this afternoon." Tad meant that to sound business-like, but was afraid the emotions surrounding that first visit in thirty-four years showed through.

"What Mrs. Dett definitely does not need is a visit from her husband or any members of that church she belongs to. That's the reason for the 'no visitors' order."

"I can understand that."

"First is an autopsy. All we need is Mrs. Dett's consent."

"Why don't I take the necessary forms when I see her this afternoon?"

"I was hoping you would say that. Perhaps I should come along in case she has some questions you can't answer."

"Which would be just about any question." Tad had long ago been told you know you're getting old when police officers are younger than you are. That must mean you are really old when your attorney is young enough to be your daughter, if you had daughters. But he was increasingly impressed with her professional bearing. "Suppose her husband objects to an autopsy."

"Tough," she said. "All it takes is one person who has custody of the body. We'll make sure that's the boy's mother. He can protest all he wants. Won't do him any good."

❦   ❦   ❦

Doctor Rashood had cleared the way, and Father Tad and Attorney Killian breezed past the third floor nurses station, no questions asked. He brought a box of Fanny May candies and a half dozen white roses surrounded by red and green accents of various sorts, guessing that Miriam wouldn't have much of either. He guessed wrong. Every department and every shift of hospital employees had chipped in, and the room was awash in flowers, cards and sweets.

Miriam was in a chair watching television, an animal show of some kind. She quickly clicked it off and stood. Nearly forty-eight straight hours of sleep and the tasteful application of cosmetic brushes had transformed her from the zombie of a couple nights before, to a woman who could be the one he remembered from thirty-four years before. Gray hair and her delicately lined face were strong reminders of fifty years, at least half of them unpleasant.

Tad kissed her cheek gently. Her eyes hadn't changed. Behind the sadness surrounding them, the color and sparkle remained. "Hi, Miriam."

"Hi, Tad."

"Ah, where can I put these? You seem to be good for the flower and candy business in Millen County."

"Aren't they wonderful?"

"Oh, and this is Ellen Killian."

"I'm pleased to meet you, Mrs. Dett. Please accept my sympathy. I can only imagine how devastating it must be to lose a child in such an accident."

"It was no accident, Mrs. Killian," Miriam said. "Won't you both sit down?"

Tad had expected to spend at least a few minutes on pleasantries before getting to the business at hand. It was plain that Miriam had little else on her mind but the death of her son.

Tad got directly to the point. "I have to admit, there are a number of questions about Tony's death that should be answered."

Miriam, too, got straight to the point: "We need to find out who killed my son, so I know who I have to kill." That was a most effective conversation-stopper. Tad had no reply. Years of theological study had not prepared him for such gut-level morality.

Ellen stepped in. "The reason why we're here, Mrs. Dett, is that we believe we must, first of all, learn conclusively the cause of Tony's death. Neither the coroner nor the district attorney has seen fit to order an autopsy. However, you, as the mother of the deceased, may request an autopsy, and it will be carried out."

"Where do I sign?" Miriam demanded.

"Right here. And if it is all right with you, I will ask that the body be taken to Madison where it can be examined by pathologists at University Hospitals."

"Any place but Millen County," Miriam said.

The attorney left with the paperwork and promised to see that the autopsy take place yet that day, or early Monday morning. Results may be known immediately, or it may take several days, depending on what they find, she said.

Tad and Miriam sat in silence. He felt that, as a priest, he should try to dissuade her from her murderous path, begin rounding off the edge of her hatred. But he knew it was pointless just then. Besides, he had an even bigger problem.

"Wanda and I haven't yet been successful in obtaining custody of your two younger daughters. As we understand it, you want them to live temporarily with Wanda until some of these things are resolved?"

"Yes."

"That's fine with Wanda and her husband. Wonderful couple, by the way."

"I should have listened to her."

"Yeah, well, right now we're not sure where the girls are. We believe they're presently staying with Mr. and Mrs. Stark."

That news had the result Tad feared. "Betsy and Maria are staying with the Starks? In the death house? You want those butchers to kill my daughters too?"

Tad wished that Ellen Killian was still there. He wished Wanda was there. He wished he was still in Rome. "Your husband is under a restraining order keeping him away from the girls. We're doing all we can to have the children moved to the Goodfeller home. First we have to be certain they are in the Stark house. Then we will have to get a court order to have them moved. This may take a while."

"Meantime, they may be dead."

"I doubt they are in any physical danger at the present time."

"Neither was Tony. Now he's dead."

"Good-bye, Miriam. I'll see you tomorrow." Tad thought, a good priest would stand over her, put his hand on her head, bless her and bring her peace. Somehow, that didn't seem the right move under the circumstances.

The autopsy did nothing to change anyone's verdict on cause of death; not the coroner's, not the district attorney's, not Miriam's. The immediate cause of death was brain damage from intra-cranial bleeding that resulted from a fractured skull. The fracture was located at the hairline above the left eye. The skull showed three other contusions. There were significant contusions on the boy's back, buttocks and the backs of his legs, as well as on his elbows and upper and lower arms. There were bruises and lacerations above both his eyes and his mouth. His nose was broken.

The autopsy report was delivered to Attorney Killian's office just before 10 AM Tuesday. Tad read it and agreed that it was inconclusive. The injuries could have occurred in a fall down a flight of stairs, particularly if the stairs were not carpeted. On the other hand, they could have been the result of a horrible beating. Miriam had requested the autopsy. She would have to see the results.

On their way out, Bruce Bestman was waiting in the law firm's lobby. "Hi, Father, hi Ellen. Where you headed?"

"Ah, well, hi Bruce, we're …"

"We're on our way to the hospital," Ellen said.

"To see Miriam Dett, I'll bet," said Bruce.

"Well, as a matter of fact …"

"I'd like a copy of the Dett youngster's autopsy report too," Bruce said.

"Well," Tad said, "I don't think we ought to …"

"Don't forget, we have a deal on exchanging news," Bruce said. "Look, I know Miriam well. ER nurses and newspaper people have a way of running into each other. Give me a copy of the report now. Ask her if it's okay. If it isn't, I'll shred it. No point in making a freedom of information circus out of this. Right?"

Tad hesitated. Ellen shrugged. "Okay," he said.

Ellen was able to report progress in the effort to remove the daughters from the Stark home to the Goodfellers'. The girls were in school on Monday, delivered there by teacher Gloria Stark and her husband. They returned to the Stark home at the end of the day, once again with the detective's protection.

From Ralph Goodfeller came the report that Myron Dett had visited the Stark household, presumably to see his daughters, in defiance of the restraining order, for two hours on Monday evening.

Ellen also had papers for Miriam to sign requesting that the Dett daughters be removed from the Stark household and move in with Wanda and Ralph Goodfeller. Just to be safe, she had drawn up an affidavit for Doctor Rashood's signature attesting to Miriam's soundness of mind and ability to make such a decision. Early Wednesday morning she obtained Judge Valders' signature to effect the transfer.

Having the necessary paperwork was one thing. Carrying out the mother's wishes was something else. Tad phoned Sheriff Moses for an appointment. He had two matters to discuss with him, he told the office secretary. First was the transfer of the Dett daughters. Second was the possibility of an inquest into the death of Tony Dett.

He took Ellen Killian with him. He had no idea how much of a bill he was running up with the law firm, nor where he would get the cash to pay it. But now was no time for parsimony.

"Ellen, honey, how's the best-looking damn lawyer in all Millen County?" Sheriff Moses engulfed her in arms the length and breadth of some mature tree trunks. Ellen looked like she might throw up.

Sheriff Moses looked like he had made a career of posing as his namesake. He was large in every proportion, most notably his head, blanketed with gray, wavy hair that he let grow well over his ears and flowing straight back as if in a strong wind or a shouting match with the Almighty. "And you must be the new Catholic priest," he said. "Three churches. You must have your hands full. Attendance holding up?"

"Hello, sheriff, I'm pleased to meet you. Yes, I've been here almost six months, and indeed attendance at all three is doing very well."

"Well sit down. Hey, Myron," he called to the dispatch desk in the hall outside his office. "Get the young lady and the good father some coffee. Or would you rather have a Coke or something? Sorry I can't offer you a shot, padre. Rules against alcohol on public property, you know."

"No, no. That's fine. Nothing, really." Tad said.

"Now then, what can I do for you," the sheriff boomed.

Ellen handed him the order from Judge Valders placing the Dett daughters with the Goodfellers. "We would like you to enforce this court order.

He read it and called again to the dispatch desk outside his office. "Deputy Dett, come in here."

The priest and lawyer shook hands with the dispatcher. He looked as frightened as he did in the hospital room.

"Judge says your daughters have to go stay with your wife's boss," Sheriff Moses said. "What do you think about that?"

"Well, I don't know, that is, I'm not a very good cook and all …"

"And also, you're under a restraining order not to see your daughters. Same judge."

"Yeah, that's true …"

"Well I think it's pure and unmitigated bullshit," the sheriff said. "The big question is what are you going to do? Take this shit or stand up for your rights?"

"I guess I'll stand up for my rights."

"Bet your ass you will. Ellen, honey, go back to Judge Valders and tell him the lawful, natural, devoted father of the Dett children has no intention of relinquishing his duties and privileges as head of their household. In short, the good judge can stick this order up his ass."

"Do I take it, then, that you do not intend to enforce either of Judge Valders' orders?"

"That's putting it more polite than I would."

All that and they hadn't even gotten to the subject of an inquest. Tad could see that Ellen's strength of personality was no match for the sheriff's. He wasn't sure about his own, but he couldn't leave this meeting without some challenge to the alpha male in the room. Nothing in his experience had prepared him for this sort of in-your-face negotiation. In the echelons of theological study and ecumenism where he had plied his trade for three decades, disagreement was invariably prefaced with the acknowledgment of the other's good intentions. Even in Vietnam, he rarely saw the source of the machine gun or mortar fire that sought to end that complex and messy argument in the way of mankind since Cain and Abel.

"The other matter we want to discuss with you, sheriff, is that of an inquest into the death of young Tony Dett."

"No inquest," the sheriff stated.

"But the statutes call for an inquest when a death may have been due to unexplained or suspicious circumstances."

"It's up to the district attorney to order an inquest."

"Right. I was wondering where you stand on this matter, based on your wealth of law enforcement experience."

"I have discussed it with the district attorney, and we agree there's no reason to believe the lad's death was anything but an unfortunate accident. No inquest."

"But the autopsy report. It's pretty hard to believe all those injuries could have been caused by a simple fall down the stairs."

"I believe it. The district attorney believes it. Cause of death: accident. No inquest. Case closed."

Tad asked the obvious question: "Isn't it possible that your judgment may be affected at least a little by the fact that the two major suspects in the case are employees of yours, Adam Stark and Joshua Flint?"

"Suspects?" Sheriff Moses shouted. "Suspects? It was an accident, plain and simple. There are no suspects in an accident. Right, Ellen honey?"

"Sheriff," she said, "it's our position, representing the mother of the deceased boy, that there are enough unanswered questions in this case to warrant an inquest. We shall pursue this matter to the full extent of the law." She rose to leave. Tad followed.

"Anything else you want to talk about today?" the sheriff called to their backs.

Back at the law office, Ellen explained. "My last comment was mostly bluff, and I'm sure the sheriff knows it. He can recognize bluff if anyone can. We have two very tenuous courses open if we want to pursue this. One is to go after a writ of mandamus to get a judge to order the district attorney to conduct an inquest. I don't think there's a strong enough case, at least at this point. The other is to go to Madison and try to get the attorney general to step in. Again, they'd be reluctant, because it right away suggests the sheriff and D.A. are corrupt."

"Looks to me like they are."

"Maybe. But any judge around here, and probably the attorney general as well, would point to a low crime rate in Millen County and tell you that's the result of good law enforcement. That's why the two of them keep getting reelected."

A third course of action developed, with no impetus on the part of the attorney or priest. Like a break in a dam, it threatened to sweep them and many more along as it gathered force. It was the March 25th edition of the *Millen County Reporter*, page one. Editor Bruce Bestman had been talking with Miriam.

> *Mother of dead youngster*
> *charges courthouse cover-up*
>
>   *Miriam Dett, mother of Tony Dett, 10, who died Friday after what author-*
> *ities said was a fall down stairs, claimed Wednesday that Sheriff Hollister*

Moses and District Attorney Merrill Brewster are "guilty of gross dereliction of duty."

She told a reporter that, despite serious questions raised by an autopsy of the child, the two have failed to pursue their investigation in order to protect two of the sheriff's employees.

The story went on from there, accurate in every detail that Tad could discern.

CHAPTER 12

It had been almost three weeks since Tad had visited with his mother, and he was feeling guilty. They had developed something of a routine, having dinner together on Thursday evenings. But the responsibilities of his profession, including the previous Thursday's inaugural small group discussion meeting, were cutting into his evenings, and he had postponed their dinner twice. Postponements weren't difficult, as they seemed to be running out of things to talk about. She appeared to be giving up her efforts to convert him to her fundamentalist religion, and he saw no way under present circumstances to bring her around to his way of thinking.

This time dinner was at her place and she was cooking. He brought the ingredients, hoping thereby to help her meager budget without making a big production out of it, and at the same time control to some extent his fat and calorie intake, which had ballooned since his landing in Wisconsin. He was a bit overweight in November, quite a bit overweight by late March. The menu was spaghetti and meatballs made from lean ground beef. Ruth Coburg had other ideas. In the tradition of mothers the world over, she baked a fresh loaf of bread and a coconut cream pie for her son. Start the diet tomorrow.

He had a lot of questions that his mother might be able to answer, but his approach was delicate. "How are things in Holy Scripture church?" he asked. "Membership and attendance holding up well?"

"Oh, my yes. Another family joined last month. From West Charleton. Brought up Presbyterian. We can't wait until summer when they can be baptized in the Midewiwin."

"I don't see Doctor Don around much these days. Is he still your pastor?"

"Of course. He's here every Sunday. During the week he's usually around. He travels a lot."

"Where does he go?"

"I don't know. Down south, I've heard. Illinois sometimes. Doing the Lord's work."

"You like Doctor Don, don't you?"

"I love Doctor Don. The man's a prophet. He showed me the way to the Lord."

"Do you know the Starks, Adam and Gloria Stark?"

"Holy people, both of them."

The spaghetti was ready, drained and on their plates. They paused for silent thanksgiving for their food. His version wasn't adequate blessing for her food. Hers would have been good enough for him, but for reasons known only to Ruth, she insisted on silent prayer—praying for his conversion, Tad guessed.

Over the delicious but entirely superfluous coconut pie, Tad broached the subject that had occupied his time and thoughts for a week. "Did you read this week's *Millen County Reporter*?" If she had, she was bound to have some strong feelings about the story, because her son's name was mentioned prominently. If she hadn't read it, he thought he should get her ready for it.

"Yes, I read the paper this morning."

"I suppose you saw the article about the boy who died after supposedly falling down stairs?"

"Yes, I saw that article."

"What did you think about it?"

"You should stay away from that woman."

"You mean Mrs. Dett? She's an old high school classmate. She asked for my help. She's trying to cope with a terrible tragedy. Her son died a horrible, violent death."

"She's a tool of Satan. She's possessed by the devil."

"All she's doing is asking that the sheriff and district attorney do their jobs. There should be an inquest into the circumstances of the boy's death."

"It was an accident."

Ruth reached for her Bible, on the table where her husband's plate had lain three meals a day for over fifty years. She opened it and quickly found her answer. "'Withhold not correction from the child: for if thou beatest him with the rod, he shall not die. Thou shalt beat him with the rod, and shalt deliver his soul from hell.' Proverbs."

Tad was stunned. Foul play had been in the back of his suspicious mind for almost a week. He was familiar with those biblical verses. But he had been reluctant to put his suspicions together with Proverbs. More unsettling now, however, were the questions of what his mother knew about the events leading to Tony Dett's death, and how she knew it.

Bruce had maintained that the editor's job was to report the news, not make the news. But, as so often happens, the act of reporting news actually creates it. District Attorney Brewster told the *Dubuque Telegraph Herald* and the *Wisconsin State Journal* for Friday's editions that he had intended all along to convene an inquest, that he had been incorrectly quoted in the *Millen County Reporter*, and at any rate an inquest was mainly a formality in the interest of thoroughness, since all indications pointed to an accident.

That's how things stood for two weeks: there *will* be an inquest. Nobody said *when*. The *Dubuque Telegraph Herald* got wrapped up in the threat of flooding of the Mississippi River and its tributaries due to an unusually heavy snow pack in eastern Minnesota and western Wisconsin. That, along with glutted granaries from the past two years' corn and soybean harvests promising hard times for the coming season, plus a string of house burglaries, kept the Dubuque newspaper and television journalists absorbed. Madison media were only marginally interested in faraway Millen County, and they were captivated by some shenanigans involving a lobbyist and a couple of Milwaukee area legislators, so their follow-up files had the Dett boy inquest near the bottom.

It was left to the local news media, meaning Bruce and Ann Bestman, to keep the heat on local law enforcement. They had one chance per week to do it. Their first was a week after Miriam Dett's startling assertion. Their immediate task was to restore their own credibility, damaged by the D.A.'s claim that he had been misquoted. The effort was not helped by his refusal to return their phone calls.

Nor could they get anyone else to comment on the record. Janice and Doug, the EMTs on duty the night of the Tony Dett incident, friends of the Bestmans, apologized. But, they explained, because of the upcoming inquest they had been instructed—by the district attorney, of course—not to comment to the press on the matter. As expected, the Starks and the Flints couldn't be reached. Myron Dett went from work to his home and back to work. Bruce got no answer to his phone calls or knocks on the door of the Dett trailer. Not that he expected any information or printable quotes from Myron anyway.

So the *Reporter*'s second story contained a reiteration of Miriam's claim of a cover-up, the district attorney's contention (as reported elsewhere) that he had every intention of vigorously upholding the law with an exhaustive inquest, and a lot of "no comment" and "couldn't be reached."

That, plus the autopsy report and a note that funeral arrangements for Tony Dett were pending.

The sheriff and his dispatcher decided to comply with one court order and Saturday morning quietly deposited Betsy and Maria Dett on the Goodfeller doorstep with most of their winter wardrobes. First thing Monday morning, a petition was filed with the court, in behalf of their father, to rescind the order and return the girls to the Stark household.

The same day, Miriam was discharged from the hospital, fortified by over twenty hours of talk therapy with Doctor Olivia Munoz and a fistful of prescriptions. Where she would go was not a serious question. The Goodfeller family home, rather than the Dett family trailer, was obvious. How she would get there was not so obvious, and it was left to Tad to handle the logistics. He hired two young, muscular entrepreneurs and their truck for the twenty-mile haul. The truck was less than half full. Tad, the bachelor priest, had accumulated more personal belongings in his lifetime than Miriam, the wife and mother, had in hers. The move was carried out under the baleful watch of the two young detectives from the sheriff's office. Tad didn't know whether the men were guarding the property of their colleague, Myron Dett, or were there in their capacity as elders in the Holy Scripture church, looking for evidence, some reason to pounce and destroy the Catholic priest who had stolen one of their members.

The *Reporter*'s next story, two weeks after the first, could only rehash the earlier stories and report that the inquest still had not been scheduled, nor would the district attorney say whether it would be conducted by Judge Valders or a court commissioner, with or without a jury. A sentence at the end of the story reported that the Dett sisters were now staying with the Goodfellers, in compliance with the court's directions.

While that legal inaction was taking place, an even more contentious question was being drawn out, beneath the purview of the law or the fourth estate. That had to do with who would be given the responsibility for dispatching the soul of young Tony Dett past the pearly gates.

On one side were arrayed the formidable resources of the Holy Scripture Universal Church of the Lord. They were convinced that only the intense prayer of their congregation, led by Doctor Don, could vault the youngster into Heaven, given the fact that he had not yet found Jesus on his own accord.

On the other side was the boy's mother, who determined that funeral services would consist of a Mass in St. Brendan's Catholic Church in Red Oak, officiated by Father Tad Coburg. The fact that someone had proposed a Catholic funeral service was bad enough, in the eyes of the Holy Scripture members. But that it was Miriam Dett who had proposed it, Miriam Dett who had turned her back on all that they stood for, Miriam Dett the tool of Satan, made the mere thought of a Catholic service for Tony an abomination.

In the middle was Winthrop Gregory, fourth generation proprietor of the Gregory Funeral Home in Bremerton. Wishing not to incur any animosity on the part of the Holy Scripture church, nor the Catholics of the county, he proposed what he considered a reasonable compromise: funeral services at his place of business presided over by both Father Coburg and Doctor Don. That sounded good to Tad, but neither Miriam nor the representatives of Doctor Don would have any of it.

Winthrop Gregory then sought the advice of his attorney, who contacted Miriam's attorney, Ellen Killian, who in turn contacted the elders of the Holy Scripture church, who retained their own attorney (from Madison), who asked for additional time to study the matter. Meantime, Tony Dett rested embalmed in a vault in the basement of Gregory's establishment.

Bruce suspected something unusual was happening with respect to the boy's funeral, mainly because it wasn't happening. Gregory would give him no information. Tad was reluctant to comment, not wishing to stir things up more or violate any confidences he had with Miriam. But when Miriam told him she would go to *The New York Times* if necessary to let everyone in the world know what screwed-up maniacs the Holy Scripture idiots were, Tad told her he'd handle it.

The *Millen County Reporter*, two weeks after Tony's death, stated simply that funeral arrangements were still pending. Tad agreed with Bruce that the way tongues wag in a small community, the *Reporter* would have to address the funeral issue in some depth in the next issue.

But that next issue had a lot to report. A spectacular, late-season ice storm started Sunday afternoon and didn't let up until Tuesday evening, and brought all activity in southwestern Wisconsin and adjacent parts of Iowa and Minnesota to a near halt. Schools were closed for three days. Many roads were impassable. Power lines were down. Most farmers had generators to run the milking equipment; those who didn't quickly learned the back-breaking skill of milking by hand. And pictures! Rarely is nature's violence cloaked in such beauty as an ice storm. Bruce risked every bone and joint in his body to record the event for his readers. Ann worked the phones—those that functioned—to squeeze into the paper all that would fit of the human drama that will be talked about in Millen County for generations.

One consequence of the ice storm was a lack of journalistic pressure on those whose job it is to bury the dead and to find how the dead died. Another week passed without a schedule for either funeral or inquest.

Finally, in the fourth week after Tony Dett's death, Bruce and Ann decided they were running out of time. Their self respect and the respect of their readers were on the line. Go after the stories they knew were theirs if they dug enough. Bruce camped in the district attorney's lobby. Ann took on the strange matter of a boy's body still unburied. Once again, the pursuit of news caused news. An inquest was scheduled for the following Wednesday, a day less than five weeks after Tony Dett died. Judge Valders would preside. No jury. A hearing was set for the day before, also in Judge Valders' court, to consider arguments by Attorney Killian, representing the mother, and Attorney Mitchell Pell of Madison, representing the father, over who shall pray the boy's soul into heaven, Father Tad Coburg or Doctor Don. A hearing on the petition to place Betsy and Maria Dett back in the Stark household would follow the resolution of those other matters.

Judge Herman Valders had presided over Millen County Circuit Court through the terms of at least eight district attorneys and a generation of trial lawyers. Tall, with close-cropped grey hair, half glasses, perpetually bronzed complexion, he was the model of how a judge ought to look. In his years on the bench, he had dealt with all degrees of ineptitude, and about every maneuver the legal profession in those parts could contrive. He would suffer neither fools nor chicanery. And not much of a legal nature would likely happen in Millen County that he had not already heard and adjudicated—properly, most citizens agreed.

When he tapped his gavel opening court on Tuesday in the first week of May, much of what was scheduled that week simply revisited situations he'd encountered many times before: an inquest into the allegedly accidental death

of a youngster in a fall; a hearing on custody of two teenage daughters of a dysfunctional couple.

But the first issue on the docket was fresh for Judge Valders, Millen County
and perhaps even for the State of Wisconsin. That was the appeal to the courts
to decide who should preside over the youngster's funeral.

Tad wondered if it was appropriate for him to attend the hearing, whether it
would be more proper to go about his pastoral business and wait for the
court's decision. But Miriam answered the question: "I need you there."

So there they sat in the circuit courtroom in the Millen County Courthouse. Miriam and Attorney Killian at the plaintiff's table, Tad behind them in
the first row of spectator seats. Winthrop Gregory and his attorney sat behind
him. A handful of citizens who simply like to hang out in the courtroom were
behind the funeral director. Across the aisle, like friends of the groom, twenty-
five or thirty members of the Holy Scripture church filled the seats behind
Doctor Don and the two detective/elders. A thoroughly discomfited Myron
Dett sat fidgeting at the defendant's table with Attorney Pell and two of Pell's
associates. He looked only forward, as if afraid Miriam's glare would burn his
beard off if he caught it head on. It might have.

Attorney Killian opened the proceedings by reading the petition asking the
court to order that Tony Dett be buried in a Catholic ceremony conducted by
Father Tad Coburg. Pell read a rejoinder asking for court direction to have
Doctor Don preside over the funeral in the Holy Scripture church. Judge
Valders then asked the attorneys individually whether Tony Dett had been baptized in either church. The attorneys consulted their clients and reported that
he had not. The judge asked if there were some compelling reasons, other than
the parents' conflicting wishes, why he should rule one way or the other. Killian said no. Pell began reading a passage from the Book of Deuteronomy, but
the judge cut him short with the admonition that it is not within the court's
jurisdiction to interpret the Bible. The judge then asked whether some compromise could be reached, say a joint ceremony in some neutral venue. Certainly, said Killian. Never, said Pell. We seem to be at something of an impasse,
said the judge. That's why we're here, said the attorneys. The judge then asked
if the attorneys had researched precedents. Yes, we have, your honor. Then,
Judge Valders ruled, I direct you to file briefs, which I would like to receive by a
week from today, and I adjourn this case until the Friday after that. Slam, went
the gavel.

The attorneys stood, gathering papers into their brief cases. Miriam stood, turned, wrapped Tad on her arm and marched him past Doctor Don and his assembled flock.

"I never had the privilege of meeting your son, but I'm reasonably certain that he's comfortably ensconced in heaven at this very moment. I don't believe a ten-year-old is capable of, let's say, incurring God's wrath."

"Pissing God off."

"Well, yes. What I'm trying to say, Miriam, is that it really isn't worth fighting over Tony's burial service. I don't think God cares."

"I care."

"That's another matter then." Tad hadn't imagined that their first real, private conversation in so long would begin with an argument, and a rather dumb argument at that. In the weeks since he was summoned to her hospital bedside early that March morning, their conversations had been confined to everyday matters, largely by his desire not to intrude in her psychiatrist's regimen. Not that this conversation could be considered truly private. A booth in the Shell truck stop outside Red Oak is not exactly a confessional.

Tad studied her as they dug into their lunches: turkey club sandwich and iced tea for her, cheeseburger and Diet Coke for him, cole slaw and a mountain of french fries for each. Religion—Catholic or Christian Fundamentalist—had not been good to Miriam. "I guess I don't understand why you care who presides over your son's funeral," he said. "You don't seem ready to leap back into the Catholic faith."

"Damn right."

"Then why? Poking a stick in Doctor Don's eye?"

"That's a gentle way of putting it. Shoving a fence post up his ass is a better way to describe it."

Tad reflected for the fortieth or fiftieth time in the last month how inadequately his scholarly life had prepared him to deal with gut-level, emotionally burdened religious belief. And non-belief. If he had gone into pastoral work right out of the seminary, or maybe been a Navy chaplain, he might be better able to handle this. But no, he chose the Holy Trinity.

"I think you should prepare yourself for the possibility that the court may rule in favor of your husband and the Holy Scripture—"

"Then we appeal."

"More likely, the judge will throw the whole thing out as not being a legal matter at all."

"We appeal."

Tad decided this was not the time to bring up the delicate matter of paying all those legal bills. He hadn't received an invoice from Killian's firm, but sensed it may already be stressing his limited resources. "Tomorrow's the inquest. That should be interesting."

"I can tell you right now how it will turn out," she said.

"Making a bet?"

"Accidental death."

"I don't see how that can be. Those injuries …"

Miriam reached across the table. "Okay, let's bet. Dinner at the Sandstone." Tad took her hand and shook it. It was soft and warm, just as he remembered.

"Tell me about your daughters."

"Betsy's thirteen, Maria's fifteen. They're going to hell."

"Do you mean that in a spiritual sense, or in a, ah, worldly, metaphorical sense?"

"I don't know about the spiritual sense, if there is such a thing. I mean they are headed in altogether the wrong direction. I can't do anything with them. Cigarettes, beer, pot. And they aren't even old enough to drive. Considering the house they're growing up in, it's not surprising. Myron thinks it's perfectly natural, the way everybody behaves. Totally out of control."

"How about your son? Tony."

"Poor little guy. Talk about being jerked around. Sensitive kid, smarter than hell. But while I'm trying to develop his talents, get him interested in reading, music, science, his old man's trying to make another redneck out of him. So one minute he's a happy, eager, loving kid, next minute he's cussing his head off at you. Or was."

Until then, Tony was simply the deceased, the victim, the Detts' dead son. Now Tad could picture a young human, laughing, sulking, asking questions, dirty face, full of wonder, a boy who might have looked like him but for a twist of fate.

"Your oldest daughter?"

"Darlene. Twenty years old. Waitress. Married, no kids. Her husband's a patrolman in the sheriff's department. Darlene's a decent girl, but not very ambitious. She and her husband are members of the Holy Scripture church."

"Is your husband a member of that church also?"

"How much do you know about Myron?"

"I've heard he's a real, well, I've heard him described as a 'bad ass.' But on the few occasions that I've seen him, he seemed more like a frightened animal, maybe a rabbit or a deer that can't find a place to hide."

"He's all that and a lot more. Take everything you've heard about him, and everything you've observed, multiply by ten, and you've got Myron."

"He doesn't seem like the type to join a fundamentalist sect like the Holy Scripture."

"Myron will do anything Holy Moses tells him."

"Who?"

"Holy Moses. Sheriff Hollister Moses. Somebody started calling him 'Holy Moses' in grade school, and he's been 'Holy Moses' ever since. Even uses it on his campaign posters."

"And Sheriff Moses, Holy Moses, told Myron to join the Holy Scripture church, so he did?"

"He's not actually a baptized member. He just sort of hangs around. Couple other guys from the sheriff's department do too. I guess because the boss tells them to."

"Somehow, I can't picture Sheriff Moses as holy," Tad said. "And certainly not a follower of Doctor Don."

"Holy, he ain't. And as for follower, I'm not sure who's following who. My guess it's the other way around."

That was a lot of information for a brain to process, even one accustomed to processing large quantities, as Tad's was. He dipped a french fry into a pool of ketchup on his plate and nibbled on it, while he tried to fit the characters—her family and the overbearing lawman—into her life as he was trying to understand it.

"What about you? Victim of all the rotten schemes and dirty tricks the gods and fate can devise. Every right to be a confirmed cynic when it comes to religion. How did you manage to hook up with the Holy Scripture people?"

"A high school friend introduced me to it."

"So you joined?"

"It had what I needed. Doctor Don and his people had something I could grab onto. Something to be sure about."

"The Bible?"

"Right. It seemed to have answers. For the first time since high school, things made sense. I could believe. What I didn't understand, someone would explain. I got caught up in the emotion. You'd be surprised how you can lose yourself, become part of something immense and important, when everybody's holding hands and singing and swaying and shouting 'praise the Lord.'"

"No, I'm not surprised," Tad said.

"And I found friends. People I thought were genuinely interested in me as a person, not as an emergency room nurse, or the wife of that maniac Myron, or the mother of those incorrigible kids."

"What happened? What changed?"

"They did. One day somebody decided I shouldn't work on Sunday. Well, for god's sake, I had to work nights because we needed the extra money. And the early hours of Sunday morning is peak time in ER. Somebody's got to be there."

"You mean they asked you not to help sew up accident victims just because it's Sunday?"

"Not asked. Demanded. Then they said I should tithe to the church. A tenth of my salary and Myron's. Can you believe it? So Doctor Don can bop around the country preaching and doing whatever he does when he isn't here? It would have come directly out of grocery money."

"What happened when you wouldn't quit and wouldn't tithe?"

"I was shunned."

"Beg your pardon?"

"I had to sit off on one side during Sunday services. A good twenty feet from the rest. And during study sessions, Gloria Stark was assigned to preach directly to me and me alone for a full hour. I took that for two weeks and quit."

"I don't think that's what Jesus had in mind when—"

"They had scriptural passages to back them up. But I didn't give a shit. My Bible went out with the trash."

Miriam lit a cigarette. Tad had to ask the question that had kept him awake on many nights in recent weeks.

"Miriam, did you really mean what you said about killing the person responsible for your son's death?"

Her answer didn't come as quickly as he wanted. Thirty years ago he could have looked into her eyes and had his answer. This time there was no eye contact. It took two long pulls on the cigarette before she responded. "Probably not."

"You don't sound convinced."

"I'm not."

CHAPTER 13

✿

District Attorney Brewster told Judge Valders he would call seven witnesses in the inquest, and he did. None of them offered any fresh information.

Doctor Rutgers of the pathology laboratory at University of Wisconsin Hospitals read the autopsy report, describing the extent of Tony Dett's injuries, and the cause of death the severe blow to the skull.

Tad sat with Miriam in the second row on the defense side of the spectator section. Attorney Killian flanked her on the right. Members of Holy Scripture church filled the spectator seats on the prosecutor's side. Tad wondered fleetingly if any of them had day jobs, but reflected that his own presence was a stretch of his pastoral job description. All waited for the key question from the district attorney. "In your opinion, Doctor Rutgers, could the fatal injury be caused by a fall down a flight of stairs?"

"I suppose it could."

"In your opinion, is there any reason to believe that the fatal injury, and the other injuries that were not the immediate cause of death, were caused by some force apart from a fall down a flight of stairs?"

"Do you mean 'Was there any evidence on the victim's body to suggest that forces other than a fall may have contributed to the injuries?'"

"That is exactly what I meant."

"Then the answer is 'no.'"

"Is it your conclusion, doctor, that the death resulted from an accident?"

"I'm sorry, sir, but I am not empowered to make such a judgment. That is the purpose of this inquest. I can only report the results of my medical examination."

Tad heard a snort from Miriam and "that son of a bitch" in a voice that could not have reached more than three feet from her mouth. He leaned and just as quietly advised her that the pathologist was doing his job exactly as the law dictated. But he saw what she saw, that Doctor Rutgers no more believed it was an accident than the invention of the computer was an accident. And he thought he detected a trace of disbelief even on Judge Valders' stoic countenance. But the answer stood unchallenged and went into the record as such.

The next four witnesses were the Starks, Gloria and Adam, and the Flints, Judith and Joshua. No surprises there. They seemed well-rehearsed, although their stories were simple, and the D.A.'s questioning was gentle. Gloria's testimony was interrupted twice by sobs, and Judith dabbed at her eyes with a tissue, dramatic flourishes that caused Miriam to grab Tad's hand and sink her fingernails deep enough to draw blood.

The two detective husbands were all business, right out of the Joe Friday school. Their stories as witnesses to the incident were the same as their wives', without the dramatics. Then they put on their law enforcement personae and reported the details: number of steps on the staircase, distance from top to bottom both vertically and horizontally, distance from the victim's bed to the top of the stairs, height of the banister, lighting, composition of the carpeting on the steps—elements of a standard police investigation, conducted by themselves. Joshua Flint corroborated all that his partner had said.

To the surprise of Tad and Miriam, Attorney Killian declined to cross examine. District Attorney Brewster was thanking Flint for his expert police work and professional attitude at a time that must have been terribly emotional, when Judge Valders intervened.

"I have a couple of questions for this witness," he said. "First of all, was there any chemical analysis done on the stairway carpet following the, ah, accident?"

"Does your honor mean was the carpet tested for blood stains?"

"That. Skin. Bits of the boy's clothing. Anything that would substantiate the vivid descriptions of the previous witness regarding the victim's plunge down the steps."

"We made an inch-by-inch inspection of the carpet—"

"We?"

"My partner, Detective Stark, and I. Yes, your honor. We found traces of the boy's blood on several of the steps."

"And did you preserve those traces as evidence in this case?"

"We saw no need for it, your honor. You see—"

"Has that carpet been cleaned since the incident involving Tony Dett?"

"No it has not."

"Then we could call the state crime laboratory in to examine it in detail to see precisely where on the various steps blood was found, so that we might more accurately reconstruct the accident. Could we not, Detective Flint?"

"Ah, no we could not your honor. The carpet no longer exists." The last sentence trailed off into a mumble.

"What? An important piece of evidence, maybe the only physical evidence that would substantiate your claims of an accident, no longer exists?"

"You see, your honor, Gloria—Mrs. Stark—was quite traumatized by the accident. The carpet was a continual reminder of that tragedy. So the Starks had it removed and new carpeting installed on the stairs."

"And where might the old carpeting be?"

"I guess in a landfill someplace, your honor. With a court order we could have it exhumed."

Judge Valders only *thought* he had seen it all before in his career on the bench. But he was certain he had never ordered a landfill reopened so a piece of old carpeting could be retrieved from under six weeks' worth of a county's garbage, and he was pretty sure no other judge in Wisconsin had either. He let the courtroom buzz run its course and the two detectives dangle for a moment wondering how they could comply with such an order. Finally, "Never mind, Detective Flint," he said. "The picture of you and your partner with shovels in a landfill is rather appealing. And while it may teach you something about thorough police work, I'll let it go. For now."

The final two witnesses were emergency medical technicians, the EMTs who answered the 911 call that night, Janice Wilkins and Doug Merton. They provided the expected answers to the D.A.'s expected questions, which were obviously phrased to validate on the record the testimony of the witnesses who had been present in the Stark home that night. Janice Wilkins was not content to answer only the D.A.'s questions. Three times he cut her off in mid-sentence when she tried to stray from the questions. Finally, Judge Valders intervened.

"Mr. Brewster, nobody is on trial here. Our purpose is only to learn as best we can what happened in the Stark home the night the Dett boy died. I'm prepared to bend the rules just a bit if it allows us to reach that end. Ms. Wilkins, you seem to have something on your mind, and I would be interested in hearing it."

"Well, your honor," she said, "a couple things struck me as unusual when we arrived at the scene. First of all, I can't see how anyone could receive the kind of injuries that kid had just from a fall down a flight of carpeted stairs. I don't think a little old lady with osteoporosis could get hurt that bad on those stairs."

"Yes, go on Ms. Wilkins," the judge said.

"The other thing is, when we got there, the kid was lying on a sofa with towels underneath him. But nobody seemed to be paying any attention to him. They let Doug and me in. Showed us the kid. Then they all went out in the kitchen to talk."

"Could you hear what they were saying?"

"No."

"Anything else?"

"No. It just struck us as kind of peculiar, given how bad the boy was hurt."

"Thank you, Ms. Wilkins. I will take your comments under consideration."

"What do you think?" Tad's question was directed at Killian, although he fully expected an opinion from Miriam as well. They were standing alongside his car in the courthouse parking lot, soaking up one of God's nicest gifts—warm, late afternoon sunshine on one of the first really spring-like days in early May. Killian had been engaged in a lengthy cell phone conversation and was excited.

"Things are falling into place for us," she said.

"Judge Valders is going to rule homicide and put those bastards behind bars for life?" Miriam said.

"I'm betting Judge Valders is going to rule accidental death, but that isn't going to make any difference. We got the testimony we wanted. That record is gold."

"What are you talking about?" Tad asked.

She held a folder over her mouth. "The detectives are watching us. Might be lip readers. Let's meet next Monday morning at ten. Jake Nicholas' office in Platteville. He's our main litigator. We'll have the transcript by then, and maybe even the judge's decision, for what that's worth."

"You haven't answered my question. What's going on?"

"Wrongful death suit," Killian said from behind the folder. "Big bucks. Really big bucks."

The many perils of the Dett family were taking too much of his time, in Tad's estimation, time that he should be devoting to his three parishes. Routine duties were taking far more time than he had calculated, leaving little for his scholarly pursuits via Internet, phone and mail. And all that had left him with little time or energy to go on the religious offensive in his corner of the state, to light a fire under those who profess to follow the teachings of Christ. Doctor Don seemed to have that territory all to himself. Of those many responsibilities, Tad was reluctantly admitting that he found the Dett family saga most interesting. Whether that was because it represented the proper role of a pastor and the role suited him, or because it was part of some thirty-four-year-old unfinished business, he didn't know and wasn't ready to speculate.

He did know, however, that it was time to back away from things a bit. He hadn't had a genuine day off since he hit Wisconsin running six months before. Trout season was opening Saturday, and he intended to be on the bank of the Midewiwin when the sun came up.

Friday evening was spent in the time-honored pastime of fishermen everywhere—tinkering with his gear, arranging and rearranging his tackle box, winding a new spool of monofilament line onto a new reel, imagining the huge fish that have spent the winter dreaming of sumptuous meals of precisely what was in his bait box.

Thirty years had passed since Tad had handled a fly rod. He had once been pretty good at it, and he felt the skill would return after just a few casts. He also knew that this early in the season, casting a fly would probably be a waste of time, and he was prepared to dunk worms and night crawlers under the stream banks and into the riffles.

The Midewiwin, or more precisely, the Davies Branch of the South Fork of the Midewiwin, wound through flat, fertile meadow lands, flanked on both sides by sandstone cliffs and steep, wooded hills punctuated with rock outcroppings. Tad had selected the section between Town Line Road and County Highway MM, about a mile downstream from where the stream passed through the Coburg family property. His inquiries had confirmed that the fourth generation Ingolstadts, who owned the land, had no objection to people fishing there, that the herd grazing the meadow consisted of Holstein steers and heifers—no bulls to be wary of—and that the Department of Natural Resources had stocked the stream with brown and brook trout a month before. Even the weather cooperated: a cold drizzle masked the movement of fishermen on the banks and kept all but the most dedicated at home cleaning their garages. Tad had a half mile of the Davies Branch to himself.

Those were just the conditions he needed, not necessarily to catch fish, although it's generally better to catch fish than not catch fish. They were the conditions for real introspection. For a thousand years, Christians have been building elaborate churches and cathedrals for a variety of reasons, one of which was prayer. But for millennia before that, humans found in nature—the woods, the rivers, the mountaintops—the environment they needed to look deep inside themselves. As a youngster, Tad had found it on the banks of the Midewiwin, although he didn't recognize it at the time. In the Navy, the dark and dangerous rivers of Vietnam performed somewhat the same function. In his twenty-plus years as a priest, retreats with the monks in a simple monastery were as close as he came to finding what he found in silent, moving water.

Tad's first decision on Saturday morning was to leave the flies in the tackle box. His collection, purchased the day before, was not large. An easterly breeze would make targeting the flies more difficult, given his thirty years of rustiness at fly fishing. Underbrush, low hanging willow trees and fallen tree branches would have taken all the fun out of it anyway. So it was good old worms, two dollars a dozen at Ernie's Bait and Tackle.

They proved effective for the first couple of hours. He had two ten-inch browns and a slightly larger brook in his creel by mid-morning. A dozen or more had been thrown back to grow up, along with twice that many pesky little suckers, redhorse and bullheads not worth keeping and cleaning. When worms seemed to lose their appeal, Tad tried some of the artificial lures—small frogs, poppers, daredevils—which, he recalled from thirty years before, could be effective for smallmouth bass. They weren't. Time to break out the boloney sandwich and hot coffee from his backpack.

He sat on a log alongside the stream, where it wound close to the steep hill. The drizzle had become a light, all-day type rain. His glasses were beaded with rain, but he could see all he needed to bait a hook and find the right spots to put it in the water. A large oak provided some measure of shelter to eat lunch, and his only concern with the weather was protecting his sandwich. His boots and head-to-toe rain gear worked as advertised.

The two discussion group sessions he had conducted, following the highly successful effort organized by the Bestmans, troubled him. The first one worked, he concluded, because of the chemistry among the participants, all selected by Bruce and Ann. They were young, educated, bright and stimulated by disparate ideas and opinions.

The second session consisted of a more random selection of parishioners. Tad had gone through the membership lists of each parish and picked out people he knew were attending Mass regularly. It took more than thirty phone calls to find four couples and two single people willing to try this novel idea of talking about their religion for an evening.

The session was, if not a disaster, at least a waste of time for eight of the ten participants. The problem was the Plumms, Peter and Mary. They were dogmatic anti-abortionists. Tad tried repeatedly to steer the discussion into other aspects of morality, the evening's agreed-upon topic. To no avail. The Plumms quickly diverted discussion back to abortion. When Monica Riley ventured that she probably fell more into the pro-choice camp, Peter and Mary came at her from both sides of the room, demanding to know how she had the temerity to receive Communion on Sunday, and where she would be if her parents were pro-choice. Monica said nothing more that evening, and Tad wondered if he would ever see her or her family at Mass again. Roger Langely raised the matter of capital punishment, only to be put in his place by the Plumms, who contrasted the killing of innocents to the killing of people who deserved it, and that's that. Margaret Stauffner, mother of nine and well past menopause, suggested that if the church were a bit more realistic concerning contraception, there might be no demand for abortion. The Plumms' answer to that was rooted in the majesty and straight-from-heaven wisdom of the pope. Nothing more from Mrs. Stauffner that evening.

The last discussion group was again drawn from the parish rolls. This time Tad sought to select the participants carefully, based on what he knew about the people—their ages, occupation and families. However, he didn't know much about them, and the group of ten wasn't very well matched. The subject was liturgy. George Meiningen was absolutely, dead certain that the church's problems began with Vatican II, and that returning to the Latin Mass and turning the altar around to face away from the people was all it would take to restore the Catholic Church's grandeur—*an odd viewpoint*, Tad thought, *given that Meiningen wasn't even born until Vatican II reforms were well underway.* That provoked a lengthy silence, which Tad broke by asking about church music.

Bob Zurn remarked that the campfire-type songs composed in the late sixties and early seventies, when the church tried to get with it, were never any good to start with and even worse—musically—today. Nobody argued with that, although Tad guessed it was because nobody knew what he was talking about.

Ellen Killian said "Father, I know you aren't allowed to agree with me, but I have to say the church will continue to atrophy until it starts ordaining women priests."

"Ellen," Tad said, "I agree with you. So there."

That was more than George Meiningen could handle. "What kind of priest are you? Don't they teach you in Rome that Catholics are obligated to obey the Vicar of Christ on Earth in all matters of faith and morals? The pope says no women priests, so no women priests. Simple as that. Or married priests. And no homosexuals receiving Holy Communion, and no artificial birth control or remarriage after divorce. You're either Catholic or you're not."

Tad guessed that Bishop Ardito would get a nasty letter from Meiningen soon. But there wasn't much the bishop could or would do to punish him more than he already had.

That was about all that came from the discussion of liturgy. That, plus the overall impression that his parishioners don't care much one way or the other about the ceremonies surrounding their beliefs.

Tad finished his sandwich, tore open a small package of store-bought chocolate chip cookies and hunched over to protect them while he ate. His mother's were much better.

He had reported the results of the discussion sessions over lunch with Bishop Ardito—at Delitalia in Madison, just a few blocks from the bishop's office—the day before. "I guess I'm not surprised or discouraged," the bishop had said. "In a country as diverse and quarrelsome as the United States, we can't expect the church in America to be any different. The days of sheep blindly following the shepherd are long gone. Democracy and blind obedience don't mix. Let's hope it stays that way. God doesn't want sheep in heaven. He wants people who decided they wanted to be in heaven and figured out a way to get there."

"I'm not sure my friends in Rome agree with you entirely," Tad said.

"Of course not. They have a vested interest in a servile laity. But I'll give them the benefit of good intentions. They're going with what they've been taught, a top-down culture from the Middle Ages. With a pretty flimsy foundation in Scriptures. Agree?"

"Well, yeah, for the most part ..."

"You don't have to agree with your bishop. You just do what I tell you. And I'm telling you that your job right now is to light a fire in southwestern Wisconsin. Make the Catholic Church relevant. And not just for those who show up for Mass every weekend."

Tad thought he ought to tell Bishop Ardito about his involvement with the Dett family and its many-faceted legal problems. He hadn't known where to begin, and the bishop saved him the trouble. "Got to go. Late for a one o'clock." With that he was gone, leaving Tad to finish his salad and Diet Coke, uncertain as ever about his job. And his relationship with Miriam, the Dett family and the Holy Scripture Universal Church of the Lord.

His Saturday morning on the trout stream had the restorative effect that fishing is supposed to. He had no fresh answers, but the questions seemed a little less perplexing. And he had fresh trout in his creel, waiting to be cleaned and fried for dinner that night.

He dumped the leftover worms on the back lawn, stowed his fishing tackle in the garage, hung his wet rain gear in the basement and was preparing to clean his catch. First, check the answering machine.

As always, there were a half dozen or more calls, most having to do with Mass times. One informed him that an elderly parishioner had entered the nursing home in Bremerton and could he stop to visit him next week. The last one, the most recent call, timed by the machine at 2:33 PM, jolted him.

"Father Tad Coburg," the call began, with heavy, sarcastic emphasis on "father." Tad didn't recognize the voice. "Millen County people have always been able to take care of our own problems without interference from representatives of foreign countries. With all due respect (more sarcasm), we ask—politely, mind you—that you stick to your own business. Papists are not welcome in Millen County. We put up with Roman priests, as long as they don't interfere with our lives. This is a suggestion. If another suggestion becomes necessary, it will not be so polite. And by the way, enjoy your two brown trout and one brook."

Tad played the message three more times, hoping to recognize the voice, or gain some other clue as to its source. His instinct was to erase the message, but he didn't. He thought of calling the sheriff, Holy Moses. Not a good idea, he guessed. Same with the district attorney. He thought of sharing the message with Bruce Bestman. Maybe.

Tad's fish-cleaning skills had atrophied over the years, and he was left with mutilated but still tasty fish. He put them in the refrigerator before hustling off to Bremerton for the 5 PM Mass. He would hurry back, fry and eat the fish and say the 7:30 PM Mass at St. Brendan's in Red Oak.

When he returned to the rectory from that frenzied schedule, it was almost 9 PM He pushed the playback button to listen to the strange, chilling phone message one more time. It was gone. Had he erased it inadvertently? One tap on the delete button while the message was playing would have done it. Tad hoped he had made that mistake, but was afraid that he hadn't.

CHAPTER 14

When Judge Valders read his decision in court Tuesday on the matter of Tony Dett's funeral services, his reasoning was so clear you wonder why it took so long. Nothing in the briefs filed by attorneys for either side was persuasive. Because his order restraining Myron from any contact with his son was still in effect and unchallenged, the boy's mother's wishes would prevail. Father Tad Coburg would preside in Catholic funeral services. However, the judge left the door opened an inch. In the event an appeal is filed within forty-eight hours, the Catholic services would go ahead, but the burial itself must await the results of appeal. If an appeals judge rules for the father, then a second funeral service would be held, which is what the judge proposed as a compromise on the first day of this strange case, and which was agreed to by the mother but not the father. Slam.

More stirring and murmuring in the courtroom from the Holy Scripture contingent. Once again, Miriam paraded her priest past them triumphantly. Tad distinctly heard at least two of Doctor Don's followers snarl "papist."

Tad had suggested they wait no longer and hold the funeral service the next day, Wednesday. Nope, said Miriam. "Some of my friends at the hospital will need a couple days to arrange their schedules. Friday."

"How about Thursday."

"Friday."

He wondered if Miriam had colluded with the Bestmans on the matter, because Thursday's issue of the *Millen County Reporter* led with the Tony Dett story, illustrated with a head and shoulders of the boy, probably a school class photo. A four-column, six-inch photo of Miriam and Tad exiting the court-house on Tuesday, a photo he did not know was taken, cemented his role in the matter for the citizens of Millen County.

Most of page one and much of pages two and three rehashed every known detail of the story, including the judge's skeptical remarks at the inquest, Myron's restraining order and the developing links between the boy's death and the Holy Scripture Universal Church of the Lord.

A sidebar in the upper left of page one reported that Wednesday morning attorneys for Myron Dett had filed an appeal of the judge's decision. What that would do for prospects of a second funeral for Tony Dett was not known at press time.

In total, it was sensationalism, drama and pathos worthy of any big city paper.

"Bruce, I can't believe you'd blow up this poor family's troubles and a simple funeral service to sell a few more copies of your paper. It's totally out of proportion." Tad was on the phone and angry.

"Relax, father. Was there anything in the stories that was incorrect? Or even out of context?"

"No, well, it's the whole thing. Wasn't there anything else that happened in the county this week?"

"Actually, no."

"And my picture ..."

"You've been in the front row through this whole affair. The judge won't let me take pictures in the courtroom. So the courthouse steps are next best. Sorry, but you're a big part of the story."

Tad considered telling the editor about the strange phone message and the whispered epithets in the courtroom, but guessed they would only find their way into follow-up stories. "Bruce, I'm just interested in helping a very troubled family through some extremely difficult times. That's my job. You don't make it any easier by splashing my picture all over the county."

"I understand that, father. But trust me. If you believe that truth conquers evil, like scissors cuts paper and paper covers rock, then you have to believe I'm doing the right thing."

"It's just not that simple."

"Trust me, Father Tad."

❦   ❦   ❦

His first clue that this was not to be an ordinary funeral for a ten-year-old accident victim came when Tad looked out the rectory window Friday morning. It was still two hours before the Mass was to begin, and already two television stations had their vans with satellite uplink antennae set up. A half dozen cars were in St. Brendan's parking lot.

Right away he knew that the standard homily he had prepared, the one intended to comfort bereaved family members and reassure them about meeting the deceased in the hereafter, wouldn't do. He would be talking to an audience considerably wider than the boy's mother and sisters.

But first, prayers with the immediate family at the Gregory Funeral Home in Bremerton. Open casket. Usually, the most difficult time for the family. Tad was called upon to intervene in a brief incident on the front steps of the funeral home. The Starks and the Flints insisted on attending the private service. Winthrop Gregory conveyed to them Miriam's wishes that they not. They contended that Myron Dett invited them. Tad said "No. Period."

Myron was there, restraining order or no restraining order. He clearly would rather have been anywhere else. Tad guessed that he had not slept well since his son died. He had either lost considerable weight, or the shirt and suit were borrowed from a bigger man.

The couple's two teenage daughters wore dresses of tasteful length, no cosmetics, and their brown hair was brushed back and held in place by plastic headbands.

Their oldest daughter, Darlene, was accompanied by her husband, the sheriff's department highway patrolman.

The Goodfellers, Wanda and Ralph, the only non-family members, were present at Miriam's invitation.

They stood surrounding the casket: Miriam and Myron facing each other with the boy's body between them; Maria and Betsy next to Miriam; Wanda and Ralph directly behind them. Darlene and her husband were next to Myron.

Tad stood at the head. His experience with funerals had begun only when he arrived in Red Oak as pastor of the three Wisconsin parishes. At those services, a couple dozen in all, the dominant emotion was sadness, usually for an elderly person who had lived a good life but would be missed and remembered fondly. Twice, the deceased was young, under thirty, victim in one case of cancer, the other a traffic accident. In those, the inevitable question of "why?" was added to the grief. Once, a West Charleton mother of five young children succumbed to Lou Gehrig's disease, and to all the usual emotions was added a large measure of compassion for the husband and children, tempered by the sense that she was finally relieved of the incredible cross she bore with her disease.

But in this small parlor in the Gregory Funeral Home, more issues were plainly present. The boy's father and mother stood, neither looking across his body at the other. Miriam's expression was that of any mother seeing her dead son for the final time. Her tears flowed unchecked. Myron wasn't crying; for him that may have been impossible. Tad couldn't tell from his appearance what was going on inside.

Maria and Betsy were impassive, or tried to be, fortified by Wanda's hands on their shoulders. But tears trickled down their cheeks despite all their efforts to squeeze them back. Tad wondered if it was the presence of their father that prevented them from giving in completely to their obvious grief for their young brother. They would not look at their father.

Darlene leaned on her husband sobbing. He held her, but stared straight ahead, tight-lipped and dry-eyed.

Tad had arrived twenty minutes before the others to become acquainted with Tony Dett and try to sort out his own complicated emotions, as well as find the right prayers and scriptural passages for the occasion. He was a handsome boy, the product of the best of both parents' genes. Tad had no trouble imagining in his face the intelligence and sensitivity Miriam had fondly described. Or the redneck crudeness she ascribed to his father. *I would have loved that kid and been proud as hell if he were mine,* Tad thought. *And devastated by his death. What's wrong with Myron? How can he still function in these circumstances?*

Even with the twenty-minute head start, Tad wasn't ready to do his best at casket-side. He thought he ought to have some words of compassion, or encouragement. Or something that might help the eight, who were seeing their son, brother, friend for the last time. But he had no suitable words of his own. He plodded ahead, "Let us now pray in the words our Savior gave us, 'Our Father, who art in heaven …'" He wondered if anyone in the room was paying any attention to the words, really meaning what they were saying. Yes, the Goodfellers. Maria and Betsy, probably not. Darlene and her husband, maybe. Miriam? She was, no doubt, miles away. Myron? Who knows. *I'd like to talk to him some time.* "Eternal rest grant unto him, O Lord, and let perpetual light shine upon him." He concluded the brief ceremony. *I could have been a tape recording for all the consolation I was to this family.*

In just over twenty-four hours, Bruce Bestman had accomplished what Father Tad hadn't come close to in more than six months—fill St. Brendan's Church. The Tony Dett case had caught the community's attention.

Tad waited at the front of the altar with the Mass servers, a boy and a girl not much older than Tony. Television cameras ("stay out of the way, this is a religious service, not a political rally," Tad had told them) worked from the side aisles.

He looked over the assembled crowd and recognized many from St. Brendan's and a few from his other two parishes. Many were unfamiliar, and he wondered whether they were moved by the poignancy of a boy's death, or by the mystery surrounding that death. The media had dwelt at length and dramatically on both, as well as the protracted legal battle over the funeral services.

Tad spotted the Starks and the Flints among the crowd standing at the rear. Sheriff Moses had found himself an aisle seat, half way back. Ruth Coburg sat next to him. No Doctor Don. The six family members plus the Goodfellers, joined now by Wanda's mother, were in the front pew—Miriam at the center aisle, Myron at the far right.

Music from the choir loft gave no hint of the organist's professed nervousness at playing before such a large crowd and the news media. The nine-voice choir, including four men and two women who played hooky from work that morning, had practiced late last night and sounded as good as Tad had ever heard them. In an earlier generation, dolorous chanting in Latin would have magnified the somberness associated with death, especially a child's death. Today, the message was joy at the youngster's entry into paradise. Mindful of Bob Zurn's counsel, Tad had suggested opening with "Jesu, Joy of Man's Desiring" and concluding with "Song of Joy," Bach and Beethoven being remote from the campfire and as good as liturgical music gets.

Pallbearers—four were Miriam's co-workers at Memorial Hospital, two were EMTs—wheeled the casket down the aisle. The choir finished as it arrived at the foot of the altar. Time for Father Tad to perform.

He breezed through the conveniently scripted prayers at the opening of the funeral ceremony and the opening Mass prayers, an event he'd presided over, with variations, some 7,000 times. But, like an examination in school, or a visit to the dentist or a plane ride to a place you weren't sure what you'd find when you got there, it was time. There was no putting it off. Five hundred people, television news crews and newspaper reporters waited expectantly for his homily, his eulogy for a boy he'd never met but felt oddly close to, his words of comfort for the mother and sisters and all those grieving, his lesson for the world from this crazy situation. He had no idea what he would say.

"Family and friends of Tony Dett." Family consisted of six people, if you include Darlene's husband. No way of knowing how many of those seated in St. Brendan's were actually friends of the deceased. Probably only a few. The scattered youngsters of his approximate age likely were classmates. The real audience was not the mass of faces, but the handful in the front pew. Miriam. Betsy, Maria, Darlene and her husband. Even Myron. Tad was supposed to make some sense for them of Tony's senseless death. Christ dying for our sins, His resurrection—the standard fare of Christian funeral homilies—"all well and good," Ann Bestman had told him, but "total yawners," more so on this strange day.

"Why did Tony Dett die?" he began. "Ten years old. In good health. Nearly everyone here today is older, and we're still alive.

"I'm not asking *how* Tony died. That's for the experts and the justice system to figure out." Tad didn't want to, but he couldn't help a quick look at the Starks and Flints in the back, and they caught him at it.

"The question is *why*. The experts and justice system can't help us there. Tony Dett. Young, bright, sensitive. He might someday have been a teacher, a lawyer, a doctor, an inventor. He might have been a president of the United States, a senator, a baseball star or famous writer. He might have been the father of any of those." Tad's eyes wandered to Myron, despite his efforts not to. Myron's eyes were aimed approximately at his knees.

"Did God snuff out Tony Dett to punish him? I can state most emphatically and certainly that he did not. Tony no doubt sometimes did things that most of us would consider bad. All ten-year-olds do. All twenty-year-olds and fifty-year-olds like me and all eighty and ninety-year-olds, we're all sinners. We do things and say things and think things that don't square with the Ten Commandments or the rules of society. Am I right?" Tad's experience as a teacher and the sound system transmitter on his belt let him wander as he spoke. The last was delivered halfway down the center aisle.

He put his hand on Sheriff Moses' shoulder. "I can't speak for everyone here, but I don't always follow all the rules in the motor vehicle code, sheriff. One of these Saturdays, I'm afraid you're going to nail me racing between

Bremerton and Red Oak trying to make the seven-thirty Mass on time." That drew the expected chuckle from the crowd. Holy Moses smiled gamely and shook his head. "And mom, remember that chocolate cake that disappeared so mysteriously forty years ago?" She smiled. Tad guessed they were pleased with being singled out, but uncomfortable about being born-again followers of Doctor Don caught so visibly among heathen Catholics.

"Will God punish me for hitting seventy on that straight stretch of county highway M near the Schaefer farm? I doubt it. Did God punish me for polishing off almost a whole chocolate cake when I was ten years old? I must report that I got awfully sick, but that was simply the laws of nature at work and not divine justice.

"The point is, God doesn't punish us. Why would he? He created us. Why would he snatch that life from us simply because we sometimes don't live up to his hopes for us? God loves us. Why would he wreak vengeance on us? Why would he deliberately make us miserable? People punish people. We punish ourselves. But God doesn't punish us. So let's put that notion away. Tony Dett didn't die because God was punishing him."

Tad's eyes scanned the audience, specifically to catch a reaction from the Starks and the Flints. He saw nothing to suggest agreement or disagreement. He walked to the front. Now was the time to do what he could for Miriam and her grieving daughters.

"That still doesn't answer our question. Why did he die so young, so full of promise? We asked the same question when John F. Kennedy was killed. And Martin Luther King, Jr. We asked it when Tony's grandfather, Elmer Baumer, a kind and loving man that Tony never knew, died suddenly and tragically on a highway a few miles from his house, a road he'd driven thousands of times before." The thought occurred to Tad that if Elmer Baumer hadn't been killed in that accident, there might be no Tony Dett to mourn. Fortunately, the mind and mouth don't always work in lockstep, and the thought flitted off.

"The closest any of us can come to an answer to that profound question 'why' is simply that Tony and his grandfather, President Kennedy and Doctor King had finished their jobs on earth."

Tad looked around his audience. They—and he—wondered where all this was leading.

"The next question, of course, is 'What were their jobs on earth? What did God expect of them?' Over a lifetime, many things. President Kennedy and Doctor King accomplished much, and God probably welcomed them into heaven and said 'Well done.' One of Elmer Baumer's jobs was to produce a family. He did a fine job at that. I knew Elmer Baumer and his family, and I'm sure God met Elmer at the gates of heaven with a high five."

Help me, Lord, I'm getting all tangled up. Myron continued to look at his knees. "We don't know what Tony's job was. I guess the answer lies within each of us. What did Tony Dett mean to you? Maybe you didn't know Tony. Maybe you're here because you know Miriam, or Myron. Or one of Tony's sisters. You feel their sadness, and by your attendance you're letting them know that their grief is yours as well. So let this sad time serve as your own wake-up call. Ask yourself how well you're doing your job here on earth. What does God expect of you? Are you living up to His expectations?"

Pretty lame. You can do better than that. Try this:

"Next question: Where is Tony Dett today? His body is in that casket. Where is his soul? Answer: His soul is with God in heaven. How do I know that? Simple. God created us with the sole purpose of joining him there after life on earth. The only way that's not going to happen is if we deliberately choose not to. Could you believe for one second that a ten-year-old boy is going to choose not to go to heaven? Of course not. Case closed."

Not terribly eloquent. At best, three on a scale of ten. It likely didn't impress anyone in that front pew. With the exception of the Goodfellers and possibly Darlene and her husband, I doubt any of them believe in God, much less heaven and a person's choice in the matter. Anyway, what can they expect from a college professor? If they want a learned, reasoned lecture or discussion, I'm their man. But throw in such a heavy load of emotions and they really ought to have someone else.

Time to wrap this up. He stood directly in front of the Dett family, hands leaning on the 100-year-old oak pew, to speak to them alone. Wondering what he would say. It came. "Thirty years ago, I was asking the questions you're asking: Why do people die? Why do I live and they don't?" He looked from one to another at the four Dett women in the front pew: Miriam, Betsy, Maria and Darlene. He had their attention. Darlene's husband was inspecting his left thumbnail. Myron was still captivated by his knees.

Tad plunged on. "Why do people die? Thirty years ago, I wasn't talking about a brother or son. I was in Vietnam, and I was asking those questions about my buddies, my Navy comrades, my Army and Marine Corps friends. One week we'd be in a tent on the Mekong Delta, drinking beer, laughing, playing poker. Next week one of them might be dead. Maybe two.

"Bobby Robards was a Navy corpsman. His job was to treat the wounded on the battlefield and get them back to the aid station. He was from Cincinnati and a good friend of mine. One Sunday morning his platoon was in the middle of a fire fight. He was treating a wounded Marine, when the Vietcong dropped a mortar round right on top of him. Killed him instantly. But the Marine lived. Not many of us are lucky enough to die saving someone's life." Tad paused, surprised at what had just come out of his mouth. He was moving into territory he'd avoided for thirty years.

"One night we'd be sitting on the fantail of a Navy river boat in pitch darkness, confiding in whispers our love for our families, our girlfriends, our hopes and plans for the future. Wondering why we were halfway around the world from everything that's important, just trying to stay alive. Scared like no one should ever be scared. One burst from an unseen Vietcong machine gun in the jungle on the river bank and we'd be headed home. In body bags."

Oh boy, whatever got me started on this? It's one thing to relive in the darkness and silence of your own room that hellish war with its body bags and its heat, mold, hunger and thirst, bone-aching fatigue, skull-breaking explosions, unforgettable stench, and the death of your comrades. It's something else to open those wounds in front of 500 people, television cameras and a grieving family that it's your job to console. But the thoughts and the words kept coming.

"Josh Chudik was my closest friend in Nam. From Chicago. We were together from boot camp. One sunny morning he was standing right beside me on the river boat when a machine gun raked our deck from bow to stern. No warning." Tad had to stop. His eyes were swimming and his voice was cracking. He took a couple of deep breaths and swallowed. Now even Myron was looking at him.

"Josh was killed instantly, a week before he was scheduled to be rotated back to the States. I was only wounded. The difference was inches.

"Senseless deaths. In a war that none of us understood or believed in. For thirty years I've been trying to find the answer to that question 'why.' And you know something? I still don't have the answer." Tad had to stop and blow his nose. He wiped away two teardrops that had defied his efforts to contain. "Thirty years of theology study and I can't answer that simple question 'Why do young people die?'

"Myron, Miriam. Darlene, Maria, Betsy. All I can tell you with certainty is that your son, your brother, is with God today and he's enjoying eternal peace and happiness. But your job here on earth isn't finished. Make Tony proud of you."

There. A weak ending to a feeble sermon. He paused briefly, convinced of his failure. Why do young people die? Questions like that are the essence of all religions. Over the thousands of years that humans have been pondering them, answers have always outnumbered the questions. Those claiming to have answers are usually sincere, sometimes charlatans. Answers are often flawed. Flawed answers have been at the root of untold hatred and wars. But humans still ask. Why do young people die? Perhaps having no answer is the best answer, the only answer.

Suddenly, Maria and Betsy stood and threw their arms tightly around Tad's neck, catching him leaning and nearly pulling him into the front pew. He felt their hair on his ears, their tears on his cheeks; smelled their Tic-Tac breath. Then Miriam, then Darlene, a spontaneous group hug in front of all those people and television cameras in St. Brendan's Catholic Church.

How long it lasted, Tad had no way of knowing. Seconds, minutes, long enough. Nothing like it in his experience. Nothing like it on the scholarly circuit. Nothing like it in St. Brendan's long history. Something streamed from somewhere, through layers of cotton and flesh, arms and bodies, five people healing each other.

Tony's funeral in St. Brendan's was the first event in which Tad was the principal participant but had to watch TV news to find out all that went on.

The emotional conclusion to the sermon that he felt was so awful captured the media's fancy. Channel 8 in Dubuque led its 6 PM news with a shot of the embrace and the anchor's voice-over: "Tony Dett's funeral recalls the horrors of Vietnam for Father Coburg. That tops our news at six."

Cut to the attractive mid-twenties anchor. "Good evening, everyone, I'm Monica Brody. The Tony Dett funeral this morning drew more than 500 people to St. Brendan's Catholic Church in tiny Red Oak, Wisconsin, population 675. They heard the pastor, Father Thaddeus Coburg, tell of his experiences with death on a Navy river boat in Vietnam thirty years ago, as he groped for an answer to why Tony Dett died at the age of ten."

Cut to Tad, choked with emotion. "Josh was killed instantly, a week before he was scheduled to be rotated back to the States. I was only wounded. The difference was inches." The video footage showed Tad wiping a tear and trying to compose himself. He didn't remember being quite that discombobulated. "For thirty years I've been trying to find the answer to that question 'why.' And you know something, I still don't have the answer." Tad saw himself blow his nose and wipe away tears. "Thirty years of theology study and I can't answer that simple question 'Why do young people die?'"

Channel 8's lone cameraman in the church maneuvered for position, violating instructions to remain on the side. He zoomed in as the Dett women huddled around the priest. On the edge, still in the picture, was Myron, clearly wondering what he should do, what was his role. Tad thought he detected some wish in Myron to be part of that giant hug, but held back by forces that anyone could only guess. Darlene's husband was not in the frame.

Anchor, voice over: "Our reporter Amy Colstead was in Red Oak."

Establishing shot of hearse pulling away from church, zoom in on Amy on steps of church: "Nothing about the Tony Dett case fits any pattern." (Eight or ten quick shots of the service, including long and two quick close-ups of people attending, pallbearers and casket, the choir singing, Mass servers and priest at the foot of the altar, people receiving Communion.) "It took a circuit court decision to even allow this funeral to take place. Then over 500 people show up. The presiding priest, Father Tad Coburg, breaks down in the middle of his eulogy, recalling the deaths of young comrades in Vietnam." (The embrace scene again.) "Tony Dett's mother and sisters join the priest in venting their collective grief. Finally, the hearse" (another shot of hearse leaving church) "pulls away from St. Brendan's with the body of ten-year-old Tony Dett, headed, not for a cemetery, but back to the funeral home. There the body will remain, pending a court decision on whether a second funeral should take place, this one in the fundamentalist Holy Scripture Universal Church of the Lord in West Charleton, the church of the boy's father. (Cut to reporter) Amy Colstead, Channel 8 News, reporting from Red Oak."

"This just in," said the anchor, "Late this afternoon a judge in the case ruled the death of Tony Dett accidental. Channel 8 reporter Brad Fischer is live with us from the Millen County courthouse in West Charleton."

"Yes, Monica, Judge Valders has ruled the death accidental. He said the testimony presented at the inquest last month left him with no alternative but to rule the death an accident. However, in his decision he reprimanded the investigators and prosecutors, saying their presentation of the case was much less than adequate and left a number of unanswered questions. The judge's decision does not give any indication what those questions are. Now, we tried to contact Tony Dett's mother, Miriam Dett, and her attorney. But neither was available for comment. Brad Fischer, Channel 8 news, West Charleton."

Channel 4's coverage was similar, although not quite as polished, with the funeral Mass interrupted at one point by footage of a local Little League baseball game, B-roll obviously intended for a story in the sports segment. The possibility of a return engagement in the Holy Scripture church was not lost on

Channel 4. They didn't get a news crew and satellite uplink to the Millen County courthouse, so the inquest verdict was merely reported by the anchor.

Lacking the visual impact of television, the *Dubuque Telegraph Herald* chose another angle, that being the differing theological points of view readers could expect when and if the case goes to round two at the Holy Scripture church. Father Coburg had conveniently set the agenda:

> *Catholic viewpoint: God does not punish people. People punish people. We punish ourselves.*
>
> *Fundamentalist viewpoint: God does indeed punish people, as noted many times in the Bible, particularly the Old Testament; e.g., Deuteronomy, chapter 32—"When the Lord saw this, he was filled with loathing and anger toward his sons and daughters.... 'Emaciating hunger and consuming fever and bitter pestilence, and the teeth of wild beasts I will send among them, with the venom of reptiles gliding in the dust.'"*
>
> *Father Coburg stated quite assuredly that the youngster's soul was already in heaven. It will be interesting to see if Doctor Don, the charismatic pastor of the Holy Scripture fundamentalist church, tackles that question.*
>
> *The Catholic pastor also stated that a person dies when his or her work on earth is accomplished. The fundamentalist position leans heavily on rebirth in Jesus being the key to redemption, and downplays to a large extent the value of good works for personal salvation. It is another significant variant between the two faiths to watch debated as this case unfolds.*

Judge Valders' ruling on the cause of death didn't surprise Tad. What he had himself ignited in the church did. *Good grief, the last thing I had in mind was a shootout with Doctor Don. I was just trying to bring some comfort to a grieving family.*

Tad received two phone calls in the St. Brendan's rectory that evening. The first was from Father Donovan, Bishop Ardito's secretary, reporting that the bishop had some things to discuss and could he meet in the bishop's office Monday morning.

The second was from a man who did not identify himself and whose voice was only vaguely familiar, who told him to get his papist ass back to Rome as fast as he can and stay forever away from Millen County if he knew what was good for him.

CHAPTER 15

Attorney Ellen Killian was standing around on the steps of St. Joan of Arc Church in West Charleton after the 7:30 AM Mass on Sunday, waiting for Tad to finish chatting with parishioners. Finally, the last one headed off and she was able to break the news. "We file tomorrow morning."

"I'm sorry, Ellen. File what?"

"Wrongful death. Total one hundred million dollars."

"You mean, in Tony Dett's ..."

"Yup. I thought Miriam Dett might have told you. She signed the papers yesterday."

"No, she didn't tell me, that is, I haven't seen her since the funeral."

"Miriam and her three daughters are plaintiffs. The oldest daughter was a last-minute addition to the list of plaintiffs. Defendants are Gloria and Adam Stark, Judith and Joshua Flint, the Holy Scripture Universal Church of the Lord, Doctor Don, Sheriff Hollister Moses and others, as yet unnamed—we're leaving it open in case investigation and testimony suggest there may be more involved in the kid's death. And, oh yes, the Bremerton school district."

"But Ellen, you can't prove—"

"We don't have to prove that someone pounded the life out of Tony or shoved him down the steps or even paddled his bottom. He died from wounds that occurred while he was in their care. How he got those wounds is beside the point. At the very least, the plaintiffs were extremely negligent."

"Those people don't have a hundred million dollars."

"Of course not, but Miriam and her daughters will get all they have and all they ever will have, besides a big chunk of insurance money from the school district."

It took the rest of the morning and most of the afternoon to reach Miriam. When he did, they agreed to meet at the Sandstone for dinner—on him, payoff on the bet they had made about the inquest verdict.

"A hundred million dollars. Aren't you a little uncomfortable getting rich off the death of your son?"

"Not really. Happens all the time," Miriam said.

"What on earth would you do with a hundred million dollars?"

"Oh, I won't get anywhere near that. The Brabender folks say—"

"Who?"

"Brabender. Law firm out of Milwaukee. They specialize in suing hell out of people. Best in the Midwest, they say. Killian's firm brought them in. Anyway, we'll probably settle for much less than a hundred million. Something like ten million. Then, by the time the lawyers get their take, the girls and I'll be left with, I suppose, six or seven million. Divide that four ways, it's not as much as it seems at first."

"Where does Myron fit into this?"

"Wisconsin's a marital property state. He'd get half. So we're getting rid of him. I'm filing for divorce tomorrow."

"Divorcing him so he doesn't get any of your millions?"

"No. Just doing something I should have done years ago. I think even you would agree he's a candidate for divorce if anyone is."

"I won't dispute that."

"The Holy Scripture people are going to have a royal shit fit tomorrow. Getting sued for a hundred million dollars, then finding out their fallen sister is suing one of their people for divorce. Satan has taken over Millen County for sure."

Miriam's second brandy old fashioned and his second glass of Brunello arrived. "Cheers," she said. "Here's to being a millionaire. Wonder how many house trailers I can buy with a million bucks." The Sandstone wasn't filled, but nearly so, a good crowd for a Sunday night in May.

"Did you ever find out what Tony was doing at the Stark house that night?" Tad asked.

"As the attorneys have pieced it together, there'd been some, let's say, discipline problems with Tony at school that day. Happened a lot. He was sent to the principal's office. I was at work. Double shift, the regular three to eleven called in sick. Myron was working three to eleven. The principal called Myron and asked if it would be all right if Tony went to the Stark home overnight. He said okay. Rest is history."

Tad sipped his wine. Lots of "if-onlys" in that sequence. And it didn't take a trained legal mind to see that the Brabender lawyers had an abundance of weapons, ammunition and targets.

"Myron seems lately like a, well …"

"Like a basket case."

"Well, yes," Tad said. "He seems to be taking the death of his son particularly hard. I didn't realize he was so fond of him."

"He wasn't. He's scared out of his mind."

"Scared of what?"

"Myron was at the Stark home that night."

"He was?"

"The people across the street, friends of Ralph Goodfeller, said they saw a black pickup truck with big wheels pull up to the house about eleven o'clock. A guy in a police uniform got out, went into the house. Was in there a half hour, maybe more. Then he came out and roared off, tires squealing. It had to be Myron."

Their entrees arrived, crab cakes for Miriam and a New York strip steak for Tad, baked potato and fresh asparagus. They ate in thought.

"What's going to happen to Darlene when the Holy Scripture folks find out she's suing them for a hundred million dollars?" Tad asked.

"Darlene may hold the world's record for naiveté. I asked her that same question. 'They'll understand,' she said. 'They know it's nothing personal.' That's crap. They'll shun her like they shunned me. The only difference is she's got a husband in that church that she'd like to keep. My guess is she'll pull out of the lawsuit. I'm afraid her husband can be very, let's say, persuasive."

"Are you worried about her?"

"Absolutely."

Tad decided it was time to tell his boss about the whole Dett family situation, going all the way back to high school. It took three quarters of an hour.

"From a legal viewpoint, I'd say the Dett women are in pretty good shape," the bishop said.

"You can see the dollar signs in Miriam's eyes. They've got a good case. But a lot will depend on how much money and insurance the defendants actually have. Except for the school district, probably not much. Miriam's main goal is to see the Starks and the Flints living in a trailer park for the rest of their lives."

"That's not a very charitable attitude."

"No," Tad said. "But right now Thomas Aquinas or Jesus himself couldn't change her mind."

"I can understand that. Tell me, did you mean to stir up an ecumenical hornet's nest by your eulogy last Friday?"

"Of course not. I just wanted to offer some consolation to a grieving family. I didn't plan it. The words just tumbled out."

"Not to be recommended as a way of preaching, but if it doesn't come from the heart, you're not much good as a pastor. Nevertheless, between the legal and theological implications and all the emotional drama, you've got the news media salivating. I've had calls from Chicago, Milwaukee, Minneapolis and New York newspapers, *USA Today*, CNN and all three major networks."

"Wow. What do you tell them?"

"My director of communications reads them a prepared statement declining to comment on the legal questions, and stating that Father Coburg has my unequivocal support."

"Do I?"

"Definitely."

"Thanks."

"One other question," the bishop said. "You and Miriam. Any rekindling of your past relationship, the feelings you had for each other in high school?"

Tad had to think about that. He wanted to answer truthfully, but he didn't know what the truth was. "I hope not," he said.

Driving back to Red Oak, Tad was troubled by the bishop's seeming indifference to the frightening phone calls and their anti-Catholic references. "Lunatic fringe," he called them. "Even within that fundamentalist church down there, I'll bet it isn't more than a handful who still believe all that pre-Kennedy junk about the Vatican taking over the United States. Or could even tell you what the term 'papist' means. Ignore them. Not worth wasting your time or energy."

Easy for you to say.

Routine visits with patients in the hospital and a nursing home in West Charleton and another nursing home in Bremerton took the rest of Monday afternoon. When he returned to the rectory about five, there were sixteen messages on the answering machine.

One message was from his mother, reminding him of their scheduled dinner at her house next Thursday evening. One was from Miriam, asking that he call her at Wanda's place before 10 PM. Fourteen of the messages were from news media. Bishop Ardito had predicted a media spectacle and urged Tad to cooperate with them as best he could, but not comment on any legal proceedings, and to take pains to avoid the appearance of picking a fight with the Holy Scripture church.

The most important of the news media came first. "Hi, Bruce. I didn't get a chance to thank you for turning out half of Wisconsin for the funeral on Friday. If I ever become famous, I'll hire you as my publicist."

"I got news for you, father. As of last Friday you already are famous, and you don't need a publicist. Now, how come all the really big news will be old news by the time the *Millen County Reporter* publishes on Thursday."

"You mean, the wrongful death lawsuit?"

"That and the divorce. I heard about the lawsuit from my barber, who heard it on the radio. I had to beg to get a copy of the news release from the Milwaukee lawyers. Killian told me about the divorce. I thought we had a deal, and your part is to make sure I'm not on the outside looking in."

"You're right. I should have alerted you."

"Why file the suit on Monday? Why not Wednesday, so people can read it in their hometown paper first?"

"That's the lawyers' business. But point well taken."

"So, what do you have for me for Thursday's paper?"

Tad considered mentioning the threatening phone calls, but recalled the bishop's admonition about stirring up trouble and he set the notion aside. He also thought about the report of Myron's presence in the Stark house the night of Tony's death. Instinct stopped him. "Nothing comes to mind, Bruce, but I consider myself properly chastised. I promise to keep you and your paper in mind as this drama plays out."

"I'll keep reminding you."

His call to Miriam confirmed his caution. "You haven't told anybody about Myron being there that night, have you?" she said. "I should have told you that our lawyers want to keep that information confidential right now. They don't want the enemy to know how much we know."

"No, Miriam, I haven't told anyone." He had forgotten to mention it to Bishop Ardito. "And I certainly will keep it quiet. But I wish you wouldn't refer to the defendants as 'the enemy.'"

"Whatever. You may get some phone calls from news reporters."

"Fourteen, at last count," he said.

"Our lawyers say you shouldn't comment."

"They're right and I won't. Not about legal business. But I may comment about religious matters if it seems appropriate."

"Be careful. We're dealing with some really nasty people."

The calls to the remaining news media followed the bishop's and Miriam's guidelines. Polite refusals to comment on legal matters, magnanimous disclaimers about the right of everyone to believe and worship according to his or her own conscience, and strong assurances that whatever Tad's own beliefs, he had no intention of disparaging the beliefs of fundamentalist Christians. After three or four such interviews over the phone, he was beginning to think he could run for public office, so polished, articulate and charming was he.

Two armloads of groceries were about all Tad could handle on his mother's rickety porch steps. Two armloads were far more than they could eat that evening, but plenty to keep Ruth going for another week.

Months ago, when he had gone over her finances with her, it was clear that the income side of the ledger needed a lift. A small social security payment and rent from some grazing and crop land covered basic food needs, property taxes, heat and light, insurance, gasoline and repairs. And not much more. She talked about getting some work at Wal-Mart in West Charleton, or maybe the nursing home in Bremerton. But Tad knew those were temporary solutions. One day she would have to leave the farm.

He set the groceries on the porch floor as he fiddled for his key. A good door lock was one concession she had made to her son from wicked and dangerous Rome. But she rarely locked it.

"Hi, Mom. Mom? Hey, Mom? Ruth?" He set the groceries on the kitchen table. "Mom? Hello?" The downstairs bathroom and bedroom were empty. The bed was made. Upstairs, deserted. One more check: The garage was empty; her well-traveled Dodge was gone.

Tad sat at the kitchen table. *Wrong day? No. She had left the message on his machine just last Monday. Maybe she went out to do some shopping and got to gabbing with her friends at the IGA. Shouldn't I have seen her there? Not necessarily. She'll be along soon. Might as well put the groceries away and start cooking.*

Six o'clock came and went. Seven o'clock. Tad ate his portion of the fried chicken, mashed potatoes, peas and carrots, Jell-O salad and brownies. He found a couple of plastic storage containers and put hers in the refrigerator. Still no Ruth. It was nearly dark. Curiosity turned to worry.

"Hi, Charlotte. Father Tad. Any admissions I should know about?" His call to Tri-County Memorial Hospital was one he'd normally make three or four times a week in the normal course of his pastoral duties. He tried to keep the urgency of this call out of his voice.

"No, father, a farmer out near Walton was brought in this afternoon with a heart attack. Not serious, and he lists Methodist as his religion. Only that and a minor motorcycle accident. So have a good relaxing evening. Talk-ta-ya-soon."

Tad wished he knew the names of his mother's friends. Any of them. Over the course of their conversations, she had mentioned a few. But darned if he could remember a single one now.

The voice at the sheriff's department was familiar. "Hello, Deputy Dett, this is Father Tad Coburg. How are you this evening?"

"Uh, fine, sir."

"Deputy, have there been any accidents reported today, either on the highway or elsewhere?"

"Let me check the log, sir. Car hit deer on County X, 5:30 AM, no injuries."

"What kind of car?"

"Tan 2002 Suburu Outback, sir."

"Anything else?"

"Motorcycle skidded and hit utility pole, 10 AM in downtown West Charleton. Driver conveyed to the hospital, treated and released."

"That's it today?"

"Yes sir. That's it. Quiet day."

"Thank you, deputy. Ah, does Sheriff Moses happen to be around?"

"No sir. But Detective Stark is here. Would you like to talk to him?"

"Thank you, deputy. I don't think so. Have a nice evening." Tad was beginning to think his evening wouldn't be so nice. He called his answering machine. No messages that gave a hint of his mother's whereabouts.

He called the sheriff's office again. "Deputy Dett, could you reach Sheriff Moses for me, please, and ask him to call me on my cell phone? Thanks."

It was nearly 10 PM when Holy Moses phoned. "What can I do for you, padre?"

"Sheriff, I'm at my mother's place outside Red Oak. We were to meet here for dinner, but she wasn't here when I arrived, and I haven't heard from her. I'm getting concerned. Could you have your patrolmen keep an eye out for her? She's driving a blue Dodge, not sure what year."

"Glad to help. We can look the plates up. We get these calls a lot. Tough when your parents get old. They tend to forget where they are. Don't worry. We'll do all we can to find her."

"Thanks, sheriff. I'll stay here at the farm tonight. Call me if you learn anything."

It was a long night. Kind of like being parent of a teenager who is out with the car well after the agreed-upon curfew. The phone didn't ring. Nothing on TV to take his mind off his worry. He prowled the house looking for something to read. He always had two or three novels going at any given time, but they were back at the rectory. So was his laptop, which precluded messaging with colleagues around the world, or even checking his e-mail.

He thought about calling the bishop, but hesitated to bother him, and he didn't figure the bishop could do anything to locate Ruth Coburg. He thought of calling Miriam, but by that time she would be at work and probably should not be bothered.

He prayed a lot, as hard as he had prayed in a long time. He couldn't help reflecting on the discussion group meeting, the night Tony Dett died, and the questions the participants had about the extent of God's intervention in daily activities. Micromanaging, as Frederick called it.

Sometime around 3 AM he nodded off on the living room couch. He was awakened at five-fifteen with the sun hitting him in the face. When he realized where he was and why, he quickly checked outside. No Dodge. The phone hadn't rung. Now what? He was due in West Charleton for a 7:30 AM Mass, which meant a hurried trip to the rectory for a shower, shave and clean clothes. He made it.

After Mass, he stopped at the *Millen County Reporter* office. Bruce and Ann were both there.

Bruce greeted him. "Father, if you don't mind my saying it, you look like hell."

Tad returned the compliment. "You don't look like a respectable publishing executive with your baseball cap on backwards."

"Something troubling you? Want me to hear your confession?"

"Something is troubling me, but I need advice, not absolution." Tad told the publishing couple what he knew of his mother's disappearance, now fifteen hours or more old.

"You've alerted law enforcement, such as it is. Unfortunately, Sheriff Moses and his crew are known to be rather selective in their diligence. And right now you're not high on their list of friends," Bruce said.

"We can put something in the paper," Ann said. "Problem is, we don't publish another issue for almost a week."

Tad's next stop was Attorney Killian's office. She offered to make some inquiries with the FBI and State Patrol, as well as law enforcement in neighboring counties in Wisconsin, Iowa and Minnesota.

Two more days passed. Tad did his own share of driving the back roads in search of her tired old Dodge. Miriam was sympathetic. She suggested there must be a logical explanation—visiting friends or relatives, for example—and offered to keep an eye on hospital admissions.

On Sunday evening the call came. The voice was unfamiliar. "Reverend Coburg, your mother is safe. She is staying with friends. You can guarantee her safety by getting on an airplane within forty-eight hours and returning to Rome. For good."

Caller i.d. identified the caller as "unavailable." No matter. The Roman reference narrowed the field enough for Tad.

He tapped in the sheriff's department administrative number. "Deputy Dett," he commanded, "put me through to Sheriff Moses wherever he is. Now." It took less than a minute.

"All due respects, padre, you caught me right in the middle of a good shit," the sheriff said.

"All due respects, sheriff, my mother has been kidnapped. Shitting time is over. You get your ass over to my house in Red Oak right now." Tad surprised himself, and perhaps the sheriff as well, with how easily that inelegant language slipped into his priestly vocabulary.

"I'm sure this can wait 'til morning," Sheriff Moses said. "I've had a busy day and I'm about to turn in. Why don't you stop by my office in the morning and—"

"I've had a busy day, too, sheriff. I work Sundays. So pull up your pants, get in your shiny car and get over here. Kidnapping, sheriff. Kidnapping. My next call is to the FBI if I don't see you here in thirty minutes." Tad surprised himself again with his boldness, and he was even more surprised twenty-five minutes later with its effectiveness.

"Come in, sheriff. I'm glad you recognize the urgency. Coffee?"

"Black."

They settled into chairs in the rectory living room. The sheriff seemed comfortable there; Tad guessed he'd had business with Father Schmidt over the years, not unusual for persons in their positions. "Well, padre, tell me about this alleged kidnapping."

"Call me Tad."

"Sorry, Tad. My days in the Border Patrol."

"I'll call you sheriff," Tad said. "Can't quite get used to calling you Holy. My days in the Vatican, you know." He noted the lawman's hair was even longer than when they'd first met, but any resemblance to Charlton Heston disappeared in Holy Moses' thick jowls.

Tad told him about the phone call, but had the uneasy feeling it was not news to the sheriff. He told him about the message on the answering machine on opening day of trout season, and again he received no indication of surprise.

"Tad," the sheriff said, "let's stop using the word 'kidnapping' until we know that's what it is. Kidnapping implies she's being held somewhere against her will. We don't know that's the case."

"Then why didn't she call me herself?"

"Maybe she just felt better having someone call for her."

"Why would she want me to go back to Rome?"

"Maybe she believes it's in your best interests to do so."

"Let's quit dancing around the subject," Tad said. "Doctor Don and his Holy Scripture church followers want me out of here. For reasons I can't figure out. They're holding my mother hostage, whether it's with her complicity or against her will. Call it kidnapping or call it extortion, what's the difference? They're both against the law."

"You don't even know if it's Holy Scripture church that's been making those phone calls. Could be some of your own people."

"That's ridiculous."

"You've managed to alienate some good Catholics by your campaign to get women priests, by allowing Protestant hymns to be sung at Catholic masses, by hanging out with homosexuals."

"Nonsense."

"Then again, those calls might have nothing to do with religion at all. Lots of folks object to your church sticking its nose in civil matters. Separation of church and state."

"What the hell are you talking about?"

"I'm talking about trying to do the district attorney's job, getting an autopsy of little Tony Dett and a coroner's inquest when the district attorney and the coroner had already examined the evidence and determined that his death was accidental. That's not priest business. That's law enforcement business. You should know better."

"That was his mother's doing."

"You're her counselor, spiritual advisor and who knows what else now. Looks to me an awful lot like meddling, in direct violation of the first amendment of the constitution."

"Sheriff, I can't believe you're serious."

"Folks around here think the last straw was the outrageous lawsuit you talked Mrs. Dett into. That's church sticking its nose in state business on a grand scale."

"Do you really believe that?"

"I'm sworn to enforce the laws and constitution of the United States of America, and that's the way I read it."

"Isn't kidnapping against the laws and constitution of the United States? How about extortion? How about enforcing those laws?"

"I will when I have reason to believe such a crime has been committed."

"I just told you it was."

"You gave me second-hand information that your mother is safe, and that her continued safety can be guaranteed by your stepping on an airplane and returning to Rome. That doesn't sound like a crime to me."

Ten minutes after Sheriff Moses left, Tad's cell phone rang out the first four bars of Handel's Hallelujah Chorus. Bruce. "What was that all about?"

"How did you know ..."

"My brand new police scanner. Birthday present from Ann. Holy Moses just called Dett and said he was on his way back to the office."

"Okay. Here's what happened."

CHAPTER 16

❀

Monday, clergy's day off, afforded Tad a chance to back off and try to think through the bewildering situation, without the distractions of what he was paid to do.

The Dett mess wasn't the only family problem he had to confront as pastor of three rural parishes in peaceful, bucolic southwestern Wisconsin. Each week seemed to produce fresh ways for ordinary people to screw up their lives. Tad too often found himself in the midst of squabbling spouses, parents and children, in-laws, psychologists and social workers, lawyers and the courts. Little in his years as a priest had prepared him for the role. His comprehensive knowledge of the theology of the Holy Trinity was little use. He found his clearest thinking and most reliable judgment on long, solitary walks in the country. Not bad for the cholesterol level either, although they hadn't done much to knock anything off the twenty surplus pounds he carried around.

This particular Monday he decided to try some trout fishing as a way to get closer to nature and listen for God's guidance among the birds and insects and breezes in the trees and the gurgling of the upper reaches of the Midewiwin. The spot was in the northeast part of the 160-acre Coburg farm, the hilly, wooded corner.

Tad parked his car near the farmhouse and checked, hoping to find his mother in the kitchen and her car in the garage. No Ruth. He got his fishing rod and tackle box out of the trunk, put on his hiking boots, sprayed himself thoroughly against insects, and set out through the pasture to the creek.

Most of the pools and riffles that he recalled from childhood, likely spots to dunk a worm for trout or smallmouth bass, were so overgrown with underbrush as to be useless for fishing. He wondered if the DNR could offer any advice on cleaning up the banks to make that section of the creek fishable; maybe a project for St. Joan of Arc's Boy Scout troop. If he wasn't in Rome by the end of the week.

Steep hills closed in on the creek, hills so dense with brush under the tall trees that travel was next to impossible, progress upstream was measured a step at a time. Whoever invented the cloth that goes into standard American jeans must have had the thorny flora of southwestern Wisconsin in mind. Tad's heavy canvas gloves spared his hands the worst of the brambles, as he cut some of them and pushed others aside, only to have the sinewy, barbed cousins of the domestic raspberry spring back to grab him by the foot. The job was made no easier by the tackle box and fishing rod.

His memory had not failed him. The limestone ledge, overhanging the shaded eddy that was reputed to house a trophy trout, existed. There it was, about 100 tortured yards from the meadow where the Coburg herd once grazed. Tad yanked brambles from the stone ledge and tried it out. Oddly, the twin indentations in the rock fit his posterior as comfortably as they had when he was a youngster and his bottom was considerably leaner.

Tad took the water bottle from his belt and drained half of it in a couple of swallows. He watched a wren poking through a thicket across the creek, nabbing insects to take home to her brood. Blue jays cussed at each other high in the canopy. The creek, the hills, the woods were as he remembered, now choked with vegetation, but splendid as ever. Better, since he now had the jungles of Vietnam and the cathedrals of the world for comparison, with the former on the bottom of the scale and St. Peter's in Rome at the top. Definitely approaching St. Peter's in grandeur. It was, indeed, the place for solitude, contemplation, prayer, a place to sort out the bewildering religious and temporal forces at work against him.

Disagreements over theology were not new to him. That's what colleges and professors are for, after all, to discuss, dispute, argue as a way to find truth. Father Tad had been in his share of theological debates, sometimes heated to the point of blood pressure emergencies. But they invariably ended with a hug and at least grudging acknowledgment that the other was honest in his or her beliefs and had a right to hold them and a duty to champion them.

That was one difference between all his previous religious controversies and this one. Doctor Don and the Holy Scripture church didn't seem prepared to accept the possibility that another point of view, another interpretation of scripture, might have merit.

The other distinction was that this quarrel didn't seem to be as much biblical as it was personal. Father Tad Coburg was the issue.

What do I do about it? Cut and run? Returning to Rome has a lot of appeal. But that's not my way. It's not what Bob Ardito expects of me. It would accomplish nothing. It would still leave Mom in the clutches of Doctor Don. Challenge the preacher from the pulpit? A letter to the editor?

Tad, you've never sat down and talked with Doctor Don. You haven't spoken more than a dozen words to him. You've listened to his thunder and formed your judgment without asking him a single question. Let him know you're no threat to him or his church. That's your way. Invite him to dinner. He likes the Sandstone.

See? An answer! St. Thaddeus' Basilica did its job.

Now about his own parishioner, George Meiningen, and his contention that the Latin Mass and the altar facing the people were the beginning of the end of Catholicism. And the single-minded anti-abortionists, Peter and Mary Plumm. If there's opposition within his own church, as Sheriff Moses contends, it probably starts there. Meet with them. Get those matters out on the table.

The church and state issue? Sheriff Moses was probably just throwing dust in the air. There can't possibly be anything to it.

Tad felt better. Time to see if that fabled lunker trout really exists. He took another long, refreshing pull on the water bottle, and reached for his tackle box. A polished boot slammed his knuckles and pinned his hand to the box. "What the hell!"

"Stand up." Tad turned and looked up at two uniformed soldiers behind him, arms folded and looking down through wide, mirrored sunglasses. Camouflage visored caps matched their starched and pressed camo field utility uniforms. He clambered to his feet, nearly falling off the ledge into the Midewiwin.

"God damn," he stammered.

"Not good language for a man of the cloth," said one soldier, a couple inches taller than Tad. The other was taller yet.

"Scare a man half to death," Tad said.

"You're trespassing."

"Beg your pardon?"

"You are trespassing on private property."

"I'm sorry, but you're wrong. I happen to know this is my mother's farm. I know every square foot of it because I grew up on this farm. The property line is a good hundred yards farther up the stream."

"You're right about the property line," the taller of the two soldiers said. "But you're incorrect about the owner. Mrs. Coburg has deeded it to the Holy Scripture Universal Church of the Lord."

"What?"

"You deaf? I said this farm is no longer in the Coburg family."

"I don't believe——."

"Now get your papist ass off this land before we throw you in either jail or this creek."

Tad looked at the pair. Either looked capable of carrying out that threat. Two of them would be no contest. The voice on the answering machine last Thursday belonged to the taller of the two.

Tad saw the wisdom of a hasty retreat. He picked up his fishing rod and tackle box and began the walk downstream, tripping and stumbling, dropping his tackle box twice. Without looking, he knew they were a step behind him.

They followed silently, never more than two feet from him, as Tad, trying to appear unrattled, half ran to his car, opened the trunk and threw the fishing gear in. He started the car and drove off, tossing a half wave to the impassive soldiers, in a feeble attempt to salvage some dignity.

Back at the rectory, a shower, salami sandwich and a beer did little to generate reality out of the surreal episode. Tad replayed his conversation with the soldiers, if it could be called a conversation, and he couldn't even come up with anything that he wished he had said. He wondered if it really happened, but sore knuckles, the many scratches on his arms and a painful right ankle, twisted on a rock in his retreat from the Midewiwin, were proof enough that it wasn't a bad dream. Only then did he realize that he did not recall seeing a vehicle of any type that could have gotten the soldiers to the farm.

He called Attorney Killian. "Ellen, open a new file. You're representing me now. I have reason to believe that my mother is being held—willingly or not, I don't know—by the Holy Scripture church. I also have reason to believe that she has deeded over her farm to that church, again willingly or not, I don't know. Any way to check that out? Thanks. Call me on my cell phone." The conflict with the Holy Scripture church had taken on a new dimension. No telling what technology may be at their disposal, and tapping his phone at the rectory did not seem far-fetched. He'd heard that cell phone conversations aren't necessarily private, but guessed eavesdropping on that may be more challenging than tapping a land line.

The next call was to Father Donovan at the chancery office in Madison. "Hi, Frank. I need to meet with the bishop. At least an hour. As soon as possible. Okay, ten-thirty tomorrow will be fine." If the Holy Scripture folks were listening to that cell phone call, so much the better.

"Do you think your mother acted on her own volition when she signed over the deed," Bishop Ardito asked. "Or do you think she was under some sort of pressure?"

"Who knows? I doubt that anybody threatened her like those two thugs threatened me. They may have told her they'd kill me if she didn't sign the deed. But something tells me that wouldn't convince her either. No, Doctor Don probably found some passage in the Bible that did it."

"Religion is capable of causing people to do some really stupid things," the bishop said.

"Amen."

"Tad, I'm not going to order you to stick around when your life and your mother's life may be in danger. If you want to go back to Rome, you're free to go."

"I'd love to be back in Rome. Thanks for your offer. But I'm not leaving under these circumstances."

"I didn't think so. The question now is what can we do about it?"

"We?"

"Of course. I got you into this mess. I'll provide all the help I can."

"Thanks. I have a feeling the best course right now would be to do nothing. Act like everything's normal. When they find out that kidnapping my mother and swindling her out of her farm can't get rid of me, they may let her go. In any case, I can't believe they're capable of causing either of us actual physical harm."

The next morning FedEx delivered a package to St. Brendan's rectory. It contained a variety of electronic communications devices and gadgetry, along with instructions on their use.

Attorney Killian reported that papers had been filed the previous Friday with the Millen County Register of Deeds transferring title of the Coburg farm to the Holy Scripture church, as represented by the church's board of trustees. Doctor Don signed for the board of trustees. All appeared legal. Tad's only recourse, she said, appeared to be a petition to the court asking that the transaction be set aside on the grounds that his mother was mentally incapacitated or under duress.

Tad was sure it was one or the other, or both. He also knew that cash from the farm would be all that would keep her self supporting, should Holy Scripture church fail her. He told the attorney to start drawing up the necessary papers.

He tried Bruce Bestman, calling, as he did to Ellen Killian, using his cell phone, but got only the paper's answering machine. It being late Wednesday afternoon by then, he guessed the editor was seeing to the printing of the week's edition.

He called Miriam at the Goodfeller home. Only Ralph was there. He said Miriam was working a double shift and wouldn't be back until morning, but he would tell her he called.

Tad was surprised to find Bruce among the dozen or so faithful at the 7:30 AM Mass Thursday morning in Red Oak. The editor didn't wait for the priest to remove his vestments after Mass. With a grand gesture, he handed him a copy of the *Millen County Reporter*. "Your own personal copy. Careful, ink might still be wet."

The Bestmans had been busy. The headline told Tad the couple had ratcheted up the conflict with the Holy Scripture church:

"Kidnapped?

Priest says 'yes,' sheriff says 'no.'"

Tad skimmed the first few paragraphs, enough to see that the local journalists had done their reporting and writing well. His eye caught a sidebar:

"ACLU weighs in on

Church-state clash"

"What's this?" Tad demanded.

"Go ahead and read it," Bruce said. "The ACLU said your advice to Miriam Dett on legal matters raises serious concerns about where spiritual advice leaves off and you start manipulating the legal system to wipe out the opposition."

"Bruce, that's crazy. Whose idea was that?"

"I simply acted on a hunch. Called this ACLU guy in Madison. He was up to speed on the whole situation. I'm sure I quoted him accurately."

Tad sat down and read the stories. Twice. He could find nothing to challenge, except the whole notion of devoting most of the newspaper's front page to the matter.

Finally, he decided it was best to have the editor informed and on his side, rather than letting him rattle around the community, creating issues where there aren't any and being manipulated by the sheriff and the Holy Scripture church.

"Bruce, we're dealing with something that's a good deal more sinister than a legal dispute. Or a theological disagreement. Let me tell you what happened to me last Monday." He described his encounter with what appeared to be soldiers, but who weren't wearing insignia or rank. "I was, quite frankly, scared out of my wits."

Bruce appeared startled. "Jesus. Any idea who those guys were?"

"Of course not. Never seen them before."

"You talk with the bishop? I mean, nobody would fault you for going back to Rome, if for no other reason than your mother's safety."

"I talked with the bishop. He's behind me a hundred percent. He gave me the option of going back to Rome. I turned it down."

The editor was silent. "Bruce, I've told you, I've told the bishop. I may tell Miriam if I feel it's necessary for her safety. But right now, nobody else. In particular, not local law enforcement. Do you understand?"

"Sure do."

"And for now, please. Nothing in the paper about it. Okay?"

"Agreed."

"Do one more thing," Tad said. "Get yourself a cell phone and pager."

"I have them."

"Get new ones. Change them every couple of weeks. And keep me informed about their numbers. I'll do the same."

The Bestmans had indeed scooped local and national media and caught their attention. The growing magnitude of the story was evidenced by the calls Tad received from print and TV reporters. His answers were polite and noncommittal, as before.

That day he made another trip to Madison. This time was to Gander Mountain fishing and hunting outfitters for his own camouflage wardrobe, "getting ready early for the deer bow hunting season," he fibbed to the clerk. The binoculars he bought were considerably more powerful than bow hunters normally use. A display near the cashier's counter caught his eye, and a hunting knife, an afterthought, rounded out his purchases.

✳   ✳   ✳

"Miriam, I need to talk to you. What's convenient?" Tad was calling on one of the three new cell phones in the package the bishop had sent him. He was to use none of them more than two days in a row. His own cell phone was to be for church-related matters only. Miriam was at work, a double shift that Saturday night. She was using a hospital phone, which Tad was almost certain would not be tapped.

"Stop in at the hospital. We'll have coffee in the cafeteria."

"That must make a couple thousand acres the Holy Scripture church owns in that part of the county," she said. "They've been quietly buying up farms all around the area."

"Are they into agriculture?"

"No. Hardly any of their land is much good for farming. Seems they go out of their way to get hold of worthless land."

"Is that common knowledge in the community?"

"I doubt it. I was baptized on some of their land, and we had a picnic. One of the members mentioned it was the church's land, but said only church members and God were supposed to know."

"Interesting." *Now there's a story for the* Millen County Reporter. *But first, I need to know where my mother is. Alive? Safe? Prisoner or happy volunteer in the service of the Lord?*

Sunday afternoon and evening were spent preparing for Monday. Phone calls. Studying maps. Checking gear and figuring out how to use it. Around 10 PM, he drove to the Goodfeller home in West Charleton. He walked in carrying filled, paper grocery bags on each arm. A half hour later, he left Wanda, Ralph, Miriam and the two daughters and drove back to the rectory in Red Oak.

Monday morning, a half hour after Ralph returned home from chauffeuring the Dett girls to school, Ralph again backed his Ford S-10 pickup out of his attached garage and headed out of town, toward Red Oak. While he was in Hardee's having coffee with the usual bunch, a man in a T-shirt, walking shorts and hiking boots stopped in the parking lot, looked quickly around, got into the S-10 and disappeared. Ten minutes later, Ralph stood, tossed two bucks on the table, stretched and said "Gotta go, fellas. The wife's got a long list of runnin' around she wants done today. See you tomorrow." He got into his truck and drove off.

Tad was scrunched down in the front seat of the truck, trying to pull camouflaged coveralls over his hiking boots, and not having an easy time. "Anybody see me get in?" he asked.

"Don't think so."

"How long before we get there?"

"Maybe twenty minutes." Tad wasn't sure his contorted, overweight body would make it.

"We got a passenger in the back seat," Ralph said.

"Hi, Tad," said a now-familiar female voice.

"Miriam, what are you doing back there?"

"I'm coming with you. That is, if I ever get straightened out again." The back seat of an S-10 is meant to carry a folded-up worker on a bench seat, or maybe a couple of small children. Not a fifty-something nurse, trying to stay out of sight.

"You certainly are not coming with me. You crazy or something?"

"I know that part of the county. I'm coming."

"You're not."

"Am too."

"Kids," Ralph interrupted. "Knock it off."

The two rolled-up passengers were silent as the pickup bounced along Town Line Road. "Are we there yet?" came the voice from the back seat.

That was enough to break the tension, and Tad fell to adjusting his plan to accommodate a partner on the patrol, a partner who may or may not know the territory, but who was certainly out of condition for the hills and underbrush ahead.

"Two minutes," said Ralph. Tad grabbed the backpack containing water, energy bars and electronic gear.

The truck slowed, then stopped. "Out," Ralph said. "Be back same place in four hours. Call if plans change." They had decided not to put Ralph's home or cell phone numbers into Tad's cell phone memory. Just in case. And they weren't sure the phone would work in the deep valleys of that isolated part of Wisconsin.

In seconds, Tad and Miriam were half climbing, half sliding down a steep embankment and hiding in a concrete culvert. It once was a place for cattle to cross under the road. The pastures hadn't been used for years; weeds and brush covered both ends. They couldn't stand straight up, but they could argue without being seen or heard.

"I'm here. You and I are together for the next four hours. We can stay in this musty ditch, or we can go looking. Which is it?" Miriam's case was compelling.

"Okay," Tad said, "we go. We'll follow this old cow path up the right side of this ravine."

"No. The left side."

"Right side."

Miriam grinned. "Fine. Right side."

"You look ridiculous in that camouflaged suit," Tad said. "Where in the world did you get it."

"It's Ralph's. Ten sizes too big, but it'll do."

There may be no more creatures of habits than cattle. And fifty or more generations of Holsteins following the exact path daily had left a groove in the hillside that will take nature eons to erase. It made foot travel for the middle-aged reconnaissance team much easier.

They walked silently for an hour, Tad vigilant, but not sure what he was watching for. Miriam followed. The pasture had sprouted patches of brush since the cattle stopped feeding there—mounds of wild roses, beds of Canada thistles, sumac and buckthorn thickets—affording a measure of concealment. They rounded the side of a hill, near the top, and Tad decided it was time for a break. No argument from Miriam.

They sat and leaned back against a three-foot limestone outcropping. Tad broke out the water bottle. It would have to be enough for both of them. It was one of those June days that make long, cold Midwestern winters worth abiding. Cottony white cumulous clouds loafed across a sky that was as blue as it ever gets. A hawk soared high in giant figure eights, in no more hurry than the clouds. It was warm enough to provoke mild perspiration, but dry enough that it didn't matter.

The view from their hillside bleachers might have been painted. Tad and Miriam looked over a valley of prairie grasses waving lazily in the southwesterly breeze. Wild flowers—yellow, red, violet, white—punctuated the scene.

"There must be a thousand shades of green in that one frame," Miriam said.

Tad had never thought about green being anything but green, but she was right. He took another sip of water. "Want a Granola bar?"

"No, thanks," she said. They sat, absorbing the view. "There is absolutely no sign of human activity out there. No farms, no fences, no roads, no cattle, and we're only ten miles from Red Oak, Wisconsin."

Tad was conscious of her shoulder touching his, and her perfume, same as she wore in high school. This is not the way his friends in the infantry used to describe reconnaissance missions. "Why did you come with me today?"

"Because I know the area. I can help."

"Okay, where are we?"

"I have no idea."

He looked at her. She leaned forward and kissed him. On the lips, gently.

Tad was silent. A gopher stuck its head out of its hole, looked around, and snapped back in when Tad moved his hand. "Why did you marry Myron?"

"I thought I loved him."

"Why did you stay married to such a scoundrel?"

She was silent, long enough for the gopher to regain its courage and venture out of its hole and into the grass. "See those flowers out there? The white ones?"

"I see them.

"Pretty?"

"Not particularly."

Miriam reached and picked one of the white flowers. She held it about two feet from his face. "Pretty now?"

"No, still kind of ordinary at best."

She held it six inches from his face. He had to tilt his head back so his bifocals could focus on the flower. "Now is it pretty?" she asked.

Tad saw it. The flower wasn't one flower but hundreds of tiny, white petals laced together, each petal a masterpiece.

"Queen Anne's Lace," she said. "A member of the carrot family. You have to look real close to see it. Some people call it a weed, others call it a wildflower. The beauty isn't in the whole, the beauty is the individual parts."

"Are you saying you saw some things in Myron that were beautiful?"

"Sure. But he's still just a weed."

Tad let the parable sink in. "Are you still planning to kill Myron?"

"I might. Either him or one of those spooks. Somebody killed my son, somebody else let them kill my son. I may have to kill all of them."

"Miriam, do you really mean that?"

"I kind of half mean it. I don't know. And you especially don't know. You've never been a mother."

Tad stood. "Let's move out."

Four hours in the remote hills of Millen County, with Miriam Dett in tow, didn't produce the kind of information Tad had hoped it would. It didn't lead him to his mother. But it did provide enough to disturb him, information that he did not point out to Miriam.

He learned, for example, that those hills, owned in one way or another by the Holy Scripture church, were by no means as deserted as they looked. The cow paths he and Miriam followed had been trodden on by humans many times since the cattle departed a decade earlier, even since the last rain three days ago. That didn't take Daniel Boone to figure out.

Tad sat in the waiting room outside Attorney Ellen Killian's office. He needed to share his knowledge and concern with someone besides his boss, the bishop. Local law enforcement was out. Bruce Bestman, maybe. But it might show up in the newspaper prematurely.

"Come in, Father Tad. Coffee? Soft drink?"

"Nothing thanks, Ellen."

Bringing Ellen up to the moment on his adventures with the Holy Scripture church and with the soldier-types that presumably worked for Holy Scripture took over a half hour. Ellen took notes vigorously.

She sat tapping her teeth with her pen, glasses pushed up over her auburn hair. "Hmm. It doesn't look at this point that any laws have been broken."

"Unless you include kidnapping. And maybe defrauding a widow out of her farm."

"Hold on, father. I should rephrase that: We don't have any solid evidence that a law has been broken, except for the fact that your mother has disappeared, and that you have received a phone call that you can—how did you put it?—'guarantee her safety,' if you go back to Rome. I don't know if a judge or jury would consider those exact words extortion or proof that she was being held against her will, but they certainly raise suspicions."

"Whatever you want to call it, something strange is going on in those hills, and I'm damned worried about my mother." Tad's voice was rising.

"Okay, okay. We can't expect any help from local law enforcement. But we're not without options." The attorney listed several ideas and suggested they get together again in a week, next Tuesday.

"Not good enough. Let's make it this Friday, three o'clock, right here in your office."

❉   ❉   ❉

Early afternoon the next day, Tad received a phone message from the nursing home in West Charleton, reporting that his former pastor and mentor, Father Nicholas Schmidt, had suffered a massive stroke that morning and had died. Tad was happy for the saintly man, relieved of a body that was little use to him anymore, and reunited with the mind that had drifted away. Tad reported the death to the bishop's office, and in less than two hours received a call from that office stating that Bishop Ardito himself would preside over the funeral Mass in Red Oak on Saturday.

Nice of the bishop to do that. But it isn't going to make the Holy Scripture folks any easier to live with. They want their papist priest to get his fanny out of Red Oak and back to Rome. Instead Rome comes to Red Oak.

CHAPTER 17

The Friday meeting with Attorney Killian began promptly at 3 PM and was still going when hunger began to tickle their insides about six-thirty. "Pizza?" she suggested.

"Good. If you have time, let's keep moving."

For the first hour, they had gone over the complexities of getting the courts to declare that Ruth Coburg had either been bamboozled out of her farm or was incompetent to freely deed it to the Holy Scripture church. Killian felt it was a waste of time, but reluctantly agreed to prepare and file the paperwork, contending that she had been cheated. "If nothing else," Tad said, "it will serve notice on those folks that God doesn't automatically grant their every wish, especially if it involves coveting their neighbor's goods."

Next came evaluating the intelligence that Killian had accumulated, an impressive amount in such a short time. It appeared that the Holy Scripture church controlled more than the couple thousand acres that Miriam had guessed.

A substantial collection of parcels consisted of farms owned by that church or by entities outside Millen County. Those entities were all tax-exempt religious organizations, several located as far away as Alabama. Some organization, or more than one, had been buying up properties from retiring or bankrupt farmers, claiming tax-exempt status, boarding up the farmhouses and letting the land go fallow. None of the land was in the federal Conservation Reserve Program. Some farms, Killian guessed, were acquired in the same way the Coburg property was. All were contiguous.

Killian opened another file folder and pulled out an inch-thick stack of aerial photographs. "Behold the Coburg farm and its neighbors, seen from 2,000 feet up two days ago. You did say money was no object, didn't you?"

"No, I didn't say that. But it's too late to quibble."

It took a half hour for them to orient themselves and figure out what they were looking at. Eventually, they were able to match the eleven-inch by fourteen-inch photographs with the six-foot-square Millen County map on Killian's office wall.

"What's that car doing on that dirt road? It isn't even on the map."

"Look again," Killian said. "It's a pickup truck and there are three of them. I'd guess about a hundred yards apart, going in the same direction."

"Empty. And are those people standing next to that creek?"

"Looks like it to me."

"What's that big rectangular thing?"

"Can't tell from this shot." She flipped through more pictures. "Here, from another angle." She whistled. "It's a tent. Big one. I'd guess fifty feet long and twenty feet wide. Camouflaged, but not very well. Three or four people standing around it."

The pizza came and was consumed without thought, as the lawyer and priest poured over photographs of the county they thought they knew. Their suspicions were such that juniper trees became sentries standing at attention, an abandoned corn picker became a rocket launcher and a trash dump behind an old farmhouse was viewed as a dugout command post. All returned to reality when seen in pictures taken at a more oblique angle. Tad and Killian weren't entirely convinced the tent was a tent, but couldn't come up with any other explanation for the shape. If it was indeed a tent, it would not be out of character for a fundamentalist church to have one, but odd for it to be set up in the middle of nowhere and camouflaged.

By 9 PM they had concluded that strange things may be taking place on the land owned by the Holy Scripture church. But not strange enough to warrant a look by the Federal Bureau of Investigation. "There's no evidence that a federal law has been broken, and certainly there won't be any invitation from local law enforcement," Killian said. "And the Bureau of Alcohol, Tobacco and Firearms would be even less interested in a confrontation with another fringe religious group. FBI and ATF are both still smarting from the Branch Davidian fiasco."

Tad gnawed on a discarded pizza crust and studied the photo with the tent. "I'm going in there," he said.

"You're crazy."

"My mother's there. Either a captive or brainwashed."

"Is it possible she's truly there of her own free will? I mean, you and I are committed Catholics. But a lot of perfectly sane, intelligent people have decided that Catholicism doesn't do the job and other religions do."

"If I get in there and talk with my mother and I'm convinced she hasn't lost her marbles and she's sincere about her new-found religion, then I'll shake Doctor Don's hand, kiss her goodbye and walk out. Maybe to catch an early plane to Rome. One way."

For the second time in less than a month, St. Brendan's was packed. It was a different crowd this time: mainly parishioners and others with a lifelong affection for Father Schmidt. Men and women, three-fourths of them white-haired, all had been touched by the priest over fifty years.

Pastor Jensen of the Lutheran Church in Red Oak was present with his wife. Clergy representing the local Presbyterian, Methodist and Episcopal churches attended. Nobody from the Baptist church was there. Also absent: Doctor Don. In his place were the two detectives, again standing in the rear of the church.

Depending on how you looked at it, Bishop Ardito's homily was either a plea for brotherhood, understanding and unity among peoples of all religious and political persuasions, or it was a deliberate poke in the eye of the Holy Scripture Universal Church of the Lord.

"Jesus had his troubles with the Pharisees," he said. "Pharisees were a religious sect of the Jews that tried to insulate Jews from foreign religious ideas. They wanted nothing to do with Gentiles. They believed in strict adherence to the Scriptures and the rules devised by their rabbis. And so one day they laid a trap for Jesus.

"'Teacher,' they said, 'which commandment in the law is the greatest?' I'm sure you're all familiar with Jesus' reply: 'You shall love the Lord, your God, with all your heart, with all your soul, and with all your mind. This is the greatest and the first commandment. The second is like it: You shall love your neighbor as yourself.'"

The Bishop used that passage from Matthew as his standard as he chronicled Father Schmidt's lifetime of good works, showing again and again how specific acts of kindness and sacrifice demonstrated his love for his neighbor, and how his neighborhood consisted of people of all faiths and no faiths, not just his Catholic parishioners. Tad hadn't realized the old fellow had made such a mark on the community, and he was curious how his boss knew that much about the deceased priest's activities.

"So let's remember Father Schmidt as a man who loved his neighbor as himself, and who put wheels on that love. Yes, you must find Jesus. You must love God with all your being. But that's just the start. The second part is the hard part. It's in keeping the second part of the commandment that you'll find your ticket to eternal happiness."

Burial was in the cemetery behind the church. Father Schmidt had picked out his plot at the farthest corner years before.

The women of the parish put together a fine lunch in the church basement, and the room was packed with funeral-goers. Tad knew many of them and used the occasion to get to know others. Bishop Ardito worked the room like a candidate. Within forty-five minutes he had shaken the hands of fully half of Father Schmidt's friends and had spent extra time with the Protestant pastors.

Tad watched the bishop, black suit and Roman collar, make his way through the crowd, shaking hands, patting some on the elbow, blessing a few who requested it, kissing a number of women on the cheek—guessing correctly who would be flattered by a kiss from their bishop and who would feel it unseemly.

Tad became fascinated as the bishop politicked his way through the crowd toward two men standing in a corner holding plates with small sandwiches: the detectives, representatives of the Holy Scripture Universal Church of the Lord. They saw him coming, but they had not planned an escape route.

Tad was too far away to hear the conversation, but guessed it was the standard "Hi, I'm Bishop Ardito. It's impressive to see so many friends of Father Schmidt. I'm glad you could take the time to come and pray with us for his eternal rest." Or something like that.

He could see the men shake the bishop's hand and mumble something. That might have ended the incident, but for the flash of a camera. Bruce Bestman caught the three, and Tad knew it would be on page one the following week. He wondered if the detectives would draw weapons and take out the newsman. Instead, they mumbled again, set down their plates, excused themselves and left, looking like they had wandered into the ladies' restroom by mistake. Not missing a beat, the bishop turned and shook the hand of a giant farmer with a red face and white forehead, who was obviously pleased with the attention.

❋   ❋   ❋

Monday morning an hour before dawn, nine days after Father Schmidt's funeral, Tad backed his car out of the garage. He was headed for the tax-exempt land in question.

He had spent evenings the previous week pouring over the maps and aerial photos, committing to memory every road, rock, hill and gully. Friday was with Attorney Killian, his home base and sole contact with the rest of the world, going over details. Saturday he visited Cabela's outfitters in Prairie du Chien for their latest in survival gear. Sunday afternoon and evening were spent checking that equipment out, learning its operation, packing. When he went to bed Sunday evening, he was ready.

Just before he turned into Norse Road he shut off his headlights. The next mile would be in the dark and take at least twenty minutes. Deer and other critters owned the back roads at night. Add to darkness the vagueness of the location of his turnoff and the obvious need for silence.

There it was. A dirt road, overgrown almost to the point of impassibility, was cut into the woods on the left. He stopped and checked it out on foot, before pulling the Chevy Lumina into it and virtually burying the car in the underbrush.

Next: Find the tiny stream flowing under Norse Road, three-tenths of a mile—317 paces—ahead. It will be his avenue to the Holy Scripture headquarters, assuming the large tent represented a headquarters, and his mother. Dirt roads and cow paths could be under electronic surveillance. Going cross country through the dense, thorny brush would be hazardous to his skin, not to mention noisy. He found the stream, not much more than a trickle, flowing through a culvert and into the tax-exempt land, 320 paces from his car, as it turned out.

Tad stepped off the road and into the stream. He sat and waited a half hour for enough daylight to navigate downstream. The stream, by no means big enough to have a name, turned out to be not much of a bargain for foot travel. Brambles had no trouble reaching from one side to the other. Wet, mossy rocks threatened a twisted ankle with every step. Tad knew he had just over a mile to go in the stream before he could cut cross-country over a hill to a spot where he could get a good view of the Holy Scripture tent. At that point, he guessed, he could be within the perimeter of electronic surveillance and live sentries. It would be almost noon before he got there.

That time was pushed back by a gigantic thunderstorm, prefacing the arrival of hot, humid air from the south. The storm had not been predicted, and Tad wasn't prepared. He huddled in a basswood grove in a futile effort to keep from getting soaked, while winds and lightning played with the trees around him and rainfall of fire hose proportions pelted the woods. When the storm stopped, mosquitoes and deer flies took over.

Finally, just after one, his global positioning instrument told him it was time to head uphill. A century or more had passed since that land had been logged, and tall oak, hickory, basswood and black cherry trees formed a dense canopy. The result was a good deal less underbrush and easier going on foot. Tad felt like a hobbit wandering in Fanghorn Forest.

When he was about fifty feet from the spot where his calculations suggested was an adequate view of the tent and its surrounding activities, he found a thorny blackberry thicket and stood against it to urinate. Finished, he zipped up, dropped a green package into the thicket and walked to his vantage point, a sandstone ledge over a fifty-foot bluff.

His guess about the view from there was disappointing. Only a part of the tent was visible; too many trees. What he saw, looking down from about seventy-five yards away, was startling. But more startling was the command from behind him: "Freeze." He didn't need to turn to know it was the soldiers that had kicked him off his mother's property. Nor did he have to guess how serious they were this time.

Their search of his rain-drenched clothing turned up his hunting knife, binoculars, cell phone, water bottle, insect spray and two Snickers bars (also hopelessly soaked). They kept the knife, binoculars and phone, and gave the rest back. With a soldier in front and one behind him, he was escorted down the steep hill into the valley.

Tad wasn't exactly a prisoner, in the sense that he was not confined by lock and key. But he knew that to leave the tent into which the two soldiers had unceremoniously pushed him would be a bad idea. Two more soldiers, differing from the first two only in size (bigger), stood at each end of the tent, wearing starched, green camouflaged dungarees with sleeves rolled above the elbows, brown berets, mirrored sunglasses and spit-shined boots. And pistols in holsters on their belts. The men were obviously assigned to him and him alone.

The tent was standard military olive drab canvas, ten by eight feet, plywood floor, sides rolled up for ventilation, although no breeze found its way into the valley that steamy day. The tent's furnishings were vintage Nam—one cot with mosquito net and a single, folded blanket; one folding chair, and a footlocker, unlocked and empty.

He sat on the chair. He tried standing for a while. He had long ago lost the art of relative ease on eighty square feet of unpadded real estate. No books, no phones, no computer, no friends, no tasks to perform, not even a comfortable chair. Just stay and wonder how he got there, why, and what he might do about it.

He was still damp from the rain, although with the heat and humidity he might have been just as wet from perspiration. He studied his two guards. Obviously disciplined and well-trained, standing at ease, they were two utility poles with hands crossed in the small of their backs, left foot shifting occasionally but never the right, eyes behind sunglasses. Something odd about their uniforms but can't place it. Oh yes. No insignia whatsoever. Nothing to designate name, rank, unit, branch of service or even what country they were fighting for. Tad tried to strike up a conversation, starting with the weather, but they might have been deaf for all the reaction he got.

The tent Tad occupied was one of at least a dozen identical setups, about twenty feet apart. They were pitched in a compound at the bottom of a steep, wooded hill, the hill he had hoped would be his observation point, his look into the strange, military-like operations of the Holy Scripture Universal Church of the Lord. As best he could tell, the other tents were unoccupied. Whether the tents were there when the satellite photos were taken, Tad couldn't tell. They were expertly camouflaged with netting and artificial vegetation.

About four o'clock, a young soldier, sort of a post-Korean War Radar Riley, came to his tent and dropped off some dry clothes—socks, underwear, khaki chino pants and blue polo shirt. "Thanks," Tad said. No answer. The clothes fit. He left his boots off; they did a good job keeping the water out—and the perspiration in.

Two hours later the young orderly came by with a dinner tray: cold cuts, cheese, two slices of bread, cole slaw and a paper carton of milk. "Thanks." The orderly was back in a half hour with sheets and pillow and to remove the dinner tray.

"Say, ah, fellows," Tad addressed his guards, "I would be very much obliged if one of you would point me toward the rest room."

That drew a response from one. "Follow me." The second guard fell in behind Tad, and they walked to the end of the row of tents to a larger tent that served as a sanitation station: a latrine dug into the soft earth and a water barrel for washing.

❦   ❦   ❦

At 6:30 PM, Ralph Goodfeller backed his pickup truck out of his garage in West Charleton and headed south. Wanda was seated beside him. About forth-five minutes later they crossed the Mississippi River and drove into the half-filled parking lot of Dubuque Greyhound Park and Casino. He spoke briefly on his cell phone, then parked alongside a blue Buick Park Avenue, and the Goodfellers got out and entered the Casino. Ten minutes later the Buick left.

At about that same time, Father Frank Donovan in Madison packed a small overnight bag, with two pairs of underwear and socks, two short-sleeved sport shirts, pajamas, tooth brush and shaving gear. He was about to close the bag, when he paused and tossed in another set of underwear, socks and shirt.

At 7 PM the two soldiers guarding Father Tad Coburg were relieved by two almost identical guards. They had stood for six hours, and Tad marveled at their hearts' ability to keep pumping when all their blood must be puddled in their legs. The two fresh guards also wore sunglasses and were equally uncommunicative. Tad wondered at what point vanishing daylight would dictate removing the shades and whether that would provide a look at their eyes. He never found out. When he went to sleep, the glasses were still on, and when he woke at 5 AM, the previous pair of guards was already in place and shielded from sunlight.

An hour later the orderly, same guy, arrived with soap, towel and toothbrush, along with a tray with boxed juice, cereal and milk.

Enough of this nonsense. Another day of sitting in this tent with those spooky babysitters and I may be as crazy as they are. Despite the lack of bars or fencing, escape during daylight seemed unlikely, given their vigilance. Escape at night seemed equally out of the question, as it would require stumbling around noisily in dense, thorny thickets, assuming his memory could even be trusted to guide him back to his car. He almost told his guards "Take me to your leader," but instead said "Fellas, I'd be grateful if you would inform somebody in charge that nothing is being gained by holding me prisoner, so we might as well sit down and talk this out."

"Later," said one guard. That would have to suffice.

Tad whiled away the morning reading from the King James Bible the guards had provided, and watching what was going on nearby. Which became increasingly interesting. The little compound of tents—his guesses for their intended use ranged from holding uninvited guests, such as himself, to housing young-sters or families attending a Holy Scripture Bible camp—remained empty. But traffic along the dirt road alongside the compound was picking up. Four vehi-cles passed: two jeeps with soldiers identical to his guards, right down to absence of insignia; a white Taurus station wagon with what appeared to be a husband, wife and two children, and a red Dodge Ram pickup with tool box in back. Tad couldn't see the driver through dark tinted side windows.

By noon, traffic had doubled, with roughly the same mix of vehicles and passengers. And by late afternoon, it had doubled again, sixteen or more vehi-cles, some military style, some civilian pickups, some looking like families on their way to Disney World. All were headed the same direction on the dirt road, south to north. He tried to recall what lay to the north of the compound, but his memory of the maps and satellite photos was growing dim.

Next morning Tad was to the point of seriously plotting escape. On his breakfast tray was a note. "We have an appointment at 10 AM. Your compan-ion will show you the way. D." He assumed "companion" meant one of the two silent sentries. He was right, although the companion did more guiding than showing, since Tad was blindfolded for the walk that took almost a half hour.

"D" was indeed Doctor Don, and the rotund pastor was seated at a small black desk in a twenty-foot by thirty-foot green tent with a plywood floor in a secluded, wooded glen. He offered his hand without getting up. The tent was unadorned, except for an easel with a two-foot by three-foot framed painting of Jesus praying to a bright light shining through clouds. Doctor Don's desktop contained a Bible, yellow legal pad of paper, pen, desk lamp and telephone.

"Welcome to the Christian Identity and the Vale of the Terebinth. Pardon the crude furnishings," the pastor said, "we're still in the process of moving in. I can't tell you how delighted we are to see you here."

Tad considered the remark the ultimate in insincerity, until he realized it could mean almost anything. He looked around for something to sit on. That was apparently funny, because Doctor Don erupted into huge, belly-jiggling laughter. "I'm so sorry." He called to the soldier-companion. "Enoch, please bring our guest a chair." Four days of looking at his stoic guard, and only now did Tad know his name. Enoch what?

"Perhaps as men of God, we should begin our deliberations with a prayer," Doctor Don said. "How about The Lord's Prayer?"

"Fine."

Prayer concluded, Doctor Don began: "I imagine you have many questions about our little community here. Most of them I will not answer today. All will be revealed in good time."

"I have one over-riding question," Tad said. "Where is my mother?"

"That's one I can answer. In fact, I anticipated it. Enoch, please show Mrs. Coburg in."

Tad expected either a haggard and fearful mother, or a radiantly exuberant mother. Instead he saw a totally impassive mother. They embraced perfunctorily. Enoch brought in another chair without waiting for an order.

"How are you, mother?"

"Fine, thank you."

"Are they treating you well here?"

"Yes."

"Are you happy here?"

"Yes."

Tad saw the conversation going nowhere. He was doing all the asking, and her answers were minimal. Doctor Don, Buddha-like behind his desk, and Enoch, the soldier, ten feet to the side were not conducive to heart-to-heart communication. "Is there anything you'd like to tell me, mother?"

"No."

They sat with nothing to say. Occasionally he heard a vehicle—jeep or car—pass on a dirt road nearby. Somewhere in the distance, heavy equipment was moving dirt, beeping dutifully to signal its reverse gear, and a chain saw was cutting timber. "Mother, I'd like to ask you one question. If you are here on your own free will, if you are truly happy here, I want you to answer truthfully. If you are not here under your own free will and are not happy here, do not answer truthfully. Understand?"

"I understand."

"The question is, How did your father, my grandfather, die?"

Ruth Coburg was plainly shaken, either by the question itself or by having to answer it. She looked every way but at him. Her hands twisted and fidgeted. She reached into a pocket in her blouse and pulled out a tissue to dab her eyes. "Mother, look at me. Grandpa—how did he die?"

Doctor Don's eyes were flitting between Tad and his mother. Enoch stood at parade rest.

"Mother?"

"He was killed in a hunting accident."

Tad had his answer. It's what Doctor Don's people will find when they search the archives of the *Millen County Reporter*.

"Do you have anything else you would like to discuss with your mother," Doctor Don asked.

"No. I'm pleased that she is so secure and well cared for here. Good-bye, Mom." They hugged, this time with all the vigor and affection a mother and her son ought to have.

"Enoch, would you be so kind as to escort Mrs. Coburg back to her lodgings?" Doctor Don said. "Thank you."

"Now then, Mister Coburg—"

"Father Coburg."

Doctor Don grinned. "Correct me if I'm wrong, but I don't believe you are actually a father."

"Correct me if *I'm* wrong, but I don't believe you are actually a doctor—medical, scholastic or ecclesiastical."

"I was about to ask you why you are here, Father Coburg."

"Call me Tad."

"Why are you here?"

"I was about to ask *you* why I'm here."

"You've been enjoying our hospitality for two days."

"Enjoying your captivity."

"You could have left at any time. No doors, no windows, no handcuffs."

"Don, call it what you want. I want very much to get out of here. Will you direct your soldiers to give me back my clothes and gear and escort me to the nearest town?"

"I'm sorry, but I'm not authorized to issue such an order."

"Then find someone who is. I've got work to do back in town, sick people to minister to, a wedding Saturday, parishioners will show up this Sunday and wonder where their priest is. I don't have time to lie around in the wilderness doing nothing."

"When a decision has been made about your status, you will be advised."

"Decision? By whom? If not you, then who makes the decisions around here? Who's in charge? And why does a church need an army? Who are those people?"

"Tad—may I call you Tad?—Tad, did you ever give thought to entering a monastery?"

"When I came back from Vietnam I gave it a lot of thought. In the end, I decided I couldn't cut myself off from civilization like that. I needed to be part of the world."

"Instead, you cloistered yourself in the Vatican and the tight, rarified world of academic theology. Given the chance, you'd be back in Rome on the next flight."

"I'm not sure I agree—"

"All the Holy Scripture Universal Church of the Lord wants is to be alone. Like a cloister."

"Okay, I can understand that. But the—"

"To be away from Satanic influences like Catholics, Muslims, pagans, the government, news media, television, universities—"

"Now wait a minute. I disagree."

"To teach the truth about creation, to enforce God's laws about adultery and fornication, as God gave them to us in the Holy Bible." Doctor Don leaned forward and moved the desk with him, his voice rising. "It's the duty of my people to bring Jesus to Catholics, Protestants, Muslims, atheists, pagans of all kinds. And we will. Without interference from government or the Pope. We can do that from our Vale of Terebinth, in Millen County, Wisconsin.

"Here is where the will of Almighty God is revealed." Doctor Don was getting really wound up. "'Call to me, and I will answer thee, and show thee great and mighty things, which thou knowest not.' Jeremaiah, thirty-three, three. All your academic conferences, Tad, all that huffing and puffing—wasted energy, playing right into the hands of the devil." He pounded his knuckles on the Bible on his desk. "Here is all you need to know. And right here in our little community in Millen County is where its meaning is revealed to those of us who have found and worship the Lord. Here, Tad. Not Rome, not Mecca, not New York or Washington or Hollywood. Here is where we prepare for the end times foretold in Revelation, here where I'm sitting right now."

Tad had never been surprised by intensely held religious viewpoints that varied from his own. Better a strongly held view—even if you don't agree with it—than no viewpoint at all, or even a tepid view on something they ought to be passionate about. But Doctor Don looked to be on the verge of a medical crisis if the discussion continued.

"I hear where you're coming from," Tad said, "and I admire anyone who feels that way about his religion. But it still doesn't explain the armed troops all over the place. Don't tell me you're planning to sell religion at the point of a gun."

"No. That's the way of Islam, an evil, wicked and dangerous religion. It's really none of your business. But as long as you're going to be with us for a while and in daily contact with some of our military friends, I'll let their commanding officer explain. Then Enoch will escort you back to the re-conversion facility.

"Major," Doctor Don called to the back of the tent, "Would you join us."

Tad turned in his chair and almost fell off it when he saw, striding toward him in crisp fatigues, combat boots and white hair streaming from under his fatigue cap, Sheriff—Major—Holy Moses.

CHAPTER 18

After thinking it over for a couple hours, Tad decided he shouldn't have been surprised by what Major Holy Moses had told him. He knew there were groups in the United States and elsewhere who opt out of society for a variety of reasons, religion being just one: nudists, drug fanciers, nature devotees and the spiritual descendents of sixties' hippie communes, people whose ideas about life are far enough from the mainstream to prompt their withdrawal, but who are, by and large, harmless.

Sitting captive in his tent in the re-conversion compound that sultry July afternoon, Tad was chilled by Holy Moses' matter-of-fact description of his organization—the "New Wisconsin Christian-Patriot Militia." He had called it a "re-engineering of Posse Comitatus and re-birth of The Covenant, the Sword, and the Arm of the Lord." Having been out of the country for the better part of a quarter century, Tad was unfamiliar with those groups and with many of the names Moses cited in his tirade: Bill Gale, Gordon Kahl, Richard Butler, Jim Wickstrom, Lyndon LaRouche. Tad was familiar with the 1995 bombing of the Murrah Federal Building in Oklahoma City—the whole world knew about that—and the subsequent execution of Timothy McVeigh. He had not known about the execution of Richard Snell, "a real patriot" in the eyes of Holy Moses, on the same day as the Murrah bombing.

Hatred seemed right in character for the sheriff. But the depth and breadth of that malice was scary. The "power structure"—the federal government, which he called the "Jewish Occupational Government," and in particular the Internal Revenue Service, Federal Reserve System, Department of Agriculture, the FBI and Bureau of Alcohol, Tobacco and Firearms—headed the major's list. The Wisconsin Department of Natural Resources got lumped in there, along with the "New World Order," which Moses defined as the United Nations, World Trade Organization and the "Zionist international banking cartel."

That was just a start. Next came "lefty-liberals" of all kinds: university professors, news media with some exceptions, Democrats and many Republicans, abortionists, marijuana legalizers, organized labor, anyone who criticizes the Bush administration and a few others that Tad couldn't remember. They were followed by immigrants—legal and illegal—as well as "niggers," "A-rabs," "mud people," homosexuals, and anyone in America who can't or won't speak English.

From the sheriff's rambling lecture, Tad gathered that the September 11 World Trade Center and Pentagon attacks had catapulted Muslims to the top in his list of world threats, and had added gravity to the mission of the "New Wisconsin Christian-Patriot Militia."

His visits with Doctor Don and Major Moses had a salutary effect on his standing with his guards. They were more relaxed, seated now on folding chairs, walking around his tent occasionally. Tad ventured a few minor pleasantries about the weather and mosquitoes and received noncommittal replies, but replies just the same. The orderly who brought him his meals and fresh clothes loosened up a little also, although the deepest their conversation got had to do with the tenderness of the noon's roast beef sandwich. Tad was able to discern, however, that the lad was from someplace in the Deep South.

The humid weather that was ushered in by the thunderstorm on Monday hung around. His hosts tried to accommodate him by providing shorts and sandals. He suggested air conditioning his tent, but the guard missed the point of his kidding and informed him it couldn't be done.

He was returning from a bathroom break when he noted a change in his habitat: one side of his tent was rolled down. Furthermore, the side of the tent next to his, twenty feet away, was also rolled down. His guards provided no explanation, but from traffic to and from the other tent—civilian and military—it was apparent that he had a neighbor.

Around mid-afternoon, he was summoned once more to Doctor Don's tent.

This time there were two chairs facing the desk. The orderly brought a pitcher of lemonade and three glasses. Tad sat sipping lemonade for ten minutes, waiting for Doctor Don and the occupant of the other chair. He heard footsteps behind him. He turned and almost fell off his chair again. It was Miriam, in Ralph Goodfeller's oversized turkey-hunting camos, escorted by Doctor Don.

"I assume you two know each other," Doctor Don said, smiling at his sarcasm and Tad's astonishment.

"Miriam, what are you, what are, what …"

"Enough of this chit-chat," Doctor Don said. He poured lemonade for all three. "Now then, let me ask that question: What are both of you doing here?"

It took Tad another half glass of lemonade before he could recover enough to frame an answer. "I believe, Doctor Don, that we are your guests here for as long as you want us to remain."

"You're right about that. You are our guests for as long as I and others wish you to remain. But that begs the question: What brought you here in the first place? In the absence of any other explanation, might I assume that you, Tad, came to visit your mother?"

"Yes, Don, you may assume that."

"And you, dear fallen sister, Miriam. May I assume that you came seeking your lover here?"

"Father Coburg is not my lover."

"How about 'soul mate?'"

"Father Coburg is my spiritual advisor. That's all."

"We have evidence that suggests a relationship much beyond that of spiritual advisor."

Doctor Don opened his Bible to a passage he had marked. "'If a man be found lying with a woman married to an husband, then they shall both of them die, both the man that lay with the woman, and the woman: so shalt thou put away evil from Israel.' Sound familiar, my child?"

"Deuteronomy, I forget the numbers."

"Tad, here's one for you. 'Thou shalt not covet thy neighbor's house, thou shalt not covet thy neighbor's wife.'"

"Exodus," Tad interrupted. "Chapter twenty, verse seventeen."

"So the Catholic does know something about the Bible. Here's another—"

"Don, we can sling biblical quotations at each other some other time. Let's get down to the real business at hand. You are holding us prisoner. I want to know why and when this silliness will stop. We've got better things to do and so do you."

"I believe you'll both have to admit that the circumstances of your trespassing on our private, posted property appear to be beyond that of a casual stroll in the woods. The priest here, dressed like a paunchy, middle-aged G.I. Joe and equipped like a very respectable spy." That picture tickled the even-paunchier pastor, producing a solid guffaw.

"And sister Miriam in her own ridiculous costume." Another, lengthier and heartier round of belly laugh. "Double Mint twins gone to seed." Tad realized that his earlier reconnaissance with Miriam had been recorded, probably every step of the way. Doctor Don reached into his desk drawer and pulled out a half dozen eight by ten photos confirming it.

"What conclusion am I to draw from these? Priest tires of altar boys and turns to adult females?" Doctor Don asked. All humor had gone. "And what about this?" He reached under his desk and pulled out a hefty bolt-action rifle. From his desk drawer he took a half dozen cartridges, which Tad judged to be .30-06. They lay silently on the desk as the pastor's eyes bounced from gun to Miriam to Tad and back.

"It's Myron's old deer rifle," she said finally.

"Let me guess. You were deer hunting—out of season, without a license and probably for the first time in your life."

"No."

"That's a lot of gun for shooting crows or raccoons. Maybe you were after coyotes."

"No."

"What then? The only animal left to shoot around here would be people. And you know that's against the law, to say nothing about the fifth commandment."

Miriam, apparently feeling the game was over, said "I came to kill the man or woman who killed my son." Doctor Don didn't seem surprised by that admission. Nor was Tad.

They returned to their respective tents, blindfolded again, under Enoch's escort. The hot, still weather had produced no rain for several days, and the combination of traffic and weather conditions left a fine layer of brown dust over the entire area, including his tent and its contents. He wasn't looking forward to a lazy, boring night in the heat, dust, mosquitoes and biting flies of the re-conversion facility, separated from human companionship by the sides of the tent, twenty feet of dusty grass and the vigilance of the two soldiers.

The newspaper he found on the wooden chair in his tent removed "lazy" and "boring" from any further association with his stay at the facility. It was the *Millen County Reporter*. The editor had spent a lot of time in the county register of deeds office and had documented every real estate transaction that had removed, in total, more than 2,000 acres from the tax rolls. If Bruce had let it go at that, there would probably have been some minor clucking of tongues over coffee or beer around the county, then the citizens would have turned to more exciting matters.

But Bruce, borrowing from television news the old "only-time-will-tell" technique of admitting he didn't have the answers yet but stay tuned, listed the questions that were bound to stir sales of next week's *Millen County Reporter*:

- *"What is one small, fundamentalist Christian denomination going to do with hundreds of acres of vacant farmland?*

- *"What are tax-exempt organizations, presumably similar to the Holy Scripture church and located as far away as Alabama, doing with large plots of vacant Wisconsin farmland?*

- *"Why won't anyone representing the Holy Scripture church return the media's phone calls? What are they hiding?*

- *"Why won't anyone from the Millen County sheriff's department comment to the media about the strange use—or non-use—of those 2,000-plus acres? Are they investigating possible criminal activity there? If so, what?"*

- *"Why is the entire bundle of contiguous farms posted for no hunting or trespassing, with identical signs nailed to trees and posts every fifty feet around the eight-mile perimeter of the property?*

The story contained a photo of such a sign, nailed to a tree, warning people to stay away from the "Vale of the Terebinth." Tad recalled vaguely that the Vale was where David killed Goliath with a sling shot.

Tad had a question of his own: If Doctor Don knew about the newspaper stories, as he must have, why didn't he mention it earlier in the day? The answer came a half hour later when he was briskly and roughly summoned once more to the pastor's tent.

"Sit down." Not an invitation; a command. Major Holy Moses seated alongside the pastor and Enoch, the soldier, standing at attention behind them completed the martial portrait. Tad sat. "So, the papist is also a spy for the liberal news media," Doctor Don said. "Who else are you working for? The FBI? The CIA? United Nations?"

Tad remembered his Navy training for prisoner-of-war status: According to the Geneva Conventions you are required to give only your name, rank, serial number and date of birth. That would probably not carry him far in these circumstances. "I am employed by the diocese of Madison to serve three parishes in southwestern Wisconsin. I came onto your land to find my mother. With your help, I did so, and she assured me that she is well and happy here. Now I would like to go back to my parishes."

"Not so fast. You've caused us a lot of problems. Now you must help us solve them."

"Like what?"

"Two things," Doctor Don said. "First, you must convince your friend, the local editor, to stop siding with Satan and call off his crusade against the forces of the Lord."

"I can't do that. We live in a democracy. Sheriff, you know the constitution as well as anyone. Freedom of the press is as vital as, well, the right to bear arms."

"And so is the right to practice one's religion without interference from government or the press," Sheriff Moses said. "The editor doesn't seem to get that."

"All he did, for crying out loud, was publish some real estate transactions that are a matter of public record, and ask some questions publicly that a lot of people must be asking privately. That's no crime."

"It is if it interferes with our ability to practice our faith," Doctor Don said.

"You want me to lean on the newspaper editor and get him to back off?"

Sheriff Moses interjected: "By way of persuasion, you might point out that he has a wife and children, and his behavior does little to guarantee their safety. They're members of your flock. As their shepherd, you should recognize your duty to look after their welfare."

"What's the second thing you want me to do?"

Doctor Don leaned against the desk. "Convince your companion, Mrs. Dett, to cease all litigation against the Holy Scripture Universal Church of the Lord."

"Mrs. Dett is a very headstrong woman. When she decides to do something, I don't believe I or anyone else could talk her out of it."

"You're her spiritual advisor," Sheriff Moses said, also leaning forward. "Convince her."

"I'll think about it."

"You have tonight to think about it," the sheriff said. Tomorrow morning you will meet with her in my office. Detectives Stark and Flint—I believe you know them—will be present to help guide the discussion. Following that, she will give us her decision. Depending on her decision, she will be accompanied back to West Charleton or will be transferred to another facility on our property."

"And the newspaper?"

"Tomorrow afternoon you, yourself, will be accompanied back to West Charleton to meet with the newspaper editor. This is your opportunity to use all the skills of persuasion that you've polished over the years as an academic scholar. Following that you'll return here. Perhaps we can arrange a dinner meeting with your mother."

Tad lay on his cot perspiring, partly because it was oppressively hot, partly because none of the implications or subtleties of his conversation with the sheriff/major and Doctor Don had missed him. He wanted to roll up the tent side facing Miriam's tent to catch any bit of breeze that may find its way into the valley, but his captors only shook their heads. His dinner tray came: chicken salad on a fresh croissant, sliced orange and cantaloupe on the side.

The situation wasn't complex. The threats, though unspoken, were real. He knew he couldn't talk Miriam Dett or Bruce Bestman out of their actions. And even if he thought he could, he wouldn't, partly because he was convinced they were doing the right thing, partly because he felt he had no business trying, and partly because Doctor Don and Major Moses told him to.

Darkness seemed to move in earlier than it should for the time of year, but it brought no change in the sultry air. Shorts, tee shirt and sandals were more than plenty for life confined to a tent in the woods. Mosquitoes were especially ornery, circling and diving at the netting over his cot, and some finding their way inside. He doused every exposed inch of his skin with repellant. Solutions and strategies eluded him, and a low quality sleep finally settled in.

When he awoke it was after midnight. Except for the luminous dial on his watch, it was as dark as it gets on the planet. Thunder rumbled faintly in the distance. *Good. Cool things off.* He dozed off again, and woke to brilliant flashes of lightning. His captors were working fast to roll down all sides of his tent and fasten them tightly. Thunder was still coming from miles off, but it was almost continuous.

Soon the lightning was bright enough to light up the inside of the heavy canvas tent, and thunder was no longer rumbling but exploding almost simultaneously with the lightning flashes. Then came wind that, even in the sheltered valley, threatened to rip the tent from its stakes. Tad worried about that, and about the possibility of a tree or limb blowing down on top of him. Next, rain of epic intensity and hail that he guessed to be the size of golf balls pelted the tent. Forty years earlier his parents would have had him and his sisters in the basement in a storm such as this.

The hail stopped and the wind dropped from its terrible peak, but rain continued in torrents, blinding lightning and deafening thunder went on undiminished. Twenty minutes passed without any indication that the storm was moving off. Tad wondered how Miriam was holding out in the tent next to his.

That question was answered when a corner of his tent opened near the plywood floor and a drenched Miriam crawled in. "What are you doing here?" he shouted, then was glad the thunder drowned out such a stupid question. He helped her to her feet and sat her on the chair. He started to dry her off with his pillow case, but she stopped him. She stood and talked directly into his ear.

"We gotta get out of here," she said.

"That's crazy," he said into her ear. "Where would we go in this storm?"

"It's that or die. Stay here and we won't live another twenty-four hours."

"The storm'll pass. The worst is probably over already. Don't worry about it."

"It's not the storm. They plan to kill us."

"That's ridiculous. How do you—"

"Just shut up. We're getting out of here." She ducked under the tent flap and back into the storm. He had no choice but to follow.

The escapees might have saved themselves a few scratches and bruises by a more methodical getaway, but adrenaline was totally in control. They learned in the first twenty yards of flight that they had to hold hands to keep from losing each other, and to pull the other up every couple minutes, when a rock or fallen log sprung its trap. Despite almost constant lightning, finding a path was impossible. The best that lightning did was keep them from crashing into large trees. Saplings and the ubiquitous brambles did their nasty work unseen. Pain would show up when the adrenaline wore off.

Two hours later, around four, dawn was making a tentative approach, enough to give trees some definition against the sky, but not enough to provide any guidance for the two escaped prisoners in their panicky dash toward higher ground and away from the re-conversion facility. Whether their captors were being solicitous in providing light weight clothing for comfort in the heat, or whether they figured shorts, tee shirt and sandals would compound the difficulty of escape, the latter proved to be the case. Tad was a mass of lacerations and bruises from brambles, barked shins and stumbles. For reasons of modesty, Miriam had been given jeans, but the forest took its toll on her as well.

The rain continued, lightning and thunder moving slowly off to the east. They found a bit of shelter under a sandstone ledge—although they couldn't get any wetter—a place, at least, to take stock of a bad situation.

"We've got another hour, maybe two before they miss us," Tad said. "Any idea where we are?"

"Maybe when it gets lighter I'll see something I recognize."

"You've been here before?"

"Yeah. Holy Scripture church used to come here for picnics. I'd wander off—to pray, I told them—but mostly for peace and quiet."

"Do you know a bluff overlooking the area where we were kept in those tents?"

"I think we passed it a while back."

"Point me there. I need to find the spot where I took a leak last week."

An hour later Tad was back with the green fanny pack he had dropped into the bramble thicket. "Let's get going."

With the gray and rainy daylight and the maps and GPS retrieved on his trip to the bramble thicket, he was able to get his bearings. They headed west toward Norse Road, the apparent western boundary of the compound, avoiding anything resembling a road or foot path. Tad watched for cameras, trip wires and soldiers, but saw none. That vigilance and the dense underbrush limited their progress to a slow crawl. It occurred to Tad, he hoped not too late, to keep his eyes open for poison ivy as well.

Rain continued to fall, and thunder to the west suggested more storms on the way. It was nearly noon when they reached the edge of a steep bluff, which maps indicated overlooked Norse Road. From there it would be just a short jaunt to his car and the keys under a nearby rock. Wrong.

Observation skills honed on the jungle-lined rivers of Vietnam were rusty, but not lost. A hundred feet below and a hundred feet south, on a small knoll, a perfect place for surveillance and defensive weapons, were two soldiers in ponchos. He looked north a hundred feet and spotted the similar emplacement where his quick calculation of fields of fire expected it. The soldiers were on their side of the road, looking west, protecting against intruders, not escapees. Still, breaking away from the compound would involve crossing twenty feet of asphalt in the gun sights of the soldiers, who, presumably, were aware of the death sentence on the pair that had caused the Holy Scripture church so much trouble.

He pointed to the sentries, and it took Miriam several minutes to see what he saw. "Oh shit," she whispered.

The new storm was almost upon them. Thunder had gone from the rumbling to the cracking stage, and the wind kicked up. Rain, which hadn't stopped since they left the tent, intensified. Miriam motioned for Tad to follow her.

Their stumbling march took them north, skirting an overgrown pasture and staying in the woods and underbrush, although tempted to avoid more scratches and make better time in the pasture. Miriam seemed to know where she was going, and Tad was satisfied with following.

After an hour, they started down what appeared to be an old and overgrown, steep and rocky cow path. Tad learned that going downhill in sandals was harder than going uphill. They grabbed rocks and small trees to avoid butt-busting slides, and added more bruises and scrapes to their already torn up skin.

Halfway to the bottom of the hill they came to a more level and traveled path. Miriam motioned for him to follow. Soon they were at the base of a rocky bluff, and at the mouth of a small cave. The path led into it. Miriam didn't hesitate. She crawled into the four-foot-high opening, and Tad followed.

Being out of the rain was small comfort. As hot as they had been twenty-four hours earlier, the chill of the cave and their scant, soaked, torn clothing left them shaking. They sat huddled for a half hour, not talking, watching the rain and trying to get their shivering under control. Growing hunger didn't help.

Diminishing rain and thunder reminded them that they had to do something. Searchers had no doubt been hunting them for hours. Staying in the cave would accomplish nothing. Thrashing around in dense woods and brush, half naked, running from an enemy in the middle of the United States of America and a mere ten or twelve miles from their own comfortable kitchens and beds seemed preposterous and the stuff of fiction. But their bruised and scratched bodies were real enough, and their options seemed down to zero.

"How do you know they were planning to kill us?" Todd asked, the first words spoken since they entered the cave.

"Holy Scripture people came to see me, tried to talk me back into the church. One of them stayed behind and warned me we're dead meat if we stay. Guess I still have at least one friend there."

"You believe him?"

"Her. Do we have a choice?"

"Probably not. This place looks like it gets some traffic, and I doubt if it's cows or coyotes. I'm going to look inside. Wait here."

Tad started crawling deeper into the cave, not entirely comfortable with dark, tight places and not planning to go beyond the limit of light from the mouth of the cave. He had just about reached that point when his shoulder knocked a plastic object off a rock shelf. A flashlight. It worked.

He had gone another twenty feet and around three bends when he stopped, and was abruptly rear-ended. "What are you doing here?" he asked Miriam for third time in two weeks.

"Following you."

They continued for another thirty feet, and the crawl space opened into a larger room, big enough to stand up. And big enough to hold a small arsenal. Tad sprayed the flashlight over stacks of weapons, ammunition, canned rations, bottled water, even boxed boots and military uniforms. "Sweet Jesus," he said, "Quaint, rustic, peaceful southwestern Wisconsin. Not enough here to overthrow the United States government, but enough to cause a lot of trouble. Did you know about this?"

"I was here about three years ago. I didn't get this far into the cave."

"They didn't put this here for our benefit. But it's manna from heaven. Let's load up," Tad said.

"Thou shalt not steal."

"Screw that." It took them a half hour to find and put on military fatigues and boots that fit (approximately), to fashion crude knapsacks out of their torn and wet captivity clothing, to load up on rations and water and to disguise their larceny.

That they couldn't stay in the vicinity of that cave was obvious. Where they should go, or even could go, was far less apparent. Their choices were limited: up the hill, down the hill or sideways. Rain was stopping. A quick study of the maps showed them that uphill would take them more into the center of the Holy Scripture land holdings. But uphill seemed to make the most sense; better to be looking down on pursuers as they struggled upward, than the other way around. Uphill they went.

At the top, woods gave way to former farm fields, now grown over with grasses, weeds, brush and small trees, nature making its comeback. The field afforded a view of the sky, which Tad hadn't seen in over a week. Rain had stopped, and a sharp line defined the slow-moving front that had kindled the storms and the blue skies and cooler temperatures following from the northwest. Already a fresh breeze had picked up, and within fifteen minutes they were nearly dry and reasonably comfortable. They stuck to the woods at the edge of the field, and selected a substantial white oak to sit against for their army ration lunch, meals ready to eat, mesquite chicken for him, seafood jambalaya for her, spiced apple for dessert.

Perhaps it was age, perhaps it was lack of conditioning, perhaps it was the safe, comfortable academic life of the past thirty years, but Tad forgot the most basic rule of survival in the land of the enemy—stay awake. Up all night, first meal in eighteen-plus hours, what were two middle-aged people supposed to do?

"Wake up, papist." The voice belonged to the soldier kicking Tad in the leg. "And the whore too."

CHAPTER 19

Tad and Miriam scrambled to their feet as ordered. Two soldiers pointed semi-automatic weapons at them. He couldn't be certain if they were the same men who had rudely interrupted his meditation on the bank of the Midewiwin a few short weeks before. The difference today, besides the weapons, was combat helmets in place of fatigue caps and skin painted to blend with the lush, green southwestern Wisconsin summer flora. One looked vaguely familiar.

"You don't learn, papist. Didn't I tell you once this is private property?"

"We're trying to find our way off your property," Tad said. "We, ah, seem to be lost."

"Lost, my ass. Get moving."

Tad attempted to pick up their homemade knapsacks containing their food and water. One of the soldiers saved him the trouble. They started off single file—soldier, Miriam, Tad, soldier—in a generally northeast direction, first across the grassy field, then into the woods and downhill. Sticking to established paths, the going was much easier than their flight in the night. In less than an hour they were on a valley floor and the bank of a river, the Midewiwin, if Tad's reckoning was correct. The river was almost overflowing its banks from the night's deluge.

They were led to a semicircle of three-foot logs, set on ends underneath a tall willow tree, and ordered to sit. Tad guessed it was a classroom of sorts, located for its inspiring view of soaring bluffs on both sides of the verdant pastures and restful waters, the perfect setting for the twenty-third Psalm. It was a valley where they should fear no evil.

But the evil they weren't supposed to fear turned up within ten minutes, in the form of two more soldiers, equipped and dressed for battle but with brown berets instead of combat helmets. As they approached, Tad lost what little confidence he had left. The two in the berets were Sheriff Moses' detectives—Adam Stark and Joshua Flint, not exactly friends of the priest. Both wore holstered pistols. Stark was carrying a rifle strapped over his shoulder. Flint carried what in military circles could be a map case, in civilian life a green, canvas attaché case.

They stood ten feet in front of the seated prisoners. The two soldiers who had captured them stood behind them.

"You bastards just don't learn," said Stark.

Tad wished he had a snappy rejoinder or a reasoned argument or some logical explanation, anything to defuse the tension and put himself on a more equal footing, but the best he could come up with was silence.

"What do you think I should do with you?"

"Send us back to our homes," Tad suggested.

"Sorry. That's no longer an option. When you put on those stolen uniforms you became combatants. You're now prisoners of war."

"Prisoners of war in the heart of the United States of America? What war? Prisoners of who?"

Tad glanced quickly at Miriam. She seemed impassive, certainly not frightened. "Look, Detective Stark—"

"Captain Stark."

"Captain. I came here to find if my mother was safe and content. I've been spending the last week trying to get off this place and back to my job. It's as simple as that. We're wearing these uniforms because it's all there was to protect us from thorns and mosquitoes."

"Mrs. Dett came here intending to commit murder. That would seem to qualify as an act of war," Stark said.

"Mrs. Dett is a mother who's still grieving over the untimely death of her son. Cut her some slack."

"Captain Flint," Stark said. "Show them the papers." Flint reached into the map case and pulled out three newspapers. He handed Tad that morning's *Chicago Tribune*. For the first time in years, maybe the first time ever, a story datelined West Charleton, WI made the paper's banner headline:

> *Federal authorities converge*
> *On western Wisconsin sect*
>
>   *Hundreds of federal agents began converging last night on an isolated area*
> *of Millen County, Wisconsin, where a religious sect is believed to be heavily*

armed and planning some as-yet-unspecified act of rebellion against the government.

Agents from the Federal Bureau of Investigation, Bureau of Alcohol, Tobacco and Firearms and Treasury Department began to surround an area of about 2,000 acres of hilly, mostly wooded land owned by a Wisconsin Christian fundamentalist sect and religious organizations from several other states.

The mobilization was prompted by numerous tips from people living in Millen County, which in turn were apparently triggered by an extensive story in Thursday's edition of the Millen County Reporter. *That story detailed the acquisition of numerous farms in the area by the Holy Scripture Universal Church of the Lord and other religious organizations, and the removal of those lands from the tax rolls.*

Citizen reports to the Wisconsin attorney general's office over the weekend told of extensive military traffic in the area, as well as the disappearance of at least fifteen families known to be members of the Holy Scripture church. Attorney General Wade Rivers contacted the FBI, and there were reports that the bureau was also investigating similar activities in other states. A United States Justice Department spokeswoman declined to comment.

Rivers cautioned against jumping to conclusions, but said the (see page 8A).

"What are the other papers," Tad asked.

"*Dubuque Telegraph Herald* and *Wisconsin State Journal*, both with the same malicious lies," Stark said.

"You have to admit that from the outside looking in all this military stuff does seem a little strange."

"You have to admit that it's nobody's business but ours. And it's especially none of your damn papist business."

"Captains," Tad addressed them, "let's resolve this matter quickly and peacefully. I don't know what's going on here, nor do I care. I simply want for Mrs. Dett and me to return quietly to our respective homes. If you'd be kind enough to escort us safely there, we won't bother you again."

"Except that I will kill the person who killed my son," Miriam said.

"That's the third reason why we can't turn you loose. The woman's crazy. The second reason is that the two of you are out to destroy the Holy Scripture church all by yourselves. We won't let that happen."

"And the first reason?" Tad said.

"The first reason is you are spies, and you must be treated accordingly."

"Spies? Who in hell are we spying for?"

"The news media, for one. The pope for sure. Probably the FBI and BATF as well. Wandering around behind our lines, equipped with maps and jazzy electronic gear, what else would you be? Prima facie case. Guilty based on over-whelming evidence."

"Lieutenant," Stark addressed one of the two soldiers. "You and the sergeant head back to Major Moses. Tell him the spies have been apprehended, they have confessed and are being dealt with in accordance with established policies and procedures. Nice job, men." The lieutenant and sergeant left at double time.

"Okay, captain," Tad said. "Would you mind telling us what the established policies and procedures are?"

"You've heard of Nathan Hale?"

Tad swallowed. "Yeah."

"Julius and Ethel Rosenberg?"

"Yeah."

"There's your answer."

Tad looked at Miriam. She still seemed unfazed. Resolute even. Had she never heard of Nathan Hale and the Rosenbergs?

"Captain, this is absurd. People in town know we're here. They'll come looking for us. The feds'll search every square inch of this property and they'll find our bodies and they'll figure out in ten minutes who did it and you'll be in prison for the rest of your lives."

Stark took the rifle off his shoulder. "You're only partly right. They'll find your bones. And it will take them ten minutes to guess who did it. But they'll be wrong. Recognize this rifle?"

"It's Myron's old one," Miriam said.

"Correct. His Remington thirty-aught-six. Now we only have to kill Myron with it and we'll have our trifecta. Double murder and suicide. Plenty of motive to close the book on the case, wouldn't you say?"

Tad shuddered. "This is idiotic. I spent two years in the jungles of Vietnam fighting for my country and I survived. Now I'm here in my home state and—"

"You spent two years fighting for a corrupt, godless government that enslaves its own people. Now it's time. I'd like to offer you a last meal, but you probably aren't hungry, after eating that food you stole from us. I should also offer the services of a priest, but that would be redundant."

Stark opened the bolt and reached into his pocket for cartridges. "God damn, what the hell are you doing, you crazy woman?

Tad turned to see Miriam pointing a pistol at Captain Stark and his comrade. Their side arms were buttoned into holsters. Miriam was standing and holding the gun with both hands, like she knew what she was doing.

"You shouldn't leave weapons lying around in caves," she said. "What if some children wandered into that cave? Or a middle-aged, crazy woman? Or the mother of a boy you murdered?"

"Jesus Christ, woman, you are out of your mind."

Tad's mind was reeling. He felt he should stop her, but he knew that would be certain death for both of them. He froze.

A shot. Captain Stark crumpled, blood spurting from his neck.

A second shot. Captain Flint was on the ground, a bloody gap where his left eye once was.

Miriam slumped to the tree stump, pistol dropping to the ground. Tad swayed, but put his arm around her. "Miriam, my dearest, why did you …"

"I didn't," she said, barely audible, shaking. He picked up the gun. It was cold. He wanted to sit on a stump, clear his head, find rationality in the unreal, guidance in theology, some vague notion of what to do next. His instincts told him, however, that sitting and thinking were out of the question.

"Let's get out of here." Escape meant a 100-yard dash across the open meadow, or picking their way down through the underbrush along the banks of the Midewiwin. Right or wrong, they started to run.

Miriam proved to be more out of shape than Tad. They hadn't covered fifty yards toward the wooded hillside before she stumbled, gasping for breath. Tad pulled her up. "Come on," he panted. "Can't stop."

Another twenty yards, they were puffing and stumbling past a thicket of multi-floral rose, and a camo-clad arm reached out and grabbed him, pulling him to the ground. His natural reaction was escape, but his body wasn't up to it. The wrestle was over in seconds; he was pinned and breathless. Gasping, Miriam tumbled beside him.

"God damn," their latest captor whispered. "You two slow down. For Chrissake, it's okay." Tad looked up, into the whiskered face of Myron Dett.

Whether Myron was friend or enemy didn't matter at that point. Exhaustion, both physical and mental, ruled. It took at least a minute for Tad's lungs to find enough oxygen for him to ask the inevitable: "You, were you, you shot captains?"

"Yeah. It was me," Myron said, tapping his Weatherby Accumark .300 Mag rifle.

"Hell of a shot."

"Not so great. Less than a hundred yards. They weren't even moving. I've hit running deer a lot farther than that."

Miriam's breath was starting to come in manageable gulps.

"You guys wait here," Myron said. He slung the rifle over his shoulder and crawled through the tall grass toward the river. He was back in ten minutes with both rifles on his back. "I hate to poison a perfectly good river with those assholes. But somebody'll find their bodies before they're too rotten. Now let's haul ass out of here."

They snaked their way to the woods and another fifty yards in, nestling behind a thicket of buckthorn to catch their breath and take stock. Myron had rescued their used-clothing knapsacks and the pilfered water, but had tossed the remaining rations into the river. Miriam sipped hers daintily but steadily. Tad guzzled a bottle of the warm water in three or four long swigs. He watched her watching her husband. Thirty years of hate seemed to be giving way to puzzlement.

"What the fuck you two are doing in this rat's nest," Myron said.

"I came to kill the bastard that killed Tony," Miriam said.

"Too late."

"Detective Stark?"

"Him or Flint. I never could find out which one actually whupped our son to death. Might have been both. Sure as hell wasn't a fall down the stairs." They let that sink in. Tad, from reflex, said a silent prayer for the repose of both of their souls and asked God to forgive them, knowing forgiveness wouldn't come from Miriam for a long time.

"What about you, reverend? What brings you into the camp of the enemy?"

"I came to find my mother."

"Did you."

"Yes. Now I have to get her out."

Myron chewed on a piece of grass. "Damn near impossible. How do you know she wants to get out? Most of those people like it here. Loony as that fat preacher."

"My grandfather committed suicide. She wants out."

"Huh? Don't make sense. But let me think about it. First we gotta get you two out, and that ain't gonna to be easy. When those cops don't show up for the major's staff meeting in a couple hours this place'll be swarming."

Where their flight from captivity the night before had been a blind dash through thorns and dense forest, lit only by stroboscopic lightning and accompanied by wind and rain, this march was orderly, illuminated by mid-afternoon sun filtered through stately oaks. Myron seemed to know where he was headed and how to get there, following a winding course around the sides of hills and through steep ravines. He went where deer and coyotes had gone, pushing brambles and low branches out of the way, stopping every fifty feet or so to look and listen. Tad guessed they were headed once again in the general direction of Norse Road.

Twice they stopped, and Myron scrambled up the hillside. They saw him take a device out of his pocket and talk into it. He didn't volunteer what it was all about, and they were too tired to ask.

They rounded a hill and through the trees saw a road at the bottom. "Wait here," Myron said, and he disappeared into the brush at a crawl. In twenty minutes he was back. "Here we go."

They crept toward the road, and they were almost on it when they came to a black pickup truck, facing the road, expertly hidden by limbs and brush, some apparently torn from trees by the night's storms. "Get in, and stay down," he told Miriam. "Reverend, give me a hand with this brush."

In two minutes they cleared enough for the truck to move forward. "Okay, get in, hold the door but don't slam it, stay down and get ready for a wild ride."

Myron started the V8, 340-horsepower engine, put the truck into gear and roared forward. Wild was not an exaggeration. When he reached Norse Road he swerved right and put the accelerator to the floor, shifting through all five gears in twelve seconds. Tad thought he heard explosions behind them, but was more concerned about not falling out of the truck. In ten seconds Myron slowed enough to turn left without rolling. "Yahoo," he yelled, in his element and having a blast. The truck dove through a ditch. For an instant Tad was sure they were airborne and wished for nothing more than a fastened seat belt. They started cross country through cultivated land soaked from the rains. "Thank God for four-wheel drive. Old Freddie Darmstadt's gonna be pissed at us tearing up his soybeans, but it's the beans or us. I'll have him send you the bill. You okay back there, Mir?"

Tad saw they were indeed slashing through a soybean field, with a wooded hillside on their right. He turned to Miriam, scrunched down in the crew cab, and saw a gash bleeding on her cheek, no doubt a casualty of the bounce through the ditch. They came to a rutted, muddy road and left the soybeans.

When the road wound around the base of the hill, they slid to a stop in a shower of mud. A half dozen men in black jackets and baseball caps aimed automatic weapons at them. Myron jumped out. "Chill out, guys. I got the reverend with me." Three of the men had FBI on their jackets; the other three said ATF.

CHAPTER 20

❁

"I'm sorry, Father Coburg. I know you and Mrs. Dett would like nothing more than your own beds right now. But you're the only ones who've been inside the compound, and we need to debrief you." FBI Special Agent Ahman Metcalf was from a movie set, a Denzel Washington look-alike.

"If you don't mind, can I do that flat on my back? If I don't lie down, I'll be no good to you or anyone else." Tad had reached the end of his endurance.

"First stop is first aid. If the rest of your body is as scratched up as your face and arms, you may run us completely out of Band-Aids. Then hot chow and some sleep. Same for Mrs. Dett. We're still moving people in from Iowa, Minnesota and Illinois, and we won't do any serious planning until tomorrow morning. We'll need both of you for that."

"Thanks."

"And by the way, we've notified your bishop that you're all right. And your attorney. They've been worried crazy about you."

"And Miriam, Mrs. Dett?"

"Covered. The Goodfellers haven't slept in almost a week, but they're okay now. The two youngest Dett daughters are safe with their uncle in Denver."

"Darlene, the oldest daughter?"

"Afraid we don't know where she is. That's a problem."

Tad woke once during the night, listened briefly to a family of coyotes howling and yipping happily, sounding closer than they probably were. He went right back to sleep.

A shower and shave in the FBI's mobile facilities, fresh underwear from Agent Metcalf's own duffel bag and a hot breakfast from the agency's field kitchen put Tad in a better frame of mind. A female BATF agent dug into her luggage to help restore Miriam's respectability. Metcalf's headquarters was one of three set up outside the Holy Scripture compound.

They took off in the FBI's muddy black Ford Excursion to the main command post, two miles the way the crow flies, ten miles by back roads. Tad noted that the Wisconsin State Patrol had the entire area cordoned off, an action that itself drew a handful of the curious at each intersection.

The strategy session, under a large tent in an alfalfa field, included law enforcement officers from at least seven different federal and state agencies, but no one from the Millen County sheriff's department.

"I can't tell you how glad we are to have you," Agent-In-Charge Murphy of the FBI told them.

"I'm not sure how much help I'll be. They took my maps, and I got turned around so many time in the past few days I'm not sure where anything is."

"Don't worry about that," Murphy said. "We've got maps and aerial photos as recent as yesterday. But we don't know how many people are in there, or how well armed they are. And most of all, we still can't figure out who's in charge."

"I can answer the last question. Millen County Sheriff Moses, Holy Moses. He's now Major Moses, but major of what I don't know. As to how many are there, I saw a lot of military traffic. A few jeeps, but mostly civilian pickups and SUVs with armed military personnel. I couldn't tell you if I kept seeing the same guys over and over. As for civilians, I must have seen a dozen different families, all heading south to north past my tent."

"Probably members of that church. How about weapons? Anything besides small arms?"

"Didn't see any. Just those outposts along Norse Road."

"What?"

"Pretty well hidden. You didn't know about them?"

Murphy motioned with his head and Metcalf got up quickly and went outside to talk on the two-way radio attached to his belt. "That probably accounts for the bullet holes in the back of Dett's pickup. You were lucky."

For twenty more minutes Murphy and the law enforcement brain trust questioned Tad, who wished he had been more vigilant in his re-conversion facility tent. He noted that a number of the gathered cops were taking notes, and there were many knowing glances and exchanged nods as he talked. "Now then," Murphy said, "could you describe your escape from those people?"

Tad began with Miriam's anonymous friend tipping her off and their frantic run for their lives in the storm. He described the arsenal in the cave.

"Any more arms caches in those hills?"

"I'm told there's more caves in that area, but we didn't see any."

"And how did it come to pass that you were captured, or rather recaptured?"

"We, ah, well, we fell asleep." That provoked a bit of snickering.

"What happened after that?"

Tad hesitated. "Have you talked with Myron Dett?"

"He told us that a couple of guys, Millen County detectives, no less, were getting ready to kill you. So he killed them."

"Simply put, that's exactly what happened. What I don't know is why and how Myron happened to be there at that particular time."

"Probably best you don't know that right now," Murphy said. "That brings us to the last question. Who's calling the shots in there? The church or the militia?"

"I don't know that either."

Miriam was offered the opportunity to return to the Goodfeller home with police protection there. She chose to stay in Metcalf's camp.

"Tad, I know you'd like to go back to Red Oak, but I'd appreciate it if you'd stick around for a while."

"I'm not going anywhere until my mother is out of that snake pit."

"It might get kind of boring here. We, ah, learned our lesson down in Texas, not to, ah, rush things."

"I understand, Agent Metcalf."

"Call me Ahman. How about some lunch? And a beer to go with it? I have a few cold Sam Adams for occasions like this."

"Fantastic."

"You might also be interested in this morning's papers from around the country. They should be here soon. Seems we're attracting a lot of attention."

Tad hadn't talked with Myron since they had roared into the FBI/BATF camp the day before. Miriam hadn't either. "How he managed to be at that exact spot at that exact time to save our lives blows my mind," she said. They were sitting on canvas chairs, moving to stay in the tent's shade as the afternoon wore on.

"Is what he did out of character for Myron?"

She thought long about that. "No. All he ever wanted was the one thing he could never find. Respect. He thought he found it in the sheriff's department. It's bad enough to lose a son. But it must have been a hundred times worse when he learned his heroes were the ones who killed Tony."

"So was Myron there to save us or to kill Stark and Flint?"

"He could've killed them a long time ago. I think Myron did what he did because he loves his daughters."

"And you."

"Yes me. I believe he does love me, in a Myron Dett sort of way."

It was nearing five when Tad woke from his second nap of the afternoon. He was thinking of inviting Ahman and Miriam to be his guests for dinner that evening at the Sandstone—a big T-bone, maybe, or broiled walleye. Baked potato with sour cream and chives, Caesar salad. The Sandstone's wine list had improved greatly in the past nine months, and he could think of two or three good selections for any entrée on the menu.

His reverie was broken when one of the BATF guys summoned him to the operations tent. Miriam was there. Ahman was talking with Myron.

"Tad, it seems we've run into a snag in getting your mother out of the clutches of the Holy Scripture church," Ahman said.

"Is she okay?"

"For a seventy-two-year-old woman, yes. Right now she's holed up in an abandoned root cellar a couple hundred yards up a wooded ravine from her old house. We managed to get her that far."

"I know the place."

"We've arranged a helicopter pickup. But she's not budging from the root cellar. She doesn't trust our operative."

"Who's the operative?"

"You met him yesterday. The sergeant."

"He looked vaguely familiar under his sunglasses and paint."

"Myron's and Miriam's son-in-law."

"How would you get Ruth out anyway?" Tad said. "It's got to be a quarter of a mile through rough terrain to the nearest road."

"I've took a lot of deer out of there," Myron said. "I know a way to the pickup spot she could handle. A little farther, but easier going."

"Looks like you and me, Myron," Tad said.

"I'm going too," Miriam said.

"Like hell you are, Mir. We got two daughters that still need a mama. Me and the reverend they can get along without. But not you."

"We're going in as a threesome," Ahman said. "Myron, because he knows the way. Tad, because it's his mother and she'll trust him. Me, because it's my job. We jump off at 0100."

Tad thought he was through with jungles and people trying to kill him when he was evacuated by helicopter to the Navy hospital ship thirty years before. He thought he was really through with trees and brambles and people trying to kill him when Myron's Silverado burst into the FBI/BATF camp the day before. Nope.

This time, however, he was far better equipped. Besides boots that fit and a fresh set of camos, the three rescuers sported night vision goggles light years in quality above those of the Vietnam era. Each carried a GPS, programmed to get them to Ruth Coburg's root cellar and from there to the pickup point, and to allow agents back at the command post to track them. Myron had his battle-proven Weatherby. Ahman had his government-issued AR-15. He offered Tad a .44 magnum police revolver. Tad shook his head. "I'm a priest, a non-combatant."

One AM was chosen to give them time to reach Ruth and get her to the pickup spot at first light. They assumed—hoped—that the militia lacked the training and experience to stay alert all night.

The first hour was spent heading north, a half mile west of Norse Road, putting distance between the agents' camp and their entry point into Holy Scripture territory. The half moon, which had provided weak light earlier, had set. Stars and fireflies were abundant, and on another night they would have been fun to watch.

They picked a spot to cross Norse Road that they believed was away from militia listening posts, although they couldn't be sure. Myron hustled quietly across the road and waited. No sound. Tad and Ahman followed, thirty seconds apart. They were in. After five minutes of scouting, Myron reported he had found the path.

Tad was struck by the contrast between a blind dash through the woods in the rain, and a measured patrol through those same woods in the eerie green light of infrared technology and led by someone who knows where he's going. Myron even cut the arcing, thorny blackberry brambles blocking their path, and warned his followers of low tree limbs.

After forty-five minutes, Myron whispered for Tad and Ahman to stop, while he crawled ahead. He was back in twenty minutes with the sergeant. He motioned for Tad to follow them.

Now Tad was on familiar ground, although nature had mostly taken over what was once a well-worn foot path between the farmhouse and the root cellar. Outside the four-foot-high stone arch entrance in the hillside, the sergeant stopped. "Your mother's sleeping. I told her you'd be coming, but she called me a liar. Wake her up gently. Use this flashlight. We'll block the entrance. When you're ready to leave, give us a poke and douse the light."

Tad bent and entered. The air was damp and chilly, as root cellars were supposed to be. "Mom. It's me, Tad." She was on an air mattress, enveloped in a mummy-type sleeping bag and sleeping more soundly than he expected. "Mom, it's Tad. We're leaving this place. You're going to be all right." That brought a mumbled response. She awoke, terrified as anyone would be, waking up in such surroundings to see a combat-clad soldier with face painted dark green and a voice like her son's. He held her tightly and continued to whisper reassurances. It took almost ten minutes before she began to understand that it was indeed her son, Tad, and that he had come to break her out of that prison on her own farm. It was another ten minutes before she stopped shaking. "Let's go, mom."

The sergeant melted into the darkness to the north. Tad, Myron, Ahman and Ruth Coburg began a slow walk south toward freedom.

The wait at the pickup point was longer than planned, simply because the rescue had gone as well as planned. The extra hour for contingencies wasn't needed. They huddled in damp grass in the pre-dawn chill, knowing where they were but having no idea if the Holy Scripture militia were asleep or sighting weapons on them.

At twenty minutes after four, Wednesday was providing enough light to define the landscape. Ahman's brief radio conversation concluded. "Shit. You'll have to walk out, Tad. Room for your ma and that's it." Five minutes later they heard a distant helicopter, meaning, of course, that everyone in Holy Scripture territory heard it too. Still out of sight, the helicopter made a wide circle of the Coburg farm.

When it came into view it was almost on top of them, rushing in from the south, no more than fifty feet off the ground. The pilot found the spot thirty-five yards from the waiting group and settled noisily to the ground.

"Let's go, Mrs. Coburg," Ahman said. He picked her up like a child and ran to the waiting Robinson R-22, crouching out of respect for the spinning rotor. The pilot opened the right door, Ahman placed Ruth into the seat, fastened her seat belt, shut the door and gave the pilot a thumbs up. All in less than a minute. Tad's mother, strapped into the plastic bubble of the chopper, soared out of the kingdom of the Holy Scripture Universal Church of the Lord.

Ahman raced to the waiting rescuers. "Okay, guys, feet save ass," and they dashed into the woods. The objective now: put distance between them and the helicopter snatch—two guys in pretty good shape, and Tad.

For an hour they followed Myron, through the woods on paths that only he and long-departed cattle knew. Tad remembered when the wooded hillsides were grazed by his family's Holsteins and the neighboring Dillingen family's Guernsey herd.

They kept low, moving like cats stalking mice. Tad's lungs had held out in the sprint to the woods, but he wasn't sure his thighs would carry him out of the woods. Periodically, Myron stopped the group and listened, often for five minutes or more, and sometimes he crawled ahead to check the path. Tad finally realized that Myron was guided as much by birds and squirrels as by his own ears. When the animals set up a squawk ahead, he had to find out if humans had spooked them. Tad thought, *Myron would have been a good Army Ranger, or in Marine Corps reconnaissance. Military discipline wouldn't have hurt him either. Sad how often people's talents are mismatched with their vocations.*

They came to the head end of a long ravine, where hills on both sides joined in a broad U. Myron called another halt and crept upward, disappearing into the underbrush. He was gone almost an hour. When he returned, he had a four-word announcement: "We're in deep shit."

He reported that the militia had established a perimeter defense, at least along Norse Road on the western edge of their compound. Troops with AK-47s and Ruger Mini-14s were placed alongside the road at approximately 100-foot intervals, close enough to shoot anyone attempting to cross the road to enter or leave the compound.

"If they're guarding the west side, you can bet they've got the same protection all the way around," Ahman said.

"We ain't doing any good sitting here," Myron said. "I found us a spot at the top where we can watch for a chance to cross."

Their Norse Road vantage point offered a good view of the road and militia guarding it, about a half mile north of where they had crossed in the dark the night before. "My God," Tad whispered. "I can't believe I'd ever see anything like that in the United States." As if to punctuate his thought, they heard small arms fire, two rapid bursts, to the south.

"I hope they're just sighting in their weapons," Myron said. "If that's for real, this could get awful fucking messy."

Ahman had been carrying on a quiet, earnest radio conversation for fifteen minutes. He signed off and turned to Tad and Myron. "I was on the horn with Ben Nightingale, the BATF guy. He said Norse Road seems to be the most heavily defended. But they've got listening posts all the way around. Those shots were apparently to let us know they're serious. Nobody was hurt."

"What happens now?" Tad asked.

"We wait."

"Until when?"

"Who knows. Ben's on his way to a strategy session at the CP. Myron, do you know anywhere we can refill these water bottles if we have to?"

"No problem."

"Mind telling us what exactly is going on?" Tad said.

"Okay. First of all, your mom is fine. They flew directly to the hospital in Platteville and a preliminary check indicates she came through her ordeal with no major problems. They're keeping her overnight as a precaution—with police protection, of course."

"That's a relief. If I'm not back by tomorrow, have your people contact Killian. She'll find a safe place for her."

"Good. Now, you guys will be interested to know that this little dust-up is one of at least three going on in the country as we speak. A militia group in Alabama, near the Mississippi border, is holed up in worse terrain than this. Another one's out in Montana, northeast of Missoula. Judging from phone and radio traffic, they're in touch with each other, but there's no indication so far that any individual or council's in charge of all three. From what we hear, the death of Myron's little boy and Holy Scripture church's legal problems brought everything to a head at least six months before they were ready.

"One thing's for sure. This is turning into a real news media circus. Between Wisconsin, Alabama and Montana there's over 200 reporters and cameramen, and more are arriving by the hour."

"What's the matter with these people, anyway? Holy Moses hates everyone. But do they all feel that way?"

"Some more, some less," Ahman said. You have people like Moses, who hate everybody, because hate makes them feel superior. Combine that with people so convinced their religion is the *only* true religion, and they hate people who don't believe as they do. Deadly combination."

"Is there a religious connection in the Alabama and Montana confrontations too?" Tad asked.

"There seems to be, but nobody knows for sure."

"There is," Myron said.

"What?"

"A sheriff's dispatcher hears a lot of things. A good dispatcher keeps it to himself. But when a detective kills the dispatcher's son, the rules change."

"Jesus, man, what do you know about these freaks?" Ahman said. "Start by telling us who's in charge—Sheriff Moses or Doctor Don?"

"Moses. The church was hijacked. Him and the fat pastor started out great buddies. But I heard some real shouting matches in the sheriff's office. About a year ago things calmed down some. They talked every day, mostly by phone, but once or twice a week they got together someplace."

"Did you know that an army was being assembled in Millen County?"

"Mostly I knew what Denny told me," Myron said.

"Denny?"

"Denny Wurzburg, my son-in-law. He's a traffic cop in the department. He put in a lot of extra time—which he didn't get paid for—hauling guns and ammo and stuff into caves at night."

"Why didn't you tell somebody about all this?"

"Tell who? Sheriff Moses? The district attorney? Moses has that little shit in his back pocket."

"Is the D.A. part of the militia or the church?" Ahman asked.

"Neither. Blackmail."

"You could've told Father Tad here."

"I was thinking about that. Just about ready to, when I got a call to the Stark house after my shift, the night Tony was killed. Stark told me if I didn't do everything they said, them and their wives would testify they saw me beat the shit out of my son."

"Extortion," Ahman said. "When did you change your mind?"

"Tony's funeral."

Gunfire, three short bursts of an automatic weapon, broke up the discussion and sent the three men sprawling on their bellies. "Anybody hurt?" Tad whispered.

"Wasn't even aimed at us," Myron said.

They slithered a couple yards toward the road for a better look, keeping cover behind rocks and bushes. The source of the bullets was obvious: a militia trooper, equipped for combat, stood in the middle of the road pointing a Ruger Mini-14 at the other side. He shouted something. Two television cameramen stood, turned and hauled off for points west, crashing through brush, retreating in panic.

"Hmph," Ahman said. "In an hour there'll be a dozen more news hounds here. Hold on, I feel a tickle." He reached into a zippered pants pocket and pulled out a cell phone. "Yeah, Murph ... You got us plotted perfect. It was about seventy-five yards downhill and a little south of our position ... No, I don't think he was trying to kill them, just scare hell out of them. I think he succeeded."

The FBI agent listened to what were apparently instructions from his boss. "Yeah ... Makes sense ... Where? ... Okay ... Gotcha ... Two-thirty, an hour and fifteen minutes from now."

"Here's the deal," Ahman said. "Agents are going to create a diversion down the road about 200 yards. Fire some weapons into the dirt, make a lot of noise. Hopefully, the militia in this area will converge down there, leaving this area open for us to scramble down the hill and across the road."

"Sounds good to me," Tad said.

"Wait a second," Myron said. "Denny's trying to reach me." He pulled his own cell phone from his pocket. "Yeah, Denny ... Oh, Jesus ... You're right. We gotta do something ... I'll call you back in thirty minutes ... We'll figure something out. Hang in there, buddy."

"Your son-in-law?"

"Right. We have exactly twenty-nine and a half minutes now to come up with a way to get Denny and Darlene out of there or there's a good chance we won't ever see them again. They've been holding Darlene, maybe as some kind of hostage. They found Stark and Flint's bodies, and they figured out the helicopter snatched Mrs. Coburg. They're madder than hell. Denny thinks they may be on to him. Only place he can call is from the crapper. Guy can only take so many shits before they start looking at you funny."

Ahman was on his radio already. "Murph, change of plans." The conversation lasted ten minutes, with Murphy doing most of the talking, interrupted by Ahman passing questions to Myron. "Where's Darlene now?"

"Hiding in the cow barn on the old Schwabisch farm."

"She okay?"

"Okay for a gal who's gonna give me a grandchild in five months."

"Got it, Murph," Ahman concluded. "1800 exactly. Three and a half hours from now. We all got our work cut out for us."

He gathered his two troops around his map. "Here's the new plan, fellas. Fortunately, we'll get a lift from the National Guard. As soon as you pass the word to Denny, we start heading that way."

Twenty-four hours without sleeping, fifteen hours without eating, on top of twenty years of soft academic living, Tad wasn't convinced he could handle the task ahead. But he had no choice. Back into the woods they went.

They crouched and crawled along the sides of steep hills, avoiding the eas-ier-going through the cleared and tillable lands on the tops of hills and the grazing land at the bottom. After two hours of that, they looked down on the Schwabisch farm, situated on a small rise above the North Fork of the Midewi-win. A wooden, pre-Depression house needed paint as badly as the Coburg house. It was occupied, but not by the elderly Schwabisches. Two youngsters of primary school age were tossing a Frisbee and giggling. A man, presumably the father, was unloading grocery sacks from a late model Blazer. The cow barn was between the house and the creek. Several other tattered outbuildings were scattered on the weed-choked site.

Myron hunched over his radio. "You there? ... Everybody okay? ... We'll catch up with you in the barn in about a half hour. Then we wait ... Diversion starts at five. We'll hear lots of shooting in the southeast, down by the Riedling place. Give 'em time to move troops to the shooting. Our bus arrives at six ... Wish we could move it up, but the chopper has to come from Milwaukee ... We have to be down by that old feed trough beside the creek ten minutes before that. By seven o'clock we'll be showered and eating steak, with a six-pack of Bud for each of us. Way to go, buddy. Piece of cake."

Tad's thigh and butt muscles were screaming for mercy, but held up. In just over a half hour they were in the musty cow barn, last used by cows five years earlier and slowly succumbing to dry rot. Darlene and Myron embraced, the many issues of the past eclipsed by their present peril. Ahman was introduced, and Denny told him he didn't look at all like the grubby monster that all feds were supposed to look like, according to militia doctrine.

On schedule, the shooting began about a mile to the southeast. According to plan, government weapons were to be pointed harmlessly above the militia's heads and into the hillside. Militia weapons could be assumed to be aimed at the agents. The sound of vehicles starting and roaring toward the fire fight cheered the group in the cow barn.

The sound of a helicopter, fifteen minutes before schedule, attracted their attention. Through a broken window they saw not one but three helicopters circling like moths above the one-sided fire fight near the Riedling farm. "Wouldn't you know," Ahman said. "CNN, ABC and NBC, if my guess is correct. CBS will be here in a few minutes. Just hope they don't run into each other."

Almost on cue, a fireball enveloped one of them, maybe even the same chopper that had rescued Ruth Coburg. One second later the blast rattled the barn. Pieces of metal fell from the flaming helicopter. The other two circled the scene, providing gruesome live coverage to a couple hundred million Americans and more around the world.

Ahman was on the radio instantly. "Murph, Murph, what the hell happened? ... Holy balls ... Okay, call me right back."

"Jesus," he said. "They aren't sure, but they believe it was a shoulder-fired surface-to-air missile." That information apparently reached the other two helicopters, because they banked and ran.

Denny hugged his sobbing wife. Myron and Tad gawked. "I don't believe it," Myron said.

"I guess if Islamic terrorists can have those kinds of weapons, there's no reason these guys can't get their hands on some," Ahman said.

"I just fucking don't believe it."

"I don't think the second amendment right to bear arms was meant to include surface-to-air missiles," Tad said.

"These people don't make that distinction," Ahman said. "Denny, did you ever see any weapons like that around here?"

"No, just small arms and a few grenades. But it doesn't surprise me, knowing the minds of some of those crazies."

They leaned against the wall, which bore only traces of whitewash from milking days. Denny found a moldy bale of hay for Darlene to sit on. The shooting had stopped, and they heard sirens in the distance. "Looked to me like the debris fell inside the compound, which means the fire and rescue people won't get to it, not that there's a chance anyone survived," Myron said.

Ahman was back on the radio. "Yeah, sure, Murph. I understand. No point in making a big target out of five people and the chopper crew. But we can't stay here long. Mrs. Wurzburg is supposed to be sleeping upstairs in the farmhouse. They'll catch on and word will go out and we'll have a hundred loony militia on our tail. Matter of fact, we better be out of here real quick ... Okay. Call me when you've got something."

They looked at Ahman, hoping for a deliverance plan, afraid there wasn't one. There wasn't. "We gotta get out. If we can find our way back to Norse Road, we'll let Murphy figure a way to get us across. Myron, lead the way."

The banks of the creek offered the only cover from eyes around the farmhouse. The route had obvious drawbacks. For 200 yards, five people waded, hunched over, through muddy water, often up to their knees. With Myron holding one arm and Denny the other, Darlene and her fetus made it. When the stream rounded a small hill, the farm disappeared from view, and they took cover on the bank under a willow tree.

"No point carrying around a couple pounds of water," Myron said, suggesting they all take their boots off, pour the water out and wring out their socks. Darlene's sneakers each yielded a half cup of dirty water.

"How far to Norse Road?" Ahman asked.

"Half mile, maybe a little more," Myron said. "Won't be easy going though. I shot an eight-point buck just over that ridge a couple years ago. Damn near killed me dragging that sucker out."

"Time to check in again." Ahman crouched over his radio, muttering at some length. He signed off. "No new ideas from that bunch. Best they can do is keep up the noise. Murphy knows exactly where we are, and they'll burn up a lot of ammunition on the other side of the compound. But if Moses and his people are any good at all, they'll figure it's just diversion and start looking for us where there's no shooting. Like here."

Ahman unbuckled his pistol belt and handed it to Tad. "No, thanks," Tad said.

"Take it, goddamn it. There's a couple hundred freaking idiots all around us trying to kill us. You're not going to hell because you saved my life, or Myron's or Denny's or Darlene's. Take my word for it." Tad hesitated, and buckled the pistol belt around his waist.

Darlene was wearing jeans and a green cotton, short-sleeved maternity top. Denny gave her his dungaree shirt to save her from the worst of the thorns and mosquitoes. The half mile to the hill overlooking Norse Road took over an hour to travel. "How you doing, kiddo?" Myron asked.

"Doing fine, daddy. I've got your genes."

In the twilight, Tad could see Myron's chest swell. *The guy could've used more of those strokes over the years. He'd be a different Myron today.*

The hillside between them and the road had been logged in recent years and wasn't as dense as some they had traveled. It was nearly dark, but from their cover on the top, 100 yards above the road, they could see militia patrolling, armed individuals spaced about fifty yards apart, their mission, obviously, to watch for anyone attempting to cross in either direction.

Ahman spent another twenty minutes in murmured radio conversation with Murphy and other federal officials, trying to devise tactics to safely cross the two-lane road. Planning was complicated by the fact that a number of separate but equal government agencies were involved, and by the fact that decision-making was now taking place in Washington, D.C. Further complicating planning was the fact that similar standoffs were happening in Alabama and Montana. There were also reports of militia conclaves operating in Idaho, New Mexico and Georgia.

The director of the FBI and the head of BATF were conferring almost constantly by phone from their respective Washington headquarters a few blocks apart. Treasury, Defense, the Drug Enforcement Agency, governors of three states and U.S. senators on key committees all insisted on at least a c.c. role in the deliberations. The U.S. Attorney General had left a dinner with the Vice President to return to his office and monitor developments. Any decisions had to be approved by him. The President, on Air Force One bound for Texas, was kept aware of breaking developments by his security advisors, who had to be briefed regularly by the National Security Agency. An unnamed source in the Central Intelligence Agency would neither confirm nor deny reports of links between the militia organizations and Al Qaeda. The Secretary of Defense scheduled a news briefing for 9 PM Eastern. A major objective seemed to be avoiding a snafu. The overriding concern in all planning, of course, was the 200 to 300 news media camped in the three states, all facing late evening and early morning news deadlines, desperate for tidbits, preferably exclusive, and clamoring for action against the evil fiends who had shot down one of their own.

"Yeah okay, Murph. I've got a fresh battery. Call me if you hear anything. But something's gotta happen in the morning. The Wurzburgs know more about what's going on inside than the entire United States government. Besides, we haven't eaten in twenty-four hours and Mrs. Wurzburg is four months pregnant and should be eating for two. Out. Shit."

The night went as well as could be expected for five unprepared campers. A stiff breeze from the southwest kept mosquitoes in hiding. Myron crept away to fill water bottles from a spring he knew about, and returned to report no sign of militia patrols. Still, the men agreed to two-hour shifts, with two men sleeping and two alert. They donated their dungaree tops to keep Darlene and her baby warm; she slept with Denny's thigh for a pillow. His leg slept the soundest of all.

Tad awoke to a distinctly low-tech sound: a horse clip-clopping on the Norse Road blacktop. It was almost 5 AM, and he was the last one awake. "What in the world?"

The road was still in the shadow of the hill where they had spent the night. But there was plenty of light to pick out the black, two-wheeled buggy pulled by a dark Morgan horse. A black-hatted young man, perhaps fourteen, was at the reins. "Amish," Denny whispered. "That's the sixth one that's gone by in the last half hour."

"Where do you suppose they're going?"

"I don't know. But they've come from a long way. There's only two or three Amish families within five miles of here."

The lad with the buggy had just disappeared on their left when a light blue van showed up on the right. A woman in blue cotton dress, with an archaic white cap on her head was driving. A girl about ten, similarly dressed, sat beside her. The van was moving at approximately five miles an hour, the speed of the horse-drawn buggy.

"Mennonites," Denny explained. The van passed a patrolling soldier, and the women waved to him merrily. He threw them a finger.

That van was followed by another containing a woman in a Mennonite cap and two small children. Then a wagon drawn by a pair of Belgian draft horses. A boy in black hat and girl in black dress piloted the rig.

Ahman was on the radio. "Murph, do you know what we're seeing? ... Uh-huh ... I'll be damned ... Okay, we'll stay put. But come up with something will you? We're hungry and tired and dirty ... Out."

He gathered Myron, Tad and the Wurzburgs close and explained, "It seems we're watching a peaceful protest. They intend to keep parading until it's over. Murphy's waiting instructions from Washington, and nobody out there knows what the hell to do. A dozen different agencies, all covering their asses and looking for publicity at the same time."

"So we sit here twiddling our thumbs," Darlene said.

"Not entirely. News media are congregated about a mile down the road, where it bends to the east. Apparently that's where the best camera angles are. They're having a ball shooting the Amish and Mennonites as they go by, trying to hitch rides, looking for sound bites. Amish aren't saying much, which makes the news folks even crazier."

"Do you suppose this gives us the diversion we need to get across?" Tad asked.

"Don't know, maybe if …"

"Holy shit," Myron said. He was looking at a militia trooper, on the road and twenty yards south. The soldier had his Ruger Mini sighted on the back of an Amish youngster, riding a black pony. Myron took off down the hill. He slid to a stop halfway down, rested his Weatherby on a tree stump and aimed at the trooper. Too late. One shot and the boy was on the ground with an ugly wound in his thigh. Myron fired once and the trooper went down, blood streaming from his back.

Ahman grabbed Denny. "Take your wife. Other side of the hill. North for fifty yards or so. When I whistle, you head for the road. I'll cover you. Stay low and get your asses across the road."

"But—"

"Move. Now." They did.

"Tad, halfway down the hill. You and Myron cover the other flank." Tad could see Ahman urgently calling for Murphy as he raced north. He knew that agents would be on the scene in three or four minutes, five tops, drawn by the shooting, if not by Ahman's call. Whether the agents could get permission from Washington in time to do something useful was another matter. Tad pulled the revolver from its holster. One part of him prayed he wouldn't have to use it. The other part wished he had Ahman's AR-15 and a flack jacket to supplement the moss-covered sandstone boulder that he and Myron cringed behind.

"How you fixed on ammo?" he asked Myron.

"Eight rounds. You?"

"One full load and that's it."

"Don't waste them on long shots. Wait 'til they're almost here and shoot for the chest."

The wait wasn't long. Two Ruger-armed troopers were coming at them from the south, twenty yards away, dashing from tree to tree in practiced maneuvers. Myron aimed at one tree, and squeezed off a shot the instant the trooper appeared. Bull's-eye!

Now there was shooting up the road. They turned and saw Ahman kneeling and firing off short bursts into the woods, covering Denny and Darlene as they scrambled across the road.

"He needs help," Myron said. "Keep this guy occupied." He took off, and the second trooper stepped from behind the tree and pointed his Ruger at him.

Tad stood, shot and tore a chunk out of a medium-sized oak. The trooper had to choose between a rapidly retreating Myron and Tad, a closer, stationary and more imminent threat. The moment of indecision was enough. His young face, his frightened and hate-filled eyes, seared into Tad's memory as none of the anonymous Vietcong ever had. The priest's second round caught him in the gut.

By now all thought had left him. Instinct controlled. Tad ran to the downed trooper and grabbed his Ruger, then dashed straight for the road. He was over it and in the ditch on the west side, gasping for air and thanking God for safety and forgiveness for his action and mercy for the dead trooper's soul. The shooting continued. The war wasn't over. He crouched and lurched along the ditch. He caught up with Myron, who had made it across the road and into the ditch.

"Jesus, reverend, am I glad to see you! Ahman's on the other side, pinned in that culvert twenty yards up. It ain't big enough to crawl through, and every time he sticks his head up somebody takes a shot. I got one round left."

Tad handed him the Ruger. "Reverend, you are a miracle worker. God bless the shit out of you! I'm going up there." Myron crawled away, using every inch of protection the ditch offered. Tad followed.

They came to the culvert. "Ahman," Myron said softly. "On three, up and over. Got it?"

"Got it."

"One. Two. Three." Myron stood and sprayed the woods, twenty-five yards from the road, drawing return fire and giving him his targets. Ahman stood, shooting and backpedaling across the road. In seconds he tumbled into the grassy ditch. The shooting stopped.

For a long minute, the only sounds were lungs pumping oxygen into the participants. Then the rightful inhabitants of the woods—birds, squirrels, chipmunks, frogs, crickets—picked up their chatter, incensed at the noisy intrusion into their domain.

"Everybody all right?" Ahman asked.

"A couple scratches is all," said Myron.

Tad saw that it was one god-awful scratch that was producing so much blood on Myron's left shoulder.

"Where's Denny and Darlene?"

"Here," came Denny's voice behind them. They were in a deep ditch formed by the rivulet that flowed through the culvert, not comfortable but well pro-tected.

"Darlene okay?"

"I'm okay," she said. Tad saw her, but wasn't convinced.

"That kid's gonna have one hell of a story in show and tell," Myron said.

"Kid's gotta get born first," Denny said.

"Son of a bitch, would you look at that." said Ahman. Driving down the road in tight procession were three Amish buggies, followed by two Mennonite-driven vans, followed by two more Amish buggies. The first two went on to attend to the youngster that had been shot off his pony. The rest pulled up directly above the tired and hungry fugitives in the ditch. They proceeded to lay out on the side of the road a checkered table cloth and a picnic, including cold fried chicken, German potato salad, three-bean salad, rolls, butter, lemonade, coffee and chocolate cake. It wasn't even six o'clock in the morning.

CHAPTER 21

That day's news reports on the "Millen County Standoff" had to begin with the end of the shootout: five weary warriors having a picnic on the side of the road with Amish and Mennonite women and children. "The men are busy with milking," one woman explained. "They'll be along. Cows can't wait, you know." Their caravan had grown to over a dozen horse-drawn vehicles, three more Amish youngsters on ponies and five vans with Mennonites. Some had started the afternoon before and had come from as far as fifteen miles away.

And since the women had no way of knowing how many hungry combatants there would be on either side, they had prepared plenty. It wasn't exactly the miracle of the loaves and fishes, but there was something for most of the voracious journalists. The militia had disappeared, and for all anyone knew, they were concealed in the woods observing the picnic hungrily through binoculars.

EMTs were on the scene quickly. The first to arrive were Janice Wilkins and Doug Merton who had ministered to Tony Dett on that fateful night. They tended to the Amish boy with the gunshot wound in the leg, and drove him off to Tri-County Memorial Hospital.

Myron went in the next ambulance, protesting that "it's just a scratch." Darlene, accompanied by her husband, was transported to the hospital for a checkup, although she claimed to be feeling fine after the ordeal. Four black SUVs with armed agents escorted them. The three fallen militia were pronounced dead at the scene.

Media, of course, were clamoring for interviews of Tad and Ahman—or at the very least, some decent sound bites. But FBI and BATF agents in dark jackets formed a wall and ushered them into a black SUV with smoked glass windows, and they were hustled off to the government command post. A news conference was promised for four that afternoon, in plenty of time for the evening newscasts.

Tad walked into the big tent in the FBI command post and was engulfed and nearly choked. Miriam's arms wrapped in a vise-grip around his neck. "Oh my darling Tad, I was worried sick. Thank God you're all right." Her face was wet, her hair in his eyes. Tad had a sudden, sinking feeling that nothing had changed in thirty-four years, neither her flair for the melodramatic, nor his feelings toward her.

Tad held her. "Everybody's all right," he said. "Darlene, her baby, Denny, Myron, all fine."

Her sobs trailed off and her grip loosened. "Miriam," he said, "let's, well, let's take one thing at a time. This insane standoff is a long way from over. Noon today. Debriefing. The government has to know what we know, and especially what Darlene and Denny and Myron know. There's still a bunch of armed and crazy men in there, and a couple dozen or more Holy Scripture folks, our neighbors. We don't know if they're there because they want to be, or if they're prisoners or Doctor Don's zombies or what."

Tad found an FBI agent to take him to the rectory in Red Oak for a badly needed shower, shave and fresh clothes. On the way, they stopped and found his car, which he had taken such pains to hide a week earlier. Tires were slashed, windows smashed and "papist" spray-painted on top and sides.

The debriefing was held in a conference room at Tri-County Memorial Hospital. The hospital dietary department had put together a hefty luncheon of roast turkey and all the fixings. Two large poultry feasts in a space of six hours might have seemed gluttonous. But after the erratic eating pattern of the past four days, Tad gulped it down, as did Miriam, Darlene, Denny, Myron and a dozen FBI and BATF agents.

At Tad's request, Attorney Killian was there. After apple pie ala mode, Murphy switched on a tape recorder on the middle of the table. "Denny," he began, "any idea how many soldiers Sheriff Moses, er, Major Moses ..."

"Holy Moses."

"Holy Moses. How many troops does he have in there?"

"He started with forty-five, plus himself. Take away me, Stark and Flint, and the three that got shot this morning, you're down to forty guys altogether."

"That's all?"

"That's it," Denny said.

"What in God's name made them think they could shoot down a helicopter and then defend themselves against the whole U.S. government with just forty-five men?"

"They claimed it was justified. The chopper was trespassing."

"Where did these guys come from?"

"Most of them from around here, a few from down south."

"Do you know them?"

"Most of them. Ordinary guys. Guys in the sheriff's department. A couple are in the National Guard with me. A few are farmers. One or two work in the warehouse at Distribute Dot Com. Some are between jobs."

"Married?"

"Some are. Most aren't."

"What made them get involved in such a violent and hateful business?"

"Because they're violent and hateful people."

"I don't understand," Murphy said. "If they're ordinary guys, why …"

"They're losers."

"Like me," Myron said with a grin.

"Yeah, like you, Pops," Denny said, with a solid jab at Myron's good shoulder.

"I know those guys pretty good," Myron said. "Every one of them thought they was shafted along the way. Old man ran away or was in prison. Kicked out of school or kids laughed at them 'cause they were poor or ugly. Couldn't get dates. Couldn't hold a job. Along comes Holy Moses. Tells them it's all the government's fault. Makes sense to them. It did to me. Next thing you know they're saying 'yes sir' and 'no sir' and firing a Ruger Mini at silhouettes on the side of a hill."

Murphy refilled his coffee cup. "How do they decide who's the enemy. I mean, you can't hate everybody."

"Yes you can." Denny said. "Start your list with the DNR. Anything that gets in the way of hunting and fishing the way they think they have a right to is enemy number one. Or anyone that takes your tax money and doesn't use it for fixing potholes in Millen County. It goes on from there. Once you work up a good hate for the DNR and IRS, then you can really get rolling. It's easy to find people to hate—anybody who's different."

"Amish?"

"Especially the Amish. How different can you get?"

"Denny, why did you get involved with those folks? You don't seem the type."

"Holy Moses got me involved. I just went along, because being a patrolman in the Millen County sheriff's department is a damn good job. I didn't want to lose it."

"Are you a member of the Holy Scripture, the, ah, Holy Scripture Universal Church of the Lord?"

"Stark and Flint told me to hang around with them, report anything suspicious."

"And did you?"

"Hell no. I didn't know what they meant by suspicious. They're just decent folks, a little crazy on the Jesus stuff, but harmless. Stark and Flint, now, they acted suspicious, but who do I report them to, Holy Moses?"

"Denny, thanks," Murphy said. "We'll probably want to talk more about this. Most important right now is the safety of the Holy Scripture folks. I gotta tell you, I'm stumped. Anybody have any ideas?"

Tad had one, which he outlined without any conviction as to its efficacy. FBI and BATF were even more skeptical.

The biggest arguments were over the makeup of the delegation. In light of Tad's recent adventures in the land of Major Moses and Doctor Don, and because he had most recently spoken to the two of them, he was the unanimous choice to lead the group. But he would much rather have been, let's say, drifting around in some galaxy far from the Milky Way.

Richard Jensen, pastor of Our Redeemer Lutheran Church, was the most reluctant to join the delegation, citing his wife's health and his approaching retirement. But Tad convinced him that it was a chance to do something for peace and for the safety of fellow Christians, perhaps his last opportunity in his official capacity. The pastor of the United Church of Christ joined eagerly. Others—pastors of United Methodist, Episcopal, Baptist and Evangelical Free churches in the area—were skeptical, but agreed. The Presbyterian pastor was on vacation.

The FBI and BATF agents insisted that at least a couple of well-armed representatives of each agency accompany the group. "Absolutely not," Tad said. "You want to get us all killed?" The issue was resolved by the U.S. Attorney General, who ruled with Tad when he learned about the faith-based nature of the delegation.

If the news media had its way, the procession would have stretched a quarter of a mile or more. Tad was adamant. "One print reporter—and that will be Bruce Bestman of the *Millen County Reporter*—and one television reporter. You guys decide who that will be." The FBI and BATF backed him on that, and the media compromised, with Diane Sawyer and an ABC cameraman serving as the pool for electronic journalists.

Miriam, Myron, Denny and Darlene were left off the delegation, on the assumption that it would mean instant death if the militia laid eyes on them.

All those arrangements took the rest of the day and well into the night.

Denny had advised that the shortest route to Major Moses and Doctor Don was to take Potlicker Hollow Road north from Town Line Road. It would be about a quarter mile walk, and they would find a well-traveled dirt road branching off to the left into the woods. They would pass the re-conversion facility, and after another hundred yards, they'd be at the headquarters tent, where Tad and Miriam had met with the two. They guessed the directions weren't necessary, as sentries would certainly intercept and escort them.

That was correct. Within a half hour, the pastors, representing a major portion of Christendom in Millen County, were seated in a hastily arranged semicircle of folding chairs around Doctor Don's desk. Major Moses stood beside the desk. Following introductions, Doctor Don began. "Well, lady and gentlemen," acknowledging Pastor Barbara Sedgewick of St. Matthew Episcopal Church, "I would like to offer you some coffee, but Major Moses and I are unusually busy this morning, and we must move this meeting along without some of the amenities. How can we be of assistance?"

Major Moses seemed more interested in Diane Sawyer and her cameraman, and more concerned about his appearance on television, than on any substance in the meeting. "Doctor Don," Tad said, "when we talked here in your tent last week, you told me all you want is for you and your people to be left alone to practice your faith and bring Jesus to all outside who will receive him. We respect that.

"And Major Moses, you told me essentially the same thing, with a more secular perspective. You want to be free of government interference in your lives. Did I understand you correctly?"

"Uh, yes, well, I guess that's about right." Tad had caught Moses gawking at Diane Sawyer and thinking about who knows what.

Tad continued, "The United States government may have some different thoughts, but that's between you and them. It's none of our business. Our business here today is the welfare of the people of the Holy Scripture Universal Church of the Lord."

"We're fine," said Dr. Don.

"That's nice to hear. But we're more worried about what's ahead. You see, given the tension between Major Moses' organization and the government, especially in light of the incident involving the helicopter and the deaths of its pilot and the NBC cameraman, we're afraid it could be rather dangerous here for you and your church members."

"The Lord will protect us."

"I agree. But we would like the opportunity to talk to your church families and explain the potential hazards. We'd like to propose to them that they return to their homes, at least temporarily. When tensions subside and it becomes safer here, they could return."

"No. Absolutely not."

Pastor Sedgewick stepped in. "Doctor Don, we have no intention of trying to lure them out of your flock and into ours, if that's what you're worried about. But we think they have a right to know the perils they face."

Doctor Don stood, and the camera swung to him. "'Lo, I will bring a nation upon you from afar, O house of Israel, saith the Lord: it is a mighty nation, it is an ancient nation, a nation whose language thou knowest not, neither understandest what they say. Their quiver is as an open sepulcher, they are all mighty men. And they shall eat up thine harvest and thy bread, which thy sons and thy daughters should eat: they shall eat up thy flocks and thine herds: they shall eat up thy vines and thy fig trees: they shall impoverish thy fenced cities, wherein thou trustedst, with the sword. Nevertheless in those days, saith the Lord, I will not make a full end with you.'" Doctor Don sat heavily on the small chair behind his desk.

Pastor Jensen was the first to think of something. "Um, yes, Jeremiah, I believe."

"Chapter five, verses fifteen to eighteen," said the Holy Scripture leader.

"Indeed. It's, ah, pretty hard to argue with Jeremiah," said Jensen.

"Does that mean we can meet with your people to explain the dangers they face?" Tad asked.

"Well, maybe ..."

"Alone, by individual families?"

Doctor Don looked at Holy Moses. "Major, what do you think about that?"

The major, addressing Diane Sawyer, with occasional sideways glances at the camera, said, "Obviously, the safety and well-being of the people we are charged to protect is our paramount responsibility. We are men of peace. But if the United States government, in direct violation of the Constitution and all the principles this great nation stands for, chooses to make war on its own citizens, so be it. We will have no choice but to defend ourselves. Therefore, the answer is 'yes.'" He stood and smiled at the assembled pastors and Diane Sawyer, with another glance at the camera lens. "Men and women of God, you may discuss the approaching hostilities with the sons and daughters of the Holy Scripture. If any of them choose to seek safety elsewhere until the battle is won, they may do so with our blessing."

It was late afternoon before the convoy was ready to depart the Holy Scripture compound. Each of the pastors had met with one or two of the families individually, and parents had met with their children to talk it over. Then the families met together, without the pastors, and with much furious flipping of pages in their Bibles. Bruce Bestman, Diane Sawyer and her cameraman roamed among the family groups, like teachers monitoring an exam.

Finally, Orin Kempten, a clerk at Herb's Ace Hardware in Bremerton, spoke for the group. "It is not without a great deal of misgivings that we have chosen to leave this paradise temporarily. We pray for a speedy return, and we take comfort in the 131st Psalm. 'Lord, my heart is not haughty, nor mine eyes lofty: neither do I exercise myself in great matters, or in things too high for me.'"

It took two hours for the families to pack their possessions into their cars and vans and spruce up the abandoned farm homes they had camped in. The exodus from their Holy Scripture "paradise" was led by Holy Moses himself, biblical white hair catching the breeze, walking, engaged in earnest conversation with Diane Sawyer, following up on her hint of a one-on-one interview with Barbara Walters. Doctor Don rode behind them in his sky blue Ford Ranger pickup.

At the corner of Potlicker Hollow Road and Town Line Road, they were greeted by a thousand cheering residents of Millen County, including a pep band quickly assembled from West Charleton High School students, borrowed for the moment from their summer jobs. Media were in seventh heaven. The tumultuous scene and interviews of everyone who would consent to a microphone in their face were beamed to the world from fifty vans with satellite dishes atop.

Holy Moses and Doctor Don convened a news conference before returning, per prior agreement with the Attorney General, to their nation in the woods.

The major proclaimed his vision of a society in which every citizen may live a life free of government bondage. For Doctor Don's turn, he read from the Book of Samuel about the bad things that would happen to the house of Eli and Israel's defeat at the hands of the Philistines and the loss of the ark of the covenant and the death of Eli, and soon the reporters stopped taking notes and cameramen switched off their equipment and people started drifting away, except for the members of his congregation, who listened raptly.

CHAPTER 22

"I appreciate your loan of Father Donovan. He did a nice job. People in the parishes liked him. How did you manage to get along without him?"

"Got a temp from Manpower, and it worked out great. Matter of fact, I'm planning to hire a lay person as my full-time secretary and send Donovan to a parish. Short-handed as we are, it makes no sense for a priest to be sitting behind a desk, and Frank would rather be out doing real priest work anyway."

Tad and Bishop Ardito were sipping Brunello in the Edgewater Hotel's Admiralty Room, overlooking Madison's Lake Mendota. A few pink cumulus clouds added character to the clear early evening, late July sky. Sailboats, powerboats, canoes and kayaks flecked the blue, white-capped lake. "Italy's a beautiful country," Tad said. "But my home state in the summer ranks right up there."

"No argument there. How's your mother doing?"

"She'll be okay. She's a tough old farm wife, but that helicopter ride scared her half to death. She'd never been off the ground more than the roof of the barn. I'm looking into a retirement home in West Charleton for her. Meantime, St. Brendan's rectory hasn't had better cooking in decades. She likes it there, and we have time to talk about things a mother and son should've been talking about over the years."

"What about the farm?"

"She'll get it back, but it won't be easy or soon. Killian said two other elderly members of the Holy Scripture church deeded over their farms a few years ago. They're dead now, and their kids are suing."

The waiter came and announced his recommendations. The bishop chose the flounder. Tad ordered filet mignon, medium rare.

"You think the militia will ever surrender? Tad asked.

"The feds have had them surrounded for over a week. But they need to do something soon. If the militia had one Stinger missile they may have more. And news media are working themselves into a frenzy. Every night NBC News kicks off with a live report from Millen County, Wisconsin. The governor may have to call out the National Guard."

"I'm still having a hard time coming to grips with such intense hatred in America," Tad said.

"Hate goes all the way back to Cain and Abel. Hate builds self-esteem at the expense of others. Your religion or politics is right and everybody else's is wrong. So you hate them."

"What about Doctor Don? He's spent enough time with the Bible to know the message of Christianity is love, not hate."

"Power. And status. They're frightening things. I didn't realize it until I became a bishop. Have you any idea how easy it is to start believing people when they call you 'Your Excellency?' Laughing at your jokes when they aren't funny? Hanging on your every word as if it came from God Himself? Ooh, that feels good! Doctor Don probably started down that path when he started calling himself 'doctor,' and didn't have the sense or willpower to turn back."

"I can understand that," Tad said.

"Problem is, not enough of your friends in Rome understand."

Entrees arrived, and the priest and the bishop attended to them. Two or three dinners at the Sandstone last fall had broken Tad of the European habit of eating with his fork rounded side up. The steak was perfect.

"What's next for you, Tad?"

"That's what I was going to ask you."

"I'm giving you your choice: Red Oak or Rome. It's up to you."

"My people need me here."

"Indeed they do. And the church needs you in Rome."

"But I killed a man."

"We've been through all that. Call it affirmative action. Creating diversity on the faculty of North American College. A priest who's met hate face-to-face, who's seen how ordinary people can mix malice and holiness so they can't tell one from the other."

"Who takes over my parishes, Frank Donovan?"

"No, I need him for a big suburban parish. I've got a priest coming from Nigeria in a month. I'll put him in Red Oak."

❦   ❦   ❦

Tad hadn't seen Miriam since the parade from the Holy Scripture compound three weeks before. Nor Myron or Denny or Darlene, for that matter.
He was thinking that a reunion and party were in order. Brats and beer on the
back deck of the rectory seemed fun. Miriam beat him to it. Dinner, but just
the two of them, at The Timbers in Platteville. It might have been inevitable,
but it was precisely the event that Tad had hoped to avoid.

For good reason. In her early fifties, and despite three decades of dysfunctional family life, she was still the eighteen-year-old beauty he'd achingly said
good-bye to on the Baumer front porch, the yearbook picture he'd carried in
his helmet in Vietnam, the face that buzzed around his head like an annoying
fly through thirty years of celibate priesthood. The distress he saw in her face at
the chicken display in the IGA last fall was gone.

Tuesday night, The Timbers was not crowded. Their table was against a
wall. Tad wished for more people around to discourage the conversation that
he was afraid was coming.

"How are the girls?"

"Back home. They had a good time with their uncle, and watched the whole
thing on TV. They're actually pretty proud of their father, which is an absolute
first for that."

"Darlene and the baby?"

"Doing well. I insisted she have a complete checkup up at Gundersen Lutheran in La Crosse. No problems. Ultrasounds show the baby's a boy. Denny
and Myron say they'll take him deer hunting this fall, but his grandma says
he'll be too young."

"How about Myron?"

"He's big man in the sheriff's department. When the state took over the
department, Myron and Denny were the only experienced deputies left.
They're both lieutenants now. Denny's in charge of the traffic patrol. Myron's
in charge of dispatching, jail, records and administration. Big raises for both of
them."

"Myron must be pretty happy," Tad said.

"Myron's not happy. He calls me every day. Wants me to drop the divorce
and move back with him. Every day I tell him 'no.'"

"But Myron's a changed man. No more violence. He's on the wagon. How
many times can you tell him 'no' before he reverts to the old Myron?"

"That's his problem, not mine," Miriam said.

"How can you say that? He's the father of your children, and for the first time they have a father they can respect."

"Kids can respect their daddy and still not live with him."

"But Myron saved your life. Our lives. He loves you."

Miriam picked at her salad. "So? He's just going to have to find someone else to love."

Tad reflected on his changed role as a priest. A generation ago, he would have urged the couple to remain together at all costs. Today, that was technically the official position, but in America only the most atavistic priests held to it when it was clear one party's love was irretrievable.

"Besides," she said, "I intend to marry you."

Could his rural parishes get along without him? They certainly did before he arrived. Could they get along with a Nigerian priest? There were enough good people in each of the parishes to overcome the tongue-waggers and see that it happened.

A bigger question was "Could Tad get along without his parishes?" And if he stayed, could he get the job done with Miriam circling around the edges of his emotions for the next twenty-five years? Bishop Ardito gave him until Labor Day to decide—Rome or Red Oak—after which the bishop would decide for him.

Myron seemed to be settling into his new, respectable life. His three daughters were finding more to like about him all the time. And he was loosening up, becoming a father, not the master disciplinarian that he once fancied himself. He still implored Miriam to let bygones be bygones, and she was having none of it. She maintained that he was still a handsome dude, especially in a police uniform, and it would probably not be long before an adoring Millen County lass caught his eye, so don't feel sorry for Myron.

Tad's talks with Miriam were long and inconclusive: tears and laughter, recollections of happier times, catching up on the thirty-four intervening years. Tad learned, for example, that Miriam was Millen County Unified Library System's best customer, with tastes running from lurid to the classics. And that in the late seventies she taught herself to speak a smidgeon of Hmong, for rudimentary communication in the emergency room with patients from the church-sponsored Hmong enclave in the northeastern part of the county. And that brandy had played a significant role in maintaining her equanimity under the conditions of trailer park living.

He told her about his life as an academician and his travels to the theological centers of the world, and the restaurants and theaters and interesting wines to be found in those centers. She admitted to no travel beyond a Greyhound ride to St. Louis and a dismal automobile trip, with three carsick daughters, to visit her brother in Denver. But, she said brightly, travel as the wife of a theology professor would be a different matter, and there must be scores of colleges looking for faculty with his credentials.

They bared their souls, as neither had since high school. She became the only living person to know about his first gun battle on the Mekong Delta, how he shut his eyes and ears and barfed his guts out on the deck of the PBR. He learned about the strange nun who would visit the convent rooms of novices in the wee hours to wake and "comfort" them, and the Mother Superior who didn't believe the terrified young sisters.

Yes, he told her, there are sick and dangerous priests, and apparently the problem wasn't confined to males. That said, he said, God created people horny, and horniness was an ongoing challenge of the celibate state, and the only workable solution he had found was staying up and awake, pacing, reading and watching TV, until exhaustion overcame it. She told Tad that he was the father of her son—well, not according to DNA, but according to her fantasy at the time of his conception.

They talked about their futures. He was as driven as he was in high school to do the right thing, if only he knew what the right thing was. She was resolved that thirty years of sadness, confined to a small town in the hills of southwestern Wisconsin, was enough. She had a lot more living to do, and her high school sweetheart was her ticket. Tad had a hard time arguing with that, partly because much of her misery could legitimately be blamed on organized religion.

Cuddling up with Miriam every night for the rest of his life was appealing. But after a half century of bachelorhood, could he make all those big and little accommodations demanded in marriage?

His conversations with the bishop kept coming back to him. The well-publicized issues—near-universal disregard of Rome's teaching on contraception, the second-class status of women in the church, celibacy and the shortage of priests—are mere symptoms of a more pernicious problem: intellectual dishonesty. Modest progress after Vatican II frozen by a papal view of the church and world stuck in John Paul II's Poland of his boyhood, a Curia devoted to papal authority and black-and-white morality, too stubborn or incapable of fresh looks at old doctrines and traditions. Is it any wonder the Vatican's influence is so meager, even among its own people? How can the church impact scientific issues of today, such as embryonic stem cell research, or even thornier questions down the road, when its reasoning on more gut-level moral issues, such as in vitro fertilization, is so shaky? Where better to work to renew the intellectual integrity of the church, but at North American College? Isn't that what universities are for? But if he didn't really believe in celibacy for the priesthood, isn't it hypocritical to cling to it himself? Could he have more influence on the church working outside the rigid constraints of the Vatican?

There was unfinished business in Wisconsin: the hundreds of still un-revved Catholics; the Bestmans, Ellen Killian, Charles and Frederick and their friends, eager for the leadership of their folk-hero priest; Rich Jensen and other Protestant colleagues, and the opportunity for a new burst of ecumenism; the challenge of stretching the minds of single-issue Catholics, such as Peter and Mary Plumm. And the dogmatic George Meiningen, with his own brand of fundamentalism. Could the Nigerian priest do the job?

The more he thought about it, and the harder he prayed, the harder the decision got. Man, did he pray! But apparently, God was not going to micro-manage this one.

CHAPTER 23

Tad clipped the microphone to his suit lapel, still not entirely sure what he would say. He looked over his audience, 300 or 400 he guessed, maybe more. He never had counted the number of bodies that could comfortably squeeze into St. Brendan's antique oak pews, no doubt fewer today than when the church was built, judging by today's wider, fast-food bottoms. All of the pews were filled, and a couple dozen men and younger women stood in the back. Most faces were familiar. Some had been carved into his memory by the events four years earlier that had jammed Millen County into American history books. Some he recognized as expressionless regulars from weekend masses at his three parishes. He once knew their names—most of them. No longer, but he still felt the bonds of pastor and flock. And how he missed them!

The last time St. Brendan's was this full for a funeral was for young Tony Dett, which was the last time Tad had stood before a group with so little inkling of what would come from his own mouth.

"First of all, I want to thank your pastor, Father Sam, for giving me this chance to talk to you today." The Nigerian-born priest, seated at the side of the altar, nodded and smiled. He had needed no persuasion. "So much has happened since I walked into St. Brendan's rectory that dark December afternoon five years ago." Tad walked past the casket and started down the middle aisle. He spotted Mrs. Koch, the cook, halfway back, her walker in the aisle beside her. He gave her bony shoulder a slight squeeze. "So good of you to come today, Mrs. Koch." Her tiny smile suggested his recognition might be the highlight of her year.

Charles and Frederick, the partners and entrepreneurs in the exotic world of bovine genomics, were just behind Mrs. Koch. "Guys," Tad said, "I still don't understand your business, but according to the *Millen County Reporter,* you're now employing half of southwestern Wisconsin. They shook their heads, delighted at his exaggeration.

Denny and Darlene Wurzburg were directly across the aisle. Tad had visited Denny a couple times at Walter Reed Army Medical Center, where he was learning to use his prosthesis, having lost his right leg and three fingers to an improvised explosive device in Iraq. Their son, Mike, fidgeted on his left knee. Next to the Wurzbergs, Myron Dett cradled and made silly faces at a fussy infant with bright red hair, while an attractive woman with equally red hair rummaged in a blue bag for a bottle or pacifier to stave off what looked like a good cry coming on.

Tad told his erstwhile congregation, "I'd like to hug every one of you right now, but there'll be time for that at the potluck luncheon downstairs after the services. I hope you can join us there." He walked back toward the altar, prompting a brief screech from the sound system.

"In behalf of my sisters Janie and Rose, I want to thank you for coming here today to help us celebrate the life of our mother." They had made it back to West Charleton in time to say good-by to Ruth, and were seated with Betsy and Maria Dett in the front pew.

Tad spotted a contingent of elderly. "And a special thank you to Mom's friends at Quiet Manor for the enjoyment you brought her. Life on the farm didn't allow much time for friends and socializing, and I had always sensed that gaping hole in her life. My conversations with her over the past few years were filled with news about Quiet Manor, how she shared your joys and sorrows and the good times she had with you. Thank you all for being such good friends."

Those friends knew Ruth Coburg only as a frail septuagenarian. Most of the others remembered her only slightly or not at all. To them, she was simply the deceased mother of Father Tad. He set out to change that with three minutes of anecdotes covering fifty-plus years as a loving mother, dawn-to-dusk farm wife with a special empathy for sick animals, as a helpful neighbor with a particular aptitude for just the right pie for every occasion, and as the fragile resident of an assisted living and nursing home, who took her pleasure from bringing cheer to her ailing neighbors. "She finished her life on earth, living as an angel," he said.

Tad paused, wondering where his next words would lead him. "My decision four years ago to leave these three parishes and return to Rome to teach, was the most difficult I had ever made. The most difficult until then. Since that time, I've faced more forks in my life's road, just as complex, just as heart-rending. I'm relating them to you today, hoping that my experience might guide you as you face your own excruciating challenges and decisions, as I know all of you have and will.

"Those horrible events near my parents' farm, my home, were more devastating to me than combat in Vietnam. In Nam, the enemy was someone I'd never seen before and, I hate to say this, someone who didn't even look like us. In the Millen County Standoff, the enemy—if I have to use that word—was us. Our relatives, our neighbors. People different from us only in the way they viewed their government and their God. I thought when I left Millen County for Rome I could put all that behind, that it was just a tragic aberration in our history, a lesson that could never be repeated. Certainly not in a country that claims to be based on Christian principles. But I was wrong."

Tad knew that most people in the church that day were there mainly to hear him. It wasn't the media circus that Tony Dett's funeral became, but Bruce Bestman had his notebook out. If his message went beyond the walls of the church, so much the better.

"When I returned to Rome, the winds of war were stiffening in Washington. Like so many people around the world, I could not imagine that our president's bellicose rhetoric was anything more than posturing to improve his diplomatic leverage. I watched the buildup to the Iraq invasion with a fascination and a growing dread that was, perhaps, unique among my countrymen. I had experienced personally the horrors of war, both half a world away and, literally, in my own back yard. However you look at the Iraq war from a political or geopolitical standpoint, there's no denying it has been a tragedy for the people of Iraq and the United States. Our Millen County has felt it profoundly, with the deaths of two of our National Guard soldiers and severe injuries to four others. As the news from Iraq became more and more distracting and depressing, I found it more and more difficult to apply myself to my theological specialty.

"I was angry. Our Holy Father had spoken out strongly against the Iraq invasion, but to deaf ears. The Catholic Church, America's friends around the world, the United Nations and NATO, were ignored. As a result, innocent people died. Innocent people continue to die. Innocent, ordinary Iraqis and Americans will bear the scars of this war for the rest of the century.

"Perhaps the war's worst result is the chasms that have widened among the three branches of the Judeo-Christian faiths and within those faiths. In a way, we're right back where we were a thousand years ago. Muslims, Christians and

Jews recognizing the same God, with only minor variations in the way they practice their religions. And hating each other for it. Killing each other because of the way we worship the same God. Do you understand why I was angry? Why I'm still angry?"

That probably wasn't what his old friends in Wisconsin had expected from him. Tad glanced at Father Sam. Uneasy? Agreeing? Hard to tell. He spotted Rich Jensen near the back of the church. The Lutheran pastor had retired a year after Tad left the county and just months after his wife died. He was now a volunteer youth counselor at an Ogallala Sioux mission school in South Dakota and an activist in Native American causes.

"I talked with a lot of people about my concerns—fellow faculty members and seminarians in Rome, academic colleagues around the world. I spent many hours on the phone with my boss, Bishop Ardito, who had brought me back to Wisconsin five years ago and, in a way, started my middle-age zigzag to where I am today. My good friend, Pastor Rich Jensen, offered some helpful perspectives, as did your pastor, Father Sam. I spent many long hours in conversation with my high school soul mate, Miriam, whose wisdom, experience and worldview I value more than any others.

"My question was the most fundamental question, the one humans have been asking themselves and debating since we walked out of that allegorical Garden of Eden many thousands of years ago: 'How can a person best use that single gift that God has given us, the gift of our existence?'

"For me, for thirty-plus years, the answer was in the life of a Catholic priest and academic theologian. But after the Millen County Standoff, and the spread of religious and political hatred throughout the world, including and especially the United States, that answer no longer worked. All of the agonizing, the soul-searching and the praying led me to a different path, a career that I hope will be more valuable to more people. And, I hope, will eventually lead me to whatever God has planned for those who die satisfied that they've earned His reward.

"That path led me to a small private college in Ohio that was looking for someone to head their comparative religions department. It's a wonderful place, beautiful campus, great faculty and students. They're glad to let me travel, write, and get tossed in jail on occasion for the causes I believe in. It's been a good fit for me. I've found people of many religious beliefs with the same burning conviction that any individual or organization that supports violence in the name of religion, any group that scapegoats any segment of God's humanity is not doing God's work. Precisely the opposite. People who spread divisiveness and hatred—Muslim, Christian or no religion at all—are the real terrorists.

"You may have seen me on TV, or read one of my op-ed columns in *The Washington Post* or *New York Times*, and thought 'Tad Coburg better watch it or he'll find himself in the pokey.' That's not my intent, but if it comes to that. I hope you'll visit me there. In the meantime, I believe what I'm doing is the best way I can apply my talents and experience in the service of God and mankind, the best way I can carry out the teachings of the New Testament."

Tad paused, deciding where to go from here. Nah, he thought. Not now. Not here. Just let Father Sam finish the ceremonies and move on. "I look forward to seeing and talking with every one of you downstairs after the services. God bless you all."

He unclipped the microphone, walked to the front pew and sat beside his wife. Miriam squeezed his hand. Tad closed his eyes, but couldn't hold back the tears. Once again, he was not allowed to participate as a Catholic priest in the funeral liturgy of his parent.

978-0-595-46785-3
0-595-46785-7

Printed in the United States
91290LV00005B/73-90/A